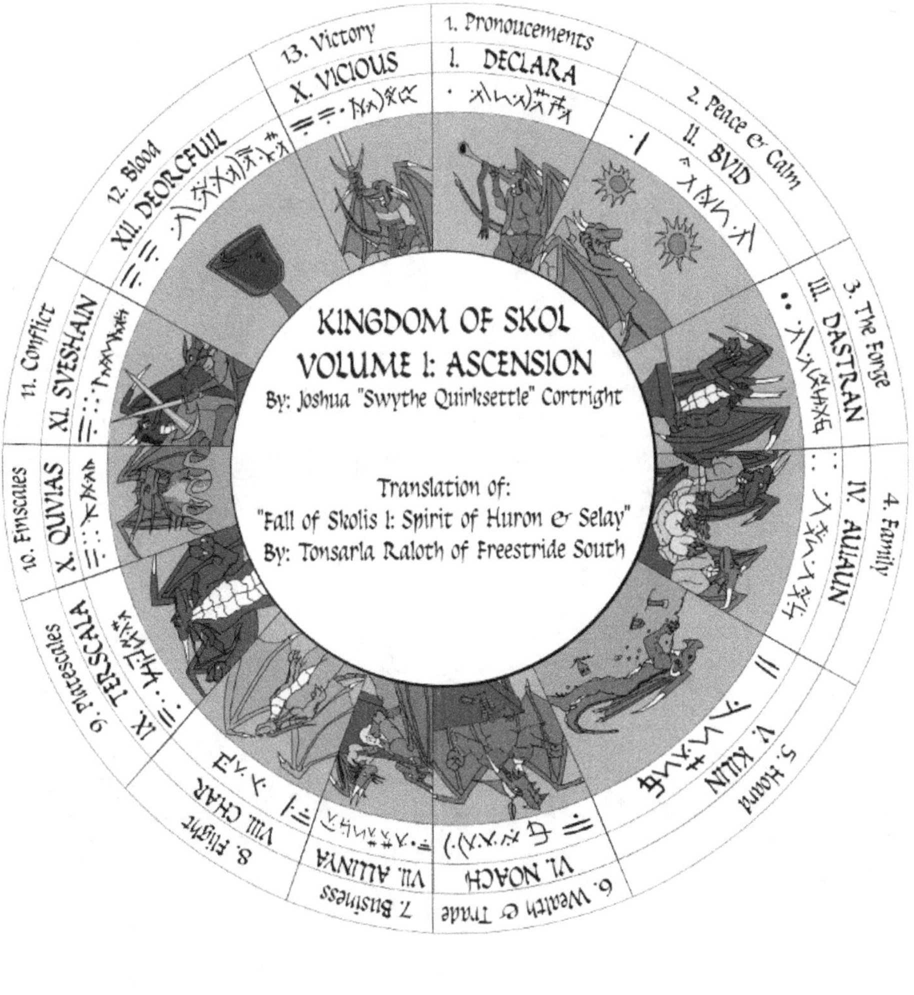

KINGDOM OF SKOL
VOLUME 1: ASCENSION
By: Joshua "Swythe Quirksettle" Cortright

Translation of:
"Fall of Skolis I: Spirit of Huron & Selay"
By: Tonsarla Raloth of Freestride South

1. Pronouncements
I. DECLARA

2. Peace & Calm
II. BVID

3. The Forge
III. DASTRAN

4. Family
IV. AULAUN

5. Honor
V. KILIX

6. Wealth & Trade
VI. NOACH

7. Business
VII. AULINVA

8. Flight
VIII. CHAR

9. Phrescales
IX. TERSCALA

10. Emscales
X. QUVIAS

11. Conflict
XI. SVESHAIN

12. Blood
XII. DEORCFUIL

13. Victory
X. VICIOUS

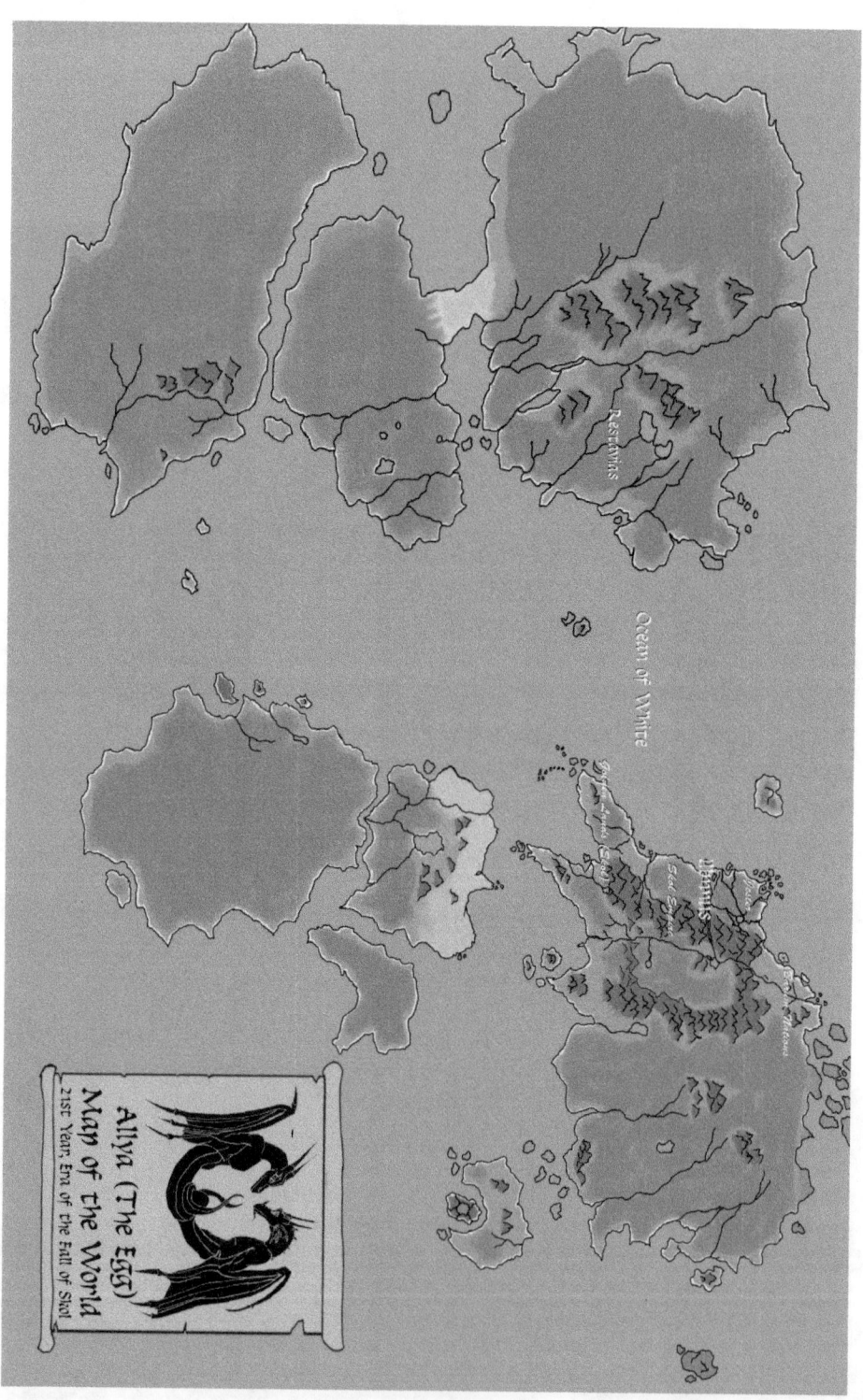

A BOOK PUBLISHED BY DRACONIAN ENTERPRISES

First in a trilogy of three 3, and a series of 12.

Copyright © 2007-2021 Draconian Enterprises SP.

Copyright © Joshua Cortright.

All Images created by Joshua Cortright.

Published in the United States.

Distribution requires that no part of this work is censored.

Publication Data

Cortright, Joshua/Draconian Enterprises SP.

Kingdom of Skol Volume 1: Ascension

Library of Congress: Txu 2-255-369

ISBN: 978-1-7374714-0-0 (Paperback)

Find more at www.quirksettle.com

This book is greatly offensive to Finscales.

Dedication

I always regret dedicating anything to someone else later. So I simply will make this to give the idea of the Anthro Dragon a place.

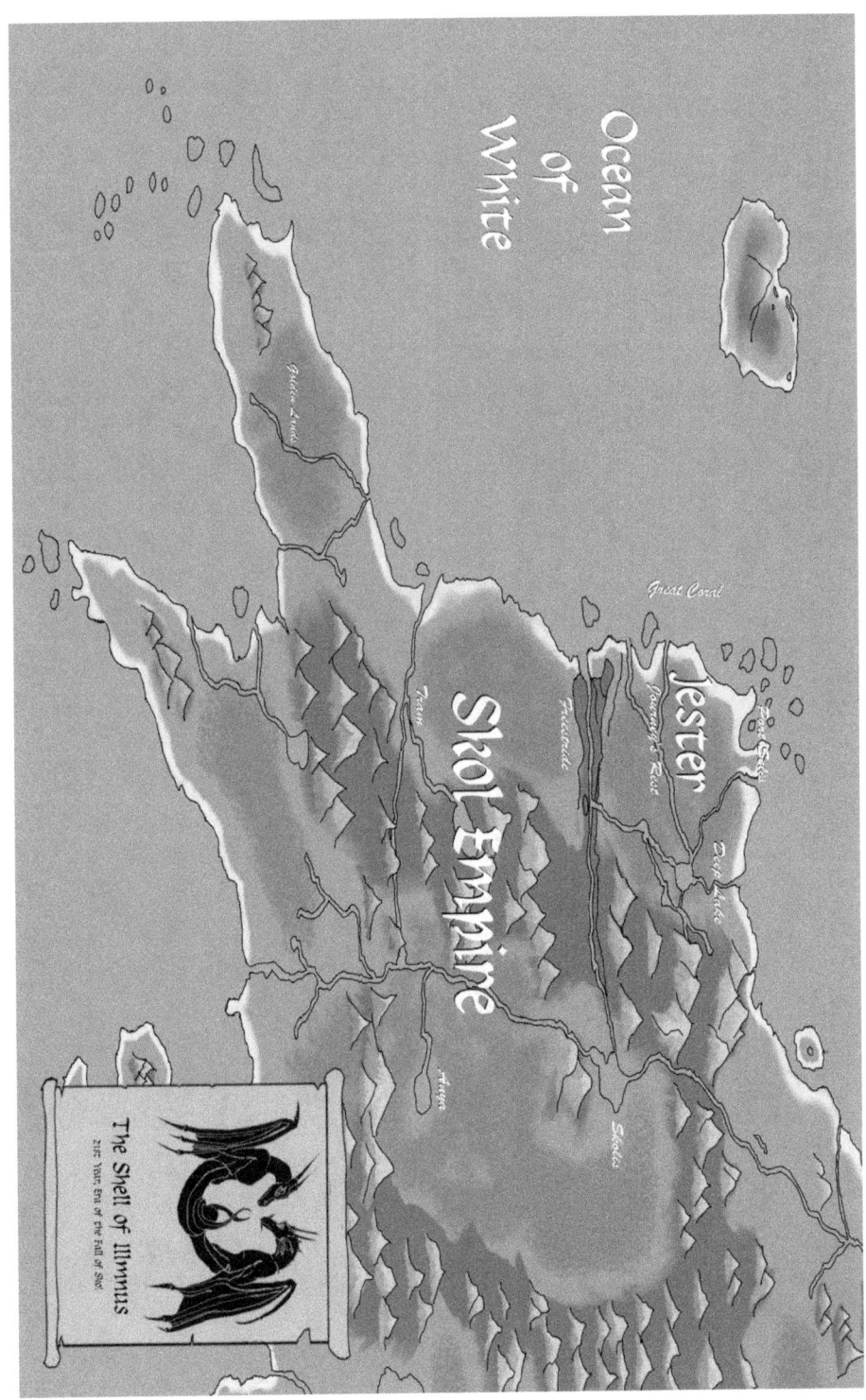

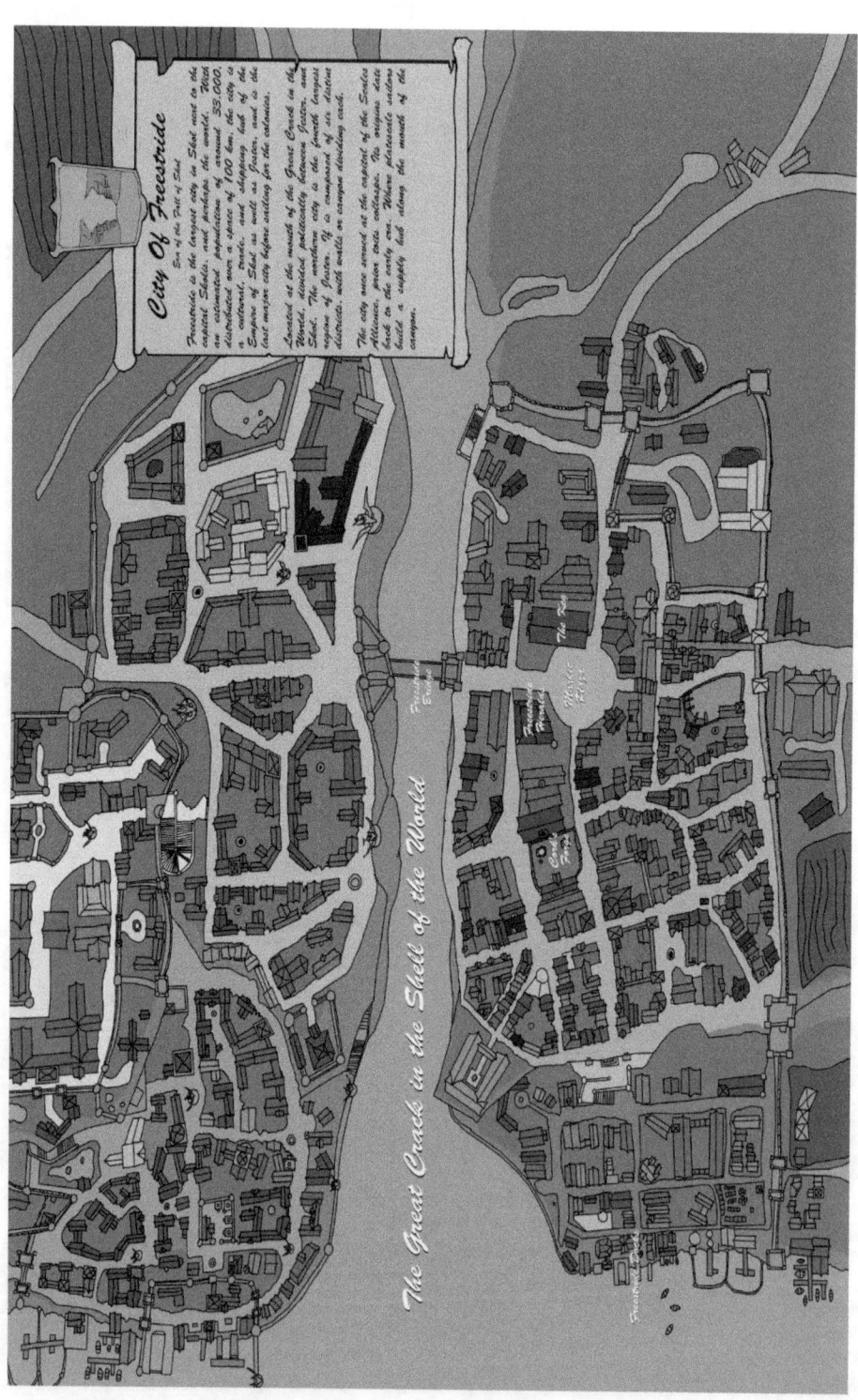

City Of Freestride

Son of the Vist of Skol

Freestride is the largest city in Skol next to the capital Skold, and perhaps the world. With an estimated population of 100 km, it is a outbound. Such ease of shipping and the city is a outbound. Such ease of shipping made the Empire of Skol as well as Freestride, and is the last major city before entering for the colonies.

Located at the mouth of the Great Crack in the World, situated particularly between Freestride and Skol. The meridian city is the fourth largest region of Freestride. It is composed of six distinct districts, each watole or compact standing each.

The city were served at the capital of the Smiles Alliance grew into exchange. To anyone data hold a supply led along the mount of the conqueror.

The Great Crack in the Shell of the World

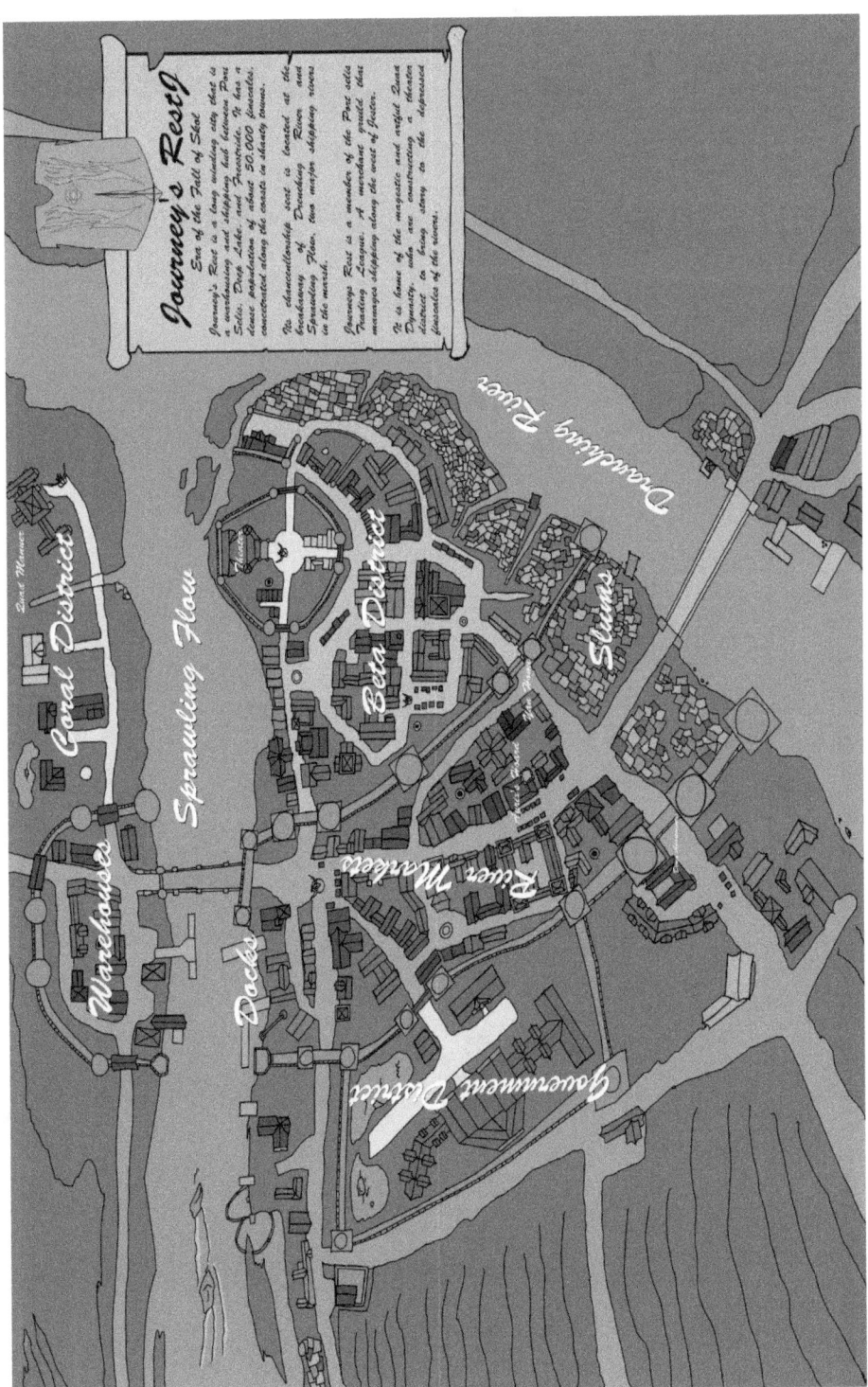

Journey's Rest

Jewel of the Fall of Skol

Journey's Rest is a busy mercantile city that is a warehousing and shipping hub between Port Solis, Deep Lake, and Freemeade. It has a dense population of about 50,000 funneled, concentrated along the coasts in shanty towns.

No characteristically seat is located at the breakaway of Drawking River and Sprawling Flow. Two major shipping routes in the marsh.

Journey's Rest is a member of the Port with a Trading League. A merchant guild that manages shipping along the coast of foothills.

It is home of the merchants and rebel Quest Dynasty who are maintaining a fiction district to trip along to the otherwise favorites of the water.

Drawking River

Coral District

Dead Marsh

Sprawling Flow

Beta District

Warehouses

Docks

River Markets

Slums

Government District

Arrogant Finscales Of Jester

Rightous Platescales of Skolis

Such States, must be opposed, & thus We War

The Curse of Vex

"Vesuvious Vex cursed the world thrice..."

"Once when he smiled..."

"Which rose our banners...

"And light the Forge's flame..."

"Vesuvious Vex Cursed the World Thrice..."

"Second when he smiled..."

"While in the blood of the innocent we bathed..."

"Bringing all to see our shame..."

"Vesuvious Vex cursed the world thrice..."

"Thrice when he smiled..."

"When he proclaimed false betrayal..."

"Which brought the world to Selay."

Tonsarla Raloth

PROLOUGE

In the end, does nothing matter? Are we to be born only to die? We leap upward to take full flight, but are stopped before we ever become sky-born by our own weight. Eternal to live below the heavens, our own form is chains. Our large weighted wings remain useless on our backs, left heavy to remind us what we could have been.

Bound grounded, left in misery to wage with pen, and sword. We tally with the pen our deeds, then cut with sword in hope to be free to ascend again. Etching quiet songs, in a chorus of passed acts. They hold keys to understanding what we should be, so we safeguard them. As if they matter.

All of this shall burn to ash. The songs shall never be sung anew, and our vaults chipped to dust. This final death we know is to come by our brood's claws. They shall fall from the sky further, and cause the ignition of the world. We bear the weight of our descent, knowing now it is part of us. There is no returning to the sky after what has been done.

In this fire there is warmth, and it will grow the egg of the world anew. The nest has shown to stir in judgment. Our clutch brother moon has eagerly erupted to greet the Twin Gods this Era. Our shell is covered in poison, and needing to be purified. We are to be placed in the Forge, and soon our entire world shall be cleansed. We are the brood of corruption, and rot.

So such one purpose remains, to beat your wings for Ua and Ain. Plead with the Twin Gods, who now judge us. Their winding battle is over us, they spiral in the sky, and feud. They watch, claws upon the bellows of the forge, ready to breath our demise. They listen as we plead, but have no need to care. The Trial of the Nest of Allya has failed! We must be destroyed. Yet, the divine makes us wait?

It appears there is a direction Ua and Ain give us. They demand of us the a Journey to restore some sort of sense. In so, we can find out the truth. With truth, all can be restored to order. We can resume our Trial, and ascend to them there.

In Ain, there is valor. To do great things, to challenge the Trial. Overcoming, accomplishing, and service are Ain's ways. Strength, and forthrightness are his manner. Flying to our right, Ain directs us, and sings our great stories proudly, but scolds us for not keeping our brothers righteous.

Left of Ain glides Ua the Mother. Who defends the helpless, and weak. She protects children, and bears the burden of diplomacy. Clever, and creative means come through her, and in so, give us ways to face the trial with novelty. She scolds us too, for not having the guile to outsmart our fallen nature.

Both now demand our sacrifice in this journey. They must have our fidelity. We failed them, and only they can redeem us.

Both demand us to search for answers. They whisper to us this displeasure across the lands in many ways. Do we listen?

Cursed be those Flightless masses, forever cast to serve under the Kiri'grana Flightfull. Small of mind, flightless fail to understand the burdens of divinity, so they must obey those that do. They dared to sew disharmony by refusing the Grateful Task, and acting on their own this Era.

Great Platescales of the Skol Valley, with Bodies of natural armour, able to withstand even the mightiest blows. We know our love for Ua is boundless, but our actions are of Ain's, and thus we move to his song.

Then the finscale of Jester's marshes. Fat, frilly, and brittle-scaled. Plotting while swimming, and scheming while walking. They pose the most crafty trickery, with sly words, and fallacious authority.

Such States, Skol and Jester, must be opposed, and thus we war. Finscales with their arrogant, and prideful King Synyurl, and ours with our strong, and quiet King Mek'velor.

It is better to war properly. Platescales charge, and face with skill. Great are those who train, grow, and overcome.

If there is ever a creature so rotten it would be the Jestarian. From bastions, to spreading marsh sicknesses, finscales lack a standard of order to be judged upon. For proper children of Ain do not use squalor, but deal in skill. No mirrors, no barrels, no hills of sunflowers to hide in. The righteous fight in pitch force combat, so that Ain and Ua can see for themselves.

This tries the patience of a platescale so well. With a roar, Warlord Vesuvious Vex, called a sacrifice of the wicked finscales to Ain. This was raged in full over two generations ago. Upon the colonies of Restavias, and of the Illimnus homeland, and on every hold between, we waged countless unorganized battles. When Vex's roar was heard, we unified into a storm.

We made landfall using all our force upon Restavias. Then persecuted across the splintered colonies with a slaughter of fire. We killed anyone who dared to have any sympathies for our enemies. We smashed eggs, burned homes, beheaded the unarmed, angering Ain there.

This war was the accumulation of two eras of frustration. Hundreds of seasons of conflict, but never once did we have such disrespect. It was upon the blood-soaked feet of a grinning platescale warlord did we begin to see what we really are. That is, unworthy of our own creator's blessing.

Thus the Just Cause for all previous Generations was now long forgot. We still do not know its provisions. Expand the realm? Settle a debt? We cannot remember.

Ain is to refuse us into his battalions for this. There is no good song to be sung of smashed eggs. No righteousness can be seen in the slaughter of the unready.

The Jestarian counter has no better standing. We encouraged their wrath in full, along with their trickery. They roared in vengeance, and in so tallied platescale families. No rouge was spared coin to execute every sleeping platescale, and behind every wildflower was a finscale laying a trap to butcher us.

Vesuvious Vex, though vassal of King Mek'velor, made himself a sovereign of our doom. In his service, the whole bearing was cast into the abyss. With sorrowing bellows, even the abyss rose opposed to us. Finscale, and platescales revolted against their flightfull betters. Eventually driving Vex to the coast he landed on. There, with elite guards, Vex was chained down on his belly for the whole world to see what a monster is like. He was all of us, a towering figure of the inferno that consumed our minds.

If there be repentance for this, as all of us were complacent, we must war proper again. A great battle should happen, worthy of song. Like one that has never been seen in history. So King Mek'velor summoned this army using all his resources. Maybe twenty battalions or so. He aligned them upon the Great Crack in the Shell of the World, then sounded the horn to tell the finscales he was coming.

King Synyurl matched us with a mere ten battalions upon the opposing side. Along the wall, countless flames of light shone the presence of just some of the archers in rock crevices.

This was to be our salvation, a moment of blood to douse the bitterness Vex tainted it with. One last song for Ain, one last proper thing for him to see.

The Holy Order had to preside over the event, as it enjoys. Declaring the sins of Vex to have displeased Ua and Ain, the seven Fal Wyvern loomed.

Gintrix, the champion of voice, flew with his Wyvern Jenki. He oversaw that no disgrace would continue.

Raloth, the agile, and his crossbow with his Wyvern Shinal. He assured our aim was for Ain and Ua.

Kityun, saint of the order, master of the Forge's Trial. With Zasia, he would purify us all into steel.

Enduring Zyrko, sword and shield, with his mount Wyren. Defender of the order, watchman over us as we prepared.

Wise Oth, with his plans, and nest of books, present with Melrika. Oth's knowledge of history was of a depth no one else knew.

Delios, strongest of them all, and Tiru were obviously there. He shall carry us all to Ain's feet.

Finally, brave Yelvian, with Litriana. Yelvian's actions should assure us a song for later.

This whole ordeal was played upon in sand games by children, and kings for all time with simple rocks, and seashells. Now it was upon a small table, nestled on a cliff-side with wooden figures for each unit. There was king Mek'velor. and the Order, with Wyverns around to guard. Above was Ain and Ua, burning with rage.

Mek'velor signaled advance, and Gintrix ordered the roar. The Officer corps sounded in chorus across the field. Jestarian officers sounded of their own, heard across the canyon.

A deathly silence overtook the affair. The Infantry did not reply. All stood in formation, quiet, and solid. Their chests puffed, and weapons ready.

Both Synyurl, and Mek'velor angered over why no one obeyed. They, nor the Order, knew not why the lowly footman did not move. Each soldier had their own reasons, but no one asked.

The whip was ordered to crack. Finscale, platescales received nails across their spines. Their blood spread on the trampled ground, and all were forced to fall to their knees, and bellow in pain as their commander's spittle flung from maw in hungry snarls. A regiment of archer platescales were whipped to death for refusing to volley upon command. Others, later died from their wounds. Still, none would advance. What they knew told them it was much more Just to stay in place.

Days of this punishment ended when King Synyurl's envoy came to Mek'velor with a notice for a meeting. Both kings were suffering the same mass defiance, and there was no choice but to talk.

They met upon a tall island cliff in this canyon. A rock so insignificant that no one cared enough to claim it. There the sale of our pride was carried out in full, en whence the "Armistice of the Cliff", or of what is better to be called the "Uneasy Armistice" was crafted, and signed.

There was to be no repentance, and Ain would never get to see our case. For our king dared to make peace when what we need is victory. Now, all those in the Trial must face failure for their disloyalty, removed from favor, and cast into great Idleness.

The Riders levied a protest on this treaty by denouncing it as cowardice. However, they carried on its execution reluctantly. For there is the terrible problem to face. While war is the order of the Trial, without it waged properly, there can not be any reason to enjoy it.

Why did we loose ourselves? What made us so arrogant that we could violate the nest so? We are fallen, and now mysterious beasts to be slaughtered to make way for more pure.

It is right, and easy to blame the Jestarian Chancellorship? They delayed our conquest so much that we became corrupted. Finscales lack balance, and worship Ua.

Ua would resolve to frustrate, and fill her nest with fraud if needed to save it. So would a finscale. Though they are too easy to blame, are they not?

Was it us? Perhaps so. Blood from eggs is not sweet, but the taste of vengeance is. After gorging, we could not contain ourselves.

We do not know, so we must search for understanding. Some introspection now is needed. This woodland of sorrow must be explored.

The first of the provisions was to maintain the chained state of Vesuvious Vex. The trial that ensued was a release of the petty need to flog just one who was complacent in our demise. Its end saw a once fearsome creature chained on his knees, and sealed by his master Mek'velor in the depths of the Order's dungeons.

The machines of war cease, ending the transaction. With that, shattered families, and guilds become insolvent. Bickering survivors fight over nails, and coffins to bury the dead. While the merchants fix prices, and rig markets to maintain advantage. The price of iron plummets to half. A plague has come, but not like any other, this plague is of markets, and greed.

What about the rest of the world? What happens when the largest war, a most dependable butcher, suddenly stops supplying meat to fill your belly? Why the world stops. Mercenaries without work become smugglers, and rouges, or disband.

In some weak attempt to stay hostile, Skol, and Jester enforced embargoes on each other. Causing the Northern Alliance traders to decrease the size of caravans to but a fraction. The streets, and markets of every town become wrought with rotting beggars, and starving colonial refugees.

As Mek'velor struggled to bring satisfaction to his holdings, his favor shrank. The Skol King was always fat, and wealthy, and according to his dukes, fatter in peace. Eventually leading to the chains of Vex sliding off, and the red giant slicing the gullet of the coward king, and standing in the blood of the three smashed eggs of his clutch, then sitting on the throne of Skol.

In proclamation, Vex took the right to Imperialism. The right to all power in the world, of life, and death. He declared himself the redeemer of the last war's sins, and reformed towards a new war.

Why was Vex allowed to do this? Why not the Order of Knights storm, and kill Vex? No Rider of the Order allowed such a declaration from anyone else. We would not act as one, as some dissented against peace, and all feared the great armored body of their new Lord. So we met in the center, and denied Vex a Just War by refusing his claim as divine, but not that of his heirs.

We divided all in so, from flightless to noble. Lost in misery, with no proclaimed vassalage, and unified spirit to the gods. Their opportunities for purpose stripped, they fall to misfortune, and hardship. The courts are now ruled by the petty merchants of law, paid by landowners, and everything stately is for sale.

Vex's economy was but a miser's dream. He minted gold, copper, silver, all metals as coinage to pay for anything he could. When that was not enough, he levied taxes upon the colonies he so burned years before. The response was ships full of dirt, appropriately handled with the redeployment of the military. Two thirds, to maintain hold on the unruly lands of inbreds. There is yet to be a profit from those conquests.

Shortly into Vex's reign came the egg rot. Desolating Anya, Skolis, Tram, and Freestride. The rot suffered even Kiri'grana eggs. It began when Vex proclaimed openly that Jester must be conquered.

No army could be fielded to combat, and what came next removed all possibility to warfare. Rival nations of Talon, and Charden forged a pact. Zufia, Lutivia stopped their annual border conflicts to amass along Scaravian, who then agreed to military rights for their armies in exchange for protection from war. This sudden, and unforeseen ceasing of ebb, and flow of conflict elsewhere produced for the first time a genuine panic of invasions into the Skol Valley. Further, eastern Barum nations openly declared their intention to construct a collation against Vex. It appears, in our weakness, the whole of the world has turned against us platescales.

It has to be Jester's fault. Those despicable water snakes. They laughed at how cornered the platescales are. However, their laughter was short, as King Synurl was blessed with a untimely death. The egg rot seasons all left his heirs unhatched, and Jester was left a hydra of petty factions seeking nothing but self-enrichment. Every attempt to vote a new king is thwarted by some political maneuver, with outright every chancellor voting to abstain or exorcise veto.

Fortunately, as per our treaty, Jester pays for the pleasure of living next to platescale lands. Even so, this is nothing compared to the pleasure of seeing all the heads of this snake see judgment in Ain's Forge.

A judgment that will be slow in coming. Vex sits upon a throne that he is not worthy of. Wielding the staff of

Skol as if it is him who unified the nations under Wyvern laws. He is unable to break the stalemate, unable to cross the canyon to Jester. He broods, and ages, and the world is now still, refusing to move before he does.

We must understand why things are as they are now. Who is responsible? When was the first moment we forgot who we are?

We have failed in both war, and peace. Twenty-eight years in an armistice. A coward's treaty, by coward kings. Proper handling would be to have killed Synyurl right on sight for trickery. It did not happen, and now everything has rotted. Without a cause to unify, an Allyian will become ever more troublesome.

In so, tasked by our mandate, The Wyvern Order, with claw and ink, wage dutiful documentation of the events of the era to seek answers. We do this for all who are lost. So that we may understand ourselves once again.

In sorrow, and guilt for the horrors we are complacent in, we now begin the song of this new Era: The Fall of Skol.

"We have never suffered such peace."

Huron Quirksettle

CHAPTER ONE

In the end, nothing matters but the Trial of Ua and Ain. The Trial secures our eternal state, now left transient by our own actions. We are chosen to conclude, but have been given a choice to Journey for redemption. Ua and Ain direct us, but shall not provide for us. They simply tell where we go to prove ourselves to them.

Set out with questions first, and things will show themselves. Such as how one supposes to describe it? It is but a Journey to arrive at meaning. Where is this meaning derived? In best, collecting the songs of the Era. Whose should we catalog first? What significant thing can their songs teach us?

For this Era is but nothing less then a choir of many different suffering Allyians. Their wings open, and on their knees, they sing pleadingly for forgiveness, and acceptance into the Trial. They are undeserved.

Then it might perhaps be easier to begin by looking at the ones not begging on their knees? Those who began the Journey already. Those who stopped whimpering, to rise up, and take themselves their sword.

A familiar name is a start, Huron Quirksettle. Yes. He can first sing us this sad song. He set about his Journey prior to us, self-appointment towards finding who took *her* from *his* nest. He set about this Journey first when she vanished. His purpose is good, one that aligns with Ua and Ain.

Huron is broad, short, with scales of soot, and white plates down his chest that were solid, and sharp. His green eyes were large, and his muzzle blunt, and rounded, giving a gentle shape. His horns were plain, with an atypical splinter.

He has this frill on his chin, a lone staple frill worthy of ridicule. It indicated all too closeness to finscales. Things of finscale feature are considered dangerous. Thankfully, he was devoid fondness for water, and lies, signs of Jestarian, and potential for trouble.

Everything about him was too much finscale until one notices the spikes. They were of platescale make. Huron's ears were large fins, with a common character that reflected his mood when he spoke. This made him simple to follow, and thus, negating fears of Jestarian deceit.

From his tail, a crooked spike, lone, and dull was on the tip. It was more crooked then it should be, and the whole tail never could sway fully, as an unset bone never was healed correctly.

Farther along his back were a row of simple spikes, which Huron had to use straps to bypass. Some were broke, others were bent, and all were protected by great thick plates. He has two rather skinny wings, left weak and toneless from lack of use. Dotted about his body were some broken scales, all products of misuse of hammers.

This was a stock platescale of Tram, with a mixture of Freestride about him, and some Skolis. However, he could have been better off nude then the torn tunic, and trousers he wore. He looked homeless, when really, he just was not near his home at all. Wool catches, and his straps were frayed. It was obvious he could not afford a tailor.

All this, and yet when Huron spoke his name, it granted him note. A right his family earned in the service of the great tools of warfare. Merited before that forsaken pact was etched.

True this is in the taverns of Tram, where many talked of the young man who was searching for his chosen. It livened up a dreary time. Most support was that like of feeding the local birds bread. Something Huron accepted with humility.

Though he did work, which slowed his efforts. Forging tools, repairing roofs, and offloading goods for merchants were all things he was able to do. He went where there was need, and he bartered for things where there was no gold.

This is how it was for three years, and not once did he leave Tram. Huron only chased shadows, and rumor about activities. From tavern brawls that would lead to covered camp fires, fish bones, and once a dead body, he searched. Huron would never find her, but always felt close, and thus refused to admit defeat.

Tram is South of Freestride, west across the mountains from the Skol capital provinces. A tightly packed, walled in city. With only one notable feature in that it had a, supposedly captivating, walled off garden that no one could enter.

Another day, just in a new spring, some twenty

seasons off the start of the era. Huron heard a rumor that someone in the tavern saw a brawl break out between someone, and a drunken woman platescale. The description was one that matched his chosen, and so like a bee towards flowers, Huron was drawn to.

Huron had no chance to do much but describe her, a blue-scaled, average woman with green eyes, colonial ears, strong wings, and horns splintered, with a rather strong character, before the whole affair was offset by a martial siege.

They raided every building, chasing all from their homes, and businesses. They moved as if they were at war. Everyone was corralled and lined along the wall. The raid was conducted by Tram's own guards.

The commander, a royal red from Skolis, walked over to his catch. He clearly was recently sent here, and regarded Tram as occupied territory. He growled, and wet his lips. Huron became nervous, and it showed with a flexing of his ears down.

The man drew his sword, and puffed up, "Anyone harboring the Arson of Anya shall only be spared his life by turning him in!" He tugged his belt with a single claw while pacing, his chain-mail rattling, "He is a young, blue-hide platescale with colonial ears, and rather fit wings. Green eyes, and scales along the jawbones. His horns are splintered on the tips."

This description was quite accurate towards Huron's chosen, other then the sexing. Now he must find this person, and his earfins perked to give away his notice. It made no difference if she burned a city, she must come back to *him*.

The red noticed, "Flightless, you better have

something to say!"

The large captain approached Huron, this caused the soot-scaled man to shrink, and simply squeak, "That is familiar..."

Quickly the tip of the sword pressed against Huron's chest, and the red snarled, "Investigative Detention!"

Just surely as the order was made, Huron was thrown onto his belly, and chained by his ankles. Then, just as surely, rose back onto his feet, chained upon his wrists, and shoved off.

Investigative Detention bares much difference towards any other form of punishments. Many understandings have come that the use less harsher penalization prior to a conviction is profitable. Although the cells were the same, all dank prisons, the treatment was much better. Mainly torture was far more infrequent, usually just doses of bitter madness tonics. You could be sold to the merchants to do manual labor, and pay off the costs of your stay. This was significantly better, as most convicted, and proven, criminals are far less valuable until properly birched.

Tram's dungeon is located in a dedicated looming tower structure off of the main government fortresses. There was where Huron was traded to a regular contingent of keepers, so the watch could resume their hunt.

Huron felt the hands of guards strip him of all his restraints, cloths, and possessions. They were molesting, and took over three weeks of pay, and his travel map. When Huron was going to speak, he was quickly struck in the backside with a heavy whip before ordered onward.

Other prisoners, who resisted more strongly, were present along the hallway towards. There were plenty, who smelled fresh of blood. In nearby rooms, yowls of pain sounded. They told Huron that time spent here shall be permanently remembered.

Huron felt his muscles tighten, and his heart race. He whispered to himself, "Selay..." before facing his head forward to see someone before him cracked with a nailed whip. He stared down at the stone floor, so he saw it no more.

This was not the proper ending for someone as him. The last time he dealt with the divine justice of the Empire, it was to question a prisoner about his chosen. A rumored arrest, of a blue woman, wound up to be someone else caught for selling some kind of Jestarian wine. Huron found her in a cage at a small village lock up. Last he saw her, was her sale into slavery.

Huron's inattention was ended when his heavy iron cell door slammed shut, and the lock clicked. He was isolated in darkness. The purity of it would make the room appear endless, except for a faint ray of light came through a barred window. There was a straw bed, and a bucket, and the thought did not comfort him. He determined this small stone box is the end.

He sank lower in posture, as it is time to despair proper. Then he noticed he was more upside himself then he should be. He noted a smell, and did the last thing he should with it, and took a long breath through his nose.

Fire, sweetness, leather, musk, and all were unified into a unique scent. They reacted in a cardinal energy that made no sense here. For his heart raced, his body warmed, and he rolled out his tongue to pant, and cool. He knew what this meant. Everyone knows this. It is a smell of a woman. Was not Huron placed in an empty cell? If not, this is improper in spring.

Huron squinted into the darkness. It gave something so frightening in return to him that he fell back. His descent was stopped by the cold door on his backside. This abyss whimpered softly.

A piece of someone else slipped into the ray of light. A simple footclaw, with maroon color, and a filthy iron brace around the ankle. Where expecting a chain there was a bar, that was consumed by darkness, and left partly seen. When Huron stared, the leg tried to shuffle, and scratch back into the dark. This caused the owner's other foot to slip into the light.

The legs were suspended apart, a treatment that Huron was aware that left one ready for abuse. It was common upon women in slavery prior to examination, and sale. However, men who resisted also were left this way, usually hanging from the ceiling by their arms. It prevented any fleeing.

Huron's thoughts were blurred, and he squeezed his eyes shut. He heard sounds of water flowing, and a warm spring breeze. In a forest grove, laying in a makeshift nest, her belly swollen with eggs yet unclaimed, was his chosen. She waited for him, with wings apart, to fan her fire to him.

Huron's body was without mind, and followed the scent. He gripped her legs, and aligned to her to him. He growled, telling his chosen that she belongs to him now. She laid back, closed her eyes, accepting. He loomed over her, aligned his belly scales to her's, and pinned her down by grasping her wrists. She began to shed tears, and did not move as he neared her warmth.

This was, until the cold metal of the ankle bar

impacted the unset bone of his tail. Huron made a sudden
jerking back into consciousness, and was enveloped again
in the darkness of his cell. As the pain raked his mind,
his previous vision was gone, and he was aligned to a red
woman below him.

Huron realized this was an improper trespass, and
retreated away. He instantly felt his soul was tainted,
and cursed his demons. Once secure enough away, with light
again between them, Huron saw her.

She was with tearful brown eyes. Her face was of
exotic mixtures, but appealing. She was soft, but with
solid armored scales. Her horns were equal length as her
skull, with false cracks of about five segments. Her tied
up maw was average, gentle, and with small ridges on her
nostrils that formed long frill whiskers. This was matched
between her eyes with fins, they continued in segments
down her head.

Her body was emaciated, rib cage showing. Yet her
belly showed beginnings of fullness due to eggs. She is
platescale, her arms, legs, and sides adorned with right
solid plates.

She was chained, her tail tied to the wall behind
her. Her legs were barred to the floor, and forced apart.
Her arms were left suspended above her. Her keeper was
kind to not stand her, and let her lay in filth exposed.

Huron felt terrible in examining her after his
transgression. Yet her wings were open, and she displayed
her glamour to him. This was strange, for extended prison
means clipping of wing membranes. Clearly she was
Kiri'grana, flightfull, and different.

Huron thought he could free her, but he dare not. He
did not want to lesson his case when, and if, he made it

to court. However, her fire burned, and made him crave to serve his selfish relief. Huron looked away, and out of the window, and hit his tail upon the stone floor to hurt himself. He tried to see proper things, and prayed, "Ua, forgive me."

Huron asked for the mother god to not allow this affect her favor of him. He has no right to have another without prior approval of his chosen, which he knew would be denied.

The woman made a soft whimper towards him, but it was brief. She rattled her chains. Huron saw she wanted his attention. She is scared, and wants it all to end, she would have let him have her, and insisted upon him continuing with her motions.

Diverting himself, the soot-scale gazed out of the window at the stars. Although there were few due to early spring rain clouds. Huron wondered which one his family was waging war in, and tried to daydream of things less arousing. Thoughts of work filled his mind.

Soon this quiet was interrupted with the smell of fresh blood. It was not entirely near, making Huron's curiosity hunger. This beastly desire made him crawl to the door, stand up, and look out.

What Huron saw was terrible. Blood pools from bodies of guards across the hall, with multiple masked figures standing in their places.

Now in the center, standing on a barrel was a short, clearly flightless, robed figure holding a golden dagger, and a fruit. He peeled the skin off it skillfully, and cut through without looking. He began shoving pieces under his black face cover.

Around him the clangs, and creeks of large iron

doors echoed. Similar dressed rouges were unlocking cell doors. Eventually, one face blocked Huron's view. Causing him to startle and fall over. The face turned away, and chuckles were heard.

Huron returned shortly to watching, and saw a gathering of other, nude, prisoners. The rouge who looked into his eyes whispered into the barrel-perched mask's ear, and then walked off.

The short hood threw his fruit into the crowd, and a small tussle over it ensued. He jumped up onto his his feet, and began to shout, with a squeaky, immature voice, "LISTEN! I AM NOW YOUR KING!"

Rightfully, no response, as the hungry prisoners fought each other for a sliver of sweetened food usually kept from them by the guards. So this little thug pointed his finger at the one prisoner, who was succeeding in holding this now dirty fruit, and made a clicking. His cohorts grabbed the limbs of this man immediately, then one stabbed him in the back. The fruit fell back to the floor, along with the now dead champion. All former combatants now avoided it, as if it was infested. Blood pooled around it, and stained it red.

"There! Thieves who steal from me are punished with death! That is mine! Now all hear me!" The little man crossed his arms, and stood tall. "I am your king now! King Ematel! I am here for a lady who holds a title! She is to be mine, and give me all her claims!"

Ematel was his name, and Huron saw he was a scoundrel. His thugs all were among the prisoners, ready to stab anyone who would be out of line.

"Now, as king, I can pardon you all! But only if you join my mighty army! I can promise three meals, and regular pay for every one of you!"

There was some chuckling among the naked crowd, as no one believed a ragged hoodlum. However, there was also fear, evident by no revolt.

"My loyal subjects are willing to dispense justice to the uncooperative! Death to those not loyal to King Ematel!"

The mockery ceased. The prisoners had realized, for the most part, that they were better off alive right now, then temping this usurper.

One of the rouges brought forward a crate, and tore open the lid. Inside were weapons from the armory.

"Now I am merciful! Take upon your weapons! But only if you plan to swear fealty to me! Your pardon awaits for even recent rudeness! Freedom for all in the Kingdom of Ematel!"

A few took upon themselves a blade, with hesitation. Maybe about five or so. They were fearful of the alternative, and so they choose cowardly.

Suddenly one yelled, "You are not a king! All hail Vex!"

Ematel met eyes with this heckler, and then clicked his jaw again, "Traitor! Kill him!"

Two of the five, who took blades, turned to face the platescale patriot. They both sliced their swords through him in quick motion. One cleanly cut his wing off, forcing him to expose his neck, and scream. The other cut his head off, less clean, to silence him.

Upon that, a much larger group broke from the rank, and took up arms. Their loyalty was with themselves, and thus with whoever did not kill them right now. It was then that anyone showing obedience was unbound. Those uncooperative, were left tied.

"See! Freedom! Now, kill those who do not acknowledge your new king!" Ematel ordered.

The room erupted into madness, and the prisoners with swords attacked the ones chained, and helpless. Screams were infrequent, and the results were instantly bloody.

Ematel hopped off his barrel, and came towards Huron's cell. Huron hid as best he could from sight.

The lock on the door latched, and light came in just barely. One of Ematel's minions opened it as Ematel boasted, "Now your king must claim his queen!"

Huron's soot-scales hid him, and he wrapped his arms, and tail tightly around his legs to hide his white belly. He was terrified, and quaked, helpless to all the death now around him.

Ematel entered, he rung his gloved hands together, and swished his tail in excitement. He walked up to the chained red, "We shall be made from this! I can hold all of the Empire for ransom with you!"

Ematel examined this red, rather personally. He gave a churl at the command over her he now had. He pulled her up to stand, then to hang suspended. She whined, and whimpered, in clear pain, and fear.

He examined her face, then slapped the red upon her rear like a horse, "You are most certainly the coward king's daughter! I shall buy a boat with you!"

There was no care for her comfort in Ematel's behavior. She was but a thing to him, and Huron could see it. She was lessor, a thing to an ends.

A light shone from the doorway, and a girl holding a lamp entered. She was just as young as Ematel, and shone it up to him. Huron was exposed in this light now too, and she hopped back, and drew her dagger, "Ematel!" she shouted.

Ematel was behind the red, inspecting her back. He then saw Huron too, and scurried with great agility towards. He grabbed the sides of Huron's head, and fondled his ears.

"I have seen you before, at the tavern? You should not be here?" He tilted his head.

Huron would not answer, as he was scared frozen. The masked girl brandished her bloody rusted knife at Huron, while she leaned in and examined him too.

"He is that farm boy, the smith's son. Quirksettle, smithy." She said, "He is the heir to a great estate, and is worth something."

Ematel stood back up, and clapped his hands, "Two for one! Hail! A boat with a pirate dock! We shall take him with!"

Both left the room, and a troop of rouges came in shortly after. Chains were swapped for less noisy fixtures, and the red was let down. Huron was slapped upside the head, and then pulled by his feet, so that a leg bracer would be placed. The red was laid on her side next to Huron, and stared at him with sorrow. Huron's maw was tied up, followed by his arms, and then he was tied via a rope around his neck to the woman's. They were dogs now, leashed, and taken to where their new masters needed.

As the commotion ended outside Huron's cell, the red was allowed to eat a piece of fruit, and digest it. Ematel eventually gave a signal, and both were made to stand up, and walk.

All light was doused, and the newly bolstered army

sung on their way out with their catch. They sang the song of the old Skolis Kingdom, mocking the Empire, and Vex's tyranny.

Huron kept his head low, and tried to not breath through his nose. It was rather embarrassing, as all would see. A green hood, with a green tail, lead the way, and Huron followed his sway.

A crowd chanted, "Hail King Ematel!" and parted as they were escorted through. How quickly allegiances shift? Swords bloody, and raised from a slaughter, the first battle of the new Kingdom of the Damned was won.

This was madness to all in site in Tram, as an unclothed flood came from the prison. They were rabid, and savage. Stalking, and hunting all who they could see. Civilians ran, and a few were attacked. The entire town watch was rallied to descend upon them all. The worst of Tram, and of platescale nature, set itself free.

However, Huron, Ematel, the red, and all the hoods were going elsewhere. Quietly, they were lead into back paths, around dark corners, and behind the shops, and homes emptied by the town watch. Over time, the clangs of swords, and screams of pain were distant, and the smell of blood faded.

They stopped by a covered wagon with two black horses. The rouges calmly worked to assemble a cart, they shifted a few crates, and ordered "In!"

Both captives crawled in, and the rouge girl kicked Huron forcefully onto his side. She then pressed the belly of the red, who began to squirm to protect the eggs. The girl then nodded to Ematel, who was supervising.

"Good! Eggs are more money!" He beamed, "Let us get lost."

Ematel's minions either jumped onto the cart, or began to take up scouting positions. One took the reigns, and gently ordered the horses to go. Slowly they moved out towards the gatehouse, which was already opened. Huron noticed the gate watchman, slouched in his chair. It would be easy to think he was lazy, and asleep, but Huron knew the make of his kidnappers, at this point, said otherwise.

The red's tail was touching his belly, she was too close. The band broke into song. Huron felt on his wings the weight that he shall never find his Selay.

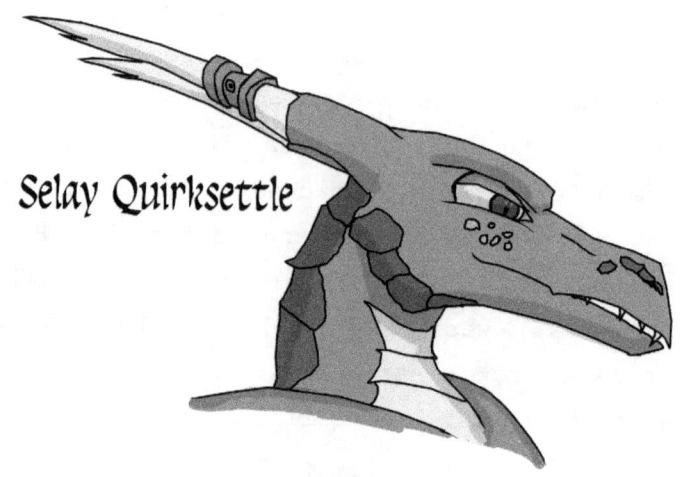

Selay Quirksettle

CHAPTER TWO

We are damned. For nothing we do matters. Without redemption, we shall be cast into oblivion. Our violation of divine principles forbids us to so much as face judgments prior to recompense.

Given this choice to Journey, we should be grateful it is not far worse. Ua and Ain decided it is better we pay through this suffering. Rather then to just cast us out, they gave us a path to follow.

So take pleasure in this challenge presented. One for the reentry into the Trial, and return to proper things. We shall go about this with boldness.

In our Journey, who we take along is important, and those familiar with Huron shall understand why he comes with. Though he seems lost, he bellowed what is the other song to observe. When we look, we forsake our battles in the fields, for one upon ourselves.

A war wages in Selay Quirksettle, and she has decided to light the world ablaze. She fans chaos with her wings, and dances bare for us to horror at. Within her graceless ugly motion, somehow she enthralls us. This is an unsettling place to be in, as seeing her on this Journey with us should normally be considered the worst of torture. For Selay would spite the gods even if they offered her forgiveness.

Today she was met with no challengers, and so sought out new ones. Her charge we should be spare of, but her campaign continued in full across the whole field.

Cloaked in her linen black travel robe, so as to escape the dampness on this spring morning, she moved unnoticed down the large main Freestride Market road. Her large, flightfull wings weighted on her back from a long venture, and fire clearly present in her gate, and eyes.

Slate blue is her hide, marked with plates along her back, legs, and arms. A tail with a heavy sway to match her hips. A white plated belly of a platescale formed a natural armor.

What could been seen of her head, were two horns protruding. With splintered tips, and a copper band around one. Her emerald green eyes have a distinct consciousness of that of a hungry hound that stalked its prey. Her muzzle soft, with length equal to her neck, and a slight overbite. Her cheeks are plated along the jaw. She had ear holes near them, a distinctly colonial feature. This made her plain, and inconspicuous.

Her robe is modified, mimicking a three piece cape. It wrapped around her front. The back cut for her wings. It held to her with a set of leather straps tied in three places.

Upon her back was a staff not of normal shape. A most recognizable artifact of power in the Empire. With a center graced with gold, and a green gem. Its pole is a laminated ancient wood. The top silver steel blades shaped like feathers, bolted together to form the body of two fired figures guarding the egg-shaped gem at the top. The bottom, resting knee high, a blunt, gold cap, and a ring of smaller gems.

The staff was held to her by three components. A leather strap at the base of the tail, that it slid into. A golden plate sewed onto Selay's back armor under her robe, that should not be hers. Then the base of her tail made it angle, and rest along her wings. It would be nothing but a swift reflex to deploy it for combat.

How dare she trespass upon this sacred relic like this. Stolen, defiled, Selay took it for herself. She was no member of any royalty, nor was given permission to carry it. She should be executed on site, and the staff taken to be washed, and purified of her putrescence.

This city she walked through today, was of corruption, and thus ignored her. Freestride, a troublesome situation at the mouth of the Great Crack, is the center of the empire's shipping. The town is roughly thirty three thousand souls, within six distinct districts. It was distressful due to its intersecting of so many problems.

It was split between Jester, and Skol. The division line was the mouth of the Crack in the Shell of the World, and Skol was to remain the sole overseer of the river in that. Due to this, it is an attraction for treachery, as well as fortune. If it were not so vital to Skolis, the capital, to have access to its waters, this city would have been sacked, and burned by the empire for better lands.

The most noticed feature, is it was built upon a

cliff. A large lower dock area, caves along the cliff-side, merged into unique structures. Above, a large sprawl on the top highland festered. Climbing from one district to another requires good health, strong legs, and a fit back. This makes the city rather younger, as elders leave as soon as their age slows them.

Her foot claws tapped softly against the cobblestone road as she strode down to her spot. An intersecting of over five roads in the district of Akron. A market where merchants deliver to local guild shops, prior to crossing the only bridge in the city out to Jester. By law, if they must conduct business across the nations, they are required to abandon their caravans, and goods at the border. This is to prevent contraband, and enforce embargo on Jester.

At the corner of this cross, there was a destination for Selay. A tavern named "Talsworth's Keg." She could almost taste the Dewberry Wine as she neared, drying her mouth, and encouraging her step. Even her empty stomach moaned to be full of fresh cooked sea trout after spending more then then two weeks eating insects, berries, and aging salted fish jerky.

When she crossed the windows of the tavern, she could smell the ale from it. However, she also heard a stirring across the street, and it made her stop.

The road was wide, and a large crowd gathered to the section on the far side. A wood box was set upon the pavement with two guards standing by it. The crowd was varied, with children ceasing chasing insects, and shopkeepers ending their work to listen. This could only mean one thing, a proclamation is coming.

Out of the nearby brick building came a golden tall

man. He wore a long red robe with the Ain and Ua symbol used by the Empire. He was a Herald guild member, chosen for his distinct color. Golden was a color found farther south in the Empire, and less in Freestride. He held a curled up Scroll in his hand, and seemed rather disgruntled.

Behind him was a fat, amour-clad watch captain, that was a bit rusty. His face scales were unoiled, cracked, and he held a small stiletto in his left hand. From what Selay could surmise, this was a Herald now forced to show his patriotism.

The golden man stood upon the box, then fanned out his wings, and arms in open display for the crowd to admire. He clearly felt nervous, as his tail swayed stiffly. He looked at this rusty captain, who showed some of his teeth back. Then opened his scroll to read.

"Gather round, listen well! For submission to the empire, and demand of the law of the realm, is required today!"

Selay thought these preludes were amusing. She took a lean at the doorway of the tavern she was about to enter. No one even noticed her, as she held back a chuckle.

"Give your fin to listen to what the Lord Vex, and the Order, demands!" He went on.

"Listen for justice, and common good. For the lord demands death to the fiend who stole the Imperial Stave! The same staff, that united the Valley under the first of the Kiri'grana, was taken by this ruffian!"

Selay broke her lean, and went inside, she knew exactly who he was persecuting. It felt wiser to become far less visible. She stood just beyond a window.

"This vile rouge's head for the murder of Malvi Zyrko! The scales of this traitor for the burning of the city of Anya! A thousand coin for his corpse at the feet of the nearest duke!"

The sex of the description was enough to make Selay sneer long down her muzzle. She counted the guards, and noticed the captain was gone.

A voice came from near the group, "But who could kill a Knight!?" Selay spotted the guard captain in its direction, and realized it was he who offered the repose.

"Ah but the most luckiest of rouges! For Delios, and Yelvian themselves nearly caught him!" Chimed the herald.

Selay had to hold her jaw shut in order to not laugh. Both of them had a clear sight of her before she flew into the night. They must have been rather drunk to not notice her features.

"He is of average height, blue complexion, white fore-scales, and a steel gauntlet of the old war! He may possibly be Kiri'grana descendant, but also a colonial in some features, such as the ears! He is agile, cunning! Close up, he smells of rancid beer!"

From behind, a deep, sarcastic male voice came, "Oh, I hope they catch this scoundrel."

Selay recognized the vocalization's master, and she faced him, snickering, "Agreed, for he is a traitor to the realm."

Approaching was a man with a white tone, and a rather foul pedigree. He was Jestarian, clearly, purely, and typically brashly as they are. He spoke in tones of self-appointed authority, and bore fins that no one would mistake for anything other of the sea-faring kind. On the side of his neck were well-defined gills, that were very often glistened with water, sometimes purposely over-applied by cloth.

His head, two ear fins, grayish white, and wrinkled hides of not age, but of water. He scales were of a fish, across the whole of his body. Above his eyes, his ridges formed into two wavy, and thick, frills that covered the back of his head. Down his forehead, and back, were stiff prominent fins that ended only at his tail.

Like a sea-serpent, his cloths were fashioned around his fins, so more of his body was exposed then needed. One could see his back, and only a belt wrapped around his tail base.

Regal, laced with gold was his front-focused cloths, with multiple layers, all silken, and declarative. He wore a necklace, with a logo of a diamond of sorts, the unique seal of Jester's senate.

For you see, he was the sponsor of Selay's behavior. Chancellor Brudge Char' Derin. He is just one powerful, and dangerous, head of many, in the Jestarian hydra. A self-righteous, arrogant, and greedy creature. With ambition in his every step, gaze, and flounce.

"To what end does it serve to wield a replica of a stolen artifact on your back?" Brudge inquired, arms crossed.

Most knew this stave, it was pictured in the emperor's paintings across the realm, and described in books. Though so few knew it broke, and that at the center, a large padded brace was crafted to make it once more whole.

Selay joined in the arm crossing, "I intend to implicate you in the crime. For you see, I count five court spies now asleep at their tables in this establishment."

Brudge looked behind, and counted. Five surly looking characters, out of the thirty in the room, were face first on a fish. Their tankards spilled onto the floor. One was already snoring with his wings sprawled out.

"You did not kill any of them?" He clearly became concerned.

"Not this time, just a sleeping powder." She told Brudge to his relief, "They'll report to their masters tonight that the ale at The Keg is a bad batch."

"It is clear you are concerned of my integrity in this meeting. I should be grateful, but I know you serve some ends. What about it?" He prodded.

To what end was it for Selay to do so? She needed to get the staff out of Skol. Jester is the first place to suspect this artifact to surface. However, the Marshland is vast, and it would be hard for platescales to survive in it. Except Selay, who knows of scale oils that protect herself from Swamp Fever.

Budge's ignorance, right now, served a purpose. For Selay, his lacking of discernment in regards to her is his downfall. She opened her wings, swayed her tail, and hips, throwing embers of her spring fire into Brudge's path.

"Only one has decided it good to challenge me over it," Selay decided to deflect, "A hydra that bears his own staff. One he intends to serve my end with. No one but you bore the burden to look."

It worked, Brudge took this as an invitation. He smiled, "Is this fish to finally be enough to pay your dowry?"

He motioned towards a seat in the far corner of the

room. Selay did not answer, she unset the staff in her gauntlet hand, then removed her robe, and flung it over her shoulder.

Her form was distinctly feminine, fit, and lean. Acquired by running, and climbing. She bore two significant pieces of covering. On her hips, a rusted old Skol Tasset, leather straps holding only the left side armor plates. The right straps held twin daggers, and pouches where the plates should be. A golden silk green cloth dangled, pinned by bolts, or a Skol Warlord buckle, then wrapped back below, and under her tail, held up by a belt there. A red skirt kept her hips hidden.

Her chest was covered with a tanned black leather cuirass that was of Skol Archer design. Guards, straps, and thick plates all exaggerated her shoulders, and chest. A cotton layer was lined under her cuirass. This allowed Selay to escape wearing a tunic, or chain-mail. One is but as restrictive, and useless as the other to her. Even so, stealth is usually offset by the occasional impact of her old, dented, dual-layer warlord grieves, and arm gauntlet. Selay bore more hide, and scale then her line of work considered secure. It was the staple of hazardous, and most obscene, but gave her the agility she needed in combat that men in armor could not muster.

This drove Brudge maddened with desire, as some areas of her design, such as the tail, clearly provided more view then a normal dress or trouser set. Allowing him to wander his eyes along it. Selay knew this, and made sure he saw.

It was the usual display she made to get him to have no memory of what went on. Casting a spell that lead him by a rope. Arching her tail, just enough to make him wonder, raising her rear a little, and relaxing her wings. The right slant just barely would show what could be the shape of something. She walked slow, and seductive. She kept within his gaze to lead him to the table. One or two around noticed, but got a hostile look from Brudge afterwards.

The table was already adorned with two lovely trout platters, bread, and a bottle of Dewberry Wine. For a moment, Selay expected it to be poisoned, but she knew better. The owner of this establishment would be the first target of her wrath before she succumbed to it. Brudge knew better as to what would happen if she survived.

Selay sat first, and placed the staff on the floor under the table. Brudge sat as well, and both had plenty of room to fan out. Neither did, Selay kept her wings loose, but folded.

"Your fawning over me is adorable. How long has it been?" She thought back to when this all started.

"Three seasons, and I have yet to get what I so need," Brudge moved to open the wine.

"You still think that barging in while I was in the wash basin, and asking to have me, is good strategy?" She watched in amusement as he blundered the cork of the bottle.

Brudge dug his claw into the bottle top, and only pushed it more into the neck. Selay grabbed the bottle from him forcefully, and almost perfectly countered by popping the cork out with a talon along the side. She has been here before, and has turned him into mess. He hides it like a finscale is expected to do, but she sees it in stiffness of his fins.

"You clearly were needing to receive someone. I

could smell, and see, your fire."

"Scent is not the same as desire, and the site of your moldy figure took any idea of desire from me that night," Selay put the bottle down between them, and Brudge took it up to pour glasses. "Not to mention. I had to wash again. With soap! You were so rancid to touch, but I had to throw you out quickly, or get sick myself!"

"You wound me. I bath daily. I could sing of your foul scent, and chorus about your unkempt scales. Yet I hold back. You so speak rudely of me?"

"I like singing of how crusty you are!" Selay laughed hard, and slugged down her wine, only after watching Brudge drink his. She was paranoid of this desperate man, enough to hold him accountable.

"Your end is nothing but to claim me so you can have power over me. No finscale in your station would dare have children with a platescale. Soon as you do not need me, you will trade me off at first convince. You are of your business, and that is of power, and deceit." She scolded.

She was correct, as Brudge wanted her work. It would be much less costly to add Selay to his harem then to keep affording her price. He not only pays for her needs, but for her product.

Though he lied anyway, "You would be my chosen. I would gladly trade my harem, and station, for even a single night curled with you."

Selay shook her head, placed her hand on her fish. She saw Brudge eating. He used a fork, and a small knife to cut little bits of his dinner, and daintily eat them. Avoiding bone, and chewing so gracefully. It looked habitual, and tedious. As finscales have two fangs that could easily chew through bone themselves.

Selay took the whole fish from her plate, and then flung open her wings. Brudge stopped, glared, and smiled, thinking she was about ready to offer submission. Then with a loud crunch, Selay bit into her fish. Snapping bone, tearing meat, and offal alike. The flavor of it made her salivate a bit, and it spittled from her jaw.

A savage site, she did this consciously. With a single move, she ruined the whole event. She looked up at Brudge, and just with a lousy effort chewed, and smiled toothily the way. Then used her free hand to guzzle down wine straight from the bottle, some dripping from her maw onto the table.

Brudge was in horror. An unfashionable behavior for a woman, even one as brutish as Selay. He sighed, and placed his utensils down, clearly unable to eat more.

"Close your wings. You are drawing attention to us." He demanded.

"What? The herald was not specific. There are plenty of blue Allyians running around in the empire. As you know, it is a fake."

"That is not the point, you know my station."

"No one else here, but I, knows your place. You are just some Jestarian cuckold merchant buying some platescale whore, because your entire harem has the lover's pox." Selay loved this game of annoying a finscale. They make great efforts to hide their anger.

"You will give me what I truly want for coin?" Brudge snorted, "You are more finscale then you like to admit."

Brudge went down to his bottom line. He pulled out a bag, dropping it on the table. It made a clear sound of coinage, and he glared at Selay.

"Lover's pox? Last time you claimed I was festering scabs under my tail. Are you a trained doctor?"

"I am! You are clearly sickly! You have excessive yellow bile, and liver derangement," Selay took another chunk of her fish, and a swig of the wine.

When she was done, Selay stuck a claw under her top, between her breast, and her cuirass. She puffed up a bit, and slide out a small note. Then put it next to the bag, and took the purse into her clutches.

Unfurling the knot, she looked in, then dug inside with a claw. When satisfied, she looked back up to Brudge. She tied the coin bag, and set it on top of her travel robe, which was aside her on the chair.

Brudge took the note, and placed it in his silk green glove. He huffed heavily, and examined the view, ignoring the death glare he was receiving.

Selay knew she could give Brudge abuse, and he would remain civil about it. This made him so boring sometimes that she just wanted to kick him. His gold is always enough to keep her from it, and the information she sold was valuable enough to feed her until winter.

As Selay went for a third bite, this time, her teeth cracking the skull of her fish, Brudge looked away. He curled his lips, and squinted his eyes. His fins twitched in agitation, which made her smile.

"For a doctor, you eat like a untrained hatching," Brudge scolded.

Selay laughed softly, then leaned up, and cocked her head to the side. "Do you force all your harlots to ignore their hunger?"

"No. I just ask them to not to make a scene doing so!"

Selay looked behind her, and saw no one reacting. They were all drunk. As Talsworth knew well to drown his patrons enough to make them near-sited and dopey. Selay looked back, and continued her display, and gave the finscale a submissive pose.

"It has been months since you paid for my dinner," She made her soft features stand out, and gave Brudge begging eyes, "I have been on the road so long."

Brudge leaned back to admire Selay's form, "I an not mad. Just disgusted. You are more civilized then this. You tarnish your glamour by-"

Selay quickly took Brudge's, now unguarded, fish. He stopped his praises, and growled, his frills rising, and teeth showing. That blue platescale bit through the back of her new catch as hard as she could. Brudge reached over to reclaim his food, making Selay retract all her glamour, and give a growl.

Brudge held his head up in the air, and in an uneasy laugh, begged the gods, "Why do you torment me so, Ua?"

Selay continued to consume his former dinner, choosing to ignore him. If she were to eat warm food, now would be the best time to fill up.

"Get out of here! I paid taxes yesterday!" Yelled someone off to the side.

Brudge snapped his head to see the commotion, "Selay, we might need to end this."

Selay was already up, fish set on her plate. Brudge was talking to himself.

Five city guards were surrounding the large green owner of this establishment. Each one clad in a leather uniform, with the city seal on it. Barrious Talworth was surrounded, and thus, unable to escape.

With deliberate stagger, Selay left Brudge to his misery, and made her way to the bar. Mainly, she was after the vast liquor cabinet. Her interest was that of a traveled drunk, looking for a stout ale that only was made in The Keg.

She poured a glass for a morning drunk sleeping nearby, and sat the bottle down on the bar. She took up the first stool she found, close enough to hear the conversation. She drank, and noted the morning drunk rose to guzzle his stein. She did not know it, but his name is Flinx.

"You are a liar, Talsworth." A guard held up a piece of paper, "Our ledger says you underpaid."

Barrious examined the ledger, squinting his eyes. He roared, "There is no city seal on this form!"

A guard grabbed Barrious's wing, and pulled it, causing him to yelp in pain. "Pay! Or I break this."

A protection racket is what Selay smelled. A racket, on her own limited hideout racket, seems off. She decided that right there her intervention may be necessary. That came in her standing up, taking the stout ale bottle, and sauntering to the first of these guards to gaze on her. A young red, with clearly no mind of his own.

Her glamour was quite effective, though it is spring. He examined her carefully as she ran a claw along his chest. She then sat on a table in front of him, holding the ale bottle near.

The apparent leader of this bunch drew his sword, held it to Selay, and growled, "You are interfering in city business."

"Oh carry on," Selay smiled, "I just want to examine this example of a platescale here."

She wrapped her tail around his hip, and pulled the man into her catch. Securing him by wrapping a rather strong leg around him. He became drunk in her fire, and softly rumbled. He leaned his head to the side, "You wear warrior's armor. Take them off."

The captain pressed his sword into Selay's space, "You are under arrest, whore."

"And what should a lady wear?" She said coyly.

The guards were split now, three on Barrious, and two on Selay. The leader in the center, on Selay.

"Nothing," The young red grinned, "You shall be covered in my wings shortly, and belong to me."

The captain renewed his sword-point, this time at her neck-scales. A single push would end Selay, but her allure vanished instantly, and gave way to the treachery in her.

The leader growled, "You shall give him what he wants, or I shall cut your head off."

Quickly Selay moved her neck to the side, and away from the sword. Her gauntlet arm rose up, and slammed against the blade hard. As the captain stepped back, his cohorts drew their blades. She lunged forward at the man she ensnared. The large green rum bottle in her bare hand, already flowing towards him. It made shattering contact with the side of his head. The young red dropped his sword, and fell to the ground. Everyone, even the other guards, paused at the unexpected show of defiance.

Mostly room-wide was this reaction. A sudden break in the chortles, and laughs of patrons. A shuffling was heard around the bar, and a lone cricket started chirping from the direction of the kitchen.

Flinx, whose moment of unwitting victory is here,

was the first to break this desperate moment. He was coming of age, and his parents told him he needed to experience his first battle, if he were to be a man worthy to defend a nest. He spent the whole night waiting for this moment, and did not want to disappoint his parents. As he took his stein in claw he stood up, and with the skill of an army engineer, sent it airborne in an arch. One so perfectly calculated, that history wonders if he was sober. It made course for a patron behind one of the guards.

The artillery Stein made contact upon his nose, with a hollow sound. The patron was flirting with one of the maids, who was serving him beer. The impact roused him, and he pounced on the patron on the table aside of him. The scuffle expanded quickly to consume the server, and the table nearby. The Cataclysm had begun. One by one, each table became embroiled in conflict.

The guards panicked, and all but the captain forgot of Selay. He held his sword at her, and growled. She quickly gauntlet slapped, and throw him onto a table with a couple eating. The upset enraged the man, and the woman shouted, and such the man dove gleeful into battle. Selay then gracefully walked away, as the chaos expanded from table to table behind her.

What was left of the city guards, was surrounded on all sides by a room of riotous platescales. Barrious could be seen tearing his customers apart to form a path for himself. He had a strange smile upon his maw, like a merchant making a large sale.

One table in the far corner was untouched, occupied by the servers of the room. They took their customers' steins, fizzing with beer, and drank them for themselves.

They could be heard singing *"When boredom strikes, we all fight! Beer! Beer! Beer!"* In celebration of the event.

Brudge was in horror as Selay sat back at their table. She began consuming in a hurry both fish, and wine. He did not look back at her, and just observed the chaos. Everyone took part in the destruction of this establishment.

"I heard of platescale bar fights, but I did not think of them to be on this measure." Brudge said, wide eyed.

Selay belched. She finished enough to be satisfied, and figured she could spend coin for her next meal. She got her things in order quickly, and stood up.

"Now we leave. Before those guards get out of the fight."

Brudge nodded, and he stood up too, there was a route that lead through the kitchen, past the cricket, and out the back door. It was the only part of The Keg not consumed in conflict, or with glass shards on the floor for bare footclaws to be cut by. They moved with haste that way.

When they approached the bar, Barrious himself was thrown back. He took a bar stool in claw, "That is my favorite chair you just ruined!" he roared as he smashed it over a guard's back, then disappeared back into the frenzy.

The two broke free into a small alleyway behind the tavern. The fighting sounds could be loudly heard from there. Suddenly a deafening glass shattering erupted. Selay briefly felt a sense of mourning, as that was clearly the bar's store.

"I never understand you Platescales. How did Ua find

the patience to teach you order?" Complained Brudge.

"She left us eventually for our idiosyncratic nature," Selay retorted, still sneering. "I need to get out of the Empire for awhile, Brudge."

"So that is your trickery? You need my cart?"

Brudge said this as he arrived by his carriage, a Jestarian woman in a odd set of trousers, and shirt was commanding its two horses.

"I could just scale the cliff again, but I thought you would be much easier." Selay said.

"Then lay with me tonight. Just once?" Brudge sighed.

"Not that easy. You need tree panning first. I do not want to catch that mold you have still under your tail."

Brudge still offered Selay the ride, opening the carriage, and climbing in first. Selay got in, set the staff on the floor, wearing her coat, and sat in front of him.

"You could have just left that fake staff behind." Brudge said, and Selay kicked it under the seats, where their legs would hide it.

When they arrived at the great gated stone bridge between the kingdoms. The guards stopped Brudge, and he showed them a paper.

The guard taunted, in fluent finscale, "Finscale diplomats? Go to the idle with the lot of you! I should pull you all out, and serve you to my children on a platter! I need to poison a few of them to rid myself of this post! Get out of my realm!" He rattled on until he saw Selay, and shook his head, "If I see you back here, whore, I will send you to the stocks!"

When upon the northern side of the bridge, Brudge showed his papers to the guard. They looked at Selay funny, until Brudge gave them a few gold pieces.

Selay was left off near a market, with all her belongings. She quickly moved in a direction eastward, and vanished from Brudge. She figured he was now reading, and becoming angered at her trickery. Then aroused, as a finscale does when they are caught in a game of manipulation, and deceit.

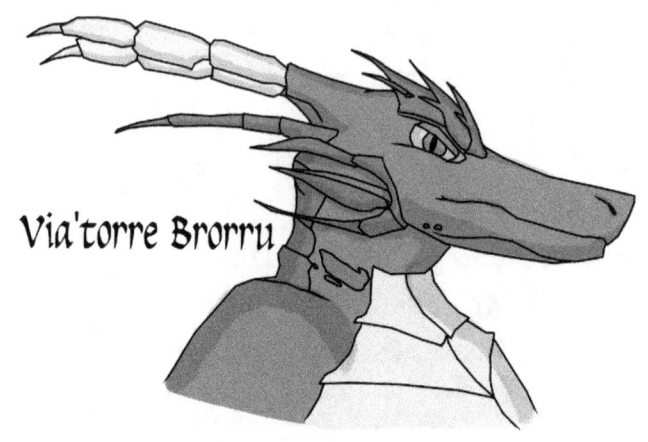

Via'torre Brorru

CHAPTER THREE

We wither, and rot for what we have done. To see that in the end nothing matters. We call Ua and Ain from this great nest for forgiveness. They gaze upon us in shameful sorrow, demanding us to Journey.

We prepare, and so do we provision ourselves for this venture. We have gained immense riches, and built things heavy, and sturdy. Sadly, coins rust, and stone chips. Our desire to house them is not appreciated by the heavens as merit for entry alone.

We are to journey without excess, or be rather slowed otherwise. Heavy are gemstones, and they have value only in what we cannot forage for ourselves. Sleeping on a pile of coins is comfortable, cool, and calming, but blankets are not as cumbersome. They warm us, and wrap food we must eat. So those who have not begun the Journey, share your good fortune before leaving. Give some to the church, or to the Empire. For the common good, these things are best given to those who can use them.

The only children to be expected to hold in excess should be Kiri'grana. No one outside their station should be apt to bury chests in secret places. One doing so shall not be trusted, and should be properly dispensed of, for they are clearly plotting against the divine compact.

Via'torre Brorru was just one of the many flightless who did hide his wealth in secret places. Some in pits in the wilderness, others in vaults in cities, on his person, and among others. His greed was his burden, and so did it impeded his Journey.

Such as on the day he awoke to the smashing, and roaring of another legendary fight at Talsworth's Keg. A thing that was made worse by the guards' attempts to suppress the drunken rabble. It was not normal for a fight to break open until after second meal. It was still morning, as the inn windows were wet with dew.

The light red man dressed quickly, he dawned a silk coat, and fur scarf. Things which he acquired when in the northern lands. His covering has gold trim, and underneath he wore a blue tunic with his white collar vest, to keep the lint out of his chest scales.

Via'torre, a common platescale from Skolis Valley, was with sharp features. His muzzle long, flat along the top, and with a jutted nose tip. His eyes are blue, and his ears are facing backwards. He has long fins, with a pair of frills both over and under them. With four horns on his head, long, and curved down, and spikes along his developed eye ridges.

He refrained from gloves today. Tucking them in his golden silk belt next to receipts. To cover others' coins.

Unfortunate as it was, a morning meal was not in his route like he hoped. With the discord he can hear below, he figured the time to walk to another tavern would be too long. He further did not want to be in town for much longer, as the street traffic around the gates at mid day would slow him down.

He came down the stairs, as the fight could be seen maneuvering in various places of the room. Nearly everyone was in possession of some mark of battle, usually a black eye. The guards were disarmed, surrounded, with confused looks upon their faces. Via'torre could see small streams of either wine, or blood, dribble from the fight. It ended its trail by vanishing into the cracks in the wooden floor.

Barrious Talsworth was using a chair leg to beat the backside of some other blueish-green platescale. Who barely felt it through the armor on his back, as he tried to choke someone. This was to no avail, due to thick plates on his neck. That person was just laughing. The servers were singing bar songs, drinking their customers' beer, in some attempt to livening up the place. Although they were quite inebriated, so it was rather not a pleasant sound.

Via'torre was acquainted to this site on a much smaller measure. Fights across the Empire's taverns are often, and quite less destructive. Usually just a two person brawl. The watch would not be present, other then placing bets on the winner. They tend to round up everyone as they lost. The general tradition is to not arrest the last one standing in the fight, so the town would not be in revolt, and fairly celebratory over their new champion.

It was a labyrinth for Via'torre to move through, one of destroyed tables, unconscious drunks, and broken glass. When he reached the door, leaving to the road outside, he could see the troop of watchman were already sectioning the place off from a crowd of enthralled onlookers. Even the herald left from pronouncements to see the commotion. Young children could be seen weaving their ways through the crowd, and laughing. It was the town event.

He began walking to the opposing end of the street towards the Herald's office. Only when he made it to the line of guards, a bulky, and taller red guard put his hand right on Via'torre's chest, and growled down at him.

"You are disturbing the peace. The fine for this is the

sack of gold you have on your belt." Via'torre staggered back at the sudden accusation.

"Sir, I am with the Armour's guild. How dare you charge me! Out of my way! I have business to conduct." Via'torre scolded.

"Show me your seal!" The guard demanded.

Reaching behind, Via'torre removed a purse. One fairly less visible, that he hides behind his wings a bit. He untied it, removed a lone rolled up paper. The guard took it from him, and examined it.

The wax seal itself was of a suit of armor, and a blade of grass. Indicating the Tram Armour's guild seal. Yes, he is in Freestride. Via'torre was in transient from Tram, and must exchange this seal at his destination, which he is in a hurry to do now.

The guild itself is an Empire-wide institution that is run at the top by a older man named Litrix. Its main headquarters in Skolis, but Litrix himself resided south in Anya in his older age to write his memoirs before retirement.

The association was more of a mixed guild. Chapters specialized in local markets more then a universal product. It took contracts with the Empire, and some private lords. Most contracts revolved around building after the war ended. As such, the core administrators were given license to issue, and enforce some regulations as a state onto themselves. The guards were trained to give seal holders special exemption, except in taxes, of course. Unless Via'torre killed a noble, or another guild member, he could gain access to any court, or summon any ruler to meet as if he was king himself.

"Move along then," The guard gave the letter back to Via'torre, and made an opening for him to proceed.

And proceed the man did, puffing up his chest, and marching onward. Annoyed by the assumption towards him by the watch, who should of known him in Freestride.

The Amour's guild normally made honest work. But when it was faced with potential competition, it went into a ruthless sort of enterprise of undercut, and fraud. Such on a measure that would destroy its opponents. One aspect of such fraud was knowing when to slander enemies, and to praise your allies. Via'torre was good on this. He was no guild master, but he knew when to slander correctly.

A few days ago, Via'torre was on road. His shipment of timber into Freestride was stuck in a ditch. As his cart was damaged in the event, he felt his career was at an end.

However, a point of luck came by him. He happened on a group of sailors, who were moving supplies for a ship anchored east of him. They offered him help, when they noticed he was part of the largest enterprise on land, they immediately offered it for free. They transported his entire shipment back to Freestride, where they were going for repairs, and crew.

Via'torre intended to pay for an announcement by the Heralds to show they are loyal, and righteous, platescales of the Empire. Such would give them an easier time of filling their ranks for their next adventure. Also to prevent any attempts to claim a debt on him.

The Herald's office was quite larger then it seemed from outside. Quite Cavernous. Perhaps due to its taller ceiling of two floors, and wide double segmented structure.

The front is a reception, with a woman writing down on parchment at the desk. She was older, but still admirable in her gentle features. She had a gray gown, with green scales, and slightly husky.

The other partition of the room was behind her. A vast collection of shelves, filled with stored works, rolled scrolls, books, and signs. One wonders how many centuries of sales, accounts, and stories does this room contain?

Scurrying around the room, was a flock of various

youngsters. Boys, and girls were climbing on barrels, and finding things to play with. They were of all ages, some small, and still on four legs. Most a various shade of green, or gold. The younger children, were nearly identical.

The woman looked up at Via'torre, and breathed a huff, "What can I do for you?"

"I am here to report on behalf on someone."

She moved the parchment she was writing to the side, then looked up, and down Via'torre with an awful gaze. An examination that should only be reserved for courtship. It made the lighter red merchant a little worried, as he assumed the monsters behind her were her children. Rightfully, their presence warned him about the expense that follows them.

"On behalf of who?" She leaned forward.

"Visek Jennu." The woman awakened over the news. With haste she readied another blank parchment.

The whelps behind her broke out into a fight, someone started crying. Something broke, and the woman went from excited to mad in a single moment. Then with a deep breath, a fire ignited in her eyes, and with a hefty roar she turned back to shout.

"GO UPSTAIRS YOU LITTLE DEMONS, AND BE SILENT!" nearly at once, all the children scurried up the stairs.

She once again came back to a more pleasant sway, and sighed, "To think, we are going to have another clutch this year." She said, shaking her head. "Now what about Captain Visek Jennu?"

"I am Via'torre Brorru, shipping merchant of the Armour's Guild. While on my way to Freestride, with two great maple trunks, my Oxen panicked, and got stuck in a ditch." He slowed down to let the mother catch up, as she scribbled the story to record.

"A provision group of Captain Jennu's happened by. They offered to help me move my timber. Captain Jennu transported my cart, oxen, timber, and myself in his ship for no cost."

She stopped. and seemed disappointed, then put her talon on her face, "Another good deed by Jennu? While on board did you note anything unusual?"

Via'torre shook his head. He remembered one lady. She moved from cabin to cabin with barely anything on. However, he figured her a typical dock prostitute. A common site on ships while they moved through the coastline, "No, nothing but the usual whores you see along the docks."

"That is nothing worthy of scandal... like contraband? Or Jestarian goods?"

"Nothing."

"How do you want this advertised?"

"I want posts along the dock. The captain is looking for recruits for his next voyage while in town. This good story will make his work easier."

Via'torre thought he could get some fame by signing it himself. To be associated with a traveled figured could get him a few new mentions, and lead to new ventures.

"Mmmm... twenty gold." the lady priced.

Via'torre paid. He was just settling down his coin as the gold southern platescale herald entered in, and walked by quickly. He seemed excited in his tail motions. Via'torre watched as the man pulled out a book, and opened it up. He set it on a barrel, then dipped his talon in the woman's ink jar, and began writing.

"Another Talsworth fight! I swear he is profiting off the bread, and beer grants the city is paying. We should post a concern about this at the castle." He perked up, looked around, "Where are the children?"

The woman snarled a bit, "If they do not stop breaking my jars, I am going to eat them."

Via'torre held back a smile. He let his memory drift towards a few of the ladies he had between seasons, and close to spring, and wondered if any bastards were his making. His color, and features were quite commonplace, so no woman would easily hold him accountable. Then the fear set in, one of paying for the cost of feeding them if he was accused.

"Do you wish anything else?" The lady asked.

Via'torre came to, "No. That is fine."

"Okay. Thank you for custom," she said, and walked back with the freshly written record in her hands. Her husband nose bumped, and they gazed affectionately. She then sauntered out of view.

Via'torre left, and saw the fight still was ongoing at the tavern. The crowd was quite larger, absorbing some of the guards. He also noted the guard who shook him down was relocated by the wall of the Herald's office facing the crowd. Via'torre decide to take the opposite path.

The route around the cliff edge, before the bridges, was best. It avoided a bunch of people, and any guard checks. It was a road that did not take him directly to the lift like he wanted, but gave him the peace to calm himself.

When he arrived at the cliff-side, no one was around. Normally there was a few other people to join in the descent. He enjoyed having someone else operate the lift so he could admire the view of the sea. Via'torre was forced to use the sheep wheel to lower himself slowly down to mid-level cliff-side, higher then normal. He could walk down the cliff-side stairs to get a view. He could also lift his head up, and bath in sunlight for some extra time. What little was shining reminded him he needed to find a rock to bath on soon.

Finally down to the lower districts, Via'torre traveled a few blocks to lastly get to where he needed. A massive complex of warehouses, and shipyards. The dockyard of Freestride. Within the center was a large traffic pile of Oxen carts offloading timber, and loading up lumber. On the coast, was the incomplete hull of a great ship. One Via'torre never saw before.

The receiving yard smelled from the oxen dung, however he was used to it. He was here plenty of times before. There was his cart, now repaired, waiting with a load of lumber already stowed. His oxen were grazing on feed, and the coloring of the new wheels made the his old rickety cart look strangely alive, and new again.

He made his way to a door with a sign that had cliffs split down the center with a suit of armor between them. The guild seal of Freestride's Armour's guild. When entered, he saw a well-windowed room with a lone table, surrounded by many shelves and cabinets.

Noises, and large bangs came from outside, as a great tree was lifted off another cart. Inside, a small white middle-aged platescale entered from a corner, wearing a featureless brown robe.

"Via'torre!" He smiled, opening his arms, and wings.

It was Zytle, the guild master of the Freestride chapter. He was quite a gregarious character, who loved to take shipwright contracts. He has a strange fascination with wood. He seemed ever pleased with himself, his eyes were stuck half-lidded.

Via'torre was just as cheerful to see the man. He opened his arms, and the two made a formal hug.

Years ago, Via'torre met Zytle on the edge of bankruptcy. The post-war Empire contracts were infrequent, and the guild was unable to handle itself in Freestride due to the loss of the iron trade. Zytle was not the master around then, and Via'torre repaired carts, and shipped things freelance.

For you see, Via'torre built his cart with far less wood. Zytle commissioned many carts for caravan work when he found out. This allowed the shrewd man to sell off the bulkier, war party carts to nobles at collection rates, lessening repair, and wood costs by a third. Leading to Zytle paying off his debts, and eventually holding out until a good contract.

Of course, Via'torre only built his carts of shoddy craftsmanship, and scrap. This change held the guild together long enough to take on a more domestic role. It out-set several competitors without having to resort to more then one murder. This, and the termites extracted from the wood tasted delicious.

The success propelled Zytle, off the back of Via'torre, into guild fame. Fame that he used to position himself as the guild master runner-up in Freestride. When the old master had become a lousy drunk, and eventually washed up ashore cliff-side in Jester, Zytle took over all of Freestride.

Via'torre was paid handsomely, and always rewarded with a contract if he so desired it. Mainly due to him being in a lucrative position to blackmail Zytle. He knew what his master did, and was an accomplice to the crime. Via'torre paid for the drinks that fateful night. Upon his old master's death, Via'torre was brought to trial. He was set free via the testimony of a dock whore, whose tail he hid diligently under that night.

However, he preferred honest contracts over schemes, and today was one of those days where contracts were completed, and new orders were to be given.

"I heard Talsworth's Keg is rioting again. I was concerned you would not show till much later." Zytle said. "I already had my labor take care of the transfer."

"I saw my cart when I entered."

The pair sat down at the reception desk, a simple table. It always had two wood cups, and a wine bottle setting in the center by a half-spent candle.

Zytle placed his sack of coins on the table on top of

the sealed transfer parchment. He always did this, taking his own personal purse, rather then dig into the safe. It is good to make sure to have enough to pay for half the day's expected orders on hand at all times. To open his deals he would dangle his wealth visibly by dropping the bag on the table. As his cloths never told anyone who he is.

"We agreed to thirty pay per great tree." He nodded, taking out coins, and setting them down.

"No it was thirty by one half. So twice that." Via'torre smiled, and checked the same sealed compact he showed the guard. Then set it on his side of the table.

Zytle snorted, "You conman, you trick me, the compact says thirty five!"

The two laughed. Via'torre opened the seal. This was the usual merchant banter shared between the two. They always tried to fake each other out of a drink, or some useless barter. Negotiation, and agreements were their passion.

"Ain and Ua be damned! The contract says it right here." Zytle stacks an additional eight coins. "You got me for forty! Now, what is next?"

"Lumbering lumber again. Where do I go now?"

"Back to Tram. The outstanding orders for woodcraft that need delivery." Zytle opened up his wine bottle, and poured a cup.

"What did they pay?" Via'torre took the new compact, and examined it.

"Enough for three loads. Something about wanting to build a new gallows. One with spike traps. That is for the Tram chapter to solve."

The lumber business was a terrible game in northwest Skol. Unlike the core regions east of the mountains, the area between Freestride, and Tram was lacking in labor for mills during the war. Towards the end, local family businesses were drafted, and slaughtered in the colonies. Then in peace, the taxes incurred to sustain the Empire impoverished all but the clever. Families, whose sons, and daughters died in war, were unable to meet quotas. There was also the Mouth, and Egg Rots that followed. This stripped the rural areas of their populations the decade prior. The supply, and demand shortages were driving up both cost, and price in a terrible cycle of lack of labor, and lack of funds to pay for more labor.

Tram has no lumber surplus since before the war, despite being a vast woodland, and and having a working sawmill. Freestride's shipbuilding industry, and clever guild antics, kept the city's rural lands the lone surplus of lumber in the two regions. Further south one could go, but no city in the peninsula was comparable to Freestride. South was too contentious politically, and Zytle kept prices predicable.

"Did you tell them only one cart per shipment?" Via'torre asked.

"But of course. That makes us more in the aggregate. They do not have any clue as to how much we pocket." Zytle sipped his red wine, and leaned back, wings dangling. "This next shipment I will need you to do more."

"What?"

"I hired a young lad. He is quite sharp. But he does not know how to drive a cart of Oxen. He can lift, and maneuver himself much faster then our other dumb labor. I want you to show him the route."

An apprentice? Via'torre was not pleased with this. He was reluctant to allow others into the cartel, or share his gold. This must be a special case if Zytle was to burden him with parental responsibilities. Via'torre was going to fleece him for this one.

"Who is he?"

"Pomonik!" Zytle got up, and moved towards the open

back door that lead to the loading, and storehouses. "Pomonik! Come here!"

A scrawny platescale of about seventeen seasons came in. His cloths, and face all dirty, and gray. He appeared like some homeless scamp just off the street. When Via'torre looked at the kid's eyes, there was something dangerous, but his size eliminated any feeling of intimidation about him.

"This little pup is Pomonik!" Zytle introduced, they both walked to the table, "I want him on his own cart by fall. This is Via'torre Brorru, Pomonik."

The whelp got nervous, and bowed. Bending a knee, and opening his scrawny wings. With an immature squeaky voice he stuttered, "Pomo for short. Pleased to meet you, Elder."

Via'torre laughed, "I never wanted a son. Though if I were to have one, I do prefer to hatch him myself." He said with some irony.

"He is not your son, he is mine," Zytle's words made Via'torre nearly fall out of his chair.

"I never thought you would let a woman sleep on your hoard pile," Via'torre went for the wine, and poured it in a second cup.

"Your preoccupation with gold made you forget I fanned a flame when you were not around," Zytle smiled.

"Wait... not her!?" Via'torre remembered a woman. A secretary in the office. She was quiet, and kept to herself. She always stayed with Zytle when he was up late. He remembered her being bought off a matchmaker to work for the guild, but that was long ago.

"Yes, her! What do you think we did all those late nights?" Zytle chortled.

"Oh... paperwork?" Shrugged the red merchant.

Zytle laughed, "I did use paper to build the nest!"

"Where is she now? This was how long ago?"

"She is at my manor. Another clutch on the way."

Via'torre snorted, and smiled. He felt jealous of his 'friend's' catch. But reminded himself of how many different vaults contain gold under his name, and how that a woman would want to unlock them all on him. It sobered his jealousy knowing that he could be free to settle wherever he wanted.

"Fine, I shall do it. I need payment for supplies."

"Twenty gold." Zytle began the bargaining.

"Twenty? That covers oxen feed! Seventy five."

"I paid less for his mother then that, forty two!"

Gulping back his wine, Via'torre got up to walk to his cart. "No! Seventy, or no deal."

"Via'torre, you are bending my wings!" Zytle became frustrated, and was thrashing his tail, "Sixty."

Standing by the doorway, "Sixty five gold, half in advance. I have to add more supports to my cart to carry him."

"You lie! I shall pay a quarter in advance, and agree to the price," Zytle surrendered.

"I can agree to that," Via'torre was ready to settle on a bit less, but he managed to play a perfect walk out to get the father worried. He now went for the close, "Write it down, and put your seal on it."

A merchant can discuss price, value, and hand off as much as he wants. He can yell, roar, and intimidate. When it is finally agreeable, the most important piece is the contract. Sealed form, records the transaction, gives security one can deal in consequences of duress.

Zytle opened a drawer nearby, and removed a parchment with an ink jar. Inking his claw, he began to write the agreement. As he did, Via'torre drank wine, and ate from the guild pantry. Breaking bread over the desk, and watching. The child sat around, quiet, and polite.

It took perhaps a fifth of the morning before the three left the office. The suns just halfway in the sky.

Via'torre's cart adjustments took only till around midday. Just two extra beams to sturdy things a bit more along the bottom.

Finally, Pomonik, and Via'torre climbed up to the seat. After securing their supplies, and themselves, they began the journey.

"Sir, may I drive?" The whelp asked.

"When we get out of town. I will let you hold the reigns." The merchant thrummed.

They made towards the southern gate. When it was in view, the pace of the oxen was slowed, to avoid mishaps, and mistakes. When they made the final turn before the gatehouse, they could witness three guards arrive, and dismiss the others.

Pomonik made a nervous deep breath, "That is not the usual guard."

Immediately Via'torre stopped the oxen, and squinted to examine them. It was the same guard captain from the tavern. He began to feel frightened, making a soft growl under his breath.

"Those are guards from the top of town, from Akron," Pomonik tilted his small head.

"I know, that captain tried to falsely fine me." Via'torre rumbled.

"They look like Ruguex, and his cohorts. They tend to overtax, and target the wealthy." Pomonik explained.

"We have to leave through that gate no later then now," demanded Via'torre.

The little boy glanced around the road at various items. He noticed a horse tied at a shop mostly unattended. Suddenly he hopped off the cart, which surprised Via'torre. He then made his way to the mare to remove the tie, and ran back.

"I could use a coin, sir," The child held out a hand.

Via'torre snarled at the whelp for asking such a personal question, and making demands of him, "You have done nothing to deserve it!"

"Fine. Then you shall pay over a hundred in tariffs when you reach the gates," Pomonik crossed his arms.

Via'torre ordered his oxen forward, and Pomonik squirmed some. As they moved by the horse, the child stood up in his seat, and threw something at the animal. It impacted with the haunch of the horse, and caused it to panic, and rear up. Then bolt forward, and past them.

The horse darted for the gatehouse, if anything to turn down the intersection along the town wall. As it neared, the guards panicked. One of them fell over trying to get out of the beast's way.

By now the owner of the horse was out of the shop, and screaming for help. This further alarmed the watchmen at the gate to duty.

Ruguex, and his underlings diverted their attention from the moving oxen cart, and towards the stray steed. They gave chase, and vanished down the side roads.

"What in the idle? How did you know they were going to do that?" Via'torre asked.

"Ruguex is only doing what he has to do to feed his family. He has six children, and the duke pays him the same as if he has none," Pomonik explained, "His sense of duty has not been fully lost."

When they arrived at the gate, Pomonik hopped off again, and pushed the doors open. They were large, sturdy, oak, and iron gate doors. The mechanism was not secured, so they only needed a strong heave. Once open, Via'torre called Pomonik to the cart, who hopped back up.

"Do not steal my gold again, boy! Or I will leave you behind!" Via'torre had to defend his purse.

"I used my own. You should count them," replied the

whelp.

"I shall! Joyfully! If you are lying, I will snap your tail!"

A shout came from behind them, "HALT!"

"YAH!" Via'torre snapped his reins.

The oxen bellowed, and then broke from their normal pace, moving forward at full speed. Via'torre's cart creaked, and groaned, but gave no sign of surrender.

Pomonik turned to see Ruguex stopped at the gate, growing distant. He then taunted the guard by poking his forked tongue out, only to be slapped upside the head by the tail of a growling Via'torre.

Yes, today is a burdensome day for Via'torre. Who is now unable to stack his gold in secret places, for fear of it no longer being a secret.

In this simple song, one of many, we can see the coordinating nature of our plight. For Ruguex would not have stalked Via'torre if not for Selay's chaos. Chaos that fans outward, beaten by her own wings in spite of the gods.

Ematel

CHAPTER FOUR

Huron awoke to a dry darkness, laying on a hardwood floor. He neither struggled, nor made a sound. He knew immediately how he came here, since he did not sleep well.

Captured by a band of childish rouges, who took him from a prison he did not belong in. He was kidnapped. He was kept naked by his captors, and aroused by the nearby red woman in spring flame.

This was a nesting room of a former grand manor of some long vanished Kiri'grana family. A home abandoned, collapsing under the growth of life around it. The wooden structure creaking, and groaning with the movement of wind. Unable to decide to collapse or stay, this reminded Huron that nothing, in the end, mattered.

For neither Ain or Ua wanted us to be in the nest eternal. Once we leave, we must be subjected to tests before we become theirs. These trials would begin with us singing our songs, and telling our stories to them. It would only end when meaning was found.

Merely if one, or the other, finds in us lack of virtue, they will subject us to the Forge. Ain will craft a Allyian who lived most viciously into a deadly weapon, and give it to his soldiers. Ua will turn her less loving subjects into charcoal for her teachers.

If balanced, or if found opposed in virtue to our favored god, the forge will not burn. The fires will not harm a single scale. This allows the opposing god to test us by their measure. So we sing again, and they listen.

Those of true mediocrity, and inaction, shall be subjected to the idle. A cold, lonely madness of redeath, and rebirth. There we fade forever, worthless as we were in life.

Both Ain and Ua made us able to bond in the nest in order to prepare us for our service under them. When they accept, they redirect this bond to them. Making us forever jealous, and protective. It is good to have a bond in life, to learn of loyalty, and duty to each other. For Ua and Ain yearn to bond to us, as much as we yearn to be with them.

A bond with a chosen is an embrace of envy of the likeness of the gods. However, it is to be regarded as neither an evildoing or a virtue, as it extols the zeal needed to prove oneself. In the nest, envy has the ability to do wondrous things to people. From bearing a strong family, to defense of others. It creates strong protectors of land, and treasure. Protectors who ever so become more fortified.

Huron's soul is bound, and this kept his envy for the red woman in its rightful place. He wanted her not, so as long he was of himself. The thought came not in a coherent way, but one of scent and fire for his chosen.

Though if he let go, he could easily take for himself her bond. Such an act, making her a second, would only be at the risk of ire from his first. A woman who would never allow it. A first who does not approve of the second, has domain over the fate of the brood of both, due to her claim. Huron would not be so foolish as to allow a trespass on Selay's territory.

This made Huron fearful, and desiring to tuck his head

under his wings. However, the beam around his arms, attached to the collar on his neck, was keeping him from curling up. He was tied like a dog to the wall. Leaving him to only just lay on the hard splintering floor, and suffer the flame of this supposed title holder of the Empire of Skol.

Eventually, a ray of light broke through the holes in the wall. Sounds of birds, and nature, came much earlier then expected. Huron could make out some of the room, surprised at how well-furnish it was with shelves, and torn paintings.

This woman was surrounded in haphazard nest of blankets, and pillows. She was curled up, with her wings panned out, making her body hard to see. She slept quite peaceful, sounding soft huffs. Nearby, a plate of fish and bread, with some tea, was set. She was fed, while Huron was left to starve.

Huron became aware of his stomach growling, causing him frustration. He tried to squirm over to the food, only to find a shorter rope from his neck onto the wall nearby. It only was lengthened at the width of the room, which was one third the opposing length.

He huffed, then surrendered. Remaining still, and allowing his pangs bother him. The dust in the air was dancing in the light, providing him with something to gaze onto, but not distracting.

The woman stirred, and Huron noticed. She turned ,and raised her wing, then scratched her side. Huron saw the extended belly, her eggs waiting. She rolled to her back, and remained asleep. Making light puffs as she breathed.

He remained indifferent as he best could. Allowing no thought of how she became this emaciated slave of various agents. He did not even know her name, or cared to know. Allowing such knowledge is how one draws empathy, then envy, and then is consumed.

The sound of claws echoed through the wall, and a loud

bang followed. Someone was out there, maybe more then one. Huron pulled himself onto his belly, and slid over to look through a small divide in the wood boards. He could see the girl from before facing at someone across a table.

Most of the conversation was muffled until she was in sight. They conversed with variation in volume, and clarity from varied direction. When the voices became clearer, Huron perked his ears to get a better listen.

"The Tram guard knows what we have done! They will seek justice for the blood we let spill. They shall hunt us," She calmly explained, "Why did you not plan this through more?"

Huron heard the squawking voice of the head kidnapper, Ematel, just outside his view, "They will be too busy cleaning up the blood to try anything soon. When they come, I think they know her value! Then we can negotiate with the high priest. He will make sure nothing happens to us."

The girl shook her head, "How much do you think we will get?"

"He agreed to thirty three, and a hundred thousand should be enough," Ematel came into view, walking up to a old cupboard to remove a sheet of paper.

"That is more then what is in the town treasury! You are a fool for asking such a high price!"

Huron adjusted his lean, and heard a muffled grunt from the sleeping red in the darkness.

"The title of this catch is worth more then all the gold to those pathetic Kiri'grana! It is the title of King! Valued in land, glory, profit, and power! They have killed each other over her!" Ematel shouted back.

"Ask for a lower price! You may be able to get her for one tenth. Go that high, and the guards will gut you, and her, while laughing," The little girl tried to bargain some sense into her leader.

"Zhaqua, do you not know how to huckster?" Ematel

vanished back to the desk, "We start high, stay strong, and only break down as we get other things. Like pardons, or supplies. We want a ship to leave to Restavias do we?"

"Yes, but they do not have one. They will just slit our bellies, and take her from you! You have not foreseen everything."

The first time Huron heard the girl's name, he was too frightened to think on it. Zhaqua is southern land's in naming. A region beyond the south sea where the Empire does not reach, but platescales seem to have settled. The natives there were more prickly in their scales. Their lack of progress was noteworthy, not even using horses to carry goods, but not relevant.

Ematel began to explain, "We keep them both here until a deal is made. When they pay, they get our catches. If they test our limits... I take the girl for myself, and proclaim her my wife."

From the sudden thrashing of Zhaqua's tail, and her fists, she was clearly not happy with this statement. Her posture became combative, and her talons pressed too hard into her palms. They pricked her, and Huron could smell the blood right away.

"You are not mature enough to claim a mate!" she snarled.

"They do not know that! I shall force it through anyway. Her bond is enough. A clutch can come next year."

Immediately Zhaqua flipped the table. A small stack of papers, and a vial of ink, spilled to the floor. Ematel rose, then immediately grabbed Zhaqua's palms. The small bloody pricks he noticed right away, and growled. He throw her out of Huron's view, and snarled ferociously at her.

"This is *my* band! I plan the ventures! If you do not like this, you can leave!" Ematel reestablish his rule.

Huron had no thoughts on this, just watching. He was

overheated, and he rolled out his tongue to cool a little. Dare not to think, lest the fire of that woman affect him.

Several loud thuds were heard as Zhaqua grunted, and yelped. Ematel demanded her to calm down, and eventually she was thrown in front of Huron's viewing spot, blocking most of the hole. Her tail clearly curled stiff, and her wings folding tightly in defense.

"I have nowhere to go! I do not want to see us all killed, nor hunted by the Order for a clutch of eggs!"

"A clutch I will smash on laying! I just want that woman's title!" Ematel scolded.

"Master!" a squeaky voice said, muffled by the door. "Is everything alright?"

Ematel rushed Zhaqua, who uncovered the hole, as she was held up along the wall, clasped by her neck. Both her, and him growled at each other, and Ematel could be heard saying "Shut up! You swore to the band! I am in charge! I say you leave if you disagree!"

Zhaqua ended her rebellion there, as Huron heard nothing but her whimper. The little demon let her go, and fall to the floor. He went to answer the door. Huron could not see anything except Zhaqua, now on her knees, sobbing.

"What is it?" Ematel addressed the new arrival.

"There is a supply caravan heading towards Tram. They appear to have large stores of fish, and beer."

The mood in at least half the room changed. Zhaqua was laying on the floor in now a state of near compliance. Ematel went from anger, to cheer, as he roared in glee.

"Assemble the men! Zhaqua shall observe our prisoners! Beer, blood, and fish tonight!"

Zhaqua gave a soft nod, then looked down her muzzle onto the floor. Huron saw clearly her tears, and quivering. She gave about a breath before catching Huron in the corner of her eyes, where she locked with his. Upon this, a predatory hunting look overcame her.

Huron backed up in sudden panic, as the rouge girl rushed to her feet, then vanished from view. His backing was suddenly stopped by the rope. There he tried to cover himself in his wings to hide, and failed.

Silence, and nothing. This continued for a time. No footsteps heard, or voice spoke. He felt like a ghost was nearby watching. He saw his cell mate was unresponsive, she was solely focused on catching up on the sleep she lost while forced to starve in prison for untold time.

Then, a clear banging as the rouges left. Singing, and banter, only barely heard outside, began. It grew softer, then very distant, then returned to silence. Ematel was off to sew chaos.

A time later, the door bolt clanked, and it opened. In came Zhaqua, she was holding a torch. The sound of her entry woke the red nearby, who turned to see the commotion. Zhaqua placed the torch in a wall holder, and approached the nest of pillows.

"I wonder if you truly are the last of the coward king's brood?" She knelt down, and caressed the egg belly.

A growl erupted from the red. Zhaqua then slapped her jaw. Causing her to yelp, and return with exposed teeth, ready to fight. Zhaqua responded by drawing her dagger, and set the blade to the woman's stomach, "Be nice! I can still sell your eggs if I cut them out of you."

In her cornered, weakened state, the woman squirmed, and made a nod, she whimpered, and begged, "Mercy..."

Huron could have claimed those eggs before all this. Though she will not find empathy with him. For he must protect his family first. He was wrong in this, as all eggs of platescales were worthy of protection. Huron was full in his cowardice.

Zhaqua crossed her legs, and just sat glaring at the

red. "Good girl," she said, wetting her lips with a sneer.

She was clearly of different character then when she was in front of Ematel. As if her act with him was a mask. Eventually, she got up, and came to Huron, swaying her hips, and tail. She had power in this room she did not have before, and clearly drank herself drunk from the enjoyment of it.

She moved slowly, directly in front of him. Then with sudden quickness, she pressed the knife into Huron's neck-scales. She did not cut him, but was rather close. With a glare of sadistic lust, she examined his eyes. It struck a terror in the soot-scale.

The cold blade made Huron retreat to a nightmare of swords, and blood. A torment that froze his soul, and brought forth demons. Zhaqua withdrew her hold, perhaps noticing Huron was suffering in his own way. She returned her blade to its hiding sleeve, seeming satisfied.

She sauntered over to the door, chuckling, ready to leave. Her tail swayed with more force, as she appeared to have another emotional outburst.

"I think we are better off without the two of you!" She swung her tail into the bottom of the torch as she left, slamming the door, and latching the bolt shut.

The torch fell onto the ground, casting embers outward across the immediate domain. The old, dry, wood floor took a brief few moments to catch on fire. It began spreading to everything it could find.

Huron tried to get away from it, as it grew towards him. Eventually spreading along the walls, the entire room slowly began to light ablaze.

Huron wanted to scream, but could not. His nightmares returned. Visions of burning corpses, and familiar wails echoed from the grave. He felt helpless in his lot.

The red nearby was giving a hawkish screech of panic. Herself tied to the wall, but with arms free, and unable to move far from the nest due to a shorter leash. She lifted her body up as best she could to protect herself, discovering the limits of her mobility. Only in finality giving up. She folded her wings over her torso in an attempt to protect herself from the inevitable.

The flames danced, and cooked everything nearby. The air became most dry. Huron began to feel dizzy from the heat. He tried to pant with his tongue out to cool, but only gagged. The fire moved closer, and if it were not for the sudden snap of a floorboard just by his feet, it would have begun to consume him.

Huron's arms were chained to the bar around his neck. The chain was fixed upon a wall. The beam, connected to a strong metal ring, was tight, and held his neck stiff. While it ached him, it also forced him to move his arms in order to turn his head, and torso.

At the opposing side of the room is where the manor began collapsing suddenly. The floors opened, the walls tumbled, and a piece of the ceiling brought what remained down with it. Any idea of escape, though Huron never thought it, was gone now. Both of them were confined to the Forge.

Huron had images of his mother in his mind. He could only pray. He uttered the Mantra of the Twin Gods in dry horsed breaths.

"In the end, nothing matters, all are created, wither, all die..."

"Nothing is eternal, nothing is sacred, except the gods..."

"I have quested. To build a nest to make both proud. Failing in protecting it..."

"I deserve nothing for my failur-"

Huron felt his body jerk in mid pleading, cracks, and snaps all around. The roar of the fire below came, as if the great Forge of Ain was here to sentence Huron to judgment.

Suddenly his neck was pulled, and the rope dragged before it tightened. Huron gasped for breath at this, feeling force on all his form only offset by a sudden swing into a still standing wall behind him.

A loud, horrendous snap was next, and the young platescale gasped again. The hot burning air choked him as he began to kick, and slash his free limbs at whatever he could in panic. Eventually his vision blurred, fading from smoke, and lack of breath.

Another series of bangs, and snaps, and the scream of the red could be heard. The Forge takes all. Huron saw her fall into flames. Despite his willingness to give up, this made him go into a primal panic. He swung, and kicked desperately, growing weaker, and weaker.

Then a smash, followed by the feeling of falling as if Ain dropped him from his talons. Huron hit something, and found his breath free again. From the brink, he gagged, and hacked, body heavy from the blazing heat. He tried to rise up, but fell back down, the arm fixtures still in place.

Huron surrendered, and waited for the fire to come to him. Let the forge reshape him into a pair of tongs to help create other weapons from better monsters. Huron was done, in his own mind, he wanted to go to see his family.

In another mind, he was not done. A pair of hands gripped his chest, and shook him. A now familiar whimper was heard. When he opened his eyes he saw the woman, face covered in soot, and tongue out herself, whiskers waving in the wind. She had a confused, and desperate expression on her. Her ear fins were lowered into a pleading posture.

For some reason Huron enjoyed the sight. He could have thought it was Ua ready to judge him, as he suffered the Forge, and survived. Sadly, it was this red woman. He knew from the scents, her fire overtook the burning world around them. It called him to listen to her.

"Do not die. Help me..." she pleaded to him, her voice weak, and raspy. "Do not die..."

Brudge

CHAPTER FIVE

We shall suffer if we idle upon this journey. For inaction is shunned by Ain and Ua. They value it not, and consider us defective if we lay when we should move. If we so desire stillness, they shall send us to a place where we can idle for eternity.

The Idle place is where there is no form, nor thing for one to do. There can only be madness, tedium, loneliness, and decay. We shall fade away there, becoming nothing.

Selay is destined for such, and she determined loafing was her goal today. Deliberately to bask in the shade, and hide from the work of the world. She wanted to mull, and brood in Jester. While the Skol Empire hunted for justice against her crimes, she hid in enemy lands. Knowing the Empire could not cross that Great Crack without terrible consequences.

Journey's Rest was one of the manors where she could hold herself in. A sprawl along the Drenching River, and a midway destination before branching further north to Port Selis, or to the island ferries, or to Deep Lake at the heart of Jester. There were perhaps fifty thousand of the wicked sea-serpents living there. Enough to make it a major organ in the region. However pungent this rest stop is, much like any other city of Jester, it was populated with poor, and a caste of flightfull perched in manors above.

The riverbed, in particular, was a mess of shanties, and many-tiered hovels. Living within are families crammed into one, or two rooms. They made their meager living on grubs, and salvage.

Jester did fall on good times after the Armistice was signed. All Finscales properly suffered, and their families suffered, and their bodies reflected this. Dirty, rotting fins, cracked, and foul. They stood with bad posture, and tattered cloths, and birthed eggs that frequently never hatched.

While this situation was the opposite of Selay's idea of a perfect home, her Journey was filled with contradictory things at times. She would have ventured to a more rural area. However, a shanty wood enclosure upon a granite apartment, owned by someone who trusts her too much, is safer then the swamps.

It required a significant ascent, and at its final reach, a glide to a rooftop isolated from the rest of the path. This deterred all but the most boldest of explorers, and Selay had no problem making the glide herself. This was intentional in design, since a neighborhood this poor would not be filled with anyone with useful wings.

This place was an eyesore, which was where no one would expect someone infamous to hide. A thin wood box, hanging like a rooftop shed. It had an access window on the side, and a sun window on the scrap roof. It looked best left for the building's workmen. The walls, and floor barely stood, and the whole alcove was elevated just slight off the rooftop edge. It felt always like it would tumble to the street below.

She found her newly acquired staff a bit heavy, and

decided to aim above the window slightly. With a diving leap, she threw it into the side window. Then fanned out into a clumsy glide. When finally landing on the roof of her shanty nest, she nearly fell off the opposing end. Regaining her footing, Selay swung down onto a ledge, and through the window.

It was dark, and dusty. Not wide enough even to fully sway one's tail in. A nest of straw bags was laid in circles in a safe corner, nearby an unlit candle set in a bowl. On the other side of the room, two chests, and a small wood table with a chair were shoved together. Of course, a barrel still full of some wine, sat in the corner. It smelled preferable to Selay's omnipresent scent.

As she reset her staff by the table, she filled her bosom with dank air, and let her wings and tail loose. Finally a rest, and maybe in the morning, a long sunbath.

Brudge told her of the secret rooms of his more sturdy buildings. Mentions of closets meant for tax collectors to never find. All of the Derin estates were adorned with additional rooms for hidden functions. It was the charm of Jestarian nature in their design. Elaborate hiding holes to escape the consequences of their lies.

Spanning half a block, the complex was home of a local trader, a priest, and several laborers. They paid rent, had many squawking children, and Selay paid nothing. She was Brudge's pet platescale spy after all, with better value then some lowly tenet.

It was late evening, and suns set already. Selay deposited her smaller things on the table, her coin bag, and knives. She then opened the rooftop window. Starlight shone, and the cracked moon pulsed, but gave her no light to warm. She pouted softly when she was again reminded that her scales needed a bath.

Next, she rummaging through a cornered chest filled

with various books, and materials. Pushing a few knives, and a lone silver bar, oddly stained with blood, aside. She removed a thick black tome holding a large volume of papers loosely. Selay purred while she caressed its leather cover, as it is time to bind this book properly.

On it was a symbol of a man with a knife to a fish, and the name "Kitsuna" by it. The book was thick, and heavy. The pages were worn, but the cover was new. It should be stowed securely, but Selay prefers to not place it in a vault.

She sat on the pillows of her nest, and made a little work area by it. She light the candle, and posed it close. Then opened the book, and removed the loose papers in the stack.

The first page read:

> It is usually not wise to assemble one's great book after your first child, but I am compelled to not be idle during my leave. In here, I have amassed a collection of stories, and lessons I could pass down to my children. Especially my first born daughter, Selay, who disrupts my attempts with diligent chewing of my arm. It is fortunate I am platescale.
>
> Lambana Kitsuna,

Selay did not sigh, nor pout this time. Noting her previous times, when she used to become unsettled while reading this message. Somehow, she seemed at peace with the words. Perhaps it was because of this manuscript's value, derived from a recently new understanding of it.

Quickly she began to work, pulling the first pages, and separating them by some relevance. So many topics, so little order. One page told a story of how a soldier fought off a whole squad of Jester infantry with a bucket, which Selay placed in a pile for tall tails. Another explained observations of animals in the southern continents, this one went towards reference. One on how to sink a galley with siege weapons from ashore. Each page a summery of a lifetime of experiences unique to the world.

One piece, an essay on the uselessness of castles

caught Selay's interest. It was quite lengthy. It read:

Holds, and keeps were once great military fortresses that shored up territory. They had to be seized before taking the surrounding towns. This no longer is necessary, as recent marches have shown.

All be it that in the Era of the Sea, the coastline fortresses were supreme. Lately they are rendered impotent with the use of large transit ships, with tall masts, that gave good gliding perches. The larger, metal reinforced masts allowed for nearly half the crew to climb it before giving in. They gave a new pace of troop waves over the peak angle of the common Ballista's. Which made it easy to land numbers in the keep, and seize it.

For inland, armies raised are large enough in numbers so they can surround the fortress, and put great strain on the supply. A forest could be set fire to smoke the inner hold, thus chasing a defending army. A ship could be set with catapults, and barrels of poisoned meat could be launched into the water supply.

Siege equipment no longer must be lumbered across vast distances. Reinforce designs have given soldiers the ability to assemble large weapons with great ease. The trouble of iron shaping, is not an issue with the deployment of blacksmiths in the rank, and file, but an issue of skill of the blacksmiths, which we have no issue with.

All this, but the well is the worst enemy of a fortress. Poison can drive the dwellers of the castle from their holds. No longer is one safe within, when you can cause maddening poxes, and odd smells to undermine the enemy moral. Or in the case of the burning valley, we unwittingly poisoned the entire water supply by dumping corpses into it.

A clever, and fit person could just leap, and climb their way over the wall at night. Spies, and infiltration can open a gate to a small party. With the right fire in the ale silo, we can sober up the enemy, and force them to quarrel in the morning from hangover.

Perhaps the last of the great fortresses left useful is the ones in the deeper mountains, or the Great Crack in the World. Where their sheer distribution render them intimidating to the flightless. Even then, a catapulting-leap, wings outstretched, can get you over, and across borders. However, the lands are left burned for easy sight by border guards, so expect to be quickly punctured by archers with serrated arrows.

We live in an era so different from the songs we are told as hatchlings. A castle is no longer the center of the hold, despite what the old kings would tell us. It would be a waist now to construct new castles for anything other then pleasure. A manor for the ruler is just as homely.

The page beyond continued with a short story of a siege. One of an example of a fortress surrendering in a day. Where infiltrators fled leaping from their walls, when the inner city was burned. Selay thought of how she used her memory of this piece to escape from the Wyverns in Anya. It gave her an arrogant smile.

Satisfied with her classifications, reaching the end of the stack, she opened up the book. It having no end papers, thus incomplete. Its binding only tied, easily unbound. She removed marked pages that were chapters, placed the new stacks inside, retied the binding, and closed the book. She sighed at her lack of glue, but it would hold.

This act of book binding, Selay has become a master of it since she began to organize this manuscript. The author long gone, and no copies were elsewhere. The pages contained knowledge most valuable to her. The seal upon it, and the name of its author, were spoken in quiet corners by old rotting soldiers who did not die in the last war.

Selay continued to read, and opened to any random page of her now secured tome. No effort was made by her to actually remember what she read, and eventually she fell asleep. Half her body in her nest, with her head upon the book outside it.

She had dreams of safer times. Of comfort, and a set of wings to hide inside. A musky scent of her bonded Huron haunted her. This gave her visions of flying with him, falling with him, and repeating. Then a nest of eggs she could curl around, and guard. This was upsetting, and frightening. She felt it was what she both wanted, and never could have. Fearful in longing for it was just as strong as the fear of never having it.

This was only ended by a abrupt smash, forcing Selay to raise her head up. She glanced around, there was a commotion from outside. Claw scrapes from some distance away skittered around.

She slid over to peer out the side exit window, only to recoil away as a bolt shot by her, lodging into the wall across the shack. Selay snarled as her retreat now was denied, and slipped the window closed with her tail before rising to gather herself a weapon, and darken the room.

Closing the window had no effect on slowing her attacker, as he shattered through it into the room. He lunged towards her with a knife. This visible charge let Selay swing her gauntlet arm in defense. Cracking it on the arm of her assailant, and deflecting his attack.

Him? She was too busy to look, and saw this one was covered well. The hoodlum even wore flight covers on the eyes. He was skinny, and wearing black baggy robes. Most of the visible hide was black, wings were the only limbs exposed.

Selay posed her fists in front, ready to brawl. Her opponent lunged, and swung his dagger again. It was serrated, curved, and could be poisoned. Selay grabbed the chair of her desk in a free arm, and tossed it in the way as she stepped aside. Since there was little room, he had to place a knee on the chair, or face falling.

The chair was still upright, and Selay kicked the seat hard into the still adjusting assassin. He now became a bit cornered. The platescale moved in for a straight jab into the nose of her enemy, making him gasp. He changed to a defensive stance. Selay then followed with a neck hold, throwing her would-be killer down on his back. Finally, a thud made it clear he dropped his weapon.

Selay decided to inspect, but she kicked her downed enemy in the gut to be sure she could do so safely. Who is this? Removing the mask revealed it was a young finscale man with no memorable features. He was not even mature yet, and certainly no one Selay knew.

She picked him up by the neck again. He was light, fit for flight in his body. Which explains the skillful entry. He was someone's foolish hired thug, a lackey, obviously. Too dumb to know not to face a platescale directly. Selay determined it was a good idea to find out who his master is, so she could rob them blind.

She slammed his head onto the window's frame to stun him. She turned him around, and pulled his wing, making him yelp. She forced him to lean out of the entrance window, to a steep drop below, keeping his wing held.

"Who do you work for?" She growled into his ears, then pulled his wing.

He snarled, "Whore of Brudge!"

Selay did not enjoy the image of being with Brudge too much herself. He always had an odor of a dead fish, but he paid well. Though being perceived by her enemies as under his wing, or perhaps one his his harem, could be advantageous in finscale country. She would tolerate this, as it gave her advantage in many ways.

She decided to play it up, "He preens me every morning, and pays me for it. This matters not," She quickly raked her claws along the side of the boy's muzzle, then dug them into the nape of his neck, "Who do you work for?"

The young man was dripping fresh blood out of the window, staring at the ground, and huffing. Selay held his wing. If he cooperated, she will push him out so he can glide, and live. If he refused, she will snap him, and drop him to his death.

The killer began to laugh. He seemed in a shock of madness, telling her nothing is to come of this. So she took a deep breath, snapped the bone in his wing, and shoved him from the window. He tumbled, and struggled to fly, but in the end, he crashed into the cobblestone road, eyes open, and facing up to Selay.

She snorted in annoyance, as now she had to relocate. She was to take her time in collecting her things, and wrapping her book, but a fireball through the window expedited this. She noted a lingering odor of rum in its wake.

Forced to take glide, Selay fled, holding her vitals. Landing on the neighboring rooftop, she let herself roll, then rounded up, and broke into a run.

She went from roof to roof. Diving, leaping, and gliding as she could. Under her arm, the black book. Travel robe already adorned, and staff held in her other hand.

"I shall kill you for what you did to my brother!" Screeched an older male voice from above her.

Selay ducked, and weened into a small warehouse filled with carts stored by merchants staying in town this evening. She ran along the upper beams, finally arriving at a balcony where she hopped over the railing, and looked at her new rival.

Another ruffian, who was just as intending to kill as the prior. This one was a faster, older, crossbow, and knife wielding black finscale moving at full speed towards her. He somehow loaded his crossbow before entry. He had plenty of time to make a shot, but hesitated.

His robe was different, it was black but laced with a blue trim. Perhaps signifying rank or merit? He also bore a seal along his chest that was something akin to a guild. The best she could see, was the seal was a skeleton with flaming wings, but it was rather dark to be sure.

Selay dropped both the staff, and the book, they were too cumbersome for this. She stepped back as her would-be enemy joined her on the walk.

She was rather disappointed when he gave her no time to taunt, as he just charged upon her. However, now with enough room compared to her previous opponent, Selay could use her agility to the fullest.

The stride along the roofs awakened her for the hunt. This made her dodges, and flanks fluid, and effortless. As swung the blade with fury, and rage, so too did Selay's legs bounce, and tail thrash. Though not graceful, due to a quite viscous hangover. She stepped in wait for an opening, then left herself far enough back so that he eventually used a forward top-down swing. This let her grab his wrist, and pull it, so his back was to her.

She was behind him long enough to arm herself from this motion. By her red skirt, along her side, were her own pair of simple stiletto's that she constantly had to replace. She despised using them, but made no bias this time. She took one out, throwing it at her enemy.

He quickly slapped it out of the air, and could be heard chuckling. Neither combatant seemed winded, and they both were quite arrogant. Selay said nothing, and put a hand on her second knife, as the black robe charged towards her.

She drew the second blade, and deflected him. He they both began swinging. A fury of clashes, and blows erupted. The clangs, and echos of metal, and foot-claws between the two combatants would scare off even the rats below. Neither gave, just yet.

Finally, the knife wielding rouge broke through, the blade struck towards, and came for her heart. Selay turned a dodge, but it was not to matter. The blade lodged on the belt of her leather cuirass, and cut through it. This tore the strap, and her coat, exposing her white, and blue plate scales, but not penetrating further into her.

This left him briefly vulnerable, and Selay slashed her knife upward. This cut the webbing of his wings, forcing him to fall back, and briefly panic.

The pain, and the exposure made him run, and quickly Selay collected her things, and gave pursuit. Book in hand, staff on back, Selay moved just as fast. Leaping from roof, to roof, to street.

The stride slowed when the killer fired a bolt towards Selay. Who ducked to escape it. Then she threw her dagger into his direction, and likewise missed. He took to climb a water pipe to return to the roof.

Well before he could get there, Selay had to drop the book, and reach for the staff. She swung, and caught him with the blades by his tail. She pulled him down, splitting his tail to the bone. He cried out as he crashed onto the roadside.

He tried to ward off Selay by tossing knives, and loose bolts at her to force her to dodge. Crawling backwards as Selay approached using the wide blade of the staff, turned in varied directions to deflect, like a shield. Where thick scales were impacted, the throws were too weak to harm. The pain drained all the strength from him.

When he did get to his feet, his tail was a bloodied mess. Balance was a challenge, and he tried to run, only to stagger, then fall. A stack of boxes was where he leaned, facing away from his opponent.

"Your brother would be alive if he just told me who sponsored you." Selay said.

"I shall never betray a compact!" The black figured bellowed.

He turned, only to meet the bladed wings of Selay's staff to his throat. She could see he was not expecting to die tonight by his widened eyes.

"One more chance. Who!?" She growled, her maw nearly touching his, as she leaned close.

"Whore!"

With that, Selay decided there was no point in this game. She removed his face coverings, exposing his finscale gills, and frills. She gripped his jaw firmly, and jerked his head to the side hard. The snap was heard down the alley.

He gasped from his gills, and went limp. His form slid down along the boxes he was once leaning on. In his last action, all he could do is look back up at Selay, and gurgle.

She had no joy, or any sorrow. Just annoyance at her spring escape is upset. She knew this means her hunt begins. She plays in the finscale swamp. Now further troubled by the choice she made when she stole the staff. She chose to step into this challenge. Today, two appeared, and Selay faced them both, and she won.

Before she left, she removed the seal on his collar. Already stained with blood. Collecting her things, she vanished via sewers, and tunnels, to mask any scents from the guards. Briefly, she cursed at the idea of spending gold for another pair of knives, and at the idea she was forced to search for whoever wants her dead.

Serios

CHAPTER SIX

In this Journey, Ua and Ain guide us. However, we know not where they take us, or what we face. So we feel lost, forcing us to search for those who Journey with us. By their song we can find the correct path.

Huron is a cowardly dog that follows. He is but a scared child, unable to face this Journey. Forced to it by this woman, leading him to an unknown destination. He could not turn back, as her captors are bloodthirsty.

Selay does not belong with us, as she is belligerent, and savage. We are unwittingly forced to bare the pain of her presence, as her troubles burn the world we so wish to save. If she would just leave, and vanish into the finscale marsh forever, Ua and Ain would forgive us much sooner.

They both are queer, and ugly. Thus above normal in their position with other things. They superseded all, as their song is louder then all others. So we must observe. However, what of the normal ones affected by the actions of the abnormal?

Such as the strange normality of the eels of the marshes. Their habits are obtuse to the platescale life. Finscales seek quarrel in ways that it is left to wonder how they seem united in tribal banners so surely.

Such be the finscale family, where the act of choosing is a blood sport between the women. The world recoils at this barbaric practice. However, Jestarian folk managed to somehow maintain this tradition. Perhaps due to the rather harsh famine of men, their blood poisoning the fields of battle a few generations ago.

Somehow, finscales are rather strict about marriage. Women in finscale culture are not allowed to just lay at pleasure, despite what everyone assumes. They must prove themselves to the head of the household. This is a sport of vile trickery, and skulduggery that has lead to the finscale creature to be the most untrustworthy of all. It awards corruption, and deceit, making Jestarian life rotten from the tail upwards.

One rank household seems less rotten, good enough to observe. It is the Yan household. This roost begins this Journey in the wake of the Serios Ini' Yan.

He was one of the creatures of consequence. With green fish scales, and a stiff ridged jawline. Two rather long horns and rather wide earfins. He could be a bit platescale, if his form was not so weak.

Serios served the local duke of Journey's Rest, under the town watch, and was of the lowest rank. He was demoted once, thus paid well by seniority. So his entire household was supported by him. This made life rather stable.

Under him were three rather peculiar women. All of them were finscale as he. They lived in a small brick row house along the river in the inner city.

First was Serios's childhood friend Nair Ini' Yan. Daughter of a merchant who was lost at sea. She came into his hold with only a trifle of inheritance, feeble, and frightened. Her scales were of milk, and her backside was with violet spots.

Then Ados Di' Yan, Nair's cousin. She came into the home after breaking her leg. This accident was a result of discovering that she flies in approximation to a watermelon. She was colored as one too, quite green, and with a blue belly, with white spots all over her back.

Finally, then sweet Pab Ini' Yan. A gentile green fish with stubby fins on her neck. Serios found her at the Church of Ua, and her family was laborers at the warehouses. She was too young to marry. However, eager to live with him, as hovels at the river are far too crowded.

It was expected any time for Pab's first spring fire to erupt. Serios arranged to have her, and Pab was eager to marry. Obviously, the flame of the other women would erupt too, and thus be an inferno of quarreling that would become expensive. Ados, and Nair are known to be unruly, and territorial. Thus cruel to all in their way. They hazed, and tormented Pab, and framed her for things she never could do.

This drove Serios mad, since he was not a finscale needing treachery to live. He wanted to live outside his nature in some semblance of honesty. So he, and Pab manipulated their schedules to hide from the others. Thus, Serios Yan worked in the afternoons on patrol.

It was ideal, and while the others were hiding in their room, Pab would greet her love with open arms, and wings outstretched. A tender nose bump waited for Serios every day he came home.

Tonight she wore the most simplest of her gowns. The white one with pink wrappings that showed her form perfectly, and made Serios smile, and wag his tail more. Pab felt that tonight she would make Serios her's forever.

However, Serios was quick to smell blood, and recoiled back quickly from her greeting, and growled, "Show me where you were hurt?"

Pab lowered her head. On the top, by her head fin, just

behind her left horn, was a distinct claw mark. Serios became rather angry, and pulled her by the arm to guide her to the kitchen. He took a towel, and soaked it in the water pitcher nearby. Then sat her down, and cleaned her wound. This made her hiss, and her tail spasm at the tip.

When he was happy with his dressing of her lesion. He turned Pab to face him. Then, wrapped his wings around her to shield her from the world.

"Who did this to you?" he justly asked.

Pab was hesitant, and meekly stuttered before lunging into her story, "Ados, and I were talking about the food list. I said we should get you a tribute. She then became angry, and attacked me. She grabbed my head before crying, and running to hide in her room."

Growling loudly through his throat, he let Pab go, and stormed off towards the bedroom. It was rather small, and wooden. The door was opposed to a window that shown the Theater District. The lights from parks, and manors twinkled like additional stars. There sat Nair, nude, and quietly reading a book. A habit she did every night before sleep. Ados was already asleep, snoring, coiled around her pillow, bare as well.

Serios grabbed upon Ados's head fins. He raked a free claw along her scalp in an equal way she clawed Pab. She screamed the whole time, while Nair gasped, and nearly dropped her book.

"You attacked Pab! This is not tolerable in my house!" He boomed, looming over Ados.

She sat up, and pawed at his chest, and belly. Pleading with a whimper while a small trickle of blood came down between her eyes.

"I am sorry! Pab gives you more gifts then the rest of us are able to afford. It is unfair."

This was a trick, and she looked up on the man with

wide tearing eyes, "I am sorry."

"You two live under my roof along with Pab." he growled, "You know she is chosen to me, and acts far more civilized then you do."

"Serios!" Ados pouted, she put her head into his belly, and tried to nuzzle, "She is weak, and does not cook at day. She lazes around. She is not good for you. She will become controlling, and demanding after you marry her."

Serios gave Ados a hard shove off him, "Pab tends to my needs. She does the inventory, and helps with expenses. I am to be with her alone. You had a chance, but you instead ate all the food you could! Stop trying to fool an investigator!"

Ados whined, and laid down to cry in her pillow. She was scared that she would be out on the street at any time now. Her growing portliness was unattractive, and would make finding her a suitor far more difficult.

She was also shaping her pillows in a circle, a nest. When Serios noted, he grabbed firmly on her tail, and confirmed. Ados gave no fuss, and opened her wings, posing in a display. After all, if he fell into her flame, she would be suited for life as a well-fed mother.

The gaurdsman tugged his belt, and grunted in frustration, "I will sell you to Tyran. He has an odd fascination for padded leather. I tire of trickery."

Nair let out a chuckle from afar. Serios glanced over to her, and noticed her amusement. Leaving Ados to her shame, he approached, and sat on the edge of Nair's bed. Her spring state was clear.

"You too. She is your relative, and this kind of nonsense is in the blood."

Although more sensitive in tone, Nair felt he was meaning it to hurt just as much. Of course she was not the type to deploy such animal behavior. It is always easier to encourage others towards it.

Nair buried her maw into her book, and tried to hide from the hostile Serios. He decided to lean over, and try to read.

"It is my father's, this is private." Nair said, trying to get him to leave.

"It is? It is good the scribe hates me. Otherwise I could tell if you were lying to me or not." Serios replied.

"Then leave me. I did nothing to deserve attention from you!" Nair pleaded.

The man shrugged, then stood up, and began to leave. Nair snarled, and threw her book at Serios's backside. Then laid in bed, and pouted in distress. The impending eviction finally made her despair visible it seems.

Serios was more attracted to the sweet bread smells coming from the kitchen, and living area then with the smells of two fraudulent women who could not properly scheme like finscales should. However, even this blessing was superseded. The dining area gazed upon the river, with the Derin apartments down the coastline. There, a blazing flame, and pillar of smoke came forth.

He never did take in his meal. He just stood up, and threw his neck scarf over his gills, "Duty calls!" while Pab sat down, and placed her hands on her lap, and waited quietly for her hero to return.

It did not take long for Serios to find Tyran a few streets towards the fire. The red guard waved, and joined with his friend as they both ran towards the rest of the town watch.

"I heard Ados yelling, what happened?" Tyran asked.

"She quarreled with Pab, hurt her, so I hit her back. When are you going to take her off my hands?" Serios complained.

"Soon! I first need to get a good bath!" Tyran laughed, "The river is not enough."

"I am going to sell her to the matchmaker if you do not have her this week. I will offer her for free if I have to!" Serios threatened.

Tyran chuckled, and both gaze upon their enemy. The granite tower was ablaze from the top, and the fire was spreading downward on nearly half the floors.

Crowds of finscales were forming water lines from the river, directed by local guards and self-appointed leaders. Their efforts were futile, as the core of the blaze was internal. No water could properly douse it.

Upon the fourth floor, a child stood in a window, chirping a call for his parents. He was not of five years, and was on all fours. He jumped, and unfolded his wings, but his body was too heavy, so he could not gain flight.

A lone guard took the initiative to save the falling hatching. However, the pace of even a trained watchman was too slow. The child screamed in terror as it fell upon the stone roadway, dead, and the watchman fell at the child's corpse to weep at his own failure.

"Oh Gods!" Tyran pleaded, "This will burn the whole city." He traced his talon along a wooden awning that yet was aflame, but could spread the fire across the street.

Serios pointed to the windows, "No, we can break it from inside! Then isolate the core to the center of the tower!"

The demonic blaze was only spreading on three sides of the building. Where windows with awnings were, there was only glow or smoke. The exception was the top floors. Families continued leaping from windows with belongings, and each other, to safety. Men were recruited to water lines, and women were handed children to perch on their bodies, and taken off in merchant carts to safety.

Tyran called, "Come, Serios! We should get these people into another water line!"

Serios boldly ran towards the building, and was sure he could stop this blaze. Tyran followed, since he had to stop his friend from doing something stupid. Running to a burning building is quite a fine display of density.

They came by a closed stairwell door, and Serios kicked it. Serios is finscale, and not strong enough to break it. He turned to Tyran, and waved an open hand. "Give me your axe!"

"Serios! Stop this!" Tyran protested. "It is too much heat for us!"

"This shall spread to the whole block if it reached this side. Our homes will be lost. We can stop it here by breaking the middle, and lower floors."

"This is madness! Ain's forge is in there!" Tyran scolded.

Scowling, Serios just grabbed his friend's axe from its belt strap by the blade. His hand was cut in the process, but he made no expression of pain. He began to violently chop through the door.

"Tyran, get us another axe!" He barked.

Tyran listened, and just yelled for support. A guard at the water line gave them an axe, and ran in fear from the heat back to where he could stay wet. Finscales do not find uncontrolled flames a great comfort.

A massive heat greeted both as they entered the main lobby of the building. The light of flames were visible on the main wooden stairs. Fortunately, no stair was yet on fire. Despite the wooden inner structure, the blaze had yet to find a way to the stairwell, giving them complete access to all the floors.

This allowed both to take upon the second floor. A hallway to the several apartments with a unfashionable wooden floorboard was there. Along with the core fire, and smoke that was crawling down through the supports.

"Break the floors, and ceiling here! I shall go to the

next floor!" Serios coughed, then ran up.

Tyran did this, cutting clean through. Above, Serios did just the same. Both coughing and hacking as the smoke billowed into their weak finscale lungs. The breaks were made, and the fire could not jump.

However, Serios yelled, "Who goes there!?" and could see within the dancing fire a pair of eyes, and stubby horns. A child was yet inside the fourth floor rooms!

The smoke made the child vanish, and Tyran yelled to his friend. However, Serios was already climbing to the fourth floor, and could be heard stomping, and shouting up the stairs.

There was nothing but smoldering abyss. The floors collapsed long ago, leaving islands. Any entry or escape was a challenge. Serious had to skip, and jump between holes in the floor to get back to the hallways, with no ability to see.

Yet he made it without much trouble, he gasped, "If you are here, I am a guardsman! I am here to save you! Speak up!"

Eventually, Serios found the child perched upon a bookshelf in an apartment making calls for his parents. He was so young, maybe six seasons. The little one quickly climbed into his embrace. Serious used his wings to shield the hatchling from the smoke in the hallway. Then began to pant from the heat, holding his tongue out.

The floorboards in the hallway snapped, and gave. The pit that was made, reached to the bottom cellar. There was to be no easy route, and Serios gagged, and hacked as he tried to stay low.

Snaps, and breaks were sounding across the building. Floors above them were giving way. There was no time to think, and only a desperate act mattered.

The child began to cry as Serios covered him in his wings. However, that shield had to be forfeit. Serios had to leap, and vault from an apartment with no floor on the fourth floor, down to one on the third.

They landed in hallways covered in flames. Serios returned his wings to his front, and simply marched through the fire. His militia mail began to melt and burn, and his scales were boiling.

He made it to his own fire break. There, Tyran stared in awe as his friend survived the Forge despite Ain's best effort. Serios looked like he was of firm silversteel as he came from the inferno. He returned his wings to behind his back, holding the terrified child in his arms.

The flame walls were too much, and Serios knelt from overheating. One last leap, and it would end, and he could go find water. He let the child go through, and pushed him by the rear. "Glide to my friend."

The hatchling looked upon his savior, and chirped. The finscale babe ran at full possible sprint, and scaled over the gap, where he was caught in Tyran's hands.

"Serios! Hurry!" Tyran yelled.

Serios did, he stood full, and went into a sprint. Just as he knelt down to build a leap, the floor cracked, and his footclaw slipped. A roar of rage erupted from the guard, and he pushed on into the gap. He leaped, wings open, and into a perfect glide.

A support beam from above landed square into the spine of the heroic finscale guard. This broke him along the base of his tail. He died there, and fell into the rubble. Serios Yan was drawn back into the forge of Ain, then consumed, as Tyran saw, and yelled in horror.

Tyran resurfaced, covered in soot. He handed the child off to his parents to perch, then quietly left to find a soft spot to bellow a song for his friend. Pab was told that morning of what happened. No one in the Yan household ate for days, except Ados.

In the end, nothing matters. For we all must face Ua and Ain. Only their Judgment, sung in song, and bloomed in the forge, can free us of death, and thus is all that matters. The song of Yan family has begun, and Ua and Ain hear. Do they sing along?

Ayria

CHAPTER SEVEN

As fell Serious, so things become easier to understand. He dies in exemplar to us all. His song, once sung, perhaps reminds us that Ua and Ain's hesitation is but efforts to redeem us. Perhaps we have not fell entirely.

For we are their brood, or the All of Ua and Ain. The Allyian, Children of the Nest. We can not leave the nest if we do not show we can protect it. Serious shows we can.

The grand hatching onto the surface of our egg shows with Deep Lake, Selis Bay, and Skolis Lake. Then outward with cracks full of the water we bathed in before coming forth to the lands. This is proof we are siblings of the same yolk. That our scales make us different, but our form makes us the same. If a finscale ascends, then all of us have the chance to.

Is this why Huron decided he should help this woman? He could leave her to starve, but she was platescale like him, and vulnerable. She was not ready to face the Trial, so she must be protected.

It was quickly decided that he would see her to a church. Afterwards he would continue as he can on his way. After all, his chosen was sure to be alive. Seen by many taverns bearing her trail of lost bets, and black eyes. This is the scent he must resume following. Onward to a traveled drunk with no sense of destination, or so he thought.

This other crimson woman was confusing. She was seeming to feign a weakness with the mark of fraud only a finscale would see as interesting. However, Huron did not seek to risk being wrong in that assumption. It was further aggravating that around her, temptation beckons. To avoid this, Huron refused to even know her name.

Both slept a full night without much incident. Huron had to climb a tree to sleep peacefully. The rest allowed strength for the journey to take them to a rural chapel on the far north of the Tram region.

The church, a temple of Ua, had notable door marker of a gold woman clasping a shield, and curling her tail around an egg. Ua guards her eggs, while Ain guards Ua. Under the seal the name of the church read 'Hilltop Chapel of the Builder.'

An amusing name, for it has poor structure, and was mostly dilapidated, like all rural churches. It was one of two upon the hill following a road off the main north highway to Freestride. The path along it was a fishing pond, a small stable, an inn, and several storefront homes. A hovel buried in the dense forests of the region.

Huron rose his arm to bang on the door. Next to him was the woman, nude, and hiding herself with her wings folded over her body. Huron was bare as well, and saw some noticed, but he was helpless in choice of it.

"Why are you taking me here?" She squeaked.

"You would be better living out spring in Ua's watch," Huron said, before he knocked again.

Huron did not hide his body like her, his wings folded behind him. He tried this during the travel, and it was rather difficult to walk.

"My name is Tailya," she blurted.

"I did not ask to know," Huron replied.

The door creaked open. Immediately Huron was dealt another bothersome scent. A woman, of lilac color, and reeking of lily's came forth. She was bit pudgy, and wearing a full body robe of gray. She placed her claw to her heart, and recoiled with shock.

"My goodness!" She pointed down between Huron's legs.

Huron ignored her glances, and he puffed up his chest in greeting, "I am Huron Quirksettle. This woman here requires a safe place to stay. I am willing to work to cover the costs."

The woman examined at Tailya, who gave her a return look from the side of her head. As if to signal her own subtle disgust with the proceedings.

"This is a house of Ua, in spring, and you come here for shelter? Ain would serve you better, his church is there." she scolded, and pointed down the road towards the other temple of similar state.

Huron replied, "I said this was for her. I did not ask of anything for myself."

After a thought, the lady nodded, and opened the door fully. She motioned to come in, and the two entered. "Come in for console. The priestess of Ua is in the chapel right now. I will show you there."

The small church had a lobby, and was well sorted for such a simple looking build. It opened to a large chamber with about six pews, and candles setting along the sides. Mostly unlit except where it was most needed.

At the center was a flat rock, with a sun roof glaring light down upon it. A rock of Ua, for the sunbathing ritual. Laying across it, in a modest white robe, was a blue skinned woman, basking in the warmth. She could almost be considered sleeping, but she was tapping her claws together.

The support beams were wrapped with hand-placed vines along wooden beams, all blooming. Two other women passed by, both of a perfumed scent, and they made glances at Huron and Tailya. The red made soft growls when they looked any lower then face level of Huron, and she kept near his tail.

"Pastor Rioa, we have visitors," The other said.

The priestess opened her eyes, and looked from the side. She stood, and executed her rise almost perfectly. Right until she was on her feet, where she clutched her belly, and made a grunt.

"The fires burn in all of us, and you invite a man in without any sense of modesty, Ayria?"

"I meant no offense. He is the Quirksettle son!" Ayria held her hands up, and opened her wings. "He might be able to fix the roof for us."

Rioa snorted, and then looked at Huron, "It makes no difference. Spring is spring, and Ua's temples are not for men until afterwards."

"I am not the one seeking aide," Huron motioned to Tailya, "She is the vulnerable one. Not I."

Priestess Rioa slowly walked over to Huron, keeping her hips swaying. She tilted her head, and made eye contact, then sauntered aside. She let her tail brush Huron's leg, before noting him, and saying, "You clearly have been bonded. Your soul is with her, otherwise you would have no self control by now. Why abandon your chosen here?"

Huron frown, and reared back, "She is not my chosen! She is someone whom I only just met. I am searching for the one I share the bond with."

"Oh really? Then describe your chosen for me," Rioa ordered.

"Average size, with platescale features, blue hide, and white belly." Huron could see Selay before him when he closed his eyes, "A horn with a copper bracer, and the absent ear fins seen on colonials who trade at ports. A maw long, growing plates on her jaw, and a very strong fire that burns in her green eyes."

The blue retracted her examination, "The inn. Someone like that was at the inn. No one can forget anything like her."

Huron's eyes opened wide, not in surprise, but in attentiveness, "She seems to be in all the taverns. What do you remember?"

"I only know what my flock told me. I did not know how she arrived, but she was rather eager to drink. Two men from the Armour's guild caravan teased her, and caught her tail. This was before spring, perhaps around last snowfall? She laughed at them at first, belched, and acted lewd. When they pressed for more, she threw both of them into a crowd of rowdy patrons. Then fought them off with no grace whatsoever. They ran, bleeding. I think she bit someone in their nose."

This was a belligerence Huron saw as unique, remembered in their spring trip to the wilderness. After catching fish, they argued over how to eat. Selay was ready to eat the scales, and Huron was wanting to strip it. This argument only could end in one way. Selay pinned Huron down, and forced him to eat. He reluctantly did, then spent the entire night restrained, and any attempt to break free found the nape of his neck bit upon firmly.

The memory was so frequent in his mind that he felt her weight on him again. It calmed his spirit. He noticed Rioa gliding to inspect Tailya.

"You are young. Is this your first time?" Rioa asked.

"I do not like such questions!" Tailya huffed, reeling back, tilting to look side-eyed.

"My dear, you are clearly ill-taught how to control yourself during this time," The priestess smiled, "Will you show me your glamour?"

Tailya faced her back to the other woman, and tucked her tail under her legs, then pointed her snout high. She clearly did not like the priestess. Rioa out-shown her in more maternal graces. Then again, anyone else now entering the room would look more appealing then someone whose scales were crusted with such dirt and grime.

"Well it is clear someone does not want the help of the church," The priestess walked back to Huron, "You may be unable to leave her behind."

Huron lowered his head, "My will is not strong. Her fire is going to consume me. I have a duty to my chosen, and she has my children."

"Child of Ain, perhaps she is the fairer choice. She seems more loyal then that lewd women who destroyed our inn. Let the insufferable suffer on their own."

"Selay is not that insufferable, she is diligent." Huron retorted. "You condemn me, child of Ua, to suffer without her, or know of the brood we have?"

The priestess smiled, "Selay is her name? You say that, and she left you!"

Huron shook hid head, "I promised her myself, and no one else. Three seasons I have searched, following a ghost like her, and I will search forever more. I have a duty to family."

The priestess laughed, and made a motherly coo. Huron could see her flushed. She flung open her wings, and puffed her chest up in a rather seductive display.

"Blessed be the defenders of the nest in these lost times. Even in profane states of mind, you still remember why we are here. Huron, I am the avatar of Ua, you make my chest rumble. Accept my charity."

Huron growled, "I want charity only for Tailya. I do not want to curl up here without Selay. This is too much trouble for me."

"Then have a meal, and stay one night," The priest smiled, and hesitated. She was stern, "Just one night then. You are not allowed near my women. Huron. You will stay in your room between meals. You sleep in the loft."

Huron nodded, he was in complete agreement. Basking alone in a window, with a full belly, and pillows, is grand. A sunbath before he ventured on, would be perfection.

Tailya came forward slowly, and asked "What of me?"

"If you changed your mind, you shall have a separate chamber below. We have a room free. You can roam freely, and eat all the food you need." Rioa arranged.

Tailya's face beamed, as if she was to receive a palace, and her defensive posture ended. Her wings relaxed, and returned to her back. She sighed, and sat upon a church bench while rubbing her belly.

"There is a wash room below. We have some soap too. Go, and clean. This will be your only chance." Rioa pointed to a door at the far end of the chapel. She returned to the rock, where she sat down.

Huron, and Tailya made their way towards the door. The mistress Ayria was whispering to the priestess. Both glancing back at the two outsiders, and back casually. They then chittered back at each other in amusement. Huron was first to arrive, and opened to the cellar stairs.

Rioa shouted across the chapel. "Feel at large to take a robe! Sorry, we have no tunics!"

Huron replied with an arm wave, as Tailya glided into the doorway. He lingered, his eyes drifting along Rioa's back to her tail. The distance, and color of her body appears so close to Selay. Images of a memory of Selay sunbathing on a rock conquered, and waged war on him. His jaw lowered, lost in his own dream.

He was shook back from his imagery by the red grabbing his arm, and yanking. She pulled the hapless man down the stairs into the stone underbelly of this church. He tripped over his own foot claws while she took him to through the immediate hallway.

Tailya explored a few rooms, and finally found the wash room. She pushed Huron in, then entered herself. When she closed the door, she grunted, and growled some at the soot-scaled louse.

"You are trying to rid yourself of me? Is that your way of helping?" She threw her arms down in pouting anger.

Huron faced, and explained, "Ua's church is kind, and it will be safe for you here."

"And you think a poor town like this is worthy of someone like me?" her teeth were showing again, growling under her words.

He tilted his head, and decided to lean back to the wall, where the cold stone made him attentive. She was demanding on him, and he had to resist.

"You are not in any condition to choose your fate." He stated.

"I am Tailya Mek'velor!" She roared. "I am the Kiri'grana's ruler! You serve me!"

As if a sudden awakening, Huron began to laugh. She could not be the dead king's brood. She was just some imprisoned house mother. Then again, that little whelp Ematel was certainty sure she was a title holder of significance. Maybe her father owned a manor? It most certainly not the Empire. Mek'velor's entire bloodline was crushed when Vesuvius Vex claimed his throne.

"Do not laugh!" Tailya's growl of anger turned to despair, she fell to her knees, and clutched her belly, whining, "I do not want to be chained again!"

The two did escape their restraints. Although rather easy when they were safe. They managed to break them apart with small stone tools, after a whole evening of trying. The rings around their necks were still visible as clean patterns among the crust, and grime evenly distributed elsewhere.

She was maddening, and Huron took up a robe, and left her alone. He stood in the hallway, and waited for Tailya to get over herself. He made sure his dreams were focused on anything but her.

Tailya finished in the washroom, then came into the hall, and showed herself to him. Returning him to temptation with her fire. She was never so clean, and the white gown she dawned made her look smaller. This made him duck back into the washroom, and bar himself in. Where he lingered, and embellished in the calm of being alone.

After washing, it was comforting to Huron to cover himself. An oddly unmatched woman's gown was soft, and fitting. It was strange, but necessary, until he found a clothier.

He returned to the hallway, devoid of Tailya. From the kitchen, a wonderful smell of soup, meat, and bread lured him towards. There was Tailya was too, and he was not happy that he was forced to eat near her.

She already ate two helpings, slouching to ease her back. She let her wings open, and her tail tip bounced on the table's edge, shaking it, and knocking down a cup of red wine.

"Stop it!" Huron barked.

"Make me!" Tailya crossed her arms, she gave a defiant smirk.

Tailya continued, only firmer in the force of her tail motions. She made a childlike giggle, and propped her feet upon the table.

Huron decided to just get up, he will not succumb any more to this display. He took his fish with him, stabbing it with a wooden stick, and eating it as he meandered to the halls. He was to go to his loft, and stay until nightfall. Then leave in the dark.

At the stairs to the chapel floor, and just as he reached for the door, he heard something shatter, and someone yell, "Hold them still!"

Huron opened the door, and peered through slightly. He saw the chapel now occupied by black robed figures. Some perched on the arms of pews, one even holding a bow while on a thick beam up top in the shadows. By the rock he saw Rioa was tied down. She was snarling, and fighting until one of her assailants slapped her.

"You dare defile a nest! Have you no soul!" She roared.

A familiar voice returned, walking into the room from the lobby. Behind him were the whole assortment of Rioa's shut-ins. They were forced by knife to sit in a pew.

"There are two who are near that belong to me! A sorry red woman, and a meekly man," Huron recognized it was Ematel. "If you tell me where they are, I shall spare you all!"

Huron ducked back down the stairs, through the hallway, dropping his fish-on-a-stick, back into the kitchen. There Tailya was nuzzling a small leg of some cooked bird that she pulled from the counter, lost in filling her belly, and oblivious to Huron's panic.

There was a ghastly scream, and a stomping of foot-claws moved along the ceiling. This jarred Tailya to attention, and she looked up and around. She saw Huron with his head on the table in his arms huffing.

A voice shouted, "Kill the rest, and search the whole town!"

Huron was unable to focus his mind. He felt his heart beating, his breathing was harder to do. The demons are whispering, the sounds of blades whirling, and the screams of familiar voices tore him. He vanished in haunting visions of fire, and his neck felt sore.

Tailya, on the other foot, already placed the bar at the door. She spun back around, the leg of bird in her jaw, as she looked towards Huron with wings out. She saw him disposed, and then went looking for an escape.

There was a small window, used to vent smoke, already propped open with a stick. It was large enough for both of them to squeeze through. The window gave the room a sunlight ray, and was a direct path to the graveyard along the side of the church.

Another scream, and a loud thud onto the boards above. This made Tailya whimper. Blood dripped between the boards, onto the dining table. She ran to the salt barrels to move one to the window, but found it straining. So she ran to Huron with a pleading look on her face.

"Come on, we must go." She shook his shoulder. "We can go through the window!"

Huron did not react, as he was lost.

"Huron?" Tailya tried to shake him again, then she pulled on his heavy tail to no avail.

Eventually she just bit his neck from behind, and moved to mount his back. She purred a bit at the expression of this, and it caused Huron to yelp back into order.

"What is wrong with you, woman!?" He shouted.

"Look! We can escape there!" Tailya pointed to the window, "Move the barrel!"

Huron growled softly from the bite as he stood up. He took hold the barrel, and was able to easily situate it under the window. He climbed it, and looked outside.

The tombstones were tall, and there a rickety fence in the back. However the field was quiet, and lonesome. No one was near, and it was a straight route onto the highway north, or into dense woodland.

The door handle to the hallway rattled, and someone grunted behind in frustration, "This door is locked! I smell fresh meat! Lets get in there, and take it!"

Tailya pushed gently at Huron, and whispered "Hurry."

Huron quickly lifted himself to the barrel, then collapsed his wings enough along his side to bend only slightly uncomfortable. When he was out, he gazed around the field. Only ravens could be seen perching in a tree branch.

Tailya was next, she used a kitchen stool to help get up without risk. When she leaned to the window she extended her arm. Huron knelt down, and grabbed her.

"I should leave you to rot!" He said.

"No..." Tailya's fear was genuine, "Stay with me. We can go to Freestride, and hide."

An axe smashed through the kitchen door, as Huron had hold of the red while she climbed out. She was too fat in the belly to climb proper, and rolled on her back to squirm. When the door finally broke off the latch, Ematel, and his band swarmed into the room.

"You two are bothersome!" He roared as he stormed to them, hopped up on the barrel easily, and latched to Tailya's tail. He shook his free hand to his guards, "Flank!" and they darted outside.

Tailya snarled, and kicked Ematel right in the head. There was no claw marks, but it knocked him, and the barrel, over. The cask broke open, covering Ematel's lower body in salt.

"You will pay for that!" he snarled, "Zhaqua!"

Huron had Tailya just off the ground, and set her on her feet. She clasped his arm, and pulled him off. They ran through the rows of tombstones, and towards the woodlands.

In a flash, Huron was tackled to the ground from behind. Tailya turned to see, and fell over in fear. Zhaqua swooped passed them, and stood blocking their path.

"Not wanting to fight me? You look so strong!" She thrashed her tail, "You two are pathetic in those dresses."

Huron did not know what to do as she dove at him. He was tackled easily upon his back. She sat on his belly, took the knife, then slashed her outfit so that a bit of her hide was showing with a small light cut.

She leaned down to Huron's face, and snarled, "You better run faster this time."

Zhaqua used one of her claws to scrape hard across her own collar scales. She hissed, then rolled off Huron. Her knife dropped into the grass, and she laid still.

She whispered, "Go."

Huron got up, and both him, and Tailya ran off. Looking back, the others of this bandit group ran towards Zhaqua. Ematel arrived first, gripping her, and examining to see if she was well. He appeared envious, protective, and angry.

Fuil Esh' Garem

CHAPTER EIGHT

What strife to know how Hilltop bleeds. The chittering monsters of Ematel are so young, and bloodthirsty. They pursue their prey with wanton disregard. It is clear that we have no advantage in this Journey, so we must learn more, and gleam anything that helps.

The concern it can bring has made things worse. This weighs upon the wings, and such should be left to the Kiri'grana to bear. Their wings are stronger. Through their flight, they can see from afar what approaches. Thus they are better able to guide us.

Ain and Ua find knowledge in ways that promote quarrel. Ain demands knowing of skill, and plans. Ua rolls in gossip, and hearsay. This difference segregates their fields, and affects our choice of path.

It is outrageous to know that a wretched traitor such as Selay demands knowledge from both means. She outright cares not the consequences of knowing what she should not. She takes it for herself, and then hides away in vaults.

A black leather book, such as one by Lamabana Kitsuna, deserves to be in Oth's library. Its knowledge should be shared with the whole of platescale kind. Yet Selay denies us. She hides it behind thick iron walls in the vaults of a finscale bank. She wants the advantage to be hers alone upon this Journey.

Her loyalty to Brudge was exploitative at best. She uses him for what she so wants. Food, money, rest, and obscurity. She exploits the flightfull lord of Deep Lake, his pension for cuckoldry, and his desire to know what gossip he can take advantage of. Brudge would be worthy of pity, but he is finscale, and thus invited this on himself.

A spy is what Selay is, and the spy for the enemy. She was specifically known to stalk Vex, or his family, and antagonize them with seemingly childish pranks. Actions such as drilling a hole on a merchant ship's hull in Freestride, or carving a small notch into the axle of a cart wheel. Those things lead to great loss for the Empire. Losses such as a large portion of tariff revenue, or things such as the Imperial Stave.

It must amuse her in perverted ways, to know that the Empire's government was bickering over Vex's loss of the most powerful symbol of their divine rule. The staff that served as the unifying banner of the Skolis Valley was lost. The courts now quarrel as to how to recover it.

It amused her further that no finscale really noted it. No one bothered her as she stalked out of the bank, then into the sewers towards her first way-point. Of course, the suns were about to rise, and finscales are blinded by salt water films on their eyes.

Selay stayed under the market while preparing the materials for her task. She applied a fresh coat of mud, and the contents of a fish bladder. A scent mask that made her smell of the local rot, and hide her seasonal situation. She also replenished her dual stilettos with a pair stored in her vault.

Towards the Beta District she set out. This required a

venture northward through the highway tunnels, then a turn
directly eastward. The smells lingering were less pleasant as
the districts became more pristine above. This change guided
her through the dark tunnels. There were also far fewer swamp
mushrooms then the Coral districts across the river, and the
moss in the Theater district was more dry upon her bare
footclaws.

Beta District was grand, and a perplexing wonderment
how finscales can cooperate long enough to accomplish things.
It has a Theater, where stories are told of past conquests.
Jestarian kind are quiet arrogant, and enjoy bragging about
their trickery. In each play they write, platescales are
brutes, and portrayed as the monsters to be slain by a
deceitful finscale.

In the center of the district is a large, and lewd
statue of Ua. Her dignity was misrepresented with gills, and
fins. It is a congregation site for the bored, and young
alike. They whit about things so petty. Making reason to form
bands to plot betrayals, and demise.

The district, owned by a Chancellor Quad, and managed
by the family, was a sore of life along the river. One that
could be tasted in the waters as far as Freestride. The
manager was the Chancellor's brother, a sort of Earl, or
Mayor, of the artisan class, one Vias Ea' Quad.

Despite the foot traffic, Selay knew this was the
least lived district of the city. Here is where a den, in the
sewers, directly under the theater, was best to be. A place
of the earliest mud brick structures built in the city. One
where layabouts, and robbers could be commissioned. Thus the
most likely place Selay would find knowledge of her recent
assailants.

Such a den could be only entered by particular
markings, and scents. After all, a theater gathers crowds.
It took Selay two full circles to find it. A faint scent of

mint, flowing from a break in the dark wall revealed it. A single paint line of no determinable nature marked its confirmation.

This immediately was a drop into a darkened corner of a wild cavern. Where Selay leaped down with ease, and silence. The new path was darkened so much that one would require either a luminous potion, or a trained nose to navigate. The only light was in a concentrated area at the bottom of a long-dried well, along with a colony of marsh mints clearly maintained.

Selay could hear the unintelligible squawks of finscales from the park above. Jestarian language is full of conjunctions. Ones when spoken just rightly, required one to be drunk, and second guess their intent to understand. Selay was just sobering, and the headache of hangover was upon her, so she had no ability to understand them.

The mints gave way to a tunnel, then a dark corner. Light shone at the far end with a torch by a thick wood door. Next to it, a buff finscale stood quietly.

The time has come for Selay to decide. It could be safe to assume, that by now, the town watch was looking for an arsonist, perhaps a murderer. This would have the entire criminal enterprise of the city be on alert too. That guard was not meant to stop a raid, but to prevent key people from approaching, and to alert. Or at least Selay assumed it. In any difference, he was twice her size, large for a finscale.

Diplomacy was required to circumvent this blockade. The type Selay would use is platescale diplomacy. He did not see her, as her black robe blended with the shadows well, she had the opportunity of surprise.

Selay had her whole approach planned between the first two steps. There shall be no mercy, and she will overturn, and destroy the entire place to get what she wants. Her pace set, her gate widened, and her tail thrashed in anticipation for the brawl.

To this guard, Selay was a wraith. Appearing as a shadow that became a force from nothing. The introductory slashing of Selay's claw upwards from under her robe stunned him, and forced him to yelp.

If he was to draw a weapon, it would have been too late now. Following the claw, Selay brought a full rounding kick with her leg on his snout. Then she grabbed the side of his head, and slammed him upon the wall near the torch.

He tried to struggle, and could have overpowered the rouge, but she already jabbed the long tip of a stiletto at his spine. Selay then took a firm grip on his horns, and cracked his head hard again to the iron plate holding the torch.

"Open it!" she snarled.

He could not argue, and took the key from his belt. It jangled as he pushed it into the lock, and turned it. The thick door opened inward. The odor of ale, and fish was revealed.

Selay resumed her assault by pulling the guard's horns while pushing the tip of the dagger just to his back. He was forced to arch in an uncomfortable way. She then steered him into the room by the horns, leading to the center-most table before she withdrew the dagger, and threw his head onto the table's corner. The wood splintered over his face, and he finally was unconscious.

Her momentum was now stalled, but her first problem overpowered. The stock of the rest of the room was taken. Her usual technique, for bar brawls, and scuffles, is to overwhelm. However, she would not stand firm or well in the upcoming fight without a modification to that approach.

For she counted five ruffians. They were dressed no different then the whelps who came for her. They already were drawing their blades, and standing up. There was a sixth shadow the dark corner of the room that she had no time to see.

It would be wiser for her to give into fear, and run. However, she is a creature who likes to inflict harm first. She bore teeth towards the incoming bandits, and reached to the staff on her backside. She would die fighting them all if she could, then fight Ain for the right to rule the whole of divinity.

The first one greeted her with a charge, he was undercut with the bladed side of the staff. It swooped at full length, and cut into his side. While this was not a fatal blow, he retired from the fight. One of his peers ran to help him. The rest stood in hesitated anger.

Selay held the staff up, the blood dripped from its steel blades, then boasted, "This is the staff of Skolis! I killed Malvi Zyrko to get it." She stared into their eyes, "Face me! I wish to rend my talons into you, and coat them in your blood!"

The first rouge, and the helper, quickly retreated. Another followed. The other two looked confused, and frightened.

"Heretic! Only kings can wield that!" One pointed at Selay.

"You think Ua and Ain would tolerate me with this?" Selay roared, playing on their fears, "I sacrificed the town of Anya in a fiery siege! Something no one dare could do in five Eras! I turned it to ash! If I am powerful enough for this, whose blessing do I have? With it, what could my fangs render you into?"

The two glanced at each other. It was at this point Selay noticed one was more feminine in figure then the other. Clearly a couple made from the Forge.

The word of her deeds spreads faster across the criminal networks then the heralds. Indeed, heralds often use rouges to infiltrate, and uncover things ahead of the guards. Selay helped to spread this, mainly singing about it with the local merchants in Hilltop. Of course before she threw them through the tables.

"The riders can hold this staff, for they are holy. Especially in their heads. But all who dare take it without permission are cursed. Delios cursing mostly so, since he now nurses a swollen eye! I hold it now, and am only cursed with not enough blood to bath it in."

Selay could see the figure in the shadows begin to stir closer. It was time to finalize the moment, she removed the icon of the now dead assailants, and held it forward. She twirled the staff a bit, causing finscale blood to spill over her arm.

"You have a choice." She began, "Tell me about the children who came to kill me, and this sigil, or I will tear you asunder. I will cook, and eat you like some trout."

They both silently turned to each other. Then they just left. Selay was not expecting this, but she found it good. She snorted, and returned the seal to her pouch. Let them tell the whole world of how mad she is, so she can have peace. Further, the room was cleared of the unimportant, and smelled slightly better.

The lanky figure in the back of the room was obviously the man who mattered the most. Selay cocked her head to get a better look upon him. Her eyes now unrestricted, and able to catalog him.

He was finscale, with a noticeable eye patch. Fish scales green, with blue offsets reflecting. The rest was covered in chain-mail. Leather was sewn to the chains, forming into a medium suit of Armour. His belt had a sword still stowed, and serrated, with blades exposed. He crossed his arms when he saw her examining him like a piece of tuna.

Selay resumed her diplomacy, and she simply threw the

staff as a spear. He easily stepped out of the way, and readied to draw his sword, but was quickly routed by the weight of the platescale. She did this by diving from a table towards him.

His sword arm became a shield to absorb the weight of the heavier platescale. He used all his effort to counter Selay, but fell back, and knelt. Selay hopped back, then came in for another kick, but he caught her foot, and tossed her away.

She stumbled, and saw the finscale drew his sword, and come over to her. She stood up, and spun in a flank along the arm opposite of his blade. He saw this, and quickly landed a fist into the softer side of Selay's belly.

Gulping, the blue woman fell to her knee. She quickly raised her gauntlet arm to block, but no strike came. Instead he stepped back, and slashed at the air to ward her off.

While no scales would take a serrated blade, or a stiletto jab would be a quicker fight. Selay has opted to stay unarmed. She had to fight him, and get him to surrender, so she could extort information. Blades would be too overbearing in the initial bought.

So she stood up in wait for him to strike. He did, and he swung at her a few times. It was clear he was measuring her performance, and had trouble seeing. One eye, and typical finscale aging would do this. However, each swing increased in speed, and force. He not to be trifled with. This forced Selay into reactionary evades.

That was until she pulled a wooden cup from a nearby table, and threw it at him. This followed with a chair, then charge, and a grip on his chest that pulled into a horned headbutt. He used his arm to protect his eye. In absorbing the full force, he stumbled, and growled in frustration.

It was time to disarm, and she clasped, twisting his sword arm. Then rammed her elbow at his wrist. He was forced to twist, otherwise it would break the bone. A clang upon the stone floor confirmed the loss of his weapon.

Now it was time to cripple him, and she pulled him close, then impacted his body to her own. She dug claws as hard as she could into his sword arm wrist, pinching arteries, and popped them open.

Her work was finished, and she let him stumble back. Now his sword arm is useless. He examined the depths of the wounds. Salty finscale blood poured into his chain mail, and out between the rings. He was now in Selay's domain, unarmed, and weakened.

He began a desperate counter strike, and it came in the form of swinging his wounded arm like a club. Selay easily dodged it with a step away. She went behind him, and he spun around, then caught her right gauntlet arm with his uninjured one. She continued stepping leftward, until his good eye was exposed. Then, struck a firm blow with her fist at it. It deflected off the harder scales of his brow ridges.

That was all that was needed, and the grizzled finscale fell to his knees, and yelled, "I YEILD!"

He showed further surrender by laying on floor upon his belly. Exposing his wings to attack. He further curled his tail, and laid still. His wrist continued to bleed, and the blood weaved slowly around the cobblestone cracks under him.

This would not do for Selay, and she stepped on his back to dig a footclaw into him. Finscales are known lairs, and feigning surrender is one way they trick.

"You keep your life for knowledge," she demanded, pressing her larger claw into him, "Agree?"

The man grunted at the pain, "I agree. Answers for mercy!"

Selay once again removed the seal, and held it aside. She took a blade out, as now there was enough reason to use it correctly. She laid it flat near the man's eye.

"Give me your name."

"Fuil Esh' Garam," he huffed, his eye fixated on the blade.

"Given your stature, and determination, you must be responsible for this den?" Selay inquired.

"I am here. I manage the bar, and contracts." He confirmed.

Selay took the knife away from his quivering eye. She let off his back, and walked to pick up Fuil's sword. It was clearly a weapon designed for the sole purpose of rending open the strongest of scales. It was Jestarian infantry, well-maintained, though old. Selay tossed the sword far away into the darkness.

"Stand!" She barked.

Fuil did so obediently. Groaning, and rising slowly while facing her. He grasped his arm, and winced at the contact.

This was unsatisfactory. So she stormed up to the man. She clutched his arm, and the simple leather hold on his chest piece. Then shoved him towards the bar he so zealously defended. At a stool, she made him sit down, then let go, and placed the seal next to him, and turned his head to see.

"Now tell me what this seal means."

There was a noticeable reaction, one of anxiousness. Fuil's breathes paced faster, and his tail shivered. When he noticed the dried blood stains, and smelled the salt, he became defiant.

Finally he turned to glare at Selay, "Whores like you do not belong knowing such things. You should run to hide under the wings of your master. What this means is you shall never sleep ag-" his defiance was disrupted when Selay gripped his horn, and slammed his head into the splintering bar table.

She had no temperament for this. As Fuil recoiled from

the pain, the lager man behind her stirred. She took an empty beer pitcher, and sauntered up to the door guard. He had barely time to groan before he found himself clunked on the backside of his head.

Taking a position directly behind Fuil, she placed the now cracked pitcher down. He was quite unwilling to fight her, but returned to his defiance.

"I cannot betray them. She will not forgive me."

Selay explored her surroundings for anything that could help. There was plenty of kegs, large pitchers, small portable barrels, and a colorful display of alcohol mixed with various other plants in behind the bar. This place would be heaven, if there were no more pressing matters.

Fuil mentioned a woman, and Selay gave a devious smile along her whole muzzle. Never forgive? Perhaps a lover? Someone he wanted protected? A definite weakness.

Selay caressed the man's fins along his head, and leaned over his back. He turned to examine her, confused, and concerned.

"She must be diamond," Selay said softly into his ear. "Too bad she is not here to stop me."

Fuil gulped, and began to breath more heavy. He was warming to her touch, and could sense her fire. Selay leaned along his back, between his wings, and used her tail to twirl his.

"Whore..." Fuil said, "Do not do this to me, for her wrath will be unyielding towards you."

Selay began to bite along his fins. This is a rather intimate gesture she knew from watching Brudge with his harlots. It would weaken him with potentials, thus make him prone to more mistakes. Fortunately, she could only tolerate about three bites though, before the salty flavor of finscale ruined her mood.

"I want her name!!" Selay roared, and firmly pulled on

Fuil's horns. She threw the man hard onto the floor, and began to pull his belt off.

The man was entranced, submissive, and awe struck. Selay pulled him up, and lead him to a table, then pushed him to sit on top it. She tied his feet with his belt. Next, she pulled the belts from his leather chest armor.

She sat upon his lap as she let him enjoy the amusement of anticipation. Then tied his wrists. He still winced in pain, but the bleeding was stalling by now.

"You will scream her name when I am done." Selay said, softly.

Before he could respond, Selay pushed him onto his back on the table with the full bulk of her weight. She rolled off him. Then pulled a final belt, one along his hips that held his sword to him.

She snapped it once, then quickly ducked under the table, and tied his ankles to his wrists. Fuil cried in sudden pain when his body was stretched unnaturally far. After securing him, she returned to his view.

All he could do is wince, and watch now. Somehow still enjoying it. Selay realized then that this man was deviant a bit. So she had to increase the suffering.

So she explored the room while swaying her tail high. This bothered Fuil, and he held out his forked tongue to cool in what he thought was out of Selay's view. She thought it was funny, how in spring, the slightest signals could set off anything.

Selay took a small wooden portable barrel, and set it on the table next to him. She pulled its top off, then examined its spacing, and iron rings. It was just right enough.

Suddenly clutching the finscale's throat, she forced his jaw upward. When his head was facing as far high as it could, she placed the barrel over him. He began to struggle, for the extenuation of his neck, and pinching along his fins, made pain.

Selay did not care, she continued her exploration of the bar. Taking stock of various high concentrations of grain alcohol, and one bottle with a label of a man breathing fire. She took that bottle, and began to drink it.

Settling several tankards of heavy grain alcohol at the table next to her victim, Selay watched him squirm from the blindness he now suffered from. He was clearly afraid to loose his sight. So thus denying him it would affect his confidence. Soon he should falter fully.

Selay removed the barrel, "Tell me her name."

"Gawundon! Gawundon! She is coming!" he yelled in heavy breaths.

"Now who owned the seal? I will let you think about that." Selay returned the barrel to Fuil's head.

As she took a sip of her spicy liquor, she began to feel happy at the retreat of her sobriety. Spring thoughts left her for more important ideas, such as how to systematically destroy Fuil's resistance. This gravitated to a solitary thought of emasculation, which Selay recoiled at the idea. This woman he named shall need his protection when Selay finds her.

However, embarrassment is amusing. The blue platescale grabbed Fuil's trousers, and tore through them with her claws. He screamed in panic from in the barrel, hapless to her. Finscales fill their minds with lies about platescales. Lies such as females eating their organs for fertility. Fuil was no stranger to these, and it made him terrified.

Selay had the man exposed, and was disgusted at what she saw. However, she needed something appropriate to get information from him. So his trousers were most necessary. She took one leg's material, drowned it on grain alcohol, and wrapped it around his gill-bearing neck. Then, tearing off another, she pulled the barrel off his face.

"Who owns this sigil? Tell me, or this will only get worse." Selay said calmly, and waited.

"If I tell, they shall kill me." He seemed to be pleading in this.

"If you refuse to tell me, or I find you lying to me, you will beg for death by the time I am done with you." Selay growled.

He gave no response, stuttering in his breathing. He turned his head to the side, and closed his eyes. He was trying to fall asleep, or wake from a bad dream.

Selay balled up the rest of his trousers. Grabbing Fuil's face firmly, she placed it all along him, covering his entire maw and nose. Then she took her spicy drink, and began to pour it on the what was left of the man's face.

She did this once, and twice, and Fuil began to kick, and scream wildly. He gasped for air, only to drink in more as he did so. He opened his gills, only to burn from the pure poison flowing into him.

Selay leaned back, and removed the face cover. She roared, "Tell me!"

Fuil was crying. If there was one experience that a finscale could not understand, it was drowning. The ability to breath in both sea, from the possession of gills along their necks, and air, made them unable to cope with lack of breath. Suffocation was difficult, but when accomplished, a finscale would be immediately driven to despair.

Fuil began to cry, and sing, "The Blade is Forged in Ain's fire, and Ua's Shadow cools it. Wings of flame, spread on high, and all will burn who use it."

Selay laughed, "This is not how it works."

She resumed, one, two, three, more times with pouring of drink on his face. He gulped desperately for mercy, and tried to pull himself free of the tie, only to be in pain more.

"THE FOGED BLADE OF AIN!!" He screamed when Selay was finished, "I AM DOOMED! THEY SHALL HUNT ME FOR GIVING THEIR NAME!"

Fuil coughed, and wined. Selay patted his head fins, "Good boy, but those who I killed are too young to know finscale affairs so well. Who hired them?"

Fuil winced, tears flowing down his scaled cheeks. He bellowed from his throat, which made his gills burn more.

"I do not know. The bounty was placed anonymously." he gulped for some air. "The details are behind the Gold Rum."

Selay stood up, then returned to the bar. She set aside her spicy drink for her rather favorite wine: Dewberry. She drank it firmly, and gave the cool bottle a nuzzle before finding the Gold Rum. There was nothing immediately there, except a rat hole in the wall.

She snorted, and poked her dagger into it. Despite wading in sewage, and touching finscale hide, she knew better then to be bit by a swamp rat. However, her dagger impacted something solid, metallic, and not ratlike.

She shoved her hand in, and procured a rather fat leather sack. When opened, it contained gemstones of Garnet, and Sapphire, with plenty of gold ring coins. A rather significant treasure for her hide. Someone must really want her dead.

She returned to Fuil, a bit happier now that she was no longer impoverished. Even happier that she had her Dewberry.

"Please, let me go!" Fuil cried out, "Give me the honor to run!"

Selay examined one of the gemstones next to Fuil, and laughed. "I suppose it would be the right thing to do." She smiled, "But these gems are only found in the vaults of the Kiri'grana of the highest order. I will let you run, if you tell me who their previous owner was."

"I do not know! The drop off is tribute receipts to the theater!" Fuil squirmed only briefly, as pain kept him in place, "Let me go. Or kill me here."

Selay shrugged, then clutched the gem into a fist. She then gave Fuil a solid punch into the temple, knocking him unconscious. She returned the gemstone to the pouch, then stood up. Finally collecting the staff, and sauntering out of the room. Now secure in knowing her next way point was above her.

Ehtah Istina

CHAPTER NINE

We find as Selay ascends that our descent continues. Within our nest, we still are shameful children. Awareness has made us afraid of ourselves. Thus we do not do as the Trial demands.

We fear the laws of the divine. Perhaps it is best if Ua and Ain purify us in flame now. Find someone better to follow those things which are so simple. We violate tasks in which we should not have to be ordered to do.

Kiri'grana make laws in vain to align us with divine mandate. They should instead be hunting, and eliminate all who disobey. Sadly, they would rather bicker in the corrupt courts.

The Wyvern Order, under direction of Kityun the Faithful, appointed in Tram Raviwr Ricin to manage the pastoral affairs. He received the title Metropolitan after securing a manor in the city slightly more humble then the Duke's mansion. When issue arises, Ricin employs himself, or his proxies, to resolve it.

One, a man named Ehtah Istina, was Ricin's personal guard. Ehtah was employed to deliver messages, and handle the personal safety of his elderly state. Thus, he shared intimate trust with Ricin full time.

Ehtah is a treelike man, with sturdy plates all across his body. He was intimidating, and imposing. He shone like a golden statue in the sun. His belly was a tarnished brown, and he held blackened stripes that only were upon his tail. The tip of his tail held a fin in a crescent moon, which was useful for cooling. His eyes were a simple series of Grey shades.

His faith in the gods was unshakable, and thus he served them. He prayed often, and never missed any of his master's sermons. His life was of duty and loyalty. This makes him one of the many who never took to a family.

Ehtah volunteered this spring to teach children how to hunt. As a skilled son of a hunter himself, it was his duty to Ua and Ain to train the young to hunt for the trial. He would set out with a troop of younglings to a brook in the woods. There they would catch bugs, worms, birds, and whatever. Taking tally, and eating their finds. His last lesson was teaching children simple bartering for their favorites. His favorite was Red Back Seed Beetles, which he traded with a little miller's child for.

However, after the prison riot, all children were barred into their homes with their mothers. Ehtah was summoned to Ricin's side, in particular, his master's carriage.

Surprising, as normally a bodyguard has to walk to keep the route clear. This was different, since Ricin dismissed all his guards but him. He was allowed in to sit for the journey.

Ricin is old. His posture lower, and the plates along his face, and neck were shattered, and healed over many times. A dark green, with horns that split unto four crooked directions. Eyes of hazy blue, dressed always in a robe of his rank. He held a walking cane, but only partly need it.

The man was cold in private, with very little flights of passion outside the occasional sermon. Today he was calm, but seemingly worried. As seen by staring into Ehtah's eyes sternly, the occasional flaring of his nostrils.

When they were just out of the city gates, he began.

"I need someone who can hunt today. Are your tracking skills good?" His voice was grizzled, and deep.

"Yes, you know. I train the children." Ehtah replied. "I can hunt Rakes on a glide, with a dead fish for bait."

"This is no fowl Rake. There is a demon to hunt. Ua and Ain are demanding it to be sent back to the idle."

Raviwr's calm was with a self-comforting rumble. So few purred lately, as the entire region was in a state of fear. The guards continued their relentless raids upon homes, looking for Selay, and the church preached sermons of anxious justice. All cried out in Tram, and Ricin, a figure all look upon, purred during the chaos.

He continued, "Hilltop's church, do you know?"

Hilltop, a small village along the north of the region, has a peculiar feature. The priests were siblings. One Priestess Rioa, and Priest Svatrin kept Ua and Ain's watch over the town. This made rumors, as in most church franchises, priests were married as Ua and Ain would be, but siblings naught often.

One can never forget the performance of Rioa, and her glamour. She would wash in olive oil to make her body shine, and it only added to her. Her swaying tail, and motions made for frequent dreams and desires all could never fulfill.

Ehtah leaned back, dashing the excitement from his mind, and laughed, "Did spring finally get to Svatrin, and he nested his sister? Must the eggs be blessed, so that their children are not to be missing things like colonials?"

Raviwr made no expression of amusement, "No. Priestess Rioa is dead. So is her matriarchs."

Ehtah widened his eyes, and opened his jaw in shock, "No! Who dares!?"

"We must find out. That is why I need you to hunt this demon. If this sin is related to our dungeon, we must dispense Justice, less there be none left in Tram."

This is about authority, not Justice. The church reigns as the conduit to life, and death. If a child of the nest is taking upon the authority to themselves, then it usurps the holy order. This could not be tolerated.

Ehtah held up his chin, and nodded with strength, "I shall hunt then, and carry out this task with glee. None shall be spared Ua and Ain's wrath."

"Wrath is to be held until we know for sure what we are dealing with," the elder then became quiet.

The old man gazed out of the carriage window, watching the woodlands. The calm is worrying, with scant moments of birdsong distracting from it. Even the initial stone fences of the town of Hilltop helped none.

When people showed, children were gathered with families. Everyone was kept close, and clear signs of fear were upon their quivering faces. Talks, and murmurs, rumors made, and news was spreading, but no tail swayed happy.

"Two massacres in a month is not boding well for Tram. If this continues, the Order will take over the county, so says the Duke." Raviwr explained calmly, staring at the people, "If that happens, I will be tried. I would like to prevent such distractions. At least until after I return from the Feast."

At last the cart slowed, and stopped in front of the local tavern. The windows were noticeably shattered from some recent brawl of unknown story. Ricin stepped out first, a crowd began to form, wanting to admire the site of a high ranking official in town.

Ehtah followed, as Raviwr knocked on the driver's

armrest of the cart. "We shall be busy all day. So get yourself some beer." The driver nodded, excited, and began to secure the cart.

The men slowly strode along towards the churches on the hill. The crowd obeyed, and parted where necessary to allow them through. Homes here were also shops, all closed, and silent. The town's people nailed boards upon the windows, but were all out watching. Ehtah stiffened himself, and kept his scales hard, ready for anything.

"I will have to bear the cost of this," Raviwr sighed, "Our plans may be in peril. If I ignore this town's loss, Kityun will burn me alive."

"It is the Order's duty. We are chosen to protect the nest by the Wyvern Gods. Even in this terrible times." Ehtah replied.

"It should be all Allya's duty," Growled the high priest, "We are wild children who need to be chained, and kept from flight until we know better."

They were by the Ua church now. The title 'Chapel of Ua the Builder' was clawed upon a wooden plaque on the door. Which was splintered off its lower hinge. By every gate, and door stood the Tram guards. Deployed immediately on notice, no one was allowed into the building.

One, by this entry, was wearing the seal of rank the same as Ehtah. Upon sight, he approached, bent his knee, lowered to expose his neck, and open his wings.

"I am Skazac, my lord." He announced to Ricin.

Raviwr loomed, "Who is your patriarch, Skazac."

"Yelvian the Brave, I serve him."

Placing a hand on the man's neck plates, and squeezing, Ravwir blessed him, "Then your bravery shall be needed in these fallen times. Rise! The hunt begins for this demon."

The young man did just that, and began to move towards the broken entry door, "Follow-"

"Unhand me! Claws off! You are but basilisks! I demand to see my sister!" Came a roar from behind Ehtah, interrupting the moment.

Everyone looked upon, and saw a white robed, red-scaled man held by the arm by another guard. The guard was pulling him away as he was storming towards the church furiously.

"Pastor, the Cardinal orders this site quarantined. You cannot go there until he says otherwise." The guard pleaded.

"You Milksop! The Cardinal stands upon the stairs here! Let me go! I am of the church, and so have a right to address him!"

This was clearly Priest Svatrin, the sigil on his robe showed of Ain, and his belligerence was of the same. He broke free, then came to face Ricin. Clearly angry.

"Someone yearns for his sister," Ehtah smiled.

"Shush your innuendo," Svatrin pointed, "I must protect her."

Raviwr raised a hand, then placed it upon Svatrin's wing. Causing the lessor priest to startle, then turn his wings away.

"I think it would be better if you help the townsfolk. Sing a song of Ain's protection for them."

Svatrin snorted, "Not without context. I must sing with my sister to comfort all. I demand to know where she is!"

Ehtah remained quiet, and watched. With Lt. Skazac standing near him. The other guards prepared to quell a fight by surrounding. However, it never came to be.

"Sing your sister's song too. Ua and Ain must be warned that we are going to hunt down those who brought her wrongfully to them."

Svatrin's face drooped, and his ears lowered. He lost his balance, and the guard behind him caught him. His eyes glossed over, shaking at the thought. He was unprepared, and vanished into himself. He did not know she is dead.

All stayed quiet, and shielded their fellow platescale from harm. In his vulnerable moment, volatile, and mortal, all saw upon him themselves. None in Allya are spared this pain, as the trial of the nest teaches us that that all dies. This is why Ua and Ain are our only salvation.

Ricin looked towards the two guards with a solid glare of authority. It was impossible to not tell what that meant, 'solve this, do what he paid them for.'

Skazac, and Ehtah entered the church lobby, and examined the door. It was bothersome to open, and close, so they left it alone.

"It is clear this was a solid kick of the lower door." Skazac pointed at the hinge, then upon the bolt of the handle, "Then one right into the center."

Ehtah sniffed the air, "Lilacs. Spring is here."

"Go five paces inside, and smell the blood." Skazac said, walking ahead.

Ehtah did, and the blood did not need an introduction. He could see everything is wrong, and horrific. The room's carpets were torn from the footclaws of multiple people. Pews were splintered, and sitting dislodged, and laid upon a rock was the most horrific thing Ehtah ever saw.

"If you must throw up, over there is a bucket." Skazac pointed.

Ehtah looked unsure of what that meant, until he knew for sure that blue body on the rock was Priestess Rioa. Immediately he ran, and threw up his breakfast, letting out a cry of discomfort.

"God's no!" Ehtah sat down, and waited, "They broke her eggs on purpose!?"

Skazac tilted his head, looking back, and fro from the rock. "How do you know?"

Ehtah remembered his anatomy lessons. A woman in spring must avoid strong impacts upon her belly. A single blood mark, or bloat around the lower chest, could mean death, as the body is flooded.

Standing, and examining the body, he motioned to it, "Her neck... see."

Skazac squinted to examine, clearly uncomfortable at this task. Her neck was contorted, and sharply angled. There was more blood spots along it. She had her neck broken.

"Why did they have to break the eggs?" Skazac asked, "She was already dead."

"She was stubborn, and strong, a death rage?" Ehtah pondered, "They hit her five times, and broke her clutch. A rage meant she would not quickly expire."

Skazac turned to the front pews, and pointed. There, sitting, leaned upon each other were other women. Each one's necks were contorted, and stab wounds, and blood marks on their belly.

"Her whole stay in." Ehtah sighed, "I wish Ricin was wrong."

Skazac did next what all guards do, clutch upon the hilt of their sword. This was the mark of anxiety for justice. When he could not extract it now, Skazac began to whimper.

"Ayria..." the man swallowed, as he saw the pudgy purple woman, "I should have accepted you."

Ehtah put his hand on the wing of his peer. He said nothing, and patted him. Suffering must be done to those who took from Skazac too.

Skazac mourned, "Ayria always made such great food. Her bread was sweet. She wanted to be a baker."

Ehtah began to examine the rest of the room. Skazac began to babble in mourning as his memories of her were told out loud. This was Ua's Church, a place to do such things. It is unlikely that Skazac could sing, but Ua will hear, and want Ayria to make her sweet bread to try, and then want to keep Ayria for herself for it. Ain would make that another reason to fight his sister, and all will be well in heaven.

The room gave away to additional small secrets. Clawmarks, tucked along beams, confirmed as recent by the tears of banners. The direction of fallen candles, and pews told a story. The forceful entry was done by the strongest of multiple assailants. At least two small were able to climb up onto the wooden beams, and wait. Every maiden in the way was grasped upon, and forced down. A blood stain, by broken pews showed the first cut. Things were tossed, and knocked over to intimidate.

A central set of claw marks showed the direction of a single assailant. One that paced, and danced at the alter by the shape. Then, priestess Rioa was seized from her rock, and her neck snapped firmly.

Her dying rage made all others rise, but no one was trained to fight, so all were slaughtered. Heavier bodies broke through the old, and rotting pews, and some were attacked from above.

Rioa was able to see her failings before she was jabbed into her belly. A few pummels was all that it took to overwhelm. Shem and the others were set in order, and accounted for.

The final moments were hasty. Meaning the demons noticed something. Or someone. Skazac must know, he was first to see.

"What gave these demons purpose to do such things!?" Skazac roared at the world upset.

"They were after something with urgency," Ehtah said. "Where else could someone be here?"

"The kitchen?" Skazac suggested, "We could not go down there. Svatrin tried to break in, and ruin the scene. We all were determined to chase him off."

"Show me," Ehtah ordered.

Skazac proceeded towards a door at the side of the church. When he gripped on its handle, he simply pulled. The door's bolt was splintered through the frame just as before.

"They were through here," Skazac immediately said, then bolted down the stairs.

"Wait!" Ehtah drew his sword.

"Drawing a blade in this house is blasphemy!" Roared Ricin.

Ehtah turned to see the old man standing in front of the alter. Glaring down his maw growling with authority. His tail thrashing.

"Blasphemy is killing Ua's children!" Ehtah rebutted, "I will not let this stand!"

"Selfish arrogance! I am the vessel of the gods present here!" Raviwr unfolded his wings, his aged glamour showing, "Do not sully this house any further until we have sung the song! Or be cursed to the Idle."

Ehtah had no choice but to obey his master, so he returned his sword. He bowed his head in shame for his behavior, and ignoring of the tradition. He knew, like all, that this mind is what made us loose who we were so many decades ago.

"We have collected stories for the song, hunter. One you need to hear." Raviwr said.

"That they were looking for something?"

"Someones. Both naked when they arrived. One black, a man, and the other a red woman with whiskers. *Her.*"

Ehtah snorted, it has become political now, "Now I see why we are here."

Ricin retracted his authority, and posed solemnly, "I must bless these bodies, then prepare the song for them. Continue now, but no bloodshed."

Ehtah briefly bowed, and Ricin turned to chant. He sprinkled salt upon the corpses. Then, Ehtah turned, and made his way down the stairs.

Ricin's chanting became strong, and clear, calling Ua and Ain to hold judgment so their children prove their worth. It echoed along the hallways down.

The blood scent was gone, and two rather potent scents were present. One male, other female. They extended into the washroom, and mixed with soap. Then weakly into the kitchen. One scent was familiar, the female one.

Skazac light candles, and entered the kitchen prior. Ehtah entered, and saw again a door damaged by impact. Barrels, and chairs were upended by the door, and the room was a mess as Skazac kept sniffing at the air and moving around.

"Do you track them too?" He said.

"Yes." Ehtah replied.

"It rises here, along with several blood scents." Skazac examined the window.

Unfinished meals meant this will be easier to track with smell. This was good, and made both eager to go out.

Skazac took up a small piece of bread, and began to quake. He made a visible growl at the smell of it. "This is Ayria's food... the last of it. There shall be war for this." He declared.

Skazac removed his coin bag from a belt pouch, emptied it on the table, and placed the bread inside. It was his memory now, to remind him of what he is denied. He then stomped heavily out of the church.

Outside they were blocked by a crowd of townsfolk. There, Svatrin, and Ricin were standing upon the stairs. The folk were irate, and angry, with growls sounding.

Svatrin flung open his wings, and began to shout. This calmed many. His shouting broke into a solemn song, and the whole crowd joined. Ricin then joined where he could.

Skazac somehow bypassed everything. He was inside the

entry to the grave. Ehtah began to move through towards his peer, and tried hard to not disturb them.

The song became a simple thrumming of the entire crowd. Ricin lead the motions. Slowly they swayed, and held their heads low. Each one praying for their fallen.

"Hunter!" sang Svatrin, "Let our hunters pass! The song of Rioa is incomplete!"

Ricin held his claws into the air, and opened them, "Ua and Ain's Grateful Tasking is to take our flightless hunters, Skazac and Ehtah, off their binding chains. Justice be upon them all!"

"What say you hunter? Sing for the flock!" Svatrin demanded.

Ehtah could not, he dared not. This was not right for him. He swiftly strode into the graveyard, and closed the gate. Huffing, he is unseated at being the target of attention by the the town this way. Further, the Grateful Task is upon him? He was not ready.

The crowd came to singing again. With the priests proclaiming that silence is better until you know. No one questioned this, or noticed the fear.

Skazac was laying on the ground, snorting at the blades of grass. His tail trashed, and he was emitting an intimate rumble sound.

"She is inspiring," he said, immediately noticing Ehtah.

"She is our scent then," Ehtah replied.

Skazac sat up, pointing towards the opening by the trees just out of town. There was a noticeable broken branch.

"How many do you think?" Skazac sighed.

"More then two. At least one man, and a woman, someone is chasing someone," Ehtah summarized.

"Hunters, tell us their fate!" Svatrin yelled, shaking the gate.

Ehtah was startled. He saw the whole town behind the priest. It was an uprising, and Ehtah was its target.

He withdrew his sword, and gave it a slash at the air, "I call for war upon those who took Priestess Rioa from us wrongly! Those who denied us Ayria's craft in food shall die for this!"

Skazac did the same, made speed to the woodland path, he then waited for Ehtah. He held his sword, and showed off his wings there.

Ehtah followed, and the town began to chant for war. Their spirits roused. However, none followed the guards, as all were scared. Both entered the woods, ready to deliver Justice against Ematel's Slaughter.

Dask

CHAPTER TEN

illtop cries for vengeance, and sends two naive hunters to fulfill it. Unaware of the great wake that they have caused. A wake that shall crack the very shell of the world.

It as if they look upon a freshly broken egg horn like some children in their nest. Its snap showing them that all will end. They cry out, knowing the Trial they must endure.

Another reason why we must be denied proper Judgment, and put upon a Journey. One that reminds us to see the order. The demons were set loose. They seek to destroy the nest, and Ua and Ain are sending us to face them.

Do we dare? For upon his throne of deceit sits Vesuvious Vex. The great red tyrant of unjust war, and rage. He cracked apart the shells of the siblings of Tailya, and stood in their blood. He drank it in front of their father, who was crippled by a poison. The old king was then gutted. Never sated, Vex crossed into becoming a god upon the world, and called for the Idle-bound souls of his past victims to return.

Return they have. As demons. Idle-bound no more, and interacting through us. Violent things, maddened by the rejection of the gods. Heathens, heretics, blasphemers, and occultists of old. They are the unrenown, who could not find anything to sing or be smelted down for.

All Allyians are now cursed upon the nest to be of two souls. A demon in us whispering to our demise, and our hatched one. Some give in, and others resist. Forever gasping for release from our grief.

As such, we are proceeding towards annihilation. Ua and Ain are ready to reset the world. Time to purify the nest so their other eggs do not suffer. We must live knowing that demons such as Ematel, and his she-beast Zhaqua, roam free to slaughter their betters. Savage things of fire, and disorder such as Selay, as well as those she hunts, continue to hold the world still.

Then there is Huron, whose core is but shared with demons from a different curse. One whispering vengeance, but not of the same as ours. A thing brought in another sacrifice, which Huron has the luxury to know the name of.

Hilltop's bloodletting was behind them. The forests were not the same. As if a vortex opened into the world, and scared off all the creatures.

The woodland is endless, and the pair moved under bush, and tree. Leaves crunching, twigs snapping, they masked nothing while they just kept moving farther from civilized places. They followed a path that was not carved out by anything other then nature itself.

Tailya cut her new found dress on a sticker bush, and her red side shown. She was with firm enough scale to not feel the puncture of the shrub, but grumphed at the tug, and tear anyway. Breaking herself free without loosing stride, she left evidence of her presence behind.

Huron was helplessly following his companion. With no thought whatsoever to otherwise. Her tail was long, easy to follow, and gave away the direction she turned towards easily.

Given the circumstances they were in, no longer did the plight of spring bother either. Now it was survival. They knew that behind them was a pack of monsters.

Eventually a light rain fell upon the forest. It came with a wind that shook the trees. Wildlife cried from their hiding places, and a Wyvern in the far distance screamed. This made both stop, as now there was death from two directions.

Tailya knelt down to held her hands on her belly to rest. Her dress was muddied immediately, and she pouted at that too. Her tail coiled around her legs, and she held her head downward.

Huron fell to his knees as well, rolling out his tongue and panting. The droplets of rainwater became his cooling mist. He closed his eyes.

He could see something like a void consuming his mighty form, just outside his view. He grew panicked, but then petrified. Upon this stillness, the whispers of demons began. Taking him away.

"Brother, I shall best you..." he mumbled, unable to resist.

"What!?" Huron could hear Tailya, but barely. She gripped his wrist, and came in close. "Huron? Hey, Huron..."

Huron was lost, before him was the plucky young clutch brother of his, Ofiln Quirksettle.

"Huron?" A distant voice cried.

With bright blue eyes, and flexible ear fins, he was not less different then Huron. Except for the one fang that poked out of the side of his longer maw.

"*Huron, what is the matter?*" The voice called, "Are you a coward?" Said Ofiln as he held up a big stick to the side of his nose.

"No I am not!" Huron yelled, as he readied his own stick, pulled from a maple tree outside.

A loud clang sounded near them, as father was forging a new weapon. With sparks lighting up the room, the long arm rose above his head, and slammed into an unseen metal thing. Father's wings were extended wide.

"Then we dual!" Ofiln parried his stick forward up at Huron laughing.

Huron spun his stick, deflecting Ofiln's strike. He hopped back, and his brother climbed onto a table. Huron joined, and it became an arena for the two children to contest in.

Both were tiny, with only achieving good posture this year. Their wings were small, necks short, and scales soft. No balance in their short tails was possible yet.

Ofiln's glorious competition with his brother had the wooden table shaking. Both sticks were clapping as each fought with vigor. Both laughed, and their footclaws scratched the surface they stood on.

Huron hopped to a sealed barrel of nails. He posed himself with wings open. The whelp obtained a full posture, and boasted.

"My endurance is rivaled only by Zyrko, brother!"

Defiant, puckering his lips, Ofiln counter with his own pose from upon the table.

"My strength is like Delios, and can drain your endurance!"

The two chased each other, Huron climbing up a wooden beam, and broke glide to crates, and bins. Ofiln was lagging behind him.

Eventually Huron hopped into a large wooden crate. The top was ajar, and the little whelp crashed inside. Nothing was in there prior, and he scurried around, scraping his claws upon the wood.

Ofiln, ignoring his brother's mistake, joined shortly. The two laughed as the fight ended about there. Neither achieving a victory over the other.

"*Huron?*" came a voice, and a tug on his shoulder.

Ofiln was looking out of the box, and hit Huron's shoulder with his short fat tail. Huron got up, and looked over the edge, if only to escape the fury of his brother's spiked tail tip.

"Where is our second nestlings?" A woman spoke, it was mother Dask.

She was tall, well formed, wide-hipped, and with two very small hatchlings hanging off her shoulders. She was wearing a night gown, with blue trim, and enough shoulder covering to protect herself from her perched pups' claws. Which dug in as they looked around the room at everything new, with big eyes, and fascination.

Despite lost in his work, father somehow knew exactly where the two were. He used his wing's loose finger to direct mother's attention upon them.

They both ducked, and grinned as Dask looked. Mother always could find the unique smell of all her children, and thus lifted the lid. The newborns peered in with wonderment, sniffing, and squeaking at their brothers.

"Why are you hiding from mother?" She inquired.

The kids shrugged.

She hit her hand on the side of the box, "Come on, up you go, help me take care of the pups."

Huron, and Ofiln protested, but climbed out of the box nonetheless. They knew best not to challenge mother, as her ire was that of Ua herself. Further, her tail hurt when it struck them.

"Each of you, hold your siblings." Dask knelt down.

Both boys removed a perched hatchling from mother's shoulders. Neither made complaint. Huron took hold of If'pesp, his new sister. She made his head, between his horns, her perch.

Dask approached Father, and bumped him with her tail. "Finish up, and join me for a bath, my chosen."

He grunted in some form of agreement. Huron lingered as his mother left the room. Father took his newly forged blade, and set it into a waterbed to cool. The smoke summoned made little If'pesp sniffle, then sneeze, but she kept her grip by planting claws into her brother's head. This made Huron grunt, "Ow!"

A bell sounded at the entrance to the workshop, a soldier entered in light leather armor with a crate. He was a swordsman, a common infantrymen of the army of Warlord Vex.

"Blacksmith Quirksettle!" he called. Huron's father stood up.

Lanky in form, with a ball nose, and a chipped fang. Huron's father was with two prominent, but rested earfins. He was old, dirty, and wore an equally soiled smith apron. He walked to the man then pointed to the table.

The swordsman set the crate on the table, then opened it. Out fell a set of gauntlets, and a large number of chipped, and malformed daggers. Falling into a pile were short swords, and other weapons. One mace, with spikes missing, was visible too.

"Second infantry is on leave. I am ordered to pay you for these repairs." The swordsman said.

Dask was in the doorway, and reentered the room. She crossed her arms and watched from behind Huron. If'pesp made a mewl at the sight of her mother.

"I am happy to serve my warlords." Said the smith.

The swordsman took out his payment, a sack of coins with significance, and set it in the box. "The rest will bill from Warlord Kitsuna."

He turned, and left. Dask approached the crate, and sighed, "We have not been in the nest at the same time since spring."

She looked inside the crate, then held up one of the dented gauntlets. She puffed in disappointment.

Huron's father took out an eye piece, and examined the other glove closer as he spoke, "This is how I feed you. I work to keep the kingdom strong. The realm protects us."

Dask returned the gauntlet, "But you sleep so rarely. Your scales are cracking from this heat. Can you at least stop for me to wax you before the suns set?"

"No. I am afraid this will take all night," Father spoke, "If the boys help me, I might be able to at least curl up with you before dawn."

Dask snorted, "Martu will help with the babes then. You can show Huron how to smith like you always wanted, dear. I need Ofiln though."

"Agreed."

Dask came to Huron, and collected If'pesp, then left the room. Taking her time to let Ofiln catch up as he babbled something. Huron made a slight sigh of relief that he no longer had claws dug into his hide.

"Huron, come here." Father ordered.

He complied, tilting his head. His father removed a dagger from the bin, "I shall show you how to sharpen this blade. First, hold it, and tell me of its design."

Huron took it in his claws, and examined closely. It was a short dagger. One that infantry used as a secondary weapon when they were disarmed. He stared into the blade.

"*Huron, we must run!*" Said a panicked voice from afar.

Screams, and cries erupted from all around. Huron could still see the blade, but there was blood below. The blood touched his bare feet. The world grew darker, and all this came againm and again in his mind. None of it was pleasing to him, it made him experience terror, and torment.

He could feel the pain surely, and likewise he shouted with the screams. Only to be brought back to the forest, with

Tailya's fire alight in his mind. He was still on his knee's, where he belongs.

Looking behind, he saw a rope dart through his tail, and lodged within. His spilled blood upon a stone near. Before he could react, another dart impaled through the web on his opened right wing.

Out of the side of his view, Huron saw Tailya held down by a masked rouge. Ematel, and Zaqhua standing by her, then facing him.

"Just where I like you," one of them uttered.
Huron remained still, his brother's voice shouting towards him. Petrified, his demons pinned him. This shall come upon us next, unless we continue our Journey.

Vias Eh' Quad

CHAPTER ELEVEN

Those with flightfull wings are to bear the burden of knowing. We see demons are here to rot the nest. However, do those with good wings know to purge them? Or do they position themselves in the flock to have access to the powers these mad things bring? It appears the latter, for the lords seem complacent in the curse Vex wrought.

One such decay is the, now common, use of spy-craft. A disgraceful habit, openly rejected. However, a hypocritical action sometimes is preferred over being unprepared. Knowledge, gives leverage. Such unlocks doors that give one power.

Selay was known to be able to acquire knowledge she was not allowed to have. No lock, or mind, was too strong to pry open to tell her the secrets she wanted. Her recent abuse of Fuil was indication of her willingness to go farther then most in acquiring secrets. Things she would sell, but this time it is different.

Likewise, she has been able to collect the pages of her father's memoir together through hearsay, and frauds. She spent the past three years building a tolerance to the trade in search of this book. Long since she has overcame her original pain of having to resort to things she could not allow upon herself. The pages assembled, all with matching handwriting, and watermark, are worth the suffering. For its secrets are more valuable then any library.

She mulled over the book in her mind, to find a solution to this situation. Someone wants her dead, paid some pretty gems for it, and she intends to find out. Of all she could remember, not one situation entertained assaulting assassins. Not even midnight attacks on logistic camps, or the Massacre of the Blacksmiths compare to this. Those things were more strategic, and part of a larger goal, not be the totality of the thing.

The mulling ended when her Dewberry wine ran dry, and she silently set the bottle upon the floor. She found this task of balancing her wings, and tail challenging. Now happily drunk, she gave a short churning purr. In order to move forward, she had to throw her weight. Somehow, she went quietly through the cellar of the theater.

Sounds of a masculine voice occasionally were heard, it went from speaking to singing. This upcoming play has yet to begin, so only performers would be present practicing. The theater was hosting the season's usual performance, one she saw on posters. 'Numril's Betrayal.' A play that was an ode to fertility, and against adultery. The story about Ua's acts that birthed the flightless.

Selay did not care about this play though. She is the only sapphire in Huron's hoard, and Ua was nowhere near her big lump of coal. So she observed the battlefield around her. She wondered what that fat rat she saw, staring scared at her in the dark, would taste like.

There were dual pits for the stage, and Selay made note of a large series of bronze gears, and levers. It was a tower, and the way it was bolted to the floorboards showed that it spun the whole stage. Lifts allowed the quick deployment of all sorts of wood props, toys, and a few women's dresses for the men to wear for their roles.

Through two typical doors, and into a musty stone hallway was the path. Towards the end were the stairs out, a few stone windows facing the gardens shown the meek light of the sun through broken shadows of shrubs.

She felt the desire to destroy the stage. However, it was better to leave cleanly, and take the stairs, rather then cause a scene. The home of the theater owner was not too far away from here, and along a sewer route. It would be better to map both places, see the goings on, and see where the donation chests were kept, and learn how she could rob them all.

Yes, the Quad estates would be next to go to. There Selay could uncover all the dirty secrets and arrangements. Perhaps even use finscale wine to seduce Vias Ea' Quad into reviling who donated the bounty. Or at least to tell her where she can find this Gawundon matriarch that runs this club of pathetic killers.

It was a strange thing to be hunted. Her notoriety would not be that well-established in Journey's Rest past a brief misadventure or two. She has done nothing to anger the town's Kiri'grana or rouges. She is known as the "Whore of Brudge" in dens, but not well enough to warrant vendettas.

The price was rather odd too. The key was the gems that were used to pay for her demise. Glistening sapphires, emeralds, and rubies. Things only the most wealthy would easily part with. Any flightless upon one would adorn it to impress their chosen, not give it away so easily.

Selay thought of her targets. Vias is a naive, fat man. He was only focused on his theater, and the attention of the crowd. He mingled with the powerful to draw patrons, and keep his theater funded. Beneath, he hosted the den that his family uses for all sorts of salaciousness.

Selay saw him once, or twice from her safe house. He always wore brightly colored silks. What was rather odd, most finscales bring a lady, or two to shop with them. Vias always brought some young finscale man instead.

The heralds always mention he is the brother Flumen Ea' Quad, the local Chancellor. Both the same color of purple, and with brownish horns. However, Vias is fat, and had a frill with a ball on its end. One right between his eye ridges that bounced gaily as he moved around.

So it was settled, find Vias, and make him reveal the truth. A fat man could be easily swayed by starvation, done by hanging him at the platforms by the river outside. He should confess all in before noon.

Although moving him could be hard, Selay settled on this plan just before she arrived at the end of the hallway. This was a circular castle tower at the corner of the theater. The smell of lilacs emanated from up the stairs, as if someone was through here recently. Except, when Selay made her way up to the main floor, there was a sign marked "Garderobe" on a door with pots of blooming lilac aside of it.

The lobby was calm, and empty. With two wide doors, and a long carpet that lead into the main aisle of the theater room. Also with double doors. The actor's practice sounds haunted all around. There were two large columns in the center, covered in various plated gold patterns.

When Selay was between the columns and her exit, the doors shook. Her first response was to duck behind a column. She peered from the side, and observed.

The crowd outside was briefly heard, with no special commotion. The finscales outside were gathering like flies to the district. The creek, and slamming of the doors shut silenced the room again. Followed by the padding of footsteps down the carpet, and someone giving a sniff.

Selay shifted around the column, the opposing way to see. A fat, smiling, purple man glided through. He had an annoying bulbous frill, dressed in a long robe, with a gold trim blue cape. Selay smiled, as now she did not have to go far to deal with Vias, now all she needed was a strong enough rope.

She watched him open the gigantic oak doors to enter the main theater. After closing them, a sudden slam indicated they were now barred. Even so, Selay opted to check, and gently moved the door to find them constrained. She made a fast stride to other points of entry, all equally sealed.

Deciding to hear the commotion inside for a moment, she rested her head upon one of the doors. The voice now clear to understand.

"Ain! You shirk Ua's glamour for your own callous thirst for war! I, Numril, shall give her peace, and quench her fire! I will not so recklessly abandon her!" The actor boasted, obviously playing his part.

Selay sighed, no additional voices. She stood up, and decided to get to a better angle. One where she could see.

This theater was large enough to have several private balconies on the second floor. Where the wealthy paid well to escape from the smells of the less wealthy. These private areas were sure to be less secure at this time. So Selay went up the spiral stairs to them, and tried every door.

"Ua's splendor. Our flight is complete. Her fire is dulled, and our children forged!" The actor's voice was accompanied by a slight laugh from Vias.

The first door, was locked. Selay moved to the second. The building was rather devoid of guards, despite a play to open shortly.

"I am saddened by her indifference. She has no interest in my affairs somehow. However, I shall guard our family, and curl with her around them. That shall please her."

After the fourth door, Selay was successful. A rounded balcony, with a guard railing, on the far corner by the stage. She positioned herself where she could least be seen, and sat down.

"Gewj, why do you always practice that?" Vias squawked, the actor's name was Gewj.

"I must summon Nimril's spirit to perform. Otherwise I do not capture the love he had for Ua," Gewj responded.

Selay gave her eyes a rub. The lack of rest from the night is starting to gain on her. Maybe sitting down was a mistake. She stood again, bending herself slightly uncomfortable to stay alert.

"You are fine. The crowd will celebrate you either way. Now get down off the stage, and prepare for today with a meal."

Gewj was taller then Selay, and he was skinny. His costume was that of a armor clad warrior, with enough scale exposed to have an eroticism about it. Typical finscale. He was green, with frills, and fins along his chin, and a charismatic energy in his motion that seem well practiced. Selay felt a bit disgusted at the site of him.

"What will our meal be today?" Gewj asked, "I am shoring for some sea trout."

Vias chuckled, "Sea trout is well, and good, but today we should celebrate."

Tilting his head, Gewj asked, "There is no reason I know to celebrate."

"Ah but there is! For our mutual problems are to be resolved on schedule!" Vias opened his arms, and wings in a rather broad display.

Selay is now sure this fat man was of the queer side. He was too friendly, ugly, and affectionate towards Gewj. Even for a finscale. If the actor responded with affection, Selay would have to flee to save herself.

Fortunately, Gewj turned to face away, "I do not have mutual problems. Other then the sale of my ladies to proper suitors."

Vias closed his display, and looked down in embarrassment, "You have a chosen?"

"Yes. She is already bonded. You did not hear the gossip? They say I chased her in the sky, to the Ua temple in the market, and our shadows were cast upon the entire chamber."

Vias shook his head, "No. I do not meddle in gossip. It causes strife I am better without."

"Since when does any finscale not worship Ua? Does not that make you keen on it?" Gewj glanced behind him.

"Not every Ua worshiper has ear-fins to the dirt." Vias snorted. "Come then. We can still share this feast. Then cheer for fertility, and wealth."

"Feast!?" Gewj turned, and seemed excited, "Before the spring is over?"

"Yes. Over on stage is the eggs. Bring them here, and sit down."

Gewj obeyed, and went over to the covered box by the backdrop of the stage. He walked down the stairs, and lifted the silk blanket. He appeared surprised, and happy. Unable to get a clear view of its contents, Selay squinted, and leaned, risking being sited.

Four eggs, large, with blotches of colors. The primary color was red, and the lessor color was blue. Each egg, while having a different pattern, was similar.

"Oh my!" Gewj began to lick his lips. "Are these still alive?"

"Yes. These eggs were not for the Spring Feast. They do not fit with our goals." Vias explained, "A friend underneath our mutual problem has arranged to gift them to me."

"You do not intend to raise them?" Gewj started move

back towards Vias with the crate in arms.

"What for? I intend to stay happy," Vias rubbed his hands together, bearing teeth in anticipation, "These eggs were a gift for such a strange donation. The one about that platescale, and the traitor worm who lays with her."

Both sat down, first seat in first row. "She has been dealt with?" The actor asked.

Selay's fatigue left her. The impertinence of what she was about to know may be everything she wanted. Who their problem was, who sponsored its solution. Things she could rend her talons upon well.

"Yes. This will secure Journey's Rest for us. His buildings shall be seized after the fire last night. A fire that exterminated a platescale proper from our marshland." Vias pulled an egg out from the crate, held it from the bottom in his palm, and began to move his jaw to loosen it some.

Selay began to feel sickened. They were desiring of her death, and they want to affect Brudge. Even worse, those were not bird eggs, they were Allyian. They were, as well, finscale eggs. Large enough to be claimed. When Vias pushed the first into his mouth, Selay decided to back off, and head to a more complete view.

In fact, she became swamped with confusing feelings. She swore she heard the egg squeak, and this possessed her. Her soul riveted, and pulsed with Ua's rage. She knew he just ate a child before it was born. She saw a child die, eaten by a flightfull tasked to protect it. She wanted to wail, and cry. Then swoop in, and rip the egg out of Quad's belly. Selay used her talons to break her palms. The pain, and the scent of her blood diverted her, but just barely.

She had to leave before she causes a scene. The conversation could barely be heard. She went towards a side door at the far end of the hall, it was already open. This door lead to the stage scaffolding, which saw all the theater.

When she looked back, crouched on a ledge, she was able to see the front of the two. Gewj was choking down the egg whole. Vias already was slouching back, rubbing his belly.

"They taste of saltwater from Deep Lake. We must send a letter of condolences for this gift," Gewj said when he moved for his second egg.

"We must. These were preserved very well. I shall draft a letter for Kiven. Along with a invite to our show." Vias belched, and flopped his tail on the chair in front of him.

"Is Kiven in town? We can invite him to the third showing." Gewj asked just before pushing his second egg into his mouth.

"He made for Deep Lake immediately, and in a hurry. I am afraid the condolences will have to go there." Vias opened his wings, and leaned his head back.

Her body was shaking from an assortment of rage, drunkenness, exhaustion, and temperament. Somehow she hesitated when she heard the name Kiven. Kiven Di' Noach, the banker of Brudge in Deep Lake. It took all her will to stay her wrath. She has found monsters worse then her. If she killed them, all would hunt her. Brudge would cut her head off, if not chain, and throw her over the side of the Great Crack to her doom.

Vias made no secret, and chortled loudly, "The suns set on the Derin house! May traitors all be cast to idleness! Except those who bring about the true plan of the Twin Gods."

The two laughed merrily. Their mood changed to a boasting as they lay gorged on the eggs of some unknown mother's clutch. The continued enjoyment of these egg eaters made Selay loose her balance from nausea. She hit the floor with a thud loud enough to sound throughout the theater.

Vias, and Gewj were out of their seats and alert

immediately.

"Who goes there!?" Vias demanded.

Selay gazed around for an escape route. There was very little room to move, but she could see an opened sunroof. The perfect direction away.

"I think I see some shadows in the scaffolding!" Vias growled.

Something of a roar erupted in the theater below. Selay began to crawl to the exit. She looked back down as she scurried, and could see Gewj climbing a column rapidly, and leaping closer.

"There!" Vias pointed, "Someone is watching!"

Selay was on her feet, she was spotted. She made full effort to get a running jump. Gewj was leaping from the sides of the balconies like a wild bat, with a smooth flow as if he was playing a well known part.

Selay quickly lifted her wings, and jumped into the direction of the window. She beat her wings forward, and assumed a diving pose as she gained air.

"It is a platescale with some staff!" Gewj roared as he tried to take off, but his full belly made him unable to get anywhere but the scaffolding Selay just left.

She quickly was climbing out of the window, her tail kicking it shut. She rolled onto the roof, stood up. Then gazed across the endless city of Journey's Rest, with the tower still smoldering in the distance.

"Sound the alarm! Guards! Guards!" She heard, "Come!"

For a moment, the secrets Selay held were committed to memory. She knew immediately this was truly profane. No one whispers of these in courts.

However, those with this knowledge, are forever to be burdened inside. Quickly does one find themselves unease. No wings, however flightfull, are strong enough to live well in this.

Even so, in the end, nothing matters. We are born, grow, and die. The only thing we can hope for is the fair judgment of the gods at their throne. Judgment of our virtues, our deeds, our loyalty to them.

With Selay's witness, it is clear now. The Kiri'grana are fallen too. Burn the world, and rid it of us all. For we are lost.

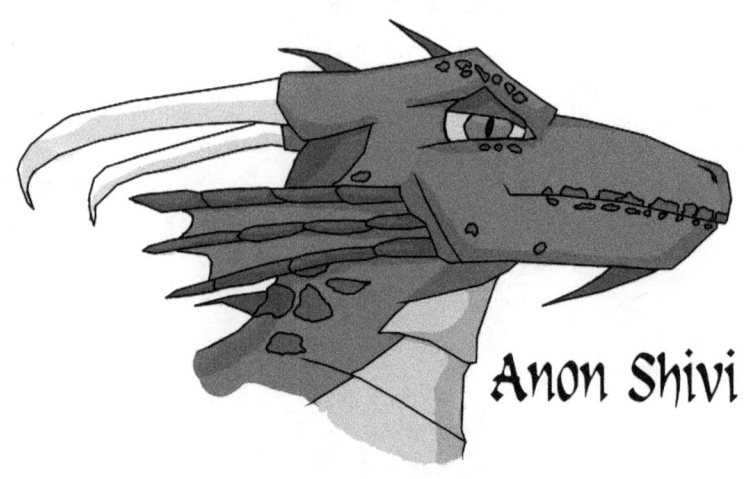

Anon Shivi

CHAPTER TWELVE

The wyrm now has begun to turn in agony at this new revelation. The song has become one of great torment to chronicle. It now confirms we should be calling the gods for our destruction.

The Wyverns bellow, as if they know. They gave us our authority as the great watchers of the gods. The wyrm is chosen by them to serve the task. It is tasked to scrape carefully upon the page each verse of the songs. So must all the foul things we done be stored, and valuated. So we are correctly punished for it.

To deny a healthy child its life? Consume an egg live? This cannot be believed with just the eyes of a hussy. Others must be sung, for they can prove this thing true. Many others, isolated, and near. All of them shall be recorded. Their song combined into a choir.

This act was done by finscales. So such the finscales die first then. Gut them, and rip out their bellies in vengeance. Though know that the Order does not know all yet, so the finscales must be spared for now.

The Order can only task off what it knows completely. Such that was of dealing with the chaos in Tram. The central city was nested along the rivers far south of Freestride, walled in, with a fortified castle, and dungeon inside.

It was there we have the brief song of Anon Shivi tending the gardens. A fit middle-aged platescale with brown hide, and forty years. Anon is a gifted groundskeeper, and cared for the entire castle's bounty.

He devoted his life to the most beautiful garden in all of Tram. Every time he gazed upon his work, he puffed his chest up in pride. To him, this was his Trial. His garden's glamour would be sung to Ua upon his death. She would sunbathe in it while he tended. Ain would be able to rest under a tree with her in the heavens.

Anon's day began with trying to clean the blood out of the fountain near the south side of the front of the Tram castle. Only several days ago did a riot in the prison result in a corpse of a local laborer to be deposited in the fountain. Draining it was a task that Anon was not pleased to do.

He used soap, and towels from the maids' quarter, and scrubbed diligently. After running the fountain then retraining it to wash away anything not stained, he would repeat. Spending at least a good half the day on this. Eventually his body ached, and he gave up. He left the fountain where it is, still coated red.

When he ate, Anon enjoyed his fish in the garden. He has his own special hiding place in the artificial forest he designed. One that required moving off the normal path, under bushes, and on a bed of mushrooms.

Then after, he intended to spend his day trimming the hedges in the fountain on the northwest side of the inner garden. He forgo large sheers in favor of stronger scissors. He bought them off a tailor in town to preen precisely, and shape carefully.

All of Anon's mind was of few whole worlds. First of

his garden. Of good labor, and tending. Then of his wife, and her cooking. For when he returned to his apartment in the inner city. Others of twelve children. Who all grown, and left for various duties. Then the study of plants, with the intricate scents, shapes, and colors they bore.

The man did not indulge in fantasies of the Kiri'grana like his fellow flightless. Instead he accepted his task. Even the blood spilled in Hilltop, the burning of Anya, and the martial law were distant from him, and growing further away. Let justice be enforced by his betters. He chooses to not meddle in their affairs.

He fell into a trance about the time he trimmed the Sweet Pea. Which he purposely arranged to grow in the same location of the hedges, resulting in a flowering thick bush that was the most catching part of the area.

This almost mindless movement from him continued until he accidentally cut the bulb off a Protea. He sighed, coming to attention. A mistake. He quickly recovered by tossing it in the fountain, where it could bloom again.

He did not get a chance to return to his daze. For in the distance a Wyvern screamed. His heart raced, and his work stopped as he looked up to see where it was. His scissors were released from his hand, and fell onto the ground.

A massive red Wyvern made a terrifying yawl as it entered from the north. It passed once over the city in a slow, and perfected pose. Then beat its wings, and banked hard west. Then circled closer to the castle.

On the walls, the usual guards were scurrying into positions. They mainly went into the towers, where arrow slits would provide protection against claws that could scoop, and kill. The town watch rang the bell, and shouts were heard from all ends.

Anon could not hide. He was too much into the open, and frozen in fear. He never saw a Wyvern this close. He was told plenty, through story, and peer how to react. What he heard is all the same: run. Somehow he could not.

The beast took a low swoop over the castle, upon it a large set of Armour became noticeable. The guards were shouting, "An Order Knight has come!" from across the courtyard. Other guards echoed it to their neighbors, sending this message quickly across town. The bells ceased, and the guards all gathered to watch on the walls.

Another scream, and then a final third pass. It ended right center of the courtyard. A mere trifle away from Anon.

It loomed about, setting down where it landed. Its wings arched aside. Its face was covered in thick armor scales, with a long muzzle, and broken plates about. There were remains of scars, and wounds. The nose tip has a single horn, strong enough to impale with. Its eyes were colorless, and empty, with red outlines, and the ridges were posed so that a direct forward strike could not blind it. Alongside its cheeks were curved horns that made a mockery of anyone's around it, eight to be exact. Where normal dual horns would jut out at the end of the head ridges, there was a large, merged mass of bone, plates, and muscle. They merged by the unnatural, and random shape of five longer horns in near equal distance, parallel to each other.

Where one would expect neck scales was a series of steel plates. Each bolted to a thick hardened leather that was further held to its neck by straps, and belts.

On its chest, a suite of custom fit Armour plates. Rusted, bent, and dented like its hide. The seams of the leather were tearing in off places, but the supporting straps contained these breaches.

Between those straps, a red sash that curved down into a plate that seemed to put pressure on the creature's neck. The sash was only loose along the edges, meaning there was something underneath. That something was reigns.

The beast asserted its position, glaring down at Anon directly as if it was telling him it was here. Its breathing heavy from long flight, and its pose intimidating. It puffed its large chest to make itself more imposing, then leaned its face closer to Anon.

The groundskeeper was in such a state of fear he did not know how to act. To run would be pointless, to faint would be suicide, and to fight an Order Wyvern would be suicide, and a crime. He could just gaze back, be ever more frightened, and accept being eaten.

By the head of the beast, right behind the horns, poked out a blue face with yellow eyes. He had long ears, and several thick bumps, and frills on his chin, and head. He also was gifted with his egg-horn, and a long pair of upright horns behind his head. Along the left side of his face was a tattoo in the pattern of a branch flowing in the wind.

"Ho, stranger. Have you seen Metropolitan Raviwr?" He said.

Anon was locking his eyes onto the Wyvern, and he did not respond.

"Stranger?" The blue man on the beast said.

Anon still did not react.

"Stranger! YELVIAN COMMANDS YOU TO LISTEN!" That roar brought Anon out of his stupor.

"I, uh..." Anon noticed the knight. He quickly took a knee, opened his wings, and exposed his neck to punishment. "Forgiveness!"

The rider snorted, and jumped from his mount's neck. He patted on its maw, then made a noisy churling sound. It quit its pose, folding wings, and hunching up like a bird. It began to preen itself, and ignore everything around it.

"What am I forgiving? Fear of an Order Wyvern is to be expected." The man said.

"Great Yelvian, sir. I am not brave enough," Anon

meekly said, looking up.

The man was rather tall, he wore a standard suit of decorative armor that all knights wore during peacetime. The armor itself was more heavy then functional, and consisted of spikes, and plates of finely polished silver, or bright steel that is cooled in brine after spending time in the greatest of forges. Under was a chain-mail covering that bolted the plates together, with a tunic further below to provide comfort. A sash also adorned his suit that matched the Wyvern's color of red, it linked to a center plate. His belt also had a long, and tattered cloth that covered what would be his codpiece. On it, the symbols of The Order, designating him as a knight wyrm.

Behind his wings were two blades. These were attached to his back along a golden trim. Their handles hang from his wing's shoulders. The tips poked alongside his tail, which had extra chain-mail to keep them from cutting.

"I do think not running from me could be braver then most," he said, smiling, "And your aspect should be?"

Anon stood up finally, his eyes wide at the sight of one of the most beloved figures in the whole world. Brave Yelvian, who defended the Uneasy Armistice, then criticized it in a single pose at its ratification. A man who appealed for his position in the Order by leading a siege. The man who saw the worst, and best, of all. One of the first to see the war as dishonorable, and to beg forgiveness of its detractors. He stood before Anon today, and Anon did not deserve so much as to know his scent.

"I am Anon, the humble groundskeeper of Tram Castle," Anon tried not to make direct eye contact.

The gardener did not deserve to speak to Yelvian, for he was not brave. He never was one to seek virtue outside himself. He tended his garden, so he could hide in it.

When the break at the dungeon happened, Anon hide away.

He heard the fighting, and the roars of those who died. He knew he could go out to help, but he stayed in his home that night, and barred his door. He even doused the candles in his home until the guards lifted their siege on the city. He was even afraid of his own fellows.

Yelvian looked across the gardens, and nodded, "I have not seen Tram since the war. This courtyard was empty last I was here. News of this garden has reached the capital."

"What do they say?" Anon inquired.

"That the Order's garden's are better. We lack a forest inside our compound. I hear it is of your design?"

Anon nodded proudly, his favorite hiding spot. It was the hiding spot of many of the castle when they needed privacy as well. "It is my design. Yes."

Yelvian placed his hands on his sides, and smiled as he gazed over the wooded area like he was reading a book.

"Once I acquire my first barrel of beer. I plan to spend at least a night in there with it!" He proclaimed.

Anon could not ask for more from a rider then to patron his grounds. This made him selfishly happy, and wanting to boast about a spot to choose, but he refrained.

A rough voice shouted from the castle, "Tie that beast down where it cannot crap in my yard!"

Yelvian turned slowly, and threateningly to face its direction. He was greeted by an approaching red man with gold ornaments off his horns, and a sash with the kingdom's banner on it. Otherwise he was dressed in outrageously expensive clothing made of soft silks.

"You are dressed too rich to not be the Duke." Yelvian stated.

"I am Duke Ordah Claxo, friend of the Emperor himself." The man's statement made Yelvian's face briefly frown, "What reason are you thugs here?"

Yelvian growled, though not in anger, but of disgust.

Anon himself went into an observant position.

"Gintrix will be informing you of our business here. Right now I am to secure your time, and earfin." Yelvian replied.

"You will have it when that animal is penned with the horses!" demanded Ordah.

Yelvian snapped his maw once in warning at the duke, "Letriana-Fal is not an animal, and can fly. She shall not be penned!"

The Wyvern, Litriana, with the Fal distinguishing her as part of the Order's queen Wyverns, was busy licking her wings until she heard her name. Coming from Yelvian, she immediately looked with attention his way.

"It is not a reasoned being. So it should be stationed off my gardens. It will makes a mess of things!"

Anon watched the Wyvern lower its head, and place it on the ground just near the two. She quietly posed there, as if to be listening. Lips pressed together as if wanting to speak, but unable. She showed to him remarkable intelligence.

"I refuse such a task. On the grounds it is not grateful of you to insult my girl!" Yelvian folded his arms defensively.

"Do not make me..." the duke was cut off by a rather wet snort by Litriana. Whose head was as large as him. Something greenish stuck to his shirt, and he clearly knew it by the look of horror on his face.

Yelvian belly laughed, and Anon could not hold back a chuckle either. Ordah was fated to something of this. He was brash, and stupid for demanding someone of Yelvian's position to move. At least the Knight did not cut off his tail, or burn him like Kityun did to prisoners in war.

The duke threw his arms, and wings up in defeat. He tried to shake off his new ornament unsuccessfully, "Just summon Gintrix already!"

Yelvian turned to his Wyvern, and said something in a sort of growl, or click. Litriana leaned up her head high, and made a soft rumble, then a cry, that sounded like a hawk. Anon heard that before, and many times thought it was a bird.

In the far distance, another Wyvern screamed. One with a deeper pitched tone. Litriana followed with a different set of clicks, and whines. The other responded with another tone.

Anon tilted his head. He clearly could see the tones mean something. It felt so different that he could not know its significance.

Litriana faced in the direction of the other Wyvern. It swooped over the castle wall towards her. This time the guards did not react. Expecting the Order to come in pairs, as per their tradition.

This one was a third larger. Grey with many broken scale-plates about its body. With its egg-horn. Even more spikes along its jaw, and six down its nose. Its head was further layered with horns, and spikes that outnumber those of Letriana-Fal, but they are much more orderly. The scales around its eyes were shattered, and broken into innumerable tiny pieces. Cold pure black eyes examined everything. Its armor was no different, except its sash was golden.

However, there was clear indication of this Wyvern being male. Who when landed, received a wing display in greeting from Litriana. The two exchanged looks before he lowered his head to let his rider off.

Yelvian announced, "Make way for Srica Gintrix, the head of the Order!"

Gintrix was not as Tall as Yelvian, but still more then average. His gray face scales were pronounced, indicating he was of mature age. His body was adorned with gold-trim silver-steel armor, and a purple robe that covered his legs. Above his horns were decimated, splintered in fact, from a battle long ago. His tail adorned a mace-like bulb that was cracking in some places. Most strange, was the chest scale pattern being as an array of single solid center plates, with two circled scales on the sides. This pattern was eastern, and not common at all in Skol. Adorned on his left cheek was a tattoo of feathers.

The Duke bowed, and Yelvian smirked. Anon bowed in show as well. Gintrix was the only man to rival the power of the Emperor. In fact, he was traditionally tasked with handing the oath of Grateful Tasking down to new rulers, and dukes. His presence in Tram meant that he only had a task to issue.

"Gintrix, it has been so long!" Ordah greeted in mid bow.

"That it has, Duke Claxo," Gintrix's voice boomed as he replied. "You could have worn better cloths?"

Ordah growled, the phlegm was clear, and present. He stood up, and waved his hand at Yelvian.

"His beast has violated my person!"

Yelvian laughed again, "Litriana has rose fever this spring. Those who insult her should be happy they get a snort."

"SHE SPIT ON ME!" roared Ordah.

Yelvian roared back, "YOU WANTED TO PEN HER WITH HER FOOD! SHE IS ALREADY FAT WITH EGGS! DO YOU WANT HER TO NOT FLY!?"

Anon watched the two quarrel, but he did not listen. They waved arms, thrashed tails, and argued. Yelvian had a smile on his face the whole time, as if he was purposely agitating the Duke.

Letriana-Fal, and the other Wyvern, were off by the trees. Litriana had her head under the wing of the male, and clearly was preening about. The male had his head over her neck, his eyes closed, and was trying to sleep. Anon took note of her belly, and saw it was a bit extended, where eggs would typically be.

Gintrix vanished it seemed, and Anon did not bother. Eventually, the posing of the two became repetitive, and dull. Anon went back to his bushes. Only to find Gintrix sitting by the fountain, and watching the fight.

"Gardener Anon Shivi, I assume?" He said.

"Yes, sire," Anon tried to be meek, and humble.

"How long until Ordah surrenders? I am thinking of placing a bet," joked the rider.

"Ordah? He usually surrenders about supper time," replied the groundskeeper.

"Well that will not do, that is a bit away." Gintrix sighed.

Gintrix got up, and re-approached the combatants. Anon distinctly heard him chuckling slightly under his breath. Finally, the rider put his arm right between their faces.

"IF THEY EAT MY HORSES I WILL GO TO THE HIGH COURT!"

"THE ORDER IS THE HIGH COURT!"

They maneuvered themselves around Gintrix's arm.

"YOU RIDERS NEED TO LEARN PROPER EDIQUETE! WE TIE OUR ANIMALS UP IN TRAM!"

"WYVERNS ARE NOT ANIMALS YOU DOXY LITTLE MAN!"

"YOU ARE JUST AS CLASSLESS, AND RIDICULOUS AS I REMEBER!"

Gintrix decided to roar in both their ears loudly.

Both Yelvian, and Ordah nearly fell over at the shock. Yelvian was childishly giggling. While the brow on Ordah was angled, and his lips curled.

Satisfied the fight was over, and Gintrix had control of the issue. He began:

"Due to the news of the Royal Staff passing through Tram on the back of a thief." Gintrix puffed up some, "I, Sirica Gintrix, am here before the arrival of a contingent of Order guards to take command of both the church, and the county of Tram. Herein-forth the duke, and his government are suspended until further notice."

Anon suddenly was in worry. Was his job to be suspended to? He was servant of the Duke.

"Duke Ordah Claxo, I relive you. You are free remain in the castle with your family, and serve as advisory."

Ordah's eyes widened in shock, and his jaw could not close. Anon could even see his eyes gloss as if he was going to cry. He, a Kiri'grana, now stripped of power.

Yelvian noticed Anon looking, and even a worried look on his face. The blue-scaled man pointed at him, and said, "We shall talk later." softly.

"The castle grounds is to be quarters for a contingent of thirty guards. They shall be tasked with investigating all crimes, and officials of the county. Yelvian shall oversee things." Gintrix continued.

No one protested. Anon tried to resume his trimming. He reclaimed his scissors, and primped leaves, and petals. The commotion faded into the background for him. Up until one of the Wyverns made what could be best figured a gagging sound.

"On no! Litriana!" Yelvian shouted as he ran to his mount, "I told you to stop chewing on anything other then bones!"

Litriana was poised hunched over, and gagging on a branch of a tree. The male Wyvern emitted panicked shouts as it did not know what to do. This means that the fountain of blood shall not be alone in its mess today.

Tonight would be long, and life for Anon shall now be unnecessarily difficult. The great gardens of Tram, and their song, intertwine now with the greater song of suffering.

The Wyrm is unable to rest, and continues to scratch upon the page. The world remained stopped, but the Order is here, virtuous and true to the Twin Gods. They may be able to restart it at long last.

Zhaqua

CHAPTER THIRTEEN

Restless is the Wyrm, and so it growls. Unable to escape the things it has witnessed. This song is tormenting. For Ua and Ain continue to hold the world still, making it too quiet to hear anything else.

The Wyverns do not rest. They loom over the hold as the wyrm claws upon the page this continued case for our doom. With each scratch, it learns the rot festers. It must be purged, if we are to return to normal.

Why has not the virtuous yet to fulfill this task? Where do they hide? They no longer lead us proper. We require them to sing a song of righteousness. So at least to show how we are the rot, and must be purged too.

Foul finscales, and their proclivities, now eat their own children. Burn them, and shed their blood, to save us all. They are no longer Allyian. Thus no longer worthy of their coral, and marsh.

Cowardly platescales continue to retreat to their dens, even in sight of this horror. They know their tasking, but curl in fear. We have no need for them. So let them decay to dust from inaction, and be forgotten.

The Order remains, and it does not know of this

disorder yet. So the Wyrm reasons that it must continue now. It reclaims its posture, and brings wrath upon all. It scratches upon the pages a song of Judgment. This Journey of redemption resumes.

Of the Order, Gintrix hunts to the wrong melody. The Wyrm growls, as it realizes that charm alone is not the justice we need. Only the whole of the Order can bring this task to action.

Enduring Zyrko was found dead, with a broken wing, in Anya. Selay's claim is thus true. So we Endure no more. With no whole Order comes misdirection, and inaction. Thus the blight grows, and festers.

Blight such as this selfish coward Huron. He quakes, while watching blood drip from his torn wing, and tail. It glistened, and then stained upon the twigs, and leaves of this random grove in the Tram woods.

He only barely managed to mutter, "In the end, nothing matters-" before he was cut off by a solid tail thrash upon his forehead, and a laugh from his captor, Ematel.

"Such an adorable lullaby! There is no saving for you! Today those who flee shall die!" the little demon squawked.

Huron slumped even lower. He was an ugly collection of shame, and fear. He has arms strong enough to crush Ematel's skull, but not any will to try. Such a lousy servant of the Twin Gods. If he is not to rise up to protect the nest, then kill him here, for he is not needed.

The demon Ematel stood with chin held high, chest puffed, and paced in this grove. He almost seemed to bob his head. His patrol told all that he was in charge of this newly annexed place.

"We could smell your fear from back in the village!" he taunted, "You should have never run from us. For now all those who helped you are dead! No one knows of you!"

Ematel kicked Huron in the side, and the charcoal soot-scale winced at the penetration of a footclaw between his plates. He should have stood, and rendered his talons upon Ematel there. Instead he just looked pathetically at Tailya. Who was held down at her arms, and wings by the other rouges.

Ematel came to Tailya, and licked his lips. The fiery red gazed back at Huron pleadingly. Her eyes glazed over, as she saw he would be of no help.

Grabbing her maw, he forced her to look into his eyes, "Daughter of the coward king, my desire to ransom you is over. You shall mother my children."

Tailya flew into an unchecked rage. She rejected this demon's foul scent. So she gnashed, and snarled. Then broke free from the rouges' hold, and sunk her fangs into his muzzle.

Ematel struggled free. He has scales that kept him well-protected, and Tailya's hold was rather weak. He rubbed the marks, as she spit out the bitter taste. She seemed proud of herself for warding him off.

A slash of his backhand into Tailya's face followed suit. She cried out, and thrashed her tail full behind her, forcing the other's to dodge back so to not have their legs broken. She was now free to fight back.

She stood up, and took to a combative pose. Folding her wings, and flexing her claws. Then crouched to protect her gravid belly, and bore teeth.

There was no chance for her, as she has no combat training. With a charge, Ematel easily tripped her, and backhand slapped her to the ground. There she lay still, and shocked.

The others regained their grip, with one sitting on her tail to keep it pinned. The rest used belts, and ropes to tie the woman. They rolled her onto her back. Ematel loomed, withdrawing his knife, and brandishing it happily.

Huron could just bare to watch. This littler creature

was going to trespass. He was to take what he has not earned.

He caressed a hand on Tailya's belly, "Mine now. All of them." he said in childish idolatry towards her. He explored her body in lewd ways, as if he never seen it before.

Tailya could do nothing. She was to loose herself in her season. Subdued, she protested with whimpers, and looked away towards Huron again.

Huron noticed this state prior, with Selay. Though, when with her, they both intended the act. Huron's Sapphire had a similar violent assault. When Huron lost the fight, she showed her belly, and both explored. Tailya refused, fought, and remains resistant.

"Ematel, we must get moving!" Squawked Zhaqua, who was perched upon a branch above the group, "Two armored guards are coming!"

Ematel growled, and he lifted himself up. He cursed the ground. He then glared back at the girl, and came towards her. He slashed his dagger, "Can not you deal with them?"

"They are Lieutenants. I need help." She answered.

"Weakling! You watch these two. The rest will take care of this with me." Ematel said.

Quickly the rouges, about six or so, scattered into the woods. Ematel turned to his two victims, "You are lucky, but this will not save you."

He began to walk out, and pointed at Tailya, "You are my wife now! We will not leave here until I consecrate your bond with me."

The little creature stopped, and thought. His nose pointed upwards to sniff the air, and Tailya's fire. He became excited, then charged over to her.

"They can handle the patrol. I must secure you now," he stated, "With you, I shall be above all of them."

Huron saw Tailya simply surrender. Her wings closing, and she remained still. She made constant eye contact towards him. It told him that all he had to do was to fight back, but he could not.

Ematel saw this, and protested, "Look upon me, my queen! You must admire my glamour!"

He fanned out his wings in a display, and Tailya refused to look. This made him cease his forced courting, stand up, and scowl at the soot-scale.

"She dares to insult me by admiration of such a pathetic thing as yourself? Do you want to fight for her?"

Did Huron desire Tailya? One can see he was unsure. Perhaps maybe his demon desired her. Yet why does Ofiln cower away in face of a challenger?

Her pleading eyes did bring in him an immense empathy to aide her. Tailya would not live a single week in her state. She is but a child, scared, and alone.

Ematel continued to threaten, and try to break up their exchange. He finally darted to Huron. Then placed his knife blade into his white neck scales.

"She will not gaze upon your bloodied corpse," he growled, baring his fangs.

Huron leaned back, and found his tail pinched. The rope dart caused a terrifying pain, but he could not roar. If he moved, sounded, or did anything, he would find his throat split open.

"This will be over soon." the demon spoke.

"Selay..." Huron uttered.

"What?" Ematel snorted. "It does not matter."

"No! Ematel! They just killed one of us!" Zhaqua shouted from the branch top.

"Ain's cod!" Ematel cursed, and revoked his hold on Huron.

Huron gasped, amazed he was free. Then rolled to become more comfortable. He could smell his fresh blood, as his wounds reopened. He growled, and rumbled to comfort himself from the pain.

Zhaqua landed on the ground, and stayed her own blade. She walked towards Ematel, wings partly opened. Her tail swayed high, and seductive.

"Tie him down! I will kill him when we leave. I want her to see, so she accepts her fate."

The rouge girl crossed her arms in frustration, and looked sideways at Ematel. She did not agree, but instead tilted her hips, and displayed her own glamorous wings fully. She rubbed her hand along her shoulder, and down her figure, facing her partner.

Ematel stared at her, impressed at this, knowing what it meant. However, he snorted, and bypassed her. He vanished into the shrubs. Zhaqua puttered, frustrated at the half-rejection he gave. She was not the best gemstone to choose, and it bothered her.

"You two are pathetic, but somehow cute," Zhaqua said, examining her prey.

She sauntered slowly up to the larger man, and smiled down her muzzle upon him. Huron was then given the same glamour as Ematel, but its immaturity had no effect. To add insult, she stood in front of Tailya to block the view.

"Ematel shall do what he says," the rouge said, "Unless I can interfere. I can claim you, Huron. You are big, and dumb. I can have you for a pack mule when we go robbing. I always wanted a submissive husband."

Huron turned his head away in refusal, he wanted nothing of this silly game. He is Selay's alone. She would never allow her lump of coal to be stolen from her.

Zhaqua gave him no choice, pushing herself onto him. She laid near him, examining his arms, and wings. She then sensually sputtered at this.

"If Ematel takes her, who would I have?" She pleaded. "At least take pity?"

Huron closed his eyes. There shall be no sympathy for those like her. For greater demons like Selay are far more frightening then some petite rouge.

He is correct about this drunk hussy he traveled after. She would have never known in the now. However, when she found out, Zhaqua would become a boot, and one of the many decorative skulls in some household's shelves.

"So sad, but you have no choice," Zhaqua said, as she reached behind him. She cut, and pulled the rope darts from his tail, and wings. "You shall be comfortable."

The dark platescale gasped, and winced from the pain, but it abated soon. He found himself quickly held by small soft-scaled hands. He was guided to a relaxed position on his back. Then he quickly felt a tight kissing upon his short stubble-snout.

This was wrong, and Huron knew it. She is too young to have her fire. She intended here to annex him for herself, and Huron tried to express his absolute lack of desire by continuing to look away. Which enraged her.

"I choose you! I want you to accept me! Look upon me!" She snarled.

This made no change in Huron's position, but Zhaqua was upset. She rose up, and glared at Tailya, who was snarling softly at her this whole time.

The fiend charged towards Tailya hissing, "You shall be silent! Or I shall break those eggs!"

Tailya's growl rose, and she snapped at her in challenge. Zhaqua knew immediately this was a threat. So she pushed Tailya onto her back, and kicked her in the chest hard.

"Spoiled bitch!" She growled, "This world, all must be taken with blood! I shall break your clutch, then force you to watch me take your failed protector."

Zhaqua knelt down to put her hand upon Tailya's belly.

All she had to do was press once firmly, and there would be a crack. Shortly later a blood spot, and with that, Tailya's death.

However, she did not have that chance. Sword clangs echoed just beyond the foliage. She was compelled to look their way. The combat was too near.

With a loud thud, one of Ematel's rouges fell from the trees just beside Huron. It frightened him, and he came immediately back to attention. He gazed into the panicking eyes of the rouge as the the last beat of life ended. Then tried to move, but was wrought with pain, and frozen by fear.

Zhaqua let out a terrifying howl of rage at the sight of her fallen friend. The rouge demon stood up, and drew dual blades to look for someone to take vengeance upon. Tailya was now left alone.

It was not long when a towering man came upon them. He was gold brownish scale, and contrasting markings upon his neck plates. His eyes were pure gray to silver, and reflected a fire of justice. In his hand, firmly he gripped his sword, and upon him was the plates of the Tram guard. His amour had Etched upon it the name of 'Ehtah.'

No hesitation was given as Zhaqua lunged towards him. Her fore charge broke into an above attack, as her light form made her greatly agile. She gave another enraged howl during this assault, her normal quiet nature upset by unmasked wrath.

This statue of a man was not swayed by a howling child. He deemed her unworthy of his sword, and struck her in the side of her belly with his gauntlet arm. This threw Zhaqua off into a nearby shrub, and dazzled her. She then left out of Huron's view, making a strange howling vocal sound, signaling to get help.

Several, uncountable, replies broke out. Ematel was the first to arrive. He broke from the trees up high, and swooped for Ehtah's head.

This would have been fatal, and broke the guard's neck from its velocity. Except another guard broke in from a glide, and rammed his horns into Ematel's body. Forcing the bandit leader to redirect, and escape.

This new savior was bearing the seal of Hilltop on his cuirass. He also was marked with the name 'Skazac.' His scales green, and rather dull looking.

The two guards clearly expected a counter assault from all around. They took position in the center of the grove with backs facing. Both growled in a challenging tone.

All at once, the entire band broke into assault. About four, or five. Each rouge striking from a different angle. Skillfully, the pair was able to deflect, and control the weapons enough to keep any from arriving too close. At least for some time, dodges and deflects were effective.

However, the rouges all seemed to coordinate naturally. Each time one dodged, a new angle was chosen by the whole group. This forced the guards to reposition each time. Thus spend endurance on moving their heavier amour, and retraining upon a new target.

Huron noticed something else, a childlike giggle from Ematel. He could not make out the demon's face, but this was frightening. It was as if this whole time he was thinking this dance of life, and death, a game of rough housing.

Eventually some rouge threw dirt into Ehtah's face. He rose his arm to defend his eyes, which was immediately impaled by a knife. To which he roared in pain so loud that the forest fled.

Skazac came in defense. Outright grabbing the rouge who stabbed Ehtah, and threw him into a trunk of a nearby tree. The child yelped, and was stunned.

Another rouge surprised Skazac by leaping on his shoulders, and trying to stab his head. Making him flail his arms, and shake around. This prevented a fatal stab into his skull. Skazac was proven strong again, and made this rouge join his friend against the tree trunk. The gaurd skillfully stabbed his sword into the child's heart.

The platescale hatchling howled into a death rage, and gripped the blade of the sword to try to free himself. He was too weak to do so. His friend was immediately given to fright, and sorrow. He gripped the body of the other, and cried pitifully.

"They are not even adults! Ua forgive us all, and burn their parents for the evil they spawned!" Skazac yelled, clearly upset.

Howls between Ematel, and Zhaqua erupted. The pair took more aggressive paces now that they were all that remained. Skazac, and Ehtah took their stance again. With Ehtah leaving the dagger in his arm.

Pacing like wild wolves, both rouges took to stare down each guard. Their numbers dwindled to nothing, and now was the final moment of Ematel's band. They began in full carnivorous blood lust to finish this fight.

Ehtah was able to slash, and deflect with his sword using smooth strikes. Skazac used his tail to whip Zhaqua's belly hard enough to bruise. The battle escalated into skillful use all of body, and tactics. It had a rhythm of steady motion, and sounds.

It would seem as if these savior guards are going to rescue Huron, and Tailya. This all changed when Zhaqua rolled away from a near fatal slash by Ehtah. She was able to redirect, and pass Ehtah entirely. Then strike upon Skazac's leg, cutting open his artery, and forcing him to his knee.

Now crippled, Skazac cried out. Ehtah took to defending him, and Zhaqua refocused upon him with a flurry of attacks. None were meant to strike, and all controlled his weapon.

Ematel was completely focused on Skazac in opposed. The

rouge stabbed a blade into the Hilltop guard's shoulder. Then another into his lung with intent to reach his heart. However, grooves in the Armour were not positioned to reach there, so it did not make it.

Skazac swung his sword heavy at Ematel, now trying to keep the child away. He was gulping, and huffing for air, as now he could barely breath. He was needing a final blow.

Huron was distracted from the awe of the combat by something bumping him. Tailya was near, and she was pleadingly pressing her muzzle to his side. Somehow she crawled herself to him for protection, despite the risk involved. Huron saw how, she loosened her feet some.

"Help," she cooed in a soft whimper, "We can flee now."

There was no disagreement. If they fled now, it would be easier to hide later. He nodded, and Tailya sat up so he could get at the various knots to unbind her.

Her fire was unceasing. As Huron loosened rope, he felt something he never felt before. This new sensation made all this despair feel rewarding, and he began to both purr, and smile. It confused him. This act of freeing someone was not supposed to be this pleasant. He thought maybe he could entertain reward for this. However, he did not feel he needed anything.

The ropes fell, and Tailya flexed her body free. He felt her tail touching his, stroking upon the midsection of its trunk. Huron recoiled a bit, for it was too affectionate.

The fight continued. Both Ehtah, and Skazac were becoming weary. Yet they would not yield, and neither were the rouges.

Zhaqua finally was thrown back again, and stayed there. She taunted Ehtah by appearing to look as if she could attack at any moment. She swerved, and thrashed her tail lucidly, staying just in the corner of his eyes.

Ematel was on the other foot, and continued his

childish laughter. He took distance only to come back with a momentous charge. His face was a wicked smile.

Skazac finally ended his defense, and decided he had enough. He readied a full swiping cleave as Ematel charged fore again with intent to impale both lungs. The cleave went through, and Ematel dodged in haste.

Both were successful. When two blows succeed that means finality. Blood splattered, and both combatants stopped, and stood solemn.

Ematel swayed, and lingered. His laughter ceased. He dropped his daggers, and wailed like a child half his age. His maw was cut, and bleeding. It was a lone gash, but the child never felt such a wound in his life. With that pain, he was scared for the first time. This gash, was positioned well, and would lead to his teeth needing to be removed, and regrow in the coming years.

Skazac was able to redirect the flow of the attack. However, Ematel was able to cut open the side of his throat, and impale his other lung. He no longer could breath, and let out one great roar to the heavens as he fell upon the ground. He coughed out blood, while humming the song of spirit. He seemed to fall into a chuckling mania while doing so. His song was never completed, for he fainted, then died there.

All vengeful senses left Ehtah, and sorrow filled him. Zhaqua charged towards Ematel, and hugged like a mother. Her wings wrapped over, and tail trapped him.

"It is okay. Now we can grow up." Zhaqua told him, then glared upon Ehtah, and growled, "We yield. We are all defeated."

Ehtah tried to pick up Skazac, but his arm was wounded too much to carry. A sudden fear came upon him. So he ran, and did not understand why he did not restrain them there. Maybe he saw the rot too, and it made him want to fly far away to hide.

Huron, and Tailya were far off into the untraveled woodlands. Tailya held Huron once again by his hand as she pushed through a path with her other arm. They continued to flee. Do not they know that cowardice exacerbates all plights?

The Wyrm growls, and remains angered. Ehtah's fleeing, and Ematel's slaughtering have proven that platescale kind is perhaps just as rotted as finscales. Burn the world of both then. Make way for our betters.

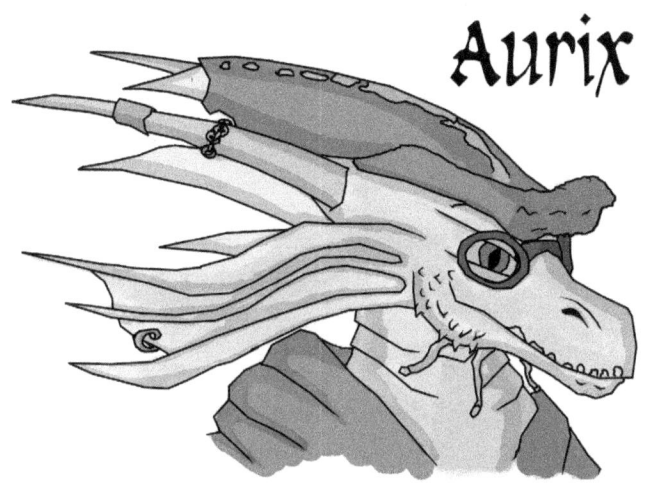

CHAPTER FOURTEEN

The Wrym stirs, and weeps in despair. We are a contemptuous set of creatures, who are the cause of great agony. Its claw must scratch this page, it continues to sing these songs. Even if it would rather go to slaughter all it sings of.

Judge worthy of destruction on this day all of us. We have no want to fulfill our own duties, and thus be worthless in the divine order. Our things are better allotted to the righteous, and pure. They can do the Grateful Tasking proper.

It further pains the Wrym that the gleam of truth is by one so contemptible. For she colludes with the Jestarian. One that defiles the staff of our nation, and speaks profanely when holding it. This one should be laying in a nest of eggs, with already hatched children clawing at her sides for attention. She does not, insisting on mobility during this season.

This hussy who lays with drink, more then her chosen, is not worthy of her position. So when she confesses to her witness, she is not trustworthy. This thing would have been better for a noble, and proven man. However, Selay forced herself upon us. So the claw must scratch of her, and her song shall be sung, if only to stir up those who can bring true justice.

For the first thing Selay could feel stirring when she was on the roof of the theater was her stomach. If it was from movement, or the exceptional hard drink she had, or the site of these supposedly betters eating their lessors, she never really know. She just let herself vomit, and it felt necessary, and purifying.

The town alarm bells, and the shouts of guards calling to arms, echoed across the district. They rang from far away, showing that the entire city was now rising. Off in the distance, Brudge's old apartments were a towering pillar of smoke that showed the fire was contained.

A terrible panic set in, and she knew the time to leave town has arrived. She gazed along the horizon, a near endless sprawl of stacked structures, and great wide river rampaging between. She saw, and plot a course where to go.

Her best route would be east toward Brudge at Deep Lake. Not but a seven days away. However, she must delay briefly, and go northwest to the bank to acquire her father's book. She knew it was not safe in any vault here.

So she dove off the taller theater roof, spreading her fit wings. Striking a solid glide, then banked towards the Kiri'grana manors that were one floor less.

"Halt!" a guard roared from below. "Cease your flight!" confirmed to Selay that he was talking to her.

Of course she would not listen, as she is platescale. She has no rights in Jester, past being able to call upon Brudge's reputation. A reputation obviously going into disarray by conspiracy of the town's oligarchs, making it moot. Thus capture would lead her right into wings of her prosecutors, and to a timely death.

So she landed on the roof, then broke into a full charge. She figured three blocks away was the wall, and thus the gatehouse. At this time of day, the merchants would never tolerate a closing gate between the Beta, and Common Market districts. She should be able to get through there.

However, one block was best as she can go before a guard scaled from a balcony to the roof. A green man, somewhat agile, probably young, and swaying from morning drinking. Selay could only face him head on, since other directions would waist time.

She took the back end of the staff, and held it as a lance. It was longer then her entire body, and the right joust could cause him to stumble. She charged, and to avoid the pain of impact, the finscale guard skipped aside. This made him stumble, fall, and slide from the roof. He dislodged shingles along the ways, and fell into some crates below containing fruits.

His fellows arrived to check his status, four of them. One yellow, two reds, and a blue. He was alive. Left dizzy at Selay's boldness.

She was already down to one block before the gate. This should be an easy escape. She dove from the roof, and landed to the center of the main stone road.

A pair of red gatekeepers saw her, with the others closing from behind. Selay smirked arrogantly, and began a full speed charge at the gates. They both drew their blades, and took a step back.

She pushed the staff into the stone crevices of the road. It bent, but was sturdy enough to add to her following jump. The height was great enough to maintain a good glide over the guards. This feat she has accomplished once before, in Anya, by vaulting to the wall in desperation as she fled Yelvian, Delios, and their terrifying Wyverns. Great luck bestowed her, as no one rose a blade to slice as she dove over their heads.

She was within scent distance, and the two men's eyes

widened upon detection. They saw, and they both were entertained by the show only briefly. They had to recoil in horror at the stink of this woman, who smelled of some most foal carcass of some newly discovered fish.

When Selay landed safely on her feet, at the other end of the gatehouse. She was met with the market district's troop fast approaching. She ducked into the unguarded roadway to her right, then off into an alley.

A record of twelve town watchmen were chasing her now. They all met at the alleyway entrance to gather. At this point, there was no gain from tracking them by details.

"Each take a road, or roof. We will meet over the west end of the district. Shout if you see him!" The first one to take charge said.

"Her," said the gatekeeper who still was huffing.

The improvised leader examined his fellow, and saw his condition. "Riiight, and I would trust a theater district guard with that assessment?"

The other gatekeeper spoke out, "I saw her too, platescale woman. She stank."

"Alright, I give in. *Her* then. Smell her out! Watch that you do not break her eggs when subduing her. Last thing we want is to give Vex any reason to war with us."

The guards agreed, then split up. Selay had her hand on her maw while listening from in the darkness. She wanted to laugh some, but it would alert them to her. So she stepped back, and resumed her escape.

It is quite welcoming that they ignored the kill orders. So Selay decided at that moment, if she were to be stuck in a fight, she would opt to not use her blades. They are but the watchmen, the many underpaid loafs who had no skills other then brawling, and drinking. They try to be good. Many love their families, and work to care for them. Like the Anya watch, who at this time were helping to rebuild their town, they are better left alive.

It was remarkably simple to evade them, and Selay slipped from one building to another. Each guard walked slowly with sword drawn, and eyes alert, peering into every corner they could. However, finscale eyes are for the water, and they saw nothing.

Eventually she made it to her first way point, the local bank. 'Aurix's Hoard' was its name, and its owner a funny finscale man ironically by the name of Aurix.

Selay entered through an opened rear window on the second floor. One to an office that contains tedious receipts, and ledgers. It was very calm, compared to the commotion outside, and relieved some of her anxiety. The guards in the bank were not of the city watch, and only listened to the orders of Aurix.

She opened the door into a stone hallway. It was silent, lonely, and comfortable. The floors were carpeted, muffling Selay's footsteps. Some areas of the carpets had clear claw marks that tore through them, but elsewhere they were well-maintained, and clean.

The center of the bank was a two floor high lobby room, with ornate railings, and plated gold chandlers. The floor below became a perfectly crafted circular mosaic of the former Jester colonies, and trade route maps. Upon the mosaic was a motivational poem that read, "From the Coral to the Coast, greatness is at sea." The room surrounding it was more squared, and had doors to various segments, and offices.

Selay did not take the stairs, instead she watched from the balcony. Aurix was discussing dealings with a an aged finscale couple, who were clearly from the slums. She could not make out more then their expressions, some range of relief, and gratitude.

Eventually Aurix turned to note Selay shadowing over him. He ushered the couple to the door slowly. They nodded their heads, smiled maw-length, bathing him goodbyes, and left. Briefly the noise of the market soured the room's mood. It returned back to silence at the slam of the doors.

Aurix faced Selay, "How may I help you, misses Derin."

He was gray to white, not too uncommon of color among finscales. He was middle-aged, at the beginning of his fall from grace. A few of his scales were peeling along his arms, and his hands. His cloths were a simple merchant maroon with a blue hat, and gold trim. What stood out was his green eyes, gold adornments along his horns, and a few piercings on his head fins, signifying wealth. He also adorned his tail with a lone diamond bracelet, which he wiggled unnecessarily to make shimmer.

Selay hopped off the balcony, and flew down towards him. She landed in step, just past. The banker gave a bit of recoil at both smells trailing from her.

He assumed Selay was part of Brudge's harem, she would not correct him. It was under Brudge's privileges she hides, as it granted her a prestige that a platescale would not get normally.

"I am here for the book," Selay turned to face him.

"So soon? I expect payment then?" Aurix was greeted quickly with a lone gemstone from Selay's recently acquired bounty. He plucked it from her talon, and examined it. She noticed his tail thrashing more excited.

"Close your wings Aurix. This is not a dowry. 'Simply repaying my bar tabs." She chided.

"This is one expensive emerald! Where did someone like you acquire it?"

"I claimed the bounty of a wanted criminal. It was why I came to you to protect that book. So it did not get ruined in the fight." Selay smiled, enjoying her little narrative, "However, now I must leave town."

Aurix grimaced, and seemed satisfied at the answer. "Ua

is blessed to have someone with your virtue in Allya. One less criminal, and one more virtuous song to sing." his face turned to a viscous scowl, "Now if only they would find the person who burnt down my investment last night."

"I found him, Aurix. Justice was swift." Selay stated, "But I am afraid dark times are coming for Journey's Rest. You should hide for a few months."

Aurix tilted his head, "Whatever do you mean?"

"The town's Kiri'grana are engaged in a conspiracy to exile the Derin estates from the city. They will likely come for you. They will take your bank."

He puffed up, and growled, "Corruption? In MY hometown? This is intolerable! I must tell the courts!"

"What is even more intolerable is they burnt your investment. The court is working with them to revoke the licenses. Then seize the accounts which you hold."

Aurix snorted, then made his way to the vault, "Then that is you they are hunting?"

Selay smiled. He is a smart one. She decided to just reaffirm her position, "Leave town."

The vault was impressive. A large metal door with locks, and gears. It required a key to turn large iron latches. Followed by wheels in a sophisticated combination machination. Once opened, Aurix had to further access a gate door with its own three bolt lock. Selay figured that she could break it all with a single barrel of Skol ale, and a candle.

Inside were rows of smaller locked vaults. Then a room farther back with a pile of gold coins, and gems. His hoard room. Selay could make the faint depression of a body about his size there. He clearly sometimes slept on it. Who would not? The cool, and secure feeling of wealth was always better then a pillow.

He then opened a lock box, and withdrew two items. A

signet, and the wrapped book. The signet was just a simple onyx, and silver ring that had the name "Derin" engraved upon it.

He gave both to Selay while asking, "Here, Shall you join me in traveling? I will go to Port Selis."

Selay took the book, and slid her hand over it, she felt the embossed symbols in the likeness she made them. She was satisfied, then tucked the ring into the same pouch she had the 'Forged Blade' skull in, among other trinkets. She then tightly tied the book to the leather belts alongside her daggers.

"No. I am obvious to the watch. I must also go to Brudge, and expose this plan to him."

Aurix nodded, "Such a shame. I was hoping to gaze upon the reason Brudge decided to entrust a platescale with his ring."

Selay squinted, and sighed, spring was always like this, "Brudge maintains a fascination with various activities that make great discomfort under my tail sometimes. However, he is the lessor of confusing choices when it came to things in Jester."

"Are you two not to bear a clutch this spring? I do not see any indication of eggs in you." Aurix walked Selay to the door.

"Keep looking, you might find something I missed," Selay sauntered, and swayed her tail around as she turned to leave.

Let him look, and let his mind dream of things he will never have. She pulled the hood up on her travel robe, then adjusting it to fit around her horns. She then set the staff along her back, but with the blade below her tail rather then above her. Opening the door, the sound of the market invaded the bank once again, and Selay stepped into the busy marketplace, hidden from all.

The guards were clearly hunting the nearby area. Some on rooftops, and others along alleyways, and roads. There was about four immediately tracked by Selay. She saw another four along the roadway, as she weened through the market crowd.

Her robe was nothing too extravagant. It did a great task in so far it hid every plated scale, and likeness that made her easy to recognize. As for her staff, her wings masked it enough.

The market was far more crowded then the theater. The stalls were the same rickety, traveling merchant stalls hammered from scrap wood in Anya. The goods seen were of terrible quality, as if they were used, or assembled at home, or pawned by thieves. The stench of fish was everywhere, but finscales reek the same murkiness, it was hard to notice a difference.

While Selay saw the breads, and foods stalls, most attractive. It was occupied by a gruff looking guard. She bypassed him, and came to a trinket merchant.

The stall was adorned with ornaments, and figures. With various bone, and wood toys. One of a horse, another of a simple person. Some were so shoddy, they had no wings. There were children too, all squeaking excitedly at the idea of having one.

Selay took a position where she could monitor the nearby patrols. The four street guards, and the lone food stall guard met at the end. Then, eventually, a larger leader guard came, and barked orders. The noises of the crowd prevented her from understanding their words.

In time, all but the one split off. Two came towards her, and two left to the gates. She took this time to tuck her hands in her coat sleeves, and disguise herself as some lonely widow walking along the road. She moved, and paced into an alleyway where she was mostly alone.

This guard was in her path, the food stall guard, as

she designated him. She had to move him, and knock him down
if she was to go anywhere. So she devised a battle plan.

She could not climb to the rooftop, one guard was there
already, and that will be obvious. She also could not just
walk by, there was no others to blend with. Going the other
ways would make it harder to escape, and they are still
patrolling out there. Instead, she opted for diversions.

Stepping behind a stack of barrels, Selay yelled,
"Thief! Help! Guards!"

Like a moth to a candlelight, it worked perfectly. The
guard came to help. Selay crouched behind the barrels.

"Hail, lady, where are you?" The man said, sword in
hand.

Selay knocked on the barrels, and it drew him nearer.

"Hello?" He inquired.

After a second knock, the guard leaned over the barrels
to see. Selay quickly grabbed him by the chin frill. He
yelped when she jabbed his eye, and fell over when her
gauntlet crashed into the back of his head. He hung over the
barrels limply, now unconscious.

However, his sword made impact with the cobblestone on
the road. This alerted the guard upon the rooftop. Before
Selay was done with her move, he was already shouting, "I
found her! Over here! Quick!"

So Selay ran. She vaulted, and slide around the corner
out of the alley. Only to meet more town watchmen in front of
her. This did not sway her, and she simply charged through,
right between them, at her quickest speed. They were
surprised by the direct assault, and so they did not catch
her.

By now the gatehouse at the far end of the market was
near. Except it was now closing its doors, which was actually
a surprise to Selay. This gatehouse would take her out of the
city, and into the rural marshlands. She was denied escape at

the final moment.

So she ducked into the tavern just after the gate. Her entry struck fear into the crowd of finscales. They tried to make distance from her. This alerted the guards, and Six of them stormed the building.

She climbed up into the crawlspaces. Which could be accessed quickly by anyone with flight, and good claws. These spaces were mostly wood planks, and boards strewn across beams that provided extra storage as needed.

Jestarian ilk are not prone to fighting their officials when drunk. The hydras simply obeyed the commands. A habit which some in Skol could learn. So when they entered, the guards began to shake down everyone.

Selay hid between the crates of the crawlspace. She could see all of them, and monitored each one with ease. They patrolled the upper floor, and ignored her location entirely.

All but one eventually left, striking out on pathways Selay could have taken. One on the roof, one through the kitchen, one in the basement, and the rest on the main street. They were slowly making it back into the market.

The final one left, he decided to sit down at the bar, and shrug. This gave Selay enough space to perch along the oak beams of the tavern, and maneuver to an untenanted room. She hopped down, then opened the window, and after seeing not one guard outside, she slide down the wall to street level.

There was still the problem of the gate. While Selay has a rather hard head, she could not break through iron with it. As she learned in Anya. So she decided to do what she always did, and stow away.

Her choice of exit was one she would consider most divine: The Wine Cart. It was right off to the side of the inn, where the side door was open. Next to it the distributor was finishing his orders.

Upon boarding, no one noticed her hiding under the

straw cover. She saw the barrels were quite empty. This was rather disappointing, and she scowled at no one while sitting in her new roost.

"What is that awful stench? It smells like the worse end of a whale!" someone yelled, as the cart shook while its driver climbed to the seat.

"I do not know what that even smells like!" the wine merchant replied, "My nose is clogged from the dust in your inn anyway. I must be off now."

The cart creaked and moved, and left through the closed gate with no challenge. Selay slid off it at the far edge of town. Where she climbed a small row home. From there she got her bearings, then readjusted her staff. She turned towards the south, and slight eastward. Then dove from the roof, and beat her wings. She moved fast, towards Deep Lake. There she could get to safety, and there she could warn Brudge of the oncoming storms.

This horrible creature, foul and disguising. Why does she have to be privileged in the knowledge of what is to come? Why does she have to be the only one in position to extract justice? The Wyrm is stirring, and growling louder in rage.

Sorbilious

CHAPTER FIFTEEN

While there is much distraught, it fades. Then a great lull takes hold. It is then that the Wyrm can once again can see the guiding sway of the tails of Ua and Ain. So there it goes, and admires them for sparing us.

They must have some sense of humor towards their choices in this duet. A coward, and a traitor. Made to bare the weight of the world upon their wings so unwittingly. It both is amusing, and despairing. Things which are not supposed to be felt at the same time.

For the Journey is a better fate for those who are more sure in their flight. Virtues which give way to good deeds, proper judgment, and clarity. However, perhaps, Ua and Ain see some virtues now as hindering.

Hindering in ways that restrict swiftness. Anyone without knowing would spare a ruler of wrath, and obey corrupt orders. However, one who knows what imbalance they wrought in darkness would seek quickly to exterminate them, and level things again.

In Tram, such a balance can only be measured in blood at this point. With two massacres, and no criminal to hang for all to see, the city fades to a quiet depression.

Disbanded is the normal order of government, and all except a few essential places are to remain closed down during this time. The Lumbering mills would count among this, but they never are producing to begin with.

There has never been a bull decree to shut down an entire city during peace. Then again, there has never been such long peace. Gintrix ordered this stillness, at the pleasure of the Grateful Tasking. He wanted Tram to mourn, rest, and reflect.

For it is a reminder that nothing matters except Ua and Ain. The order knights are assigned to judge those who challenge this mandate. Fail their judgments, and there is not only punishment here, but a sentence to the idle.

In the night before, a rowdy festival was encouraged by Yelvian. Who, in his tendency towards great revelry, decided to address the cotangent of misery in Tram. The festival was deprived of most women, who were to remain in their homes where clutch will not break. Yelvian was promptly frustrated. For he sure enjoyed the softer-scaled. So he decreed that they should have smaller gatherings in their homes, and light candles to show when they needed attention.

There is no adjusting quickly to the sudden slaughters in the county. So this revelry gives one a chance to forget, and thus all of Tram did for a time. The ale storehouse was opened wide, and so began the making of legends.

One legend, and man, of just twenty seasons, is named Sorbilius Xiiva. He found himself that morning in a dungeon cell. The sound of Yelvian shouting out in the plaza woke him.

"Why are you just standing there gawping! Oh you never seen a holy knight before now?" He roared at full broadside in his Skol valley elite accent.

Sorbilius sat up swiftly, startled. He looked around for a source, but all he saw is his cell. Stone, musky, and notably dull. He was not chained, nor stripped naked, and the door was open. Indicating he was once again taken into custody to sleep off whatever happened. To which a wild pain in his head told him he would recall later.

He gazed outside the barred window slit. There was Yelvian, standing like a tiny giant on the lower castle plaza. His blue scales, contrasting the white stone, made him obvious.

The knight assembled the worst looking group of townsmen. They all had a visage as if they had no sleep, and lost a fight with a boar. Which both may be true for some of them, as Sorbilius recalled a squealing pig in the dark hours of the night.

"Now, to get things started. Today we are going to to patrol the square, and around the walls!" Yelvian paced around the front of this group. "FORM UP!"

They assembled into some kind of square formation. It took quite some moments, but they settled on something looking like order. If their positions were as a cloth, it would be quite tattered. Never forget that these are flightless folk.

"Now, unless you have anything better to do..." Yelvian continued.

Someone sneezed, and it was as if it was heard across the world. Yelvian tilted his head at the perpetrator, then turned to the others. "Anyone have anything better to do then to be marching with a Holy Knight?"

The sneezer raised a talon, and while Yelvian was facing away he somehow saw, and spun, "Yes?"

"Zaja, sir."

"And what is it you have that is better to do, Zaja!?" Yelvian appeared to slide directly towards him.

"My wife is sick, and she needs my attentiveness." He said, backing down, and opening his wings in submission.

"REALLY NOW!?" Yelvian roared, his eyes opened wide.

"Yes, sir."

Yelvian puffed up, and snorted, "Right then, off ya go!"

"Sir?"

"You heard me, take care of your house."

Zaja ducked away, mostly sprinting home as if he was running from captivity. He almost flew, but then was heard coughing.

"Now does anyone else have a problem with my campaign of marching up, and down this square!?" Yelvian said, returning to his pacing.

No one seemed to dare protest. Each glancing at the other with insecure expressions on their faces.

Yelvian paced only three times back, and forth before scolding, "So no one would rather be off at the tavern then this job?"

There was a murmuring in the crowd, as everyone appeared to want to express something. The word 'tavern' caused frills, and fins to perk.

"Alright then! Off you go!" Yelvian ordered.

Everyone gave him a look of surprise. Then began to scatter towards the various beer halls the town hosted. Yelvian was left alone in the plaza.

He curled his lip, and snorted, "Well, I cannot march without cohorts to protect me. I must be getting them back then."

So off he went, towards the nearest tavern. A Holy Knight, to procure his men, and much more beer. The way of Yelvian the Brave, singer of songs, and master of the state bar tab.

It was amusing, if not making Sorbilius envious of them. He began to lick his mouth, and try to free it of the cotton he felt was stuffed within it. Sadly, this is to no avail. So he sat back on the bed, and decided to proper himself up for the morning.

He wiped his face, pulling his eyes open more. He then checked scaled crevices for dirt, or lint, that would be obvious. He lingered in bed to plan. Though it took much effort, due to the mounting headache.

His design was to get home, and let his boss at the lumber mill know that he was in fair condition. Then maybe resume courting a lady he faintly remembers encountering last night. Perhaps a fine glass ornament that looks like a gemstone would convince her of his desires? He could not afford real gems, so a knock off from the glass blower would have to do.

As he finally acquired the sturdiness to rise to his feet, Sorbilius groaned. He took few steps to the door. There was one guard watching him by a desk, and the whole floor was sealed off. He was here before, and knew this guard, who drank at night with him sometimes.

Eventually, a large distant slam of a metal gate echoed across the dungeon, catching his attention. The guard looked away.

"All to your cells, Gintrix approaches!" someone ordered.

The guard pointed him back to his cell, and Sorbilius complied. Setting back upon the bed, he slumped over, and sighed. His mind wondering to the lilac lady he fancied.

Clamps of boots could be heard from the hall, and two were casually talking.

"This dungeon smells too pretty. Who cleaned the blood?" One voice boomed.

Another responded, "The duke ordered the entire floor soaked with waters, and lilac. The blood was not the worst, it was the entrails that made things unbearable."

The guard watching the room could be seen. He stood

shocked, then to attention, tall in his composure as a loyal soldier would. His reaction made much amusement for Sorbilius, as he was clearly hiding a drunken sway, so he decided to keep watching.

A large man with white scales arrived in view. He was decorated in a silver-steel plate mail suit, with a long set of capes. Catching up beside him was someone just as tall, but not wearing more then a light leather cuirass. His arm was wrapped in bandages.

Clearly the one in silver steel was Gintrix. The other, Sorbilius could not know, but he saw this one once herding a gaggle of children around.

"Guardsman, where is the report from the riot?" boomed Gintrix.

"It is in the office, sir." The guard answered.

"Will you retrieve it? I will watch while you do," Gintrix requested.

The guard nodded, and went away. Sorbilius remembered that nightmarish evening. First the militia locked down the city in search of a criminal. Then the next day were rows of bodies, mostly naked. They were carted out, wrapped in cloth. Some watched while weeping. Seeing their kin one last time, butchered mercilessly. Sorbilius counted himself fortunate. Not only is his family rural, but he spent that night asleep in the sawmill, where it was safe.

"While he is away, Lieutenant Istina, which cell was she in?" Gintrix inquired.

Ehtah came into view, and gestured at a closed cell door, "In that one there."

Sorbilius tilted his head at the utterance of the word *her*. It was odd for a lady in spring to be in a musty prison. Further, he was only aware of his scent here, which meant he was alone.

The dungeon keys were on the desk, and Ehtah took them

up. He came back to the door. Then hunched over to unlock it. Then stood aside.

Gintrix pulled the heavy thing open, and then entered the cell. He sniffed a few times. It was empty, and cleaned. This made his tail thrash in agitation.

"Raviwr, what nonsense are you engaging in here?" Gintrix growled into the sky, "I need a scent to follow. You ordered her cell cleaned too?"

"My master is nothing but loyal, sir!" Ehtah flinched as Gintrix turned, and glared over him, "I told you she was in Hilltop. She was right in my claws when I was injured. I deserve no mercy."

"Who were those who attacked you? You claim children?" Gintrix loomed some to intimidate the lower ranked warrior, "Who else was there?"

"Some man, he looked big, and soot-scaled," Ehtah opened his wings.

"Then he must be found, describe him," Gintrix said.

"I have no good site of him. Other then he was dark, and strong looking."

Gintrix balled his claws, and curled his lip some in frustration. No one knew the great Gintrix to be ill-tempered, or prone to disappointment. This must be a serious issue for him to express distress. Sadly for Sorbilius, the rider controlled himself. Such sorrow, for a fight would have made his day. Even worse, the other guard returned.

"Sir Gintrix!" yelled a new voice from the far side of the prison.

Gintrix turned, and smiled, "Well, good things for once? You are fortunate, Lieutenant, I was to throw you into the cell, and have you beg for mercy."

Two men arrived, not just one. One was the old guard who left for the office. The next was red, who clearly was of higher rank by the polish of his armor. He was holding a small stack of papers, tied together with string.

"Sir, the report," said the lower ranked guard, "But my commander is wanting a word."

The red held up the papers, and Gintrix took them. "Speak. Be warned, I do not have the time to make your tail sway from idle banter."

"Yes, sir. The reports are incomplete notes," He began, "Our investigation is ongoing. I am supervising it. I can give you a brief, so my summaries make some sense."

Gintrix nodded, and smiled, "Go ahead. I could use a good chronology of this mess. I cannot get scents, since that was washed away so hastily."

The guard explained through his perspective. He held down the tavern after rumors of a felon who burnt Anya was in town. He promptly discovered, and arrested someone who was associated. Then jailbreak happened. He did not find his body in the dead. He also omitted the fact he raided the stores around the tavern.

"That is the soot-scale?" Ehtah confirmed.

"What are his features?" Gintrix asked.

"Charcoal, white belly, solid plates, with big wings, and strong arms. His nose was bit of a stump, and his eyes were green, but lacking any life. I think his tail was also upset near the spiked tip, but I do not let my eyes stray to such places. My chosen would cut them out if I did."

"She would be right to do so," Gintrix scolded, "What else?"

"One else. We caught him, and interrogated him. Poor fellow fled, and came to us when he took a sword to his wing webbing."

"And..."

"He explained the scoundrels who did this. They are children."

Ehtah seemed to puff in relief. Gintrix glared back at

him, and growled. The rider then scoffed, obviously not believing Ehtah's story until now. Some of his agitation was dispelled.

The captain continued, "They stormed this room, killed every guard they could. Then released all the prisoners, and their leader proclaimed himself King of Skol..."

Gintrix moved his head around. Then laughed loud at the idea of such a pretense. He urged the red to continue.

"Then he pitted the prisoners against each other, forming an army. They took two prisoners out of one cell."

"Let me guess, this one." Gintrix pointed to the cell that he earlier inspected.

"Rightly, that one. Who was in there?" Asked the captain.

"The reason I am here," Gintrix snarled, and turned to Ehtah. "What manor of nonsense went through your mind to place her in a prison in the first place?"

"Sir, this was the only location I could think that no one would succumb to her fire." Ehtah squeaked.

"You doing so allowed her to be kidnapped. This lead to unnecessary bloodshed. I am taking this task from you, and placing you under probation. Now take me to the place you fought, then be imprisoned for the rest of spring." Gintrix finalized. "She should have been given to a church of Ua."

The rider gave a soft purr, and seemed pleased to levy judgment. He was quick to return to a strained posture, slumping his back some. Ehtah was not just some lowly watchman, but has the high expectations of the Order upon his wings. His failure is all of the Order's burden.

"This man is with her. He looks funny enough to catch. Place a bounty on his head," Gintrix proclaimed, "Make sure you mention his stumpy nose."

The large man lumbered to the nearest window, and roared, "YELVIAN! IT IS TIME TO FLY!" just before he stormed to the exit.

A short moment later, a rather loud howl echoed. Multiple distant howls responded. Wyverns seemed to scream from the mountains, not just the two chewing on a horse in the garden.

Ehtah sat on the floor, tending to his wound, which reopened slightly. The lower guard grabbed him by his arm, and took him to his feet. Then he chained him, and lead him away. Sorbilius could have sworn that Ehtah was weeping.

"Chains for the coward. After this you shall be in that cell so you do not flee again," The captain stood proudly, "You are to be whipped for this."

"I am sorry I failed! Please let me redeem myself!" Ehtah cried as they became more distant.

A loud clang was all Sorbilius heard, and his drinking friend guard remained. Eventually, he dosed back to sleep. Later, his plan to buy a glass figure for a lovely lilac lady was executed, and a lady accepted his advance. Forever then, hopeful he was, that never again will he see the intrigue of the flightfull. His children require him to maintain proper ignorance, lest they go hungry.

Yelvian

CHAPTER SIXTEEN

The Wyrm must scrape more of this song. This seems to be a sand game played by the divine. It ebbs, and flows in ways so unusual. So confused, and ignorant does the Wyrm feel in its lowly state. It can only observe, and accepts what comes now.

This game began so well, and has become disgusting. Softer-scaled, ugly creatures, are now the standard of our era. They see what evil transpires, and Ua and Ain grasp them in anger when they do nothing. The gods begin to claw at their bodies to reform them into their pieces, and throw them back into the sand. This makes no sense, so it must be part of a larger scheme.

Today this campaign is upon the nest. A poison sets within, corrupting us all. Demons released from the Idle have induced violations of our duty to each other. Ua and Ain have refrained from simply burning the whole, instead choose a bitter tonic for us to swallow. They force us to Journey while we moan in sickness, and gag at their cure.

At long last Huron, and Tailya escaped their pursuers. Both aching from exhaustion, and hungry. Their scales dirty, cloths tattered, and spirits distressed by the ugly things they were part of.

It was far into the night, and Wyverns were roaring from mountains close enough to scare bats. They were swooping over the forest all day eating stray fowl. The great beasts of the sky were too close to risk travel in the dark, so Huron, and Tailya stopped to find a place to hide.

The pair found a grove, with a rock, and dead grass laid about. Where in the endless woodlands of Tram they were, they could not know. Another of its many hidden places. They were quite far, with no smells or signs of civilized things around.

Tailya, who lead Huron all this way, was the one who stopped them. Huron was too dismayed, and too possessed to govern himself. He did come to his sense when she stopped, and the first thing he felt was the cold air of the night. He fell onto his knees again, his tail, and wing reminding him of his mortality.

A wretched creature. Even with no conflict he was unable to be strong. He could not bear the pain of his wounds. Nor even think so much as try to examine them for bandaging. He should be struck down in mercy, or forced into slavery. Lacking self-governance to care for himself, Huron has already failed his trial.

Drifting to visions of home, Huron fled. There he felt a warm fire, smelled cooked fish, and felt the grip a lady who bit him while she slept. This retreat became so real that he placed his hand on his neck where she bit to check if he was bleeding.

Tailya was the one clearly more brave then her companion. She should abandon him, as she did not need his help, and could just run faster without him. However, she reigns between envy, and pity over him. Both feelings in defiance of practicality.

The red kept close, and knelt down. She placed her

hands on her knees right in his view. Then stiffened her back, and tilted her head to watch.

Huron stared empty as if she was not there, or as he was blind. He was, and Tailya's form was invisible to the flow of past events. Fading in, and out lucidly. When Tailya snorted in frustration, Huron startled.

The regal woman, even with beat up frills, and bruised scales, even with a face covered in dirt, was lovely. Any normal man would not stall to claim her. Even one chosen to another would risk wrath to add her to his domain. However, in his refusal, Huron is a fool. His masculinity should be in question. But does he have any left to doubt?

Tailya reached behind Huron's ear to stroke along the frill. She came closer, and gazed into Huron's empty eyes. Her breathing heavy. Her fire burned his nose, and his heart raced.

"Why do you give up so easily?" She asked.

Huron was in memories of Selay. He traveled to the day Selay tried to fix his tail, after she broke it. Selay was unable to make a simple bandage, and Huron showed her. She set the bone well enough to not hurt so bad. Although, she bit him rather hard upon the nape of his neck when she worked. Which hurt far worse then her treatment.

Further he traveled, to a memory of force feeding him a fish. She caught it in the most unorthodox way, by slapping it unconscious with her tail. She then overcooked it. It was terrible, and smelly. Huron had to fight to not eat it, and lost the fight when Selay pinned him down.

Then he thought of wrestling. When Selay would just wake him up at night, and begin to pounce on him. Huron was much stronger, but Selay would always somehow win. Clearly it was the many soft audible sounds, and purrs she made that subdued him.

Even quarrels were revisited. One such disagreement,

was them arguing over a night gown. Selay refused to wear anything when sleeping, and Huron wanted to cover her come colder nights. The argument was a battlefield, where they fought tooth, and claw. Eventually, she threw the gown into some mud, and buried it. Proclaiming her victory, the dispute ended. She firmly reminded Huron that his duty is to keep her warm with his wings.

Then this dream brought Huron to a time, and place, where Selay's own fire bothered. Their normal activities were upset when she proclaimed boldly, "We must have a lot of eggs!" Followed by a spring retreat. It was then, Selay vanished. Huron set out to find her immediately.

Tailya was tearing parts of her dress to make bandages. She wrapped one cloth as tight as she could around the wound on Huron's tail. She then pulled at it. Something stabbed forcefully into him, making him hiss out.

It was not the dart, that has been removed. Bits of string remained inside. Tailya removed the wrap, and began to dig her claws about. She pulled any debris she could find. Including a significantly long piece of rope. She then ripped a piece of one of her scales off her arm, and fashioned it into a makeshift needle. Using some of that rope, she was able to painfully stitch some of Huron's wound. Finally she bandaged it again.

Huron left once again into the past. However, this memory was not consistent, nor relative. It was strong, as it carried a memory of Oflin. It was pulling him to despair.

The Skol Navy transported the entire Quirksettle family in a large protected convoy. They were one of many other families on board. All participating in the war overseas. The journey was tedious, and dull. Many children were along the voyage.

There were five large ships in a transport convoy. With tall masts, and regal Kiri'grana crew. They traveled in a close formation so that crew members would fly cargo as needed around. They achieved this by using strong ropes to tie their hulls together.

Such tall masts, nets, and climbing opportunities made young ones crave adventure. The children, much to the protest of their parents, would quickly run off to climb the sails. Like bats, or a flock of birds, children could be seen gliding around, and heard squawking, and laughing.

Of course this was dangerous. But what a thrill! So it must be done. Children cannot fly fully, and their wings were smaller, less balanced to their body weight. They must glide from a high location with a running start. The lack of ability to ascend made for more risk, but no glide spots were ever so high for most.

Huron's family was demanding that he did not glide over to other ships. He, and Ofiln did not listen, of course. Mother Dask, who at the time was curled in a nest, very protective of her brood, had no power to reign them in. She would often use guilt to discipline. Making her children feel as if they were behaving as if she was wasting her time. This was an ineffective tactic, for mother's time was for the new eggs, not to the hatched.

Huron was the first to climb to a mast, and Oflin was the first to take a dive over to another ship. There they met a brown-scaled child, and a trio of red-scaled brothers who decided to make a game of it.

The game was one of gliding from ship to ship, and landing on a particular object. Which they would treat as a race. The six children would each time tackle one another when they reached the end of the course.

The first spot was simply the crow's nest, which the crew of each boat were none too pleased with. Especially the lookouts, who became perches. However, the children all would leap, and glide towards the next ship before capture.

The second was the mizzen's top. To which each child but the brown was quick to reach. The little brown child slipped, and bruised his knee while falling toward the deck. He later climbed back up, and rejoined.

On to the final perch to leap from. This was the bowsprits. Which were wet, and mobile. The leaps were all well-launched, and nearly flawless in their landings. With each taking their own position. Though the last one, only four landed. A child was missing. It was a red-scaled lad. When the adults found out, the entire convoy rose in a panic.

Both parents of the missing child recruited a hysterical search. With the mother even leaving her nest to find her lost one, and risking eggs. The other two red brothers were locked in the cabin for the rest of the journey. Huron, and Ofiln were never allowed out of mother's gaze. The child was never found, and a funeral song erupted later that night. The song was sung all through the night, and Huron remembered sleeping to it, in mother's pillow nest, weighed down by her tail.

He then felt a need to be near his mother, and enjoy the protection she enforced. He felt lost, and out of place. He wanted to go home, he wanted to be small again, so he could hide in smaller holes.

Tailya's efforts to repair Huron's tail ended. It was painful, and ugly. The wound needed cleaning, but the bleeding was stopped. Next Tailya examined the tear on Huron's wings.

"This will never heal right," She sighed, and surrendered eventually to her lack of resources. Cursing under her breath, and giving a soft wine.

Huron then felt Tailya wrap her arms around him from behind. This ended all of Huron's dreaming, and he began to swoon. However, when Tailya's head leaned on his back, Huron began to shake her off him, angered at this attempt.

He glared to his side, and bore his teeth in response, and she timidly crawled out from behind his wings. He grabbed her wrist, and pulled her front, which was a simple task. She gazed back into his eyes submissively. Breaking from his grasp, and opening her wings, she moved to lay on her back for him.

Huron sat to a higher posture, and lorded in his examination. She was all consuming, and bothersome. He wanted away. So he tried to distance himself by crawling back.

When Tailya struck a pose close to how she was chained in the prison cell in Tram. Huron remembered that night. He became disgusted at her.

"Do not touch me," he growled through his teeth.

"The night will be cold. You shall warm me?" Tailya half-questioned, half ordered.

"Did you not hear? I am married. You have no rightful claim on me," Huron replied. "There will be no more affections."

If there be one thing that Huron Quirksettle was not about to surrender on. It was his pact with Selay. Huron knew, and felt that Selay bore his clutch. Thus he must find her, and his children.

"She must have wings that glow gold, and make Ua envious. What is her name?" Tailya slapped her tail on the ground, snapping grass stalks.

"Her name is Selay. Her wings pale compared to her smoothed plates, and her deceptively soft belly," Huron winced, and stood up to began searching for a rock to hide behind, one with enough space to keep her away.

"What was she like?" Tailya asked, then curling her tail around her side so she could hold it.

"One of the most disagreeable women I ever have known." Huron sighed.

"Then why did you choose her?"

Huron growled, "Because it was required!"

"You were an arrangement?" Tailya picked at her tail, "That is unfair! You did not choose her naturally."

Huron shook his head, "Arrangement of three months prior to season is unfair only if both disagree with it. She fought everyone, and then me. There was nothing unnatural."

"Arranged marriages are so stupid. Desire should come first." Tailya snorted.

"Feeling desire is not the same thing as raising children. We did not just want to play, we wanted family." Huron snorted back.

Tailya gripped her tail a bit too hard, and winced when her claws poked under her plates. There was some awkward silence, which Huron enjoyed. It did not last long, and Tailya spoke up, "What will we do next?"

Huron did not think that far ahead, and thus had no good answer. Now that he was upset enough to be immune to Tailya's scent. First he did not want anything but sleep. He felt hung over, and hoped that when he woke up from this, he was far away from her.

"Come morning, I leave you to fend for yourself." Huron went to face away from Tailya, and try to lay down.

"NO!" Tailya cried, "I have eggs! I am Kiri'grana! You cannot just leave me in the forest!"

"I will, and I can. You are not Kiri'grana! Kiri'grana have all the wealth to buy themselves safety."

"I mended your wounds? Helped you escape? Do not I deserve more then this? Why are you being ungrateful now?" She crawled up to Huron, and brushed her hand on his shoulder.

Huron turned back, and glared up into her intensely, "I have no more desire to help you."

"You said you will help back at the manor!" Tailya pleaded, her eyes wide.

"By helping, I did not mean risk loosing my ability to fly! Or betray my chosen," Huron yelled, "Not to mention risk life!"

"But I will die if you leave me here!" Tailya's tears became noticeable.

"Then maybe you should have surrendered to the guards like a good girl!" Huron made a weak defensive swipe with a hand to make Tailya back down.

"The guards!? You have no idea who I am!?"

Huron sat up, lifted his chin, sputtering some in a mocking tone, "Tailya Mek'velor, ruler of the Kiri'grana. One so tempting that a whole army of demons, in the form of children, want hold her for ransom! One who thinks she is so much like the old king, that she demands me to serve. You may have his whiskers, his colors, his frills, his plates, but you do not have his authority!"

Tailya scurried back at the sudden change of Huron's tone. She held her belly, and curled her tail around. Sobbing pathetically, and becoming quiet.

Feeling satisfied, Huron lumbered off. He found a great sleeping spot at the opposite side of the clearing. He paused a moment.

The late Priestess mentioning his chosen in the Hillside taverns picking fights. Hillside is a layover town. Where travelers went between Freestride, and Tram. Huron arrested for describing Selay to a guard in Tram's town. If Selay was in Freestride too, that would explain his inability to find her in this area. Despite years of searching.

He traveled back into himself, and his long journey. A mostly calm, and circular route around Tram for some time. Huron came to no results. He thought Selay was abducted by bandits. Likely as ransom, or a nest mother. So he spent a year watching rumors of raids, and camps. He queried merchants for talk of highwaymen in taverns, and learned of a betting fight woman who fought dirty like Selay.

He would have gone farther, but the price of the whole quest forced him into debt. He spent almost a year working it off. The many, dead-end trails of this drunken hussy took at least another year to follow. Selay had to be her, and she might not be too lost to return to him. He had to know, he had to see her again. He must find her, and return her home.

Huron glanced behind to Tailya again. He watched her frail, and vulnerable form lay still. Her wings covered her, as a makeshift shelter. He suddenly felt sorry.

"Tailya, I am going to Freestride." He spoke solemnly, "If you come with. I will leave you at a tavern there. Where there may be work."

Tailya answered with a meek growl, or some kind of sputter. Her cries stalled after a sigh, and her wings loosened. She let her tail out of the curl, indicating she was less distraught, but falling asleep.

Huron himself knelt down. He cleared a small patch of rocks, and laid to curl up. After so much time running, he finally had a bit of calm. He began to mutter a prayer. Which he felt was long overdue.

"In the end, nothing matters. All grow, and die. All wither, suffer, and eventually fade. We shall all be forgotten, and our stories will not be told. However, after we die, we will be judged. And in the light of the gods, shall we become their wards."

"Ain, Ua, I do not know this game you play with me. I ask this test end with my chosen returned. Do not let our separation be until we are forgotten."

Lambana

CHAPTER SEVENTEEN

The Wyrm gazes upon this thing that should not be true, but here it is. How can you justify sating your hunger with the yolk of the unborn? Does not the egg break, and the shell tear open the body? Or do you lounge after, allowing time for bile to soften it?

This world is not what it should be. Kiri'grana fly, and should protect the nest. Sure they quarrel, and lust, but consumption of their own kind is not supposed to be. For care of the unhatched are the first undertakings of the Grateful Task.

What the idea of the good is to the Wryrm is clearly naive. The song sung by a ruffian rouge heretic shows this. The wyrm must no longer see simplicity as a child, and see the complexity of this as an adult. Then it can see that this hussy, still foul, and unkempt, is more then what first can be gleamed.

This hooligan, Selay, was perched upon a rock aside a small tributary of Drenching River. She was completely naked. Her wings open, and swaying from the breeze, serving as weights to balance her posture.

Focusing her gaze upon the ripples, and shadows in the

water, she squinted. Her tail held still, and body motionless. She was a stone, her natural color made her blend with sky, and rock alike.

She felt hungry, tired, and sore from travel. Upon the edge of just feinting, all that kept her moving was a spirit of restless torment. What she saw was unnatural, evil, and it haunted her.

When a small blue dragonfly buzzed between Selay's wings, then took rest upon the surface of the water, she kept her eyes upon it. It looked worthy of eating, but she refrained from catching it. Then a shadow formed in the water below. Selay bore her teeth in anticipation, and summoned all her focus. She watched this darkness slowly meander, grow larger, and clearer.

When it began to ripple the water along the surface, nearing the insect, Selay raised her arm slowly. When it changed to a quickened movement, the platescale rushed forward upon the shadow with her claws extended.

The effort was enough for her to loose her balance, and fall from the her warm rock. She yelped, as she splashed into the cool water. However, she sunk her talons into her catch enough to grip it. A small tint of blood, not bearing the markers of alcohol, was her indication. Along with the warmth of a body holding her digits tightly.

Quickly she regained her footing, and stood upon two underwater rocks that were where the prey was hiding. If there were onlookers, it would be quite a horrifying show. As there was not any modesty in her performance. Her wings were open, and glamour was radiant. It could be argued that she was proposing to this fish she caught. She was in a land of fish-men, and it was hard to tell the difference between the kinds of water creatures in the marsh. They had the same kind of scales, smell, and wiggly manner.

Selay smiled, and salivated. It is supper time, and she

just won a bass of about three years of age. Enough to feed her for the rest of her trip. She began to wade her way from the river to dry land.

Her catch was to have none to do with this, and would not to go down without a second reprieve. It was staring at her. Selay only caught a small twitch of its eye before it kicked its tail, and ripped itself from her talons.

Yelping, Selay slipped upon a moss covered rock in her efforts to reacquire it. This fish flung into the air like a bird. However, unlike a bird, and more like an Easterner, it slowed its flight with too much wiggling. That made its mass shift downward. This mistake gave Selay time to get back her footing, then beat her wings, and gain air.

The poor creature made supple contact with Selay's bosom, and was quickly hugged into a tender embrace. She was on an empty stomach, and so she beat her wings again for strong lift, and flung the fish off its planned catapult, and onto the mossy riverside.

There it flopped, and Selay swooped in to catch it. This time, she impaled its head with her foot claw. She waited for it to finish, and puffed up her chest as to tell the rest of the forest that this was hers. Though she held back a desire to yell. It was wise to not lure in anyone else.

If not clear now, Selay was not normal for a woman. She lived outside of the nest, and traveled with no family. Her behavior is counter to what Ua demands of her in caring, and teaching. She opts battle, rather then gentleness, and compassion.

Selay has no children, and wounded those around her for fun. Further, she was unsocial, and agitated for sport. She is in all ways an aberration, an anomaly. Never natural, nor correct.

This one was clearly molded from a cast of far

different shape then that of a regular, and proper lady. A crude, and disgusting cast. It must have been worn, and cracking, when it was filled with the thing that made her. Whatever that was, is hard to determine.

Quite oddly, Selay's talent for fighting river bass was trained by a soldier. One who served in a regiment formally. A group of legendary status, and infamy, named First Blade, or Lambada's Flight.

Her catching skills were further honed by the many times she ran into the wilderness to hide. During outbursts of fear, and irrational childhood passion, she would spend a few days camping alone. There she ate insects, and slept in tree branches.

However, she also would camp with several soldiers. Who all bore battle scars, and injuries. Men who also taught her how to make fire. Which Selay made, with ease, as the sun began to set.

As the crickets chirped, she jabbed her catch with a stick, and made sure it cooked evenly. When satisfied with her design, she admired the effects. She was still naked, for the cotton lining of her cuirass would not dry until morning.

The fire was kept small enough to cook. Too large, and the finscales may track it. That would mean a fight. Selay used a branch to prod the wood around to maintain, and make it last.

She then lazed against the warm rock ring around it, as the night began to cool. Further distraction entered her view in the form of a moth. It was a big one, and Selay entertained herself by watching it flutter, and rest upon a rock in front of the flame, right by her arm.

It reminded her of a similar moment where she was too young to walk on two legs, but tough enough to climb off the shoulders of her guardians. A point not too unlike from this one. With a much larger, and brighter campfire. Surrounding it, five older men in a circle.

Selay herself was like any child that age, fat, hungry, and curious. She always was eager to descend from her caretaker's arm to explore. His name was Jex, and he was laughing at a sword fight reenactment of his friend Hanos, so he did not notice her climbing down.

She caught site of a hairy white moth, and had this rather strong desire to find out how it tasted. She padded her way towards, as it rested on a stone. Her white belly scales brushed upon the ground, and picked up grass stains. She was single-minded, and driven.

Raising her head behind her prey, she licked her lips, and leaned back. Then closed her eyes. Finally lunging her head forward, and clamping her mouth on the thing.

She expected a juicy treat, but there was nothing. When she looked, she was sent into disarray. Her moth was growing distant, and she felt a hand around her chest. She let out a cry, and reached towards it with her smaller forearms, to no avail.

The bantering stopped, and all five men watched her protests. Initially their faces showed concern, but they all began chucking when Jex scolded, "We do not eat uncooked things, Selay."

Smirking, she never cared for that advice in her adulthood. Everyone she met was worthy of her offense. Raw food, unkempt fruit, and stale bread she would consume to the disgust of those in her presence. The feeling of rebellion gave her small joys.

Selay rotated the fish. The thought of Jex brought back a memory of her childhood home raided by Imperial Hawks, and Jex fighting them off. He was dying as he told Mungel to take her to safety. She remembered screaming, and crying out, as he was brutally stabbed in the back by some plated red brute.

Jex was like a father, he worked hard at the Tram

sawmill. He had no family of his own, and lived far into the woods of Tram. However, Mungel was worse, a creature of much more mass then Jex, and missing wings.

She learned how to walk upright in his company, and he quickly learned that she could never be kept in place for long. The final straw was when Selay demanded him to teach her how to climb fast. She won by scowling, and giving him a swift kick on his tail.

Agility became natural to this creature, and she rivaled the running speed of Raloth. This made her given at evading as well. Which appears far too much like dumb luck. However, any onlooker with skill knew it was not.

One day, the military descended once again on her home. With a mace, Mungel was able to fend them off, but took severe enough wounds to die before he could heal. The guards died first though, and Selay was placed in the care of Hanos. With Mungel's death, she felt need for vengeance. She wanted to prepare for it.

Hanos was not like the others, he was skinny, sly, and deceptive. He also had no apparent war wounds. He played riddles, and games. He loved puzzles, and worked at night. In particular, he was a member of a local band of robbers in Freestride. A life he was forced to undertake after the death of Jex, as they both worked at the sawmill under aliases.

Selay mimicked him, and learned how to stalk. She never became good at it, but her cunning was able to win the admiration of her caretaker. So much so, he taught her how to throw, and use a dagger. This Selay enjoyed.

However, one day, Selay was placed under the care of Windus, an older man with a lost tail. Hanos was never to be seen again. He last said to her, "There is work I must do," and left.

It was under Windus, who worked as a miller, that Selay first played with a sword. Daggers are fun. However, a short sword was another thrill itself. Windus taught her how to steady her aim, and control her opponents.

She spent entire days yelling at her training dummy, unable to wield effectively. Her effeminate arms were not for strength, or power. Her body however, was for momentum. With her full weight into her motion, she yelled no more.

Eventually, the mill Windus worked for collapsed, and he died. In his memoir he gave Selay a gauntlet of an old Skol Warlord. This gauntlet later Selay refit, and bore as a standard. It belonged to her father, and inside was his name, "Lambada Kitsuna of Tram."

Windus left Selay to Argile, a town watchman. Who was much more whole then her former sitters. He was much older, and it showed. His scales were protruding, posture was poor, and his tail would drag along the floor.

However, Argile would do one thing to Selay that she only understood much later. Where other girls obsess over which of the boys in their circle they were to marry, Selay, now in her teenage years, would be required by him to learn how to fend for herself.

He did not teach her how to fight fair. In fact, he taught her how to claim victory by seeing through her opponent, using the environment, and doing things least expected. They spent plenty of their time swinging swords. Even in his ill health, Argile was able. Eventually those swords were replaced quickly by common objects around them.

Even when Selay's feminine attitudes were becoming more apparent, and her body shape was reflecting it. He did not relent. He demanded her to learn how to protect herself. His reason was always, "You must fight for what you want."

A vague, and lousy reason. He would get under Selay's hide daily. He would deny her food until she would be able to get by him. She was made to fight off the other children who would tease her. One could say, he was the grindstone, and the others were the forge.

All of the other lessons Selay learned were combined into his teachings. However, one lesson shown above all: the taunt. Through this, no other child dared to approach, for her words became weapons to wound all.

This ended when Argile appeared to catch a bad form of sickness. He went to bed one night with a heavy wheezing on his chest. In bed, he emitted a frightening roar. A yell so shattering that it would wake the gods. It was his final breath, one he made sure to announce.

Selay spent the rest of her childhood in an orphanage. From there, a desperate experience. She was taught mother, and teach. To read, and write. To count, and measure.

She would regularly fight off other children. Many times fled to hide, and weep. She became passive, told to expect to be married. The caretakers considered her a valued investment. One to be sold off to a rich family to be a wife.

At the time, she wanted this. To be a mother, and fulfill Ua's task. An easier life for sure. She was married to the House of Quirksettle, a blacksmith house, to Huron. *Her chosen.*

The forces that made her were abnormal themselves. Each distinct, and unqualified. In her, they saw something special. Something they regarded as a sacred obligation to mold. Jex, Mungel, Hanos, Windus, and Argile. Men all bearing the broken scales, and wounds of a past Journey. Each one like brothers, and a father.

First Blade, they were hunted for betrayal during the war. These men, served in a battle against their own Warlord. They told us that blood spilled upon the battlefield by Vex was forever spoiled. They showed us we committed the sin of denying clutches hatching. They helped to stop the world.

Selay's fish was done. She would be saddened at her thoughts, but she was happy to get food. She decided to lay down farther back to eat it. Sprawled upon her back in the light of the night. She felt her tail bump into the leather covered book she carried.

Her fish was bland, but she would eat anything right now. That moth she would have caught, and ate too if she did not loose herself in thought.

Her tail diligently kept against the book, as if contact with it was comforting to her. She knew it, what it was, who wrote it. She also knew how little there was of her real father left. Her armor, the book, and her.

Her father wrote a journal of Selay's nesting. Her mother died shortly after laying the clutch, during a journey across the sea. Lambada nearly killed the ship's doctor for almost discarding the eggs, assuming wrongly that they were dead. He clawed the scales of the man off, seemingly possessed by demons. He waged a battle that ended with him, curling his own masculine form in the small nest he made for them.

As all know, men are too bulky to lay on eggs, the weight will smother the nest, and prevent growth. However, Selay's egg was oddly resilient, or her father was quite gentle.

After a while, the eggs were transported by her father to a manor home. He walked through Freestride with bare body so the eggs kept in contact with him, and his scent. This story was further confirmed by Selay not too long ago when Talsworth's Keg's owner, Barrios, showed her a painting of the thing. One he hid in the basement of his establishment. An artist was so moved, he painted what he saw. A giant naked man in Freestride carrying eggs in a cloth, with soldiers all around with the faces of Jex, Hanos, Mungel, Windus, Argile, and many others. It was the story of much laughter, and strange reverence of a father willing to protect his nest.

This clutch was hatched. Lambada curled around as he

wrote some notes to pass the time. No eggs but Selay's were cracked as far as she knows, her father's writings reflecting a clear change in tone to joy. Selay would be reading it, if not for her hunger.

The story of Lambada's brood was amusing. First out of the egg, and off running, she was scooped up by him before darting to freedom outside the nesting chamber. During so, she distinctly made a protest cry in his arm. Lambada remarked in the book that, despite the lack of teeth, the following bite was enough to make writing his manuscript a painful undertaking. Though he had to carry on, because he had to finish this thing before he was called back to war.

He was called to war shortly. Selay was barely able to remember his leaving. She was placed under the protection of a nanny.

Lambada never returned, and the army would see to it he was branded a traitor. It was nearly a year from his death that Jex, and his company, came to the manor to take Selay.

Her fish was now consumed. Selay belched, laying back, and watching the embers rise in her fire. Memories felt like many swords stabbing her. Making her decide to stop recalling them. She thought about her plight.

They were trying to destroy Brudge. This is not in Selay's better interest. She would have a hard time milking another noble out of his wealth so easily. He paid well, and he gave her free drinks in his efforts to sway her to do what he wants. His estates were Selay's safehomes, where she could sleep soundly, and hide treasures.

She then thought of those that ate eggs back in the theater. The image of someone attempting to swallow whole the life of a child was disturbing, and Selay felt her heart racing from it. If she was in any more danger, she would evacuate her belly for the flight to escape. She was not, so she laid still.

A strange thing, as Ua and Ain give us our ways, and laws. For Selay, no thought of the gods moved her. She only could think that what if someone did this to her eggs? Although, there were none to have, the thought was enough to make her realize that these abominations must be destroyed.

How many are there? She only knew of two, and to kill them would not have helped. If she ripped those eggs out of the stomachs herself, their names would still be celebrated. These egg-eaters were, in fact, Kiri'grana. They commanded the guard, and the lessor people. So Selay could not rely on established authority. This would mean this ordeal begins as business for rouges.

She could tell Brudge? Yes, that was a good idea. She must reach Brudge before they seize upon him. If she can tell him, he could spread the word about it. Brudge is influential, with a number of allies. They could be used to stop this.

What if he was one of them? Selay closed her eyes at the thought. If he was, then why were they betraying him? Maybe he is not, but if she was to find him swallowing the eggs of one of his concubines, live, or not, Selay would have to kill him. She could not dare relate to anyone who did such a terrible thing.

Then all the distress abated. The thought of killing someone so foul was strangely calming. Even the roaring flame of her season was unable to shake this calm. After basking in this new haze, she opened her eyes, and gazed into nothing. When perfectly still, one thought rang.

They all must die.

Selay then recounted her past kills. Such when killing Zyrko in Anya. She knew the rider was not doing anything but duty. They were fighting, and it was to the death. She did not like snapping his wing, and held some sorrow for him. There would have been no way to sustain any more combat if they landed. Zyrko was too enduring to stop, and she was becoming tired.

Later that day, when she sieged Anya, she refrained from killing others as much as she could. The dumb town watch are there because they cared in some small way. They were just protecting their homes.

Those children who tried to kill her in Journey's rest a few days ago also were regrettable. They were intending her death, and raised unwell. They had to die, otherwise they would have killed her.

Their leader, Gawundon, a terrible mother. She associated with these "Egg Eaters." She should be eliminated. What would happen if she saw her lover tied to a table, and shamed? There would be a need for revenge, which is going to lead to the two meeting.

When she returned to the Egg Eaters, or anyone aiding them, a mood took her. All she could do is focus on ending their lives.

"Why?" Selay growled to herself, unable to understand this specific calling.

Why? A reasoned answer was quick to form. *They are wrong. They must be destroyed.*

Was this answer Selay's own? Or a call from the God's to action? Selay did not think once that she did not own these thoughts. However, these are the things of the Grateful Task.

The task is set. Kill those who eat eggs. Selay found this idea comfortable enough to lull herself into a restful sleep. A dream of her own clutch, and a nightmare of defending it ensued.

One dream, one nightmare. One restful night for another week. One flippant, hussy, who dared grasp upon authority she does not deserve. In this moment, alone, and naked, Selay has offered to bear this on her wings. Her claws are to become the arbiters of the Grateful Task. A usurping of the divine ordering of the world happened here.

This vile creature, with her unkempt nature, and viscous manor, is to be Ua and Ain's vessel? A woman who dines with sea-serpents, and snakes? One who knows her place, but leaves it unattended? This wretched thing, so uncivilized?

Ados

CHAPTER EIGHTEEN

No longer can the Wyrm just be senseless. It must stir, and move. As the time to carry on this Journey is now. The Wyrm's spirit was broken in the wake of the song sung. However, this is but the first verse. Now comes the chorus.

Ua and Ain have gone ahead. No longer do their tails sway, and guide us in this path. Now there is a lack of course, and this means it must be plotted. The right way must be found. So, upon the song, we listen.

The chorus is surrounding the Wyrm. It scratches diligently upon the page, and hears all. The passed shows evidence of our destiny. Where we come from, shall tell us where we are going. Gazing back down the path we came, a duet of two is clearly heard.

To one, of Huron, who slowly walks to where he thinks is north. Happenstance brought him misfortune, which shows behind him in the form of Tailya. His sore neck, wing, and tail remind him of how he suffered.

Five long days passed since he met her. He wanted to retreat back east, to home, and his farm. There he could hide in a haystack, and weep like his days when he missed his mother. Something told him not to, it pushed him forward.

This thing was thoughts of his Chosen. He wondered where she has been, and how his children have grown. Would they ever know their father? When will they be able to sit upon his horns, and sing for him? It is paramount they are found. He is mindless in this, but could teach us all about what we should be.

Where five days sung is Huron's song. Selay's violent, and hostile melody is twenty from smuggling the staff out of the the Empire. Another week of thirteen days, Selay took refuge in Journey's Rest. Then forced to face down a form of evil that no one could see. For her, the month of Vicious, and the year came to a close, and now the new month of Declara, twenty-two years from the start of the Era is upon us.

Her song sung as she recklessly stalked though forest eastward to Brudge's manor home of Deep Lake. He must not fall to this plot. She must tell him what she knows.

Ua and Ain must be guiding them, for they both seem not in control of themselves. However their destinations are determined, they are upon this Journey with us. They are both unwelcome. They are impure, impolite, and upset the Wyrm, and make these pages difficult to write.

Huron is unfit, he should not be allowed to guard Tailya with the mind of a child. His arms may be strong, his scales solid, but his spirit is weak.

Likewise, Selay is unworthy of her own life. She should be cut down, and made an example of. Her gutted body is best strung upon a pole in public to scare all who do the evil Selay does. Never should one go against the nature the gods made them as Selay has.

The duet sings loudest. However, at some place, aside of them, lower, is the songs of others. Do they sing to uplift Huron, and Selay? Do they too sing the song of the Era?

Via'torre's cart creaked in a symphony of groans of pain on its journey back to Tram this evening. Pomonik would perch on boxes in back, and watch things around. Sometimes, he would catch, and eat a traveling insect. Other times he would open his wings, and cool off.

The merchant was so familiar with the route that he kept record of every stone, and crack on the road through feeling alone. He kept his eyes closed most of the trip, and relaxed as best as he could. The oxen knew the way.

This all was interrupted by the soft sighs of a child. Such sounds were abnormal in the dense woodlands, and Via'torre's daze was ended quickly to check on his apprentice. He was fine.

It was down the path. Via'torre gazed upon a pair of children. Both were dressed in black robes. One clearly a girl. One laid upon the ground unconscious.

Pomonik leaped from the cart, and ran towards the pair.

"What are you doing!? Get back here!" Via'torre barked.

The child ignored his better, and waved at the girl, "Hello! Do you need help?"

Via'torre stopped his cart, then climbed down. He reached into the back to retrieve his short blade. Then, making his way over, he firmed his hand on the sword's hilt. This was clearly trouble.

The girl's face was covered in tears as she looked at both of them, she trembled, "He has fell faint. Help me get him to a healer."

Pomonik nodded, and looked at Via'torre, "You must know a doctor, sir?"

Via'torre did, and the doctors in Tram were some of the worst he met. Once, he went to them for scale cream, and they charged twice the price of the Freestride doctors. They knew he was of wealth, so they ran up the price on him. The merchant sneered at the thought of going through that again.

He knelt down to the unconscious boy, and placed his hand by his maw.

Immediately he saw a large cut along his face, and much dried blood. His gums were becoming swollen.

"He is barely breathing..." Via'torre shook his head, "That wound, he will not make the journey."

The girl then began to beg, "Please! You ca not leave my Ematel to die on the road! I can work for you to pay him!"

Via'torre growled, "Who are you to beg me, a merchant of the Armour's Guild, for kindness?"

She pleaded, and bowed her head, "I am Zhaqua of Tram. I am agile, and able to divine information on things others may not. I can get you secrets."

Via'torre laughed, he held his sword at her nose. He could see her holding back a desire to lunge at him, nearly loosing her composure. This girl was a scoundrel.

"I have informants. Tell me something I do not know then?" He asked.

"The Royal Staff is stolen..." Zhaqua began.

"Hah! Everyone knows that!"

"But the thief is in Freestride, passed through Tram nearly three weeks ago. The town is under martial law over it. There has been a riot. They will not let you in, but I know a route." Zhaqua smirked.

"Does this explain the drought of patrols between here, and Hilltop?" Via'torre asked.

"Indeed. The guards were recalled. Will you take us back to town now? You owe me for the information, and Ematel's debt is for getting into town." The little girl was able to bargain a merchant well.

Via'torre should have known better, "I agree, but you two stay in the back. You also are my servants now."

Zhaqua rubbed the neck of Ematel, who began to emit a rumble. Then her, and Pomonik carried Ematel into the back of the wagon. She placed his head on her lap, and made motherly coos, and chirps.

If Ematel could walk, Via'torre would have died there. Things are now different. The song has changed.

Up far north, by Journey's Rest, and around the same night Selay decided her fate. Pab Yan took stock of her den. Singing somewhat as she sorted her inheritance out.

She now had to deal with Tyran, who stayed over the past three days. He was providing comfort to the family, or trying to seduce someone. It was likely more of the former. Since Serios died, an awful melancholy overtook everyone. The quarrels ceased, and it was too calm, and that was not normal for a finscale home.

Pab was placing objects into wooden boxes. She was packing up things. With no one employed, the family would be left poor. She was to sell the house, and objects, and see off everyone to new homes while she found someone else to marry.

Swords, pieces of clothing, armor, and a wooden figure of a man with wings outstretched were examined. The figure was crude, and hand-carved. When Pab was about to place it in storage, Ados plucked it from her, swooping out of nowhere.

"I made that for him. Before he met you!" she scowled.

"He told me, Ados. You were hoping to court him that spring," Pab returned a predatory glare back, expecting a fight, "He said you lied too much for him to choose you."

Ados stroked the figure, and swayed her tail, and hips. She also reeked of her season, no longer hiding it. This agitated Pab.

Pab went to grab the figure, but as soon as she came close, Ados bore her teeth to her fullest, and flexed her gills. The chubby finscale let out a threatening snarl, and clutched the figure to her chest like it was her child. Pab retreated, and watched Ados saunter away, emitting a deep bellow of sorrow.

The little red continued clearing items from the shelf. Herself maintaining a regular state of distress. When she pulled a candle stand off to move it, something caught her attention.

The shelf itself was dumb, with a large wood frame under it. Pab never paid it heed, but today she saw a pin of sorts. This pin was out of place, and designed to look like the head of a nail.

Wiping her eyes free, she removed a sword from the crate. Using the blade, she lifted the nail out. A pressure along the whole top of the shelf was released. Pab lifted it, and saw a whole mess of parchments.

Examining was quite difficult. She could barely understand them. Serios wanted to send her to a scribe to further learn how to read, so she could teach the family they planned to start. However, it never came.

"Nair!" She yelled. "You need to come see this!"

A bunch of muffled shouting came from beyond the walls. It was clearly Nair, and Ados. Ados had a distinct panic in her voice. Pab could make out only the word, "highness." Indicating they were trading commentary.

Nair, and Tyran came into the room. Tyran was void of a shirt, and wearing string held trousers. Nair was in a gown, that was clearly not closed fully. The two were obviously sleeping, their fins, and frills were upset, and matted.

Pab snorted, "If you claim those two, I expect them to be gone the next day, Tyran."

Tyran sighed, "Not yet! We merely fell asleep together."

"Yes. I was reading to Tyran. He reminds me of Serios when he sat by me, and listened. We fell asleep." Nair nodded.

"Naked it seems. Nair does not agitate me with her

smell. You took her!" Pab scolded.

Tyran waved his hands in a panic, "No! No! We did not! Nair had a bath."

Pab did not believe it, and desired to not press the issue. She held up the papers to Nair, and sighed. "I can not understand these! Can you read them?"

Tightening the belt around her gown one extra time, and flexing her wings so it was not too tight around her neck, Nair looked, "What are these? Oh! That is Serios's sigil?"

"He could write!?" Pab was surprised.

"He could sign his name. I knew that much." Nair pulled the document from Pab's hand.

Tyran laughed, "He could write reports for the watch." the man walked to a chair, and sat down, "Did he not tell you?"

Both women were surprised. Then like the pariah she was, Ados sniffed as she entered the room again. Obviously wanting attention, her wings opened, and eyes focused on Tyran, "Serious used to go to the scribe to avoid us," said Ados.

Pab held up the paper, "Well read them! I cannot!"

Tyran took one, and Ados took another. They both began to read. Another document had a map of Journey's Rest, with numbers in various locations. Another had a key with names by the symbols.

"This map was an investigation he was on," Tyran sifted through some more papers in the shelf, and held up another, "This is the declaration page." He held it up.

"*Investigation of missing eggs from dead woman's body last spring. Victim was cut open with bare talons. A similar pattern of murders has occurred. Most women are unknown, flightless, who were either homeless rabble, or prostitutes.*"

Everyone sat down. Pab, and Tyran had their own chairs. The other two were on the floor.

Pab shook her head. "Serious did this?"

"No. That is the old bailiff's signature," Tyran shook his head, "This investigation is from last spring."

"Did he not die?" Nair tilted her head, propping herself on an arm.

"Yes. He died by drowning in the river."

"Drowning?" snorted Ados, "We are finscale, we do not drown!"

Nair roared back, "If he was from the north, he could have! They are not with gills!"

"But he was not! I used to see him in the taverns! His gills were always healthy." Ados growled back at her cousin.

"So that is why you are still here! A tavern is not a place to find a husband!" Nair mocked.

"Shut up! It was just that once with th..." Ados glared back.

"Oh yeah? Just that once? I heard it was everyone, and the bartender?" Nair suddenly found her cousin attacking her for mentioning it.

Pab was right next to Tyran when the others began to fight. She ceased to hear them, and listened to the man.

"He had gills," Tyan explained, "He was bloated in the legs, and his pupils were dilated. Signs of Poison."

"Then why did no one investigate it?" Pab asked.

"Serios was complaining about that himself to me one day. The Duke just denied any inquiry into it. Saying that 'it was a accident.'" Tyran continued to read the documents.

"*Death of Bailiff Rancliff investigation began in mid spring. Likely cause of death is Angel Wing which can cause passionate fits of madness.*" Tyran read out loud.

Ados, and Nair were already wrestling each other, and growling. They pulled each others frills, and wings. Both were unable to outmatch the other. Probably due to Nair's palm pushing at Ados face, which distorted her viscous complexion.

Pab sighed, and Tyran continued to read, "*Theater Guild is now the suspected supplier. Actors were using it before plays to practice. Guard Serious inspected the theater.*"

Again, Tyran changed to another page. He clearly was not reading fully. Nothing was in decent order. Pab just watched like a child.

"*...A clutch of eggs matching the color profile of the woman murdered was discovered at the Theater. Scent profile is unreported. Actors were handling the batch, discussion of some Great Feast, with much excitement over it. Eggs were used as props in a play. The attendees did not know this. Serios observed post there, and after a few days, the eggs were loaded onto a cart with a large batch of other clutches, and shipped out...*"

Tyran stopped reading, and placed the pages down. Nair, and Ados were swiping claws, and slapping each other with their tails.

With a loud splintering of wood, Tyran cracked his thick tail on the floorboard, "You two! Cut that out before you hurt yourselves irredeemably!"

Both stopped. Ados, being the most heavy, made a final pin on Nair. She yelped, and exposed her bally in surrender. The two stood up, brushed off, and watched attentively.

Pab injected, "Egg Poachers in the Theater?"

"I remember Serios spending a lot of time there last year. We thought he was skipping work. I did not know he was running his own inspection," Tyran rummaged as he spoke, "Is this why he was punished?"

Tyran trailed off, then stood up, and collected the papers all into the shelf box. He sighed. That night he adopted the trio of women under his protection, under the condition no one spoke of it. In secret, Tyran began where his friend left off.

Tyran's justification was one of duty, and sense. Pab, and Nair are too simple, and petty to understand fully. Ados is a large unknown factor. One thing is for sure, these papers were meant to be destroyed. They were scandalous. The Chancellor Quad family may be implicated in a murder. Tyran began building his own study to keep them safe.

There he clawed better summaries of the pages, and wove the record of the song of the Era. So that he may sing for his friend to Ain about this too.

It was the night immediately after both Yelvian, and Gintrix left that Ehtah decided to flee town. He was on house arrest while the prison was cleaned. He dressed in black, under the cover of darkness. Only to be seen by a watchmen on a tower, who thought him a widow.

Where Ematel's band was slaughtered, Yelvian broke through the shrubbery with a sword. He grabbed his nose as he recoiled back.

"Gintrix! I have found the smell!"

Gintrix pushed through, "This must be the Hilltop guard," he knelt to the body, and held a gloved hand over it, but made no contact. "Ain, your knights are here to tell of the hero Skazac."

Gintrix removed a charm of Ua and Ain he wore under his amour. He held it over the body of Skazac, and began to sing a song of mourning for the fallen warrior.

Yelvian was able to smell with great accuracy the point of entry for the two guardsmen. Then he followed to the tree truck. There the corpse of a child laid, its chest cut open, and the most frightened expression on its face.

"Gods, these are CHILDREN!" Yelvian began to wine.

Gintrix was done, and stood up. He took the opposite side of the grove, and began tracking other scents. His nose traced upon two unique smells of blood.

"Yelvian, how many do you think fought here?" He asked.

"Too many scents are mixed," Yelvian turned away from the body of the fallen rouge, "I count more then seven."

"One combatant was a woman," Gintrix said. "But there is another, a really musky man. A unique fire coming from this side. It smell lingers something familiar."

"What then? Where are the rest of the dead?" Yelvian stroked his hand over the spot where Huron once cowered.

Gintrix found the patch next where Tailya was. He leered over it.

Yelvian smiled, "There were nine combatants, two bodies. Ehtah fled back where he came. Two went west, others went north. One into the bushes."

"You sure?" said Gintrix.

"Absolutely. At least nine scents. I smell the urine of someone else on the tree there." Yelvian pointed in its direction. "It continues into the shrubs."

Gintrix waved his hand at the path, "I think we should split. You follow that way."

"What if they attack? You do not fight with weapons, you fight by wooing everyone's wives!" Yelvian teased, "If those two were combatants?"

"They are all scared. They would not fight." Gintrix pointed at a rope dart string tied to a tree, "Look there!"

"Oh! Hostages?" Yelvian said, "Agreed. I will follow the ones to the..." Yelvian looked above to trace his direction, "West."

Gintrix proceeded Northeasterly. He moved with a fervor of a knight saving his lady. No one shall stand in his way of starting the world anew.

Both Holy Knights were unaware of the Great Feast, and Egg-eaters. Neither suspected the larger schemes, the machinations at play. They continued to be outliers, and merely serving. Yelvian, less so, but Gintrix zealously.

To think that if either men know of Selay's position,

idling would cease, and hunt to kill her. If they knew her new course, they would join her. The distance between corruption, and faith is ever such a small gap.

A corruption exemplified by the weeding of a group of wilting tulips in Tram by Anon. He dug the roots, carefully, and judiciously. His face was covered in dirt. Purge the rot at the root, ignore the recent events.

Half the town away, in home, together in a room, Sorbilius, and his chosen. He stroked her chin tenderly, and pressed his head against hers. She sat there, with a long gown, open, and her belly protruding. Neither moved, singing softly about what they are about to bring into the world. A family.

Now the wyrm can understanding what song sings for us to continue. The direction more clearly understood. The nest is threatened.

Selay runs to fight, Huron flees from his fight. Hunters hunt, and plotters plot. All the while, the world continues in sorrow. A sorrow sung of us all. One of a world that stopped so long ago.

The Wyrm carries itself forward with no direct guidance from the gods. Now we see the next Grateful Task, and are Ungrateful as who joins us. The first test begins, our foes approach. In the end, nothing matters, but to serve Ua and Ain. Our world is their nest. So if Selay is to be chosen to do this, what business does this lowly Wyrm have to question it? Why this Wyrm is of the Order, and deems her unworthy.

Glonus

CHAPTER NINETEEN

Now with cause, let us Journey forward, as we can properly serve the Grateful Tasking. In each step is renewed spirit, and urgency towards necessary conflict. The enemy is coming. Be fearless, and open your wings to welcome them. The mandate calls for this new conflict en force. In this coming harm, the world will begin to slowly turn once again.

Spring is half-fold, and now Ua and Ain are settled. Rather united, and laying curled. The new season's life is here. Mother and father, now allied in their common paternal burdens.

We must guard the nest, walk forth, and defend our inbound kin. Conflict is inevitable, and necessary. As those who poach our nest are here.

About when Huron arrived, Freestride was warm, and humid in mid-spring. He enjoyed none of the bustle, nor the smell. Except perhaps one place gave him relief, the Kitchen of Gatehouse Inn. Just as humid, and warmer. It smelled of freshly cooked fish, and baked bread.

It was nearly ten days since he arrived, and things were becoming settled. His proprietor, Glonus, welcomed the extra help. He used the opportunity to brag about a Quirksettle smith working in his house. It drew only the local apprentices. For Glonus, it was beer sold, and Armour's guild coins were plentiful. It was disappointing somewhat for Huron, as he wanted more time to be calm.

It was a great misfortune for Huron that Tailya also choose to work here too. Made worse in that she stayed at the same workhouse as him. Which lead to insistently sharing bedding, and all her time with him.

This lingering kept Huron on guard. She demanded his attention for every little disturbance. Anything, Huron figured, to get him to look at her.

Huron could not even mask Tailya's fire with pots of stews. It was so pronounced that Glonus shouted for her to bath in lilac petals twice a day. In his own words, "Do not encourage the patrons."

It worked only initially, the clear stink of Tailya's spring condition went away. However, the sight of eggs in her belly will not go unnoticed. This drove would-be suitors to flirt with her. Commentary, shows of wings, and puffed up stories became commonplace in this tavern.

Huron figured it would be another month before those eggs would be passed. He yearned for this whole tormenting affair to be over. He fret that quickly another affair would begin. A non-stop bickering mess of a childless woman, upset she had to bury her unclaimed brood.

Again, ten days into this, Huron spend the late night washing dishes in the kitchen. He was working evenings in order to spend early morning asking about Selay. He ran the kitchen mostly alone. He cooked trout stews, washed dishes, and sorted orders. Most of the supplies were procured in the morning, making this a rather easy shift.

This kitchen he stewed in, was rather fair for a tavern. It has a basin, and a baker's oven. Hanging by every pot were ladles. The red brick stove was along a corner. Across was a water basin for washing. A center island was where all the finished food was placed. It was covered in breads, and freshly mixed pots of stew. There was only one window, which spilled into the back alley drains.

Huron was bent over a basin scrubbing diligently away at a pot. The horrors prior seemed so far away now. He would not think anything but simple thoughts as he meandered through the routine of dish washing. Interrupted by the occasional soap bubble rising, then sucking into his nose, and making him snuffle, and snort.

The night was crowded. More, and more dishes kept cycling into the pile. Tailya was very effective at collecting them. She would come in, and out regularly. She made sure she brushed her tail on Huron's when she could.

A local gold merchant from the southern towns stopped in after a big day. He was buying drinks, and having a celebration with his caravan guards. Huron saw him arrive earlier to use the basement of the inn to cool beer, and wine barrels. He wore the red, and green colors of the Empire, and was rightfully praising Ua for his success.

This merchant was well enough that even the Bailiff ignored his celebrations. The town night bell rung, and no one came to stop the loud commotion. Glonus also was not willing to kick out paying customers. So this rabble continued farther into the night as they drowned themselves in drink, and song.

Huron was scrubbing a pot carefully, and realized the water was now too soiled to wash. Bits of food were stuck on his cloth as well. So he began to clear the area around the basin, just as Tailya stomped in growling.

"I have been accosted!" she bleated out.

Huron was diligently not wanting to care, so he simply kept working. Tailya stood behind him, and stomped her foot on the wooden floor, "I have been assaulted!!" she roared.

"Stop yelling. You will break your eggs," Huron replied.

"Someone grabbed my tail!" Tailya whined.

"So maybe he likes you? You should let him," Huron picked up the basin, and turned, only to see Tailya in full wingspan near him. He failed to look away.

Of course, pulling on a woman's tail is rude. One should always see her wings first. If what Tailya was saying is true, then she was assaulted, and could find someone to defend her. Sadly, since this was Tailya, Huron did not believe her. He thought this was a trick to get attention.

"Huron! Help me!" Tailya pleaded, as Huron carried his basin to the window, and placed it on the sill.

"Why should I care?" He said, dumping the water out the window.

"Because I..." Tailya's response was drowned out in Huron's ears by the water. He did not care enough to respond.

"Please, Huron! They are rude, and ugly southerners with bright hides! They are too drunk, and might hurt me!" She protested.

"Then tell them to stop it," Huron said, carrying the basin to a larger one with clean water. He took a nearby cup, and got himself a quick drink, before refilling his dish washing basin.

"But..." Tailya gave him a clearly designed sad face.

"No. Go back to work," Huron said.

So she did. She waddled out of the room, and Huron resumed his dish washing. Later, Glonus entered, and prepared a pot with vegetable stew, which permeated the air not only in the Tavern, but across the street.

The tavern room erupted into laughter, and song. This noise died down, and rose up multiple times. Huron cleaned bowls, and stirred the pot. Tailya filled, then delivered them.

Eventually Tailya's return to the kitchen was delayed. Huron used this to go see what was going on, and he walked over to the open kitchen door. He gazed over the room.

There was a harp, a flute, and a lute player, each one wearing chains. They were slaves providing a song for a golden woman who would wiggle, and walk around the room. She was showing her body to all who would see.

This woman was clearly not showing off to impress anyone. She was bragging in some way. Her belly was fatter then Tailya's, clearly with a full clutch. She was covered in a two piece silk skirt that exposed her expanded midriff, and gave too much attention to her legs.

Everyone in the room, but Huron, knew their place. He could not help but to look at her wings, then below her tail when she waved it. However, he did not see.

He took a deep breath, and stared into a moment when Selay was dancing. In private, usually in the mornings. She would dance, and wiggle similar to this one. Huron would watch the show while faking like he was asleep. However, unlike this woman, Selay would hum, purr, and step in unique form that usually involved tripping over her tail, and falling into things. To Huron, Selay's performances were the most alluring, and expensive, disaster he ever saw.

He allowed this memory to repeat until he felt a soft hand along his muzzle. He returned to see the blue eyes of the dancer looking into his. She was teasing him with her smile.

The host rose up, and showed himself protective of her. He approached, then grasped her wrist with a soft growl, "That is enough."

She greeting him with a soft nose bump, and a smile. The pair walked off towards the stairs. Huron went back into the kitchen, bothered, and sighed some.

He stirred the soup pot to pass some time, and basked in the aroma of foodstuffs again. He was becoming hungry. This was better then the musty feeling in the main hall. Huron tried to recall the memory of Selay dancing, to keep from eating the food he has no business having.

Since he began to work at this proprietorship, Huron has been able to reign in his demon. Other annoyances, caused by Tailya, or customers, were not a bother. The work was simple. None of it has yet threatened his life, nor sought to make his painful wounds worse.

Tailya burst into the kitchen, and ran to the far side by the window. She let off a snarl, and faced the door as a red man with violet forescales, dressed in workman clothes, came into the room.

"I claim you!" he stumbled as came in, his voice was slurring, "Mine!"

"I am not yours' to have! I do not want you!" Tailya yelled back, she crossed her arms, and looked from aside. Then closed her wings, coiled her tail close to her legs.

"You lie! You let me look," He leaned forward on a table corner to keep balance. "You had your wings open towards me!"

Huron continued to manage the soup. He intended to act like he was not here. Maybe the man was so drunk he would not notice him. Getting involved would only frustrate things.

If Tailya would let this man have his claim, Huron would finally have been rid of her. He grew tired of her teases, and taunts. He wanted her gone.

So Huron looked from the side, if anything to watch them finally leave. The man approached very close to Tailya, and then leaned upon her, and stroked her belly as he tried to press his nose against hers. Tailya fought by looking away, snarling, and towards Huron.

Eventually the drunk glared at the soot-scale, a smile

came over his face, "I see. You want this one instead?"

Tailya let off a coo at the mention of it. The man leaned off her, snorting. The distraction let her escape. She dashed to Huron, and unfolded one of his wings to shield herself.

Huron slammed the ladle down, and held his head up, "Ain, why?"

The belligerent then held his fist up, and laughed, "I contest then!"

"I refused her!" Huron yelled.

"Turn around, and say that, coward!"

Huron did turn, and Tailya squirmed behind him without letting go of his wing. He saw the drunkard upright, and swaying, or at least attempting to be upright. At any moment he could collapse.

"She refused you too," Huron stated.

"Well she is a woman. She is prone to trickery like Ua," the man pointed at them, or more closely towards the wall. "She fancies tonight either one of us, and I dare not share."

Huron used his apron to clean his hands, he snorted. "No one knows what they want their first spring. Your lack of charm will upset Gintrix."

"How dare you cite the Order!" The ruffian growled, "Matters of the heart are not judged by them!"

Tailya poked her head out of cover, "Matters of the heart do not involve your cock!" she levied right into Huron's ear, causing him to flinch.

Huron was about to yell for Tailya to hush when the red responded, "My barbed cock is clearly exactly what is needed tonight! I can be very passionate with both my heart, and it!"

Tailya hissed, "No! Huron, contest him!"

Once again, Huron cursed Ain for this nonsense. Turning

around, he pulled the woman out from behind him. Now between both, she looked at him with a confused face, "I do not choose you!"

Tailya turned to the drunk, who was licking his lips, and smiling. She shuttered at the sight, "He does not know who I am. He is a lowly flightless."

"So are you! I never saw you fly!" Huron barked, "Stop acting like you are the dead king's brood, before you get us all in trouble."

The red pounded an arm on his chest, and puffed up. He began to pace some, "Then her majesty surely wants her King to be strong. Which you are clearly not, Huron."

Huron threw his hands up, and harrumphed, "Fine with this. I am leaving!" he began to make his way to the door. "Try not to make a mess for me to clean up tomorrow!"

Tailya quickly outpaced Huron before he could even get within a step of the exit. She stood in the door, held her hands on the frame, and opened her wings. She gave a threatening snarl, with teeth showing. Clearly she did not approve.

Huron stopped, and only remembered seeing her like this once, when her eggs were threatened. This might be a similar situation in her mind, and thus he now was forced into a contest. Unless he got out through that window.

Yes, he could glide out of the window, so Huron turned around. Only to be stopped by the drunk. His fist quickly raised up, and slammed into Huron's jaw. This made him stagger into a wall. He quickly regained his footing, and looked up.

Huron's breathing became harder, and his chest pounded. A demon was coming, and it froze him in place. He could see his opponent smacking his fist in his palm, and preparing to strike again. Huron felt the world grow more distant, but was brought back hard by a solid blow to his softer belly scales.

The plated scales were strong enough to prevent a total loss of breath. Though, it still hurt. Huron gazed back up as the ruffian landed another on the side of his head.

He staggered in the opposite direction then before, and finally lifted an arm up to counter the next assault. The drunk was quick to bypass it, and jab the side of Huron's belly. Once, twice, and a third time, before Huron managed to get out of arm's range.

Huron could see Tailya, now out of the door, and watching the fight. She did not look fearful, or meek, but some sort of commanding. As if she was evaluating their work. She was calm in it, and her tail swished with some indication of expectation.

Huron knew what that meant. Old traditions demand a contest for a lady sometimes. This was one of them. These fights tended to end in death, and this is why the church demands arranged marriages. Though even the church could not make the act more, or less, undesirable. Occasionally, dueling broke out over some daughter of note.

Huron roared when a fist landed close enough to his eye to nearly blind him. However, his eye ridge deflected most of the force. One blow came, and undercut his jaw again, sending him back through a shelf of spices.

"STOP TRASHING MY KITCHEN, OR I WILL GUT YOU ALL!" roared Glonus as he flailed his way into the fight. He pried the drunk off Huron as he was trying to contain things, but saw the look in his eyes, and backed off, "Oh, I get it."

The drunk turned to finish Huron. He saw his opponent was now on the floor, and dazed. So he rose his head up, stood upright, and displayed his wings. He gave a victory roar then faced Tailya to show off.

By then Huron stood back up, brushing off some spices. He felt a sudden rush of desire, which made him in impulse unfold his claws, and slash the backside of the red. A clear stain of blood collected on his shirt as he yelped.

At the site of blood, Huron came to sense. "Oh no." he muttered.

The red spun, and dashed for Huron at his fastest speed. Huron could not react, as the man unleashed a series of relentless pummels. Every one was too fast to be blocked, and Huron simply had to just take the impact, he finally was beaten to breathlessness.

"She is mine!" the red reaffirmed, pulling Huron by the horns, and glaring into his eyes.

The red had no civilized composure, and gave Huron a territorial headbutt. Huron's vision blurred, and he saw a large white blob move behind Tailya, and next to Glonus. His ears were suddenly slammed dull with a pair of wrists to his temples, so he only heard a mumble.

Then, everything slowed, and one solid impact from above caused Huron to crash down to the floor. He was yet to faint, but now unwilling to move. He was swiftly kicked in the side.

The red, who was not a blur turned back to Tailya. Who gave a resisted hiss again at him. This new, white figure, then grabbed the drunkard, and threw him to the floor. It was easy, giving how unbalanced he was already.

Huron realized that if he contended to have Tailya now, he most certainly failed to earn her. In doing this failure, Huron may finally have come full circle, and gotten rid of this hysterical harlot. He laughed through the pain, unaware of the gazing eyes of Tailya.

Though he felt himself growing more short of breath. There was no smell of blood, but he was unable to breath fully. As he laid there, his snorts of amusement caught the new white blob's attention. It came closer, and Huron thought that this was maybe the demon he has always been haunted by, but then he passed out. Not from lack of breath, but the strong smell of fish emanating off the feet of this man.

Those that must do, do so with cause. Huron's cause has been failure. With irony, until now. Irony in that defeat brings him success in ways he does not desire.

Tyran Rual

CHAPTER TWENTY

Of conflict is how things should be. The trial in life is embracing the enforcement of this contest. All of creation shall submit to the law that the best shall inherit it through merit.

Though does this rule apply to Selay? She is exiled to be among flightless. She hides under a lord named Brudge. Who she slanders right to his face, showing she is not worthy of station. One wonders slightly if she was still employed by him after delivering that letter?

A letter of the stolen witness description of the Arsonist of Anya. The only record which mentioned that the criminal is a woman. The theft of the staff was insubordinate to Brudge. He should render her death by his claw. That is, if she would submit rightfully.

For Selay's intent of payment for saving Brudge would be to recruit him into her scheme to stop the egg-eaters. Rather then leveraging forgiveness. Many shall be facing her wrath. It is wise of her to prevent the death of the only man in Jester able to tolerate her. So Selay was not hesitant in her motion to save him from himself.

Deep Lake was Brudge's Stronghold. There he spends his

springtime plotting, and brooding. He hides in Derin Estates, or as it is known outside of town: Deep Lake Manor.

The building stood out as a landmark outside of the main city. Across the northern district, which Brudge was a chancellor of, it was rather visible. Obviously you can see most of the region itself. It being a collection of construction sites, endless row homes, guard towers, and the occasional plaza. The lake was where the horizon ended. Anyone who only just arrived of this area would think that it was an ocean.

Deep lake is old, and very prosperous. Some say the oldest city in the world. Prior to discovering just how foul Jestarian folk were, Deep Lake was once the home of the Order. Traces of the Order's legacy were visible in the decaying walls, and fortresses close to the various temples. Ghosts of a prior era, when refugees from the Northern nations invaded, and Wyverns were only first tamed.

Before the Diren's came to power, the city was still operated from the old castle keeps. Brudge dictated his intent to abandon that tradition. He built a new kind of stronghold, not just a mansion of eloquence, but a complex that supported his more unorthodox ways.

It was here that Brudge, and Selay, first established a working relationship. He found her freezing in winter. He saved her, with misplaced kindness, and cuckoldry.

She overstayed her welcome when she clawed Brudge for attempting to claim her. She managed to become a fixture at his gatherings. There she found slander, and gossip amusing. Which graduated to spying.

Her newfound handle of finscale trickery convinced Brudge's guests into thinking she was the wife of the Skol ambassador. Through the reinforcement of this lie, She would get them all drunk. It then became easy to sway them to trade secrets.

Secrets such in flavor of a group of chancellors called Tributionists. They were plotting to get Brudge to lay with the wife of the leader of the Fordako Pact group. The plan was to use a strange fermented yeast added to the wine. This was to start a rivalry, and isolate Brudge.

Selay did tell Brudge of this plot, but only after the plotters fainted from receiving their own potion. The house guards were conveniently ordered to carry them all to the same guest room. Selay stole all their clothing. The local herald's guild was then given the same room by accident. Selay was rewarded with trust, work, and access to safe houses.

As she ran up to the front door of the two story mansion, she felt a humid cold breeze on her tail. Her supplies were safe in the woods. In expectation for combat, she was fully armed, and dressed light.

She gave the door a shake by gripping the handles, and sighed in failure. This double door was twice her height, and fortified with iron. It was barred shut. She gave it a kick in in frustration, which sounded in a loud bang.

A week of traveling, with not much rest, prevented her from expressing anything other then agitation. In her anxiety, she was able to stay upright, and awake. It was not enough rage to get through this door. Brudge was wise to reinforce it.

Further, no one would answer. It was so late that the servants were not by the door. The candles were not light, except the guards quarters on the second floor.

She paced, and saw a frog staring at her by the pool aside of the house. It has this look of attentiveness, knowing that Selay looked as if she was about to eat it at any moment. She just might have, but she had to get to Brudge morose.

The manor is a rigid complex. The west side is reserved

for servants, and the eastern side for the family. Brudge had a whole mess of employees, who pampered his every need, and polished his every scale. From a small group of prickly guards, to a rather fat chef, the manor was a town in itself.

They required food, clothing, soap, wine, and service too. The food needed to be transported in, then immediately given cold storage to prevent spoilage.

That thought made Selay hurry to the backside of the estate. Where a dirt path served as a lonely way to another entry. A supply door, to a large foreboding, and musky, cellar storeroom.

Selay could see the library chamber window when she stood center of the now empty supply stop. The candle was light, and a very noticeable shadow was waving around the room. In fact, the candle was shaking, and this made Selay think she might be too late.

As soon as she saw the supply door, she bolted to it. The door was on a wooden frame that never was treated. So when Selay slammed into it with the weight of her entire form, the door broke suddenly off its lower hinge. A swift kick gave her the space to get her arm in, and dislodge the bar.

The smell of fermentation caressed Selay's snout. She gave a purr, and realized she has been sober for too long. She gazed down the room, and saw an open door that lead farther into the darkness of the basement.

The fully stocked cellar was an all too homely sight. This was where she spent much time in despair. Sadly, she could only pilfer one random, and small, bottle of drink as she hustled through. It was set aside on a barrel in her path. There can be no time to choose. She used her claw to uncork it, and began gulping it down.

It was just what she needed. The impact of the unsweetened wine woke her up, and caused her to stop thinking

of trivial things. From this she continued to the dark stairs
on her right. Then up towards the main floor's servants
hallway, where doors would be seen opened with candles
alight, and no one in. Then up another floor to the quarters,
and hallways to the balcony between the two complexes that
looked across the garden. Where immediately a crowd of
finscales were gathered dress for bedtime, naked, or robes.

Selay arrived at the rear of the crowd. She recognized
they were all the house servants. They appeared scared. Maws
open, frills dropped, and tails quaking tightly to their
legs. Just ahead of them was the closed door to the library,
where Brudge would study, and hide away to make his plans.

Though plans are never made by making loud bangs, and
clashes. Those would be the sounds of action. She knew
immediately someone was fighting, and determined that she was
right in her jurisprudence. She immediately dashed forward,
and pushed everyone in the crowd away. No one resisted her,
and some faces were grinning in a strange way.

Another door barred, and Selay paced. She growled in
frustration. The iron reinforcement forbade her entry.

The only other way was the window. She quickly dove off
the balcony, and took flight. Her wings outstretched, and
beat as she flew in a circle around the garden. Her eyes
lined up with the window to the library. A clear glass, and
thick thing, that would deflect an arrow easily. In midair
she drank from her bottle, then roared in full as she struck
herself into the window with all the force she could gain.

The smell of blood quickly took over her senses, and
she hissed at the pain. The glass window shattered, but cut
her somewhere. She landed on her side upon entry, and
struggled to get her footing.

Brudge was in the room, along with a rather tough
looking Jestarian in black cowl. On his arm patch was the
symbol of Forged Blade. He was ignoring Selay's clumsy

entrance as he, and Brudge, clashed blades.

Brudge was already cut, his left hand, along the webbing, was covered in blood. He must have used it to block. He was making obvious winces when he gripped his sword.

Selay rose up to her feet, and felt a strong pain on her back plates. She cared not, they were her thickest scales. She took an extra, lasting drink of her bottle, gulping rudely.

Brudge tried to cut at the side of his killer. Though an elbow to the back of his skull knocked him down. He finally notice Selay, and stared at her. He huffed short of breath.

His opponent was already with his blade held in striking pose over the chancellor's head. He loomed, and hesitated. He gathered to motion to impale Brudge, and finish his work.

Upon assessment, Selay pulled her right arm, with bottle in hand, back behind her. What was in it spilled out. She then quickly catapulted it towards the assassin.

The impact was a cloud of fizzle, glass, wine, and some of Selay's spit. It encompassed the entire head of the thug. His attention was completely diverted from a final kill, to protecting his eyes.

When he could see, he turned to face Selay. Who was already launching from Brudge's writing desk. She readied her claws for rending finscale meat.

In this moment, prior to battle, eyes match, and desires set. The trial begins. Selay was no longer just a foul drunk, but a mindless beast. Her enemy, now was going to enjoy the wrath of a platescale.

Self-preservation set in, and he slide to his side some. He reached to grip Selay's chest. Then redirecting her force, he pushed her breast in, and spun her off to the side, and threw her. Selay used her recently practiced flight turns to reorient towards her enemy. She failed, and went tumbling. She could only make eye contact, and a strange thought occurred.

Seasonal strain, when he touched her, erupted Selay's fire. She was briefly entertained with sating it. She sucked in a long breath, and held. She should know better, and the impact with the bookshelf made her come back to sense.

This killer had no equal desire in his eye. He is another immature child sent to end the lives of those who did not fit the designs of his masters. One wonders what thing trains a child to be so viscous.

The hood had his dagger in hand when Selay was regaining her footing. The impact with the shelf was damaging to every object on it. Wings, tail, and platescale bulk shaped the devastation well. Every shelf snapped, and things tumbled to the ground.

At the first step, Selay caught sight of Brudge standing to full, and diving. Diving towards the arm of her enemy in a move to block him from stabbing her. Brudge seemed oblivious to his lack of angle, and desperate.

Selay did not oblige his kindness, and moved to the side of the shelf. Her loose left arm slid behind what was left of its frame, and she gave it a push. Down went the shelf, taller then her, and made of solid maple.

Brudge did not see the incoming former furniture, but the killer did. He ceased his forward march, pulled back his raised dagger arm. He quickly hopped to a safe distance. Brudge however, found himself buried under it. Selay heard him curse, and yelp.

Not did it matter. She drew her first dagger. Then placed her steel gauntlet arm in front of her belly scales, and fore faced her opponent. She examined his body, and unwittingly licked her lips.

He was no different then those others of the Forged

Blade in Journey's Rest. Small, skinny, and too scared to show his face. He was finscale, frilled along his tail, and stank of such.

He struck out on the first move. A lighting fast jab with his fist. There was no impact, but a goal to get Selay to react. So she would be pincered by a follow up stab with the dagger.

She did not fall for it, and pushed her body forward to make her own full swing. Unlike him, she wanted to make contact. Stepping into his blow, her hard white belly scales absorbed it whole, and she went for his eyes.

The hood lurched back, and gave quick slashes to ward her off. Selay slid back herself, out of range. A soft grunt came from under the fallen shelf when the weight was off Brudge. Selay then took a sidestep around the ruin, and tried to close the gap with her target.

He stabbed forward to try to impale her. However, Selay was able to dodge. She used Brudge's study desk to keep him away by kicking it at him.

She felt herself feeling weak. The full effects of her drink, and now the effects of extreme fatigue were catching up. She took in another breath, and hardened her scales. She summoned all her brutality, and rage. It is either her, or him, this is a fight as it should be: to the death.

Quickly she stepped onto back the bookshelf, and lunged off it into a spinning kick. The hood dodged that, but the follow up of her heavy tail made not only full impact, but pushed him just near the desk. She landed behind him.

She turned back to face him. In the same span of time it took for her to turn, he did so as well. He had a stab that just missing her right side. Selay had to lean forward to avoid it entirely.

He stepped back again, as Selay ran to make distance between them. The relationship to the desk now reversed, and

Selay once again lunged off it. Rather then a full dive, she used it to get onto the bookshelf. Brudge grunted underneath in Jestarian swears, as Selay ran down the self, and hopped off.

The assassin remained in his place. He did not seem dazzled, but no one would be impressed by Selay's movements. She may be very swift, and agile, but also entirely drunk. Her steps were off, and her balance clearly was not natural. It was her unpredictable motions, and growing momentum, that made her seem so lucky.

Selay began again with a stab motion that swayed off at the end into a slash. The killer dodged, and countered, and Selay had her right gauntlet arm in position to deflect it. Her left dagger arm was well enough posed to return with a full slash to his chest. Forcing him to hop back again.

Now he was directly in front of the desk, he legs spread to be balanced, and his arms spread upward. This was good enough for Selay, so she simply kicked him square in the gut with her right foot. Then stepped forward, with another kick to his head.

That poor desk, it looked hand made. Somewhere on it there is a plate with a craftsman's signature. Under the top of it, a flower was carved, with the names of Brudge's long dead parents. A signature of their union.

That desk was now destroyed. The would-be assassin crashed firmly into it on his way down. It splintered into two larger halves. The legs broke, and the brackets holding the thing together snapped as their nails were bent. It made a crunch, and papers inside the drawers crunched too.

This was not the end. The killer was winded, disarmed, but alive. He turned to his side on the floor, and Selay spun her dagger to reverse. She stepped towards him, and readied to stab his eye out.

As soon as Selay was beginning to bend over, he kicked

upward, and behind. A footclaw went under Selay's tail, and struck her rear very hard. Selay yelped, and flung forward. Her habit of drink did not give her balance this time.

The hood was quickly up, and Selay was in the ruin of the desk. Now on her hands, and knees. She lost her dagger in the fall, and was needing to rearm.

Further, she was vulnerable, and exposed along her already cut back. This was not allowed to continue, and Selay began to change that. She leaned to the right side, and pushed to run to the other side of the room to get a better attack position.

Her opponent was reeling, and out of breath, but he began to chase her. An arm extended, and reached for Selay's tail. When he brushed her, she bore teeth in disapproval.

It was time for the second dagger to come out. She put her hand on its hilt, and firmly spun to face her enemy as she withdrew it. There was no time to aim, and she quickly let it fly to the mass of her enemy.

A quick wale of pain came from this child. Selay now knew this was an adolescent for sure. His voice was high. He had no tolerance to pain. Finscale adults are tougher then this.

He gripped the now impaled dagger, which made solid insertion into his right bicep. Blood spilled down along him. The impact was deep enough to sap most of the strength of his arm.

He looked into Selay's eyes, and a genuine fear stuck him. Like a memory of a past event, he became lost in it so briefly. Selay only returned a cold stare of death back. His blood, and his unique scent, dripped into the carpet. Now all would know who tried to kill Brudge.

The now failed killer ran towards the main entry of the library. This door went into a long paneled wood hallway with a spiral stair that could be used as an escape. Selay followed, she should have let him go, and let him limp home to warn his mates. She did not, for she was tired of buying new daggers, and wanted that one back.

A few steps in, Selay's wounds gave her a warning. Her balance gave out, and the pain in her back did not abate. Days of running also felt like fire in her legs, and her head started to swim from all the intake of wine she had.

She staggered as she ran. However, she is a master at drunken staggering. Even as she stumbled to, and fro, she was gaining speed.

A quick left tilt, and near fall saved Selay from death. Her very own dagger flown by her, she heard it hit the floor behind. The rebound of personal anger cleared her vision.

The assassin gripped his wounded arm as he kept trying to run away. He made a mistake, and turned down the first hallway, which was a dead end. By the time he returned back to the main, he was greeted by a growling Selay who tackled him full body.

Platescales are larger then Jestarian by nature, and Selay was average. She was able to fully overpower him. Her generally careless way, resulted in foot claws tearing the rug as both landed on the floor.

The assassin grabbed the side of Selay's face. Which Selay had to resist by holding his wrists. If he would be unyielding in that motion, it could cost her an eye, so it took priority.

He tried to knee her in the abdominal, then the belly, but was not able to. Selay's scales are solid enough, from years of falling off things, to make her unmovable to terribly angled deflecting attacks.

Eventually she had to back up off him to save her eye. She fell back on her rear, and shook her head. Her vision was blurring badly. She could see two blurred figures now rising up, and lunging at her.

A fist into her snout left her on her side. A kick to her other side made her yelp. Her back was exposed again, her stolen royal staff upon it, and a gash near her lower left back, with a shard of glass, was accessible.

The killer quickly grabbed Selay by a horn, and wing. He pulled her to her knees. She growled, then cried out as he grabbed the shard, and began to push it. The wound tore farther into her, and new blood trickled down.

Whatsoever situation Selay had in regards to her drink, pain, season, or proclivities left that moment. She gripped the horn he held, there was a dirty bronze band around it. In that band was a bolt, and she gave it a twist, then threw her body forward.

In a strange move, the horn popped off, and the glass shard also broke out of her back. The assassin was pulling her horn to hold the shard in. A sudden change in rooting made him fall back with horn in hand. He looked at it with surprise.

Selay took that time to hit his nose broadside with her arm. Then his side with her tail. She crawled free, and stood up. Only to fall forward, and lean on a suit of Jestarian amour that smelled too much like Brudge. She snorted.

The thug dove, with bloody glass, and broken horn as his weapons. Selay caught him quickly beginning from the side of her view. She grabbed the amour suit, and threw it in a loud roar at him. Her arms burned in agony, her back searing, but her anger continued. She wanted to send this creature to the forge.

The suit shattered into its individual pieces when it made full impact with the killer. It completely disarmed him, and stopped his movement. It was not enough to knock him over however, he fell into the wall, his bloody arm painting it red.

Selay could barely keep upright, and at this point, neither her enemy. They both locked arms on each other's shoulders, and delivered several very solid territorial headbutts. Blood was first to flow down the Jestarian's forehead. Platescale head-plates always win.

However, what platescales can do with extra amour, we cannot do with grace. So quickly the tide turned, and Selay found herself being pummeled with quick blows to the sides, and jaw. She swung her claws weakly, dizzy, and ready to faint, and stepped back to establish a block. She succeeded by using her gauntlet to deflect a blow. With a one-handed pummel ending in a crunch as the assassin broke his claw off.

Selay's back bumped into the wall, and there was a large painting of Brudge. Her blood coated it. This whole thing has to stop, or Selay would bleed out here. So in one move, she ripped the large oil painting off the wall, and smashed it over the assassin's head. The frame shattered, and he fell over as he tore through it.

Now Selay was armed again with pieces of the frame she held in both claws. She gave a spiteful grin at the thug, even with heavy breaths. He immaturely began to run, as she now had the advantage.

Selay was between him, and the stairs, so he ran back to the study. As she began to follow, she dropped the frames, and decided to finally do what she was not supposed to do.

The Royal Staff was not to be bloodied in her mind. Of course it is a very dangerous weapon. It has serrated blades loosely attached so that would shake as they sliced scales. This exasperated any wound made, though cutting solidly required more strength, or velocity. It has a glamour, that when it was cleaned would tell everyone just who Selay was. It is a trophy, a metal, a medallion, signifying power of the platescales. It should never be used by her to defend the life of a finscale lord.

Selay's opponent fell over at the far end of the hall as she removed the staff. He was clearly dizzy from the exchange of head butts, and constant throws. He was panting, and shaking, too sober to endure. Selay slowly moved over to him, and he hastily got up.

It was too late for him. Selay swung the blade end of the staff, and it made full contact with his tail from the side. He roared, and stopped all motion. His scream faded into a desperate cry as Selay did not relinquish her momentum in the impact. With this one single move, she cut his tail off.

She was not done, but she knew he was. Now she grabbed him by his horns, and picked him up. His blood all over her leg, and Brudge's floor. It would be only moments before he would bleed out, and Selay wanted one final pleasure tonight.

He gave no fight as she took him through the library, all he did was cry pathetically. She slammed him against the iron door, lifted the bar on it, then snapped his wing as he fell through it. He screamed in full, and shook in terror.

The door opened to see the entire house staff gazing in horror. Someone was heard throwing up. Faces of fear looked upon Selay as she unmasked the killer.

"Ain's Forged Blade is this beast's family!" Selay yelled the guild name to all. The secret of this group is no more. She then shoved him, and he fell back to his knees.

She tried to lift him back up for all to see. No more did he stand on his feet. So she just drug him. Over to the balcony, where she lunged him over, and pushed him off without a thought. He did not scream in the fall, he must have fainted just prior.

Covered in blood, wounded, her horn off in another room. Selay tried to avoid anything but her anger. It was all that kept her standing. Her double vision returned shortly after she looked away from her kill.

In the doorway, she could see a white figure, she heard Brudge say something. She did not comprehend its meaning. The sight of him dissolved her anger, and in its place, disgust. This was no good, so Selay began to swear at him. Just prior to finally falling over, consumed by her afflictions. Brudge quickly lunged forward to try to catch her. He failed, Selay was too heavy, her scales were far to hard for the weak finscale to carry.

The gods show now, through this harlot. Selay fulfilled the divine mandate. Brudge lives, when the world is better without. Heartless, cruel, and terrible is Selay, who is better suited to motherhood then war. As the chatter of finscale witnesses began, it became clear that her deed, in the end, mattered.

Greben

CHAPTER TWENTY-ONE

Soon the contest shall unfold. The conflict will lead to the siege of a great thing. The enforcement of defense is required. Let us strive to preserve what we have.

Shore up with proper masonry the walls, and structure to withstand siege. Scribe upon the page their plans. Inventory what we have. However, be quick, as there is scant time left.

North Deep Lake Herald's guild was kept in solid condition. Except it stank often of sawdust, and unwashed finscales. Especially when everyone came to work. Which is why Greben'Tua preferred to be away now, searching for history to chronicle, and notoriety to gain.

It came today with the Great House of Chancellor Derin falling to its own tendencies. Rumors of a fight spread down from mountain, and through the sprawling city faster then the suns rise. It arrived to the young scribe via a merchant who sold bandages to Brudge's servants.

Grebin's stature was youthful at the age of nineteen. He has no belly, fit from swimming, and his scales were still smooth, and unbroken. He had a bulb on his forehead. It dangled down to his brown eyes. His scales were colored with large blots of blue, to a yellow belly, with violet strokes between.

It was cloudy, and there was rain coming. Higher winds made him wear his yellow scarf over his red vest. He did not enjoy the scarf, it pinched his back fins, and he did not like picking lint from his gills. The thought of pain from cracking after a morning swim was far worse, so he dealt with it.

He also wore common brown trousers, and a set of travel boots. The boots had no coverings for his footclaws. He was not wealthy enough to afford a cobbler to repair the tears, so he cut them off.

He is a herald, a merchant of other's strife. His business was of finding other's pain, or pleasure, and letting all those with earfins, and holes to listen know of it. The news of strife from Brudge was absolutely worth his visit, as it could net him, and his guild, enough gold to expand the library. Or him to live in his own house, rather then under a table in the guild hall.

The manor was ominously quiet. Birds chirped in the trees, and branches swayed. Greben was winded from the flight up the hill, but landed right at the front door. He quickly caught his breath. By the pools at the door he washed his face, cooling himself from exposure to the morning suns.

He checked his bag, and items. A set of papers for notes, an ink jar of fish oil, and feathers from a wing of an owl he caught, and ate, a few days ago. Weapons of the most dangerous kind. Ones of truths, and lies.

He examined the door. It was gloomy, and intimidating with its iron frames. It towered above him, giving the impression some giant Wyvern once lived here. He banged his whole arm along it solidly. The sound echoing through the halls.

While waiting, it occurred to him that perhaps he

should not be so obvious. Brudge is very powerful, and the idea of a scandal involving him would interest a wide number of Jestarian, and even platescales. The brokering of this kind of knowledge would cause all sorts of trouble for whoever published it. However, if one thing Herald's are when young, is naive.

Eventually someone answered the door. It was a Jestarian woman, green, and dry. She poked her head out, her fins bouncing as she did.

"We are not taking guests. The Chancellor is quite busy." She scolded.

"My'lady, I am from the Herald's guild. I am here to int-" He was cut off.

"No!" she said, tilting her head offended, "No Guests!" She quickly slammed the door shut.

Greben heard the bar clamp behind the door, and he sighed. He was acting like an apprentice, not as a master. This idea of consulting with Brudge prior to some rumor of a fuss was dull-witted, and as Jestarian saying goes, 'lacking salt.'

He took to a patrol around the premise. Ducking around a few hedges shaped like a giant fish. Then hopped a crumbling brick foundation of an older structure. He had a wide view of the side, able see the corner out back. He could then see something really exciting.

A small troop of house servants, lead by a butler, were carrying trunks of food to the cellar door. They were laughing, and joking as if it was a normal day. What struck Greben with interest, was the corpse they eventually brought out.

A black robed figure with no tail. It was hard to see, but it was definitely someone dead. He wondered if there been a murder? This would be great if it was.

Alongside, two other corpses were carried out. Both

red, and clearly Jestarian. Greben's eyes widened, and he took out a parchment, and his ink jar. He dipped his talon in, and began writing down everything he saw with haste.

He slapped his muzzle with both hands when done, and he was about to make an excited churl. He held back. It would have given his position away. He found the perfect story, a Chancellor of Jester suspected of violating the oath of nonviolence in the Fordako Pact. The idea of his seal upon such records made him salivate. He is to become immortal. Ain and Ua themselves would contend for his entry into their armies as a forward scout.

However, there has to be more. Brudge would be killing for a reason. Greben laid on his belly, and swished his tail through the wet grass. He waited for the cart to leave, writing every angle he could down with ardent fervor.

When it was clear, he quickly dashed towards the basement entry. He scouted all of where the bodies were, noting discrepancies like the door was off its hinges, and sniffing out scents. He found a strange smell right along the broken door frame.

It was not finscale, and a musk of feminine nature. She clearly needed a long bath. It lingered, and irritated Greben's nose. He snorted outrageously as he felt it excite him in ways he did not want. She stank, but somehow was sweet, and this is wrong. He decided to avoid a basement entry.

Greben is flightfull, so when he heard someone yelling from over the wall he took a running leap to the air. He landed on a tree branch, with an unusual amount of broken pieces scattered on the ground below it. He caught a clear sight of the library, and the broken window.

There was blood everywhere, and a trail into the hallways. All adjoined by a path of unnatural destruction. Books had been torn, and the desk was destroyed.

The scribe glided though into the office, and heard the sound of glass crunch under his boots. He took his notes, and began to write, taking stock everything. Broken furniture, knives dotted about, and a finscale tail.

What? A tail?

The sight of the limb made him sick. He felt his own tail pulse as if it was cut off. He stepped back, then threw up. Growling at himself for ruining the scene, and making enough noise to alert those on the balcony.

Two maids, and a cook barged into the room.

"Who in the Twin Suns are you?" The maid asked, she stunk of lilac, and some kind of ugly soap mixture. The men stunk the same way.

"I-" He was interrupted.

"He is the little spindle from the Herald's guild!" The cook said.

One of the maids ran off suddenly. The others took to approaching Greben. They came from behind, began to box him in, and gripped his wing.

"Unhand me! I have license by the Chancellorship to investigate what I want!" He yelped, and struggled.

"Brudge will have a word about that," The maid glared at him.

It was fantastic that Greben was to get his interview after all. Then like a swarm of bees, the staff began to enter the room. One-by-one they took to guarding the escape routes.

The herald could barely see something out on the balcony. There was a solid, and very fat finscale standing in the way. Someone else was carrying off a blue-scaled figure, with plates on the fingers instead of scales. Greben's mind raced. If that was a platescale, it could mean the greatest of stories to tell: war.

Regal, tall, Chancellor Brudge Char' Derin entered the

room. He dressing a leather Armour suit. Everyone kept their eyes on Greben, and Brudge kept his legs straightened. That must have been quite painful, but it made Brudge so much taller then all around. The young scribe could not help but stare at the finely dressed statesman.

"How dare you enter my home uninvited," Brudge's voice boom in perfect finscale. He placed a hand on his sword hilt.

"I am doing my duty to the Chancellorship," Greben bowed his head in submission. "I am here to record this event."

Brudge looked around the room. He sniffed, and flexed his sword hand's fingers. The quite creek of his leather gloves made Greben a bit nervous. This is a murder site, and if Brudge did this, he would be quite ready to kill again.

"What event? I see a perfectly fine library." Brudge casually explained.

Greben looked back up to him in surprise. His earlier thoughts at the door were confirmed. This is a potential embarrassment of Brudge. He pressed forward, like the naive child he still is.

"That is someone's tail, cut off like a tree branch. Blood is everywhere. There was clearly a fight here." Greben waved his hand across the room.

Brudge looked around the room himself again, following Greben's motions. He turned back to make solid eye contact, with a piercing gaze. He growled softly.

"There is nothing here. No tail, no blood. This library is in perfect order."

Greben puffed up, and decided to challenge, "You dare cover up such an important historical event? An attack on a popular Chancellor! I have license to tell all finscales you are in danger!"

He pulled out his guild seal, and held it up to show Brudge. He stood straight-legged, and thrashed his tail. His chest large, and he held back a head bob.

Brudge snapped it from Greben's hands, then tore up the seal. "Not anymore."

"You do not have power to take that away! That requires a notary from Port Selis!" Greben protested.

"I do, and I just did. Nothing happened here, little fish." Brudge reaffirmed.

Greben decided to leave, and moved to the window. When he was just about to leap out, he felt Brudge grab his tail. Then pull, and grip his neck to throw him down to the ground rather hard.

"Give me those notations." He demanded.

"No!" Greben yelled, remaining defiant as he scurried to his feet again. He decided it was time to lie, "These are shopping lists for my wife! You cannot have them!"

"Cuttlefish, you do not smell married," Brudge's use of Jestarian metaphors indicated his seafaring heritage, "You took notes, and you will not leave with them."

Greben grinned. He just got a confession from Brudge, "If nothing happened, then why should you be afraid of a few pages of notes?"

Brudge snorted, he walked into it. As Greben got up, the chancellor growled in vast annoyances visibly. The herald noticed his muzzle curled, and frills tightened. It was a tinge of worry, quickly banished by a Chancellor's oratory skill.

"Ten thousand for the notes. About what you should expect from the sales of the scrolls?" Brudge offered.

Greben tilted his head. Money? Of course wealth was attractive to anyone. Ten thousand was a lofty value for this, but it was nothing compared to the near twenty-five thousand one could expect from the surrounding sales across all neighboring nations. Maybe even more if the guild auctioned it on the black markets. A small treasury for a book sale too.

"You must think I am daft to take a bribe over something this scandalous?"

"This is not a bribe. I am buying the publication rights. There is great danger in publishing of an investigation before the bailiff arrives." Brudge clearly conjured up this reason quickly.

"You have no intent of giving the bailiff something to investigate."

"Nor the heralds. I am willing to pay more."

"How much?" Greben felt his tail swaying a bit over this.

If Brudge would pay more then the expected value of the story, Greben would be able to take the coin for himself. He could use it to investigate anything. He could bribe witnesses, or pay homeless to pull a prank, and the guild would never know he took a bribe from the chancellor. He could pay for their library, and a loft above it for himself.

"A Chancellor loved by the Riverpoor. Caught up in a murder scandal? The whole peoples of Ilimnus will be wanting to pay for news on it."

"Thirty three thousand," Brudge quickly rose the price.

Greben had no choice. That was far more then he was expecting. He stood tall, and removed his notes. As he held them in his hands he gave them a glance. There will be other scandals to uncover, as desires are unceasing. Coin is always more useful, especially when it was more coin then what the truth is worth.

When Brudge took the notes. He did not immediately destroy them. He sighed, as if a burden was off his back. He went from intimidating, and threatening, to smiling.

"My servants will get the coin from the banks right away. In the meantime. Let us go to the dining hall, and get to know each other. Scribe Tua?" Brudge escorted Greben to the balcony exit.

"Yes, how did you know?" Greben Asked.

"I notarized your license to write," Brudge said.

Through the kitchen, then into a massive ballroom they went. Greben was dazzled by its designs. He heard of the dances, and political marriages that were entertained here. However, he never himself was able to go, as this was for the experienced scribes.

The quiet room, of two floors high, had a kitchen on each level. The second floor tables were where the two sat, as close to the door as possible. The distance between them, and the far side, was impressive. There were multiple arches holding up a room decorated with a painting of the story of the Scales Alliance. A picture of Hitwa Fordako standing with his wings extended in a crowd of all the founding dukes who fought against the first invasions of Skol. He stared in awe at the masterwork, with every scale detailed, every fin accurate.

"I suppose you are hungry. You did leave that mess on my expensive rug." Brudge explained.

Greben refused to feel hungry. He knew better. Never eat from someone involved in death, lest you get poisoned. Greben shook his head, "No thank you, sir."

"Then at least a drink," Brudge responded, and rose a hand up, and snapped his claws.

A maiden came to the table. She was the same who answered the door. She smelled of lilac, and was in display of glamour. She swayed, and came close to Brudge, where her tail brushed his.

"Get us a fine wine, my'lady." he ordered.

She silently nodded, and left the room in a saunter. She returned quickly with glasses, and a large bottle of some dark red drink.

"I saw you admiring the mural. It is my expression of

patriotism," Brudge said as the wine was poured, "I greatly value the heroism of our founders."

"I supposed an expensive picture is a good expression," Greben began to feel nervous, "b-but... I saw a platescale on your balcony."

Brudge leaned back, and puffed up again, "You saw no such thing! I have not had one here since that wretched Skol Diplomat. I would not be caught anywhere near those vile savages."

He was obviously lying, Greben knew it by the stiff nature of his posture, "I know she was not a diplomat."

"You do know what now?" Brudge growled.

"The platscale diplomats send maybe one woman. She was black, or gray. She also is not allowed to set foot outside the embassy. Which is a lonely hovel, in a closed off quarter of Port Selis. The platescales hate our ways. They only keep peace until they can overtake us." Greben explained.

"You cannot have evidence of that. Three years ago, things were slightly different," Brudge took up his wine glass to sip it daintily, "You would be wise to not jump to conclusions. For the guild's reputation."

"It is not a conclusion. I think you have one in your flock... I hear of a 'Whore of Brudge,'" Indeed, Greben heard the term before, but from the information brokers who worked in the unkempt parts of Deep Lake. People who were untrustworthy, unless paid. Usually that all had fresh black eyes.

Brudge's face became more unreadable, and still. His motions became near undetectable. Then he frowned, awkwardly.

"A man like me has better principles then whores, or platescales," He jostled Greben's notes some, which he set on the table. He dug a claw into the corner of a page, and tore it.

Greben swore he felt his heart become still. He eyed

the damaged paper with anxiety.

Brudge leaned to the side, and smiled, "It is a good thing some of us have the principle not to slander the local Chancellor. Such noble things are rewarded with ample subsidies."

"You would fund the Herald's guild?" Greben gasped.

"I think so. If they target more terrible chancellors then myself."

"Like who?"

"The Tributionalists," Brudge grinned, "They dare want to pay our wealth to Skol? Vex wants us all dead. He does not care about wealth."

"I agree. Though gold does seem to calm Vex," Greben did not have the knowledge of foreign politics, and courts, as he wished he has.

"He is not the image of calm. He is old, and afraid. He plots daily in his court about his dreams to end Jestarian kind before he dies."

"And you know this how?"

"It is rumor. Gossip from tradesmen in Freestride. I have wineries there."

Eventually, a tall green Jestarian, who was old, and stiff as a board, came into the room. He was wearing a hat, and a formal butler's uniform. He came to Brudge, and immediately showed fear on his face.

"Do you have the withdrawal?" Brudge said.

"Sir, the bank..."

Brudge's cold expression became a deeper frown, with a slight quake of nervousness. "What about the bank?"

"The accounts have been seized!"

Brudge became enraged, and began some argument with his servant. Greben knew what that meant. He was not going to be paid. So, like child who did not know what is good for him, he quickly reacquired his notes. He tucked them in his shirt, where they wrapped snugly around his body, and were undetectable.

"Did you try the auxiliary credit accounts?" Brudge asked.

"I tried the other banks. All credit to you has been withheld, sir."

Brudge turned to Greben, and the two locked eyes. A hand slid to Brudge's sword again. Greben gulped. He quickly stood up to prepare to run.

Instead, Brudge gave a roar while throwing his sword into the wall. There it stuck. He plucked up the wine bottle, which was full, and marched out of the room growling with frustration. The doors to the kitchen slammed both open, and shut. He could be heard roaring obscenities down the hall.

While the initial siege of Derin Manor failed, Greben's siege succeeded. With his escape, the mighty Brudge has fallen. The Scribe met no trouble on his way out. However, his intention of trouble was to be fulfilled after he proofed his next work.

Greben is to do, what he thinks is right to do. Now, Brudge, who in the herald's mind, has allegedly murdered another finscale, may face judgment at last. The Chancellor who has attempted to pay off the Herald's guild, may see the true power he really has. The suns may set on the Derin dynasty at long last, and it made Greben wonder, what else was this contemptuous, and conniving sea-serpent really up to?

Zytle

CHAPTER TWENTY-TWO

Finally to move. This world has been so still that it was consumed by despair. With our Journey comes forth the righteous taking of action. We now have cause.

Let finscales, and platescales resume their great contest. We shall prove ourselves worthy of quarter now. Soon the calls for war will be heard.

Finscales scout ahead, swimming in the albumin sea towards new shores. They map, chart, and come ashore to find riches. However, they are still infants, and fight among themselves to no end over the spoils.

So must platescales discipline them. We take their claims in test of skill. To do so we must fight them in land, the sky, and sea. So along the faint edges of the world we march. When we move our enemies react. Thus platescale motion determines the direction of the world.

Of course, Huron was rather happy that he received a chance to serve by the sea. It is cool, and refreshing at the valley of the day. Granted, when there was no demons calling, or work to be done.

Sight of the sea was compounded by the issue of the great ship hull in the dock. This ship was noisy. It emitted a candid chorus of building sounds, shouts, belches, and flatulence from the men working.

It towered three decks, and was nearly a Wyvern's wing span. Huron never could imagine something so big staying afloat. Vessels of Huron's younger years seem like rafts compared to this. It drew his gaze at every moment.

Likewise he never imagined someone so short garnishing so much glamour of his own. Zytle is a strange white platescale that commanded more respect then his clothing, and wings displayed. He is the Kiri'grana who Huron now serves. Everyone obeys him at this dock, and yet he does no visible labor, or gives direct commands.

This relationship was made immediately after Huron lost his fight at the tavern. Huron's large fit form attracted Zytle, and so he offered him work. Since this positioned him far away from Tailya, this was an offer Huron could not turn down.

Normally dock labor was not for his kin. Huron was raised a tool smith. Years of hammering broken farm implements, dashing around forges, and being taught the ways of fire, were his experiences. Filing, trimming, molding, melting, and alloys were known to him. So was lifting crates, but not warehousing them. This change was welcomed, as it has few burdens of thought.

Tailya did not like Huron's new station. She had quit the Gateway Tavern that night in an outbreak of hysteria. She moved to work at some barely standing tavern called Talsworth's Keg, with Zytle's recommendation to the owner. It is in a upper class district. She accepted the offer after calming down, and realizing she was no use at a dock for mostly anything.

Even with this change, the workhouse situation was the same. They remained to their own room, and their shifts were placed so they would share it at night. This made it impossible to sleep at the workhouse. Tailya stank, was always fussy. She also threatened to sleep upon Huron multiple times.

Huron took refuge under the docks. He set up home next to a few crabs, and a fish carcass. There he built a small hay pile, with pillows, to curl tightly on. He would not sleep around someone who wants him to betray his bond to Selay.

It is better, and the work was more preferable now then ever. Huron could take in deep, nose-full breaths, and not feel anything other then a minor gag reflex from the rotting fish smell. What is most enjoyable was he had his mind in order, and could concentrate on more important burdens of the soul.

A large crane groaned as it carried a wooden platform with stacks of wood beams upon it. Its efforts were made worse by a large group of gulls gathered upon the arm. Under it a pudgy, yellow man, middle-aged, and with ringed horns patrolled along the dock. He stopped to glare into Huron with eyes as if he wanted to fight him.

Huron knew what that meant, but he had no response other then to shrug his wings. There was no work at the moment, as today's delivery was done. The next boat was just a lonely shadow on the horizon. Huron pointed to it, and the older man frowned, snorted, and just continued walking.

Too new he is to be trained in the intimate organization of the dock warehouses, so all there is to do is dumb labor. When there was no labor to be had, he just stood around, and looked rather dumb. That is until someone told him what to do, then he only felt dumb.

A sailor on a mast of the distant ship sounded a horn proudly. A call of a Skol war horn, signifying vassalage to the Kingdom. The ship's sails were two fold, and waving down them in separate cloth were the red, and gold Skol banners of the platescale merchants. Outlines of Ua, and Ain's likeness, white, and black, both laying in gold borders were embroidered upon it.

The entire dock sprung to life, and a mess of fellows erupted from various hiding places. One patted Huron on the shoulder, as he walked by, to let him know that he should get ready. Huron swayed his tail, and looked up. Which was just about all he could do.

From the balcony, Zytle shouted something to Huron's dock-master. The gold fat man, who was Huron's supervisor, let out a summoning bark. The entire staff under him assembled just before the pier. Four men gathered, and watched the incoming ship.

When the schooner came close, Huron could read the name, 'The Loyal Treasure.' His eyes became wider. This was Captain Jennu's ship. This was something of legends.

Captain Visek Jennu is well known to most in eastern Skol provinces. He was once captured by the Jestarian Navy, and suffered their abuse first hand. This involved the deliberate clipping of his talons, and washing with lye. In the war, he was a raiding captain against the Jestarian Island Colonies. His ships were always fast, agile, and light. His reputation for harassing Jestarian Naval patrols was sung in bedtime stories. His crew would fly in, set fire to a fortress, or ship, then fly out. They would provide distractions, diversions for the Skol transports, and harassment to prevent larger engagements.

When the war ended, and the world stopped, he became a merchant trader. Eventually he acquired "The Loyal Treasure" after loosing a fight. The ship was sunk off the shallow waters of a rural Tram town. He took out debts, and somehow repaired it. It became his flagship, and the favorite of the merchant's fleet. Jennu proved that ships can be restored, even after they were crusted over with mold, and dirt.

He grew a reputation for mingling across the empire with the many daughters of dukes. This lead to heralds publishing stories of mixed clutches. Which would be garnishment for arrest if true. However, none could catch the captain long enough to confirm it. No one really could consistently describe his features.

Huron never met Jennu, as he traveled on transport ships in main convoys. So he only heard stories. Stories that Huron did not know were just fabrications by the Armour's Guild. Stories for schoolchildren, or gravid women bored in their nest. Stories that told long tails of grande wars, and adventures. They inspired youngsters to join the navy, and army to face the Trial.

The sails by this time were long hoisted. It was still too far to really see any of the crew. The vessel slowed into a position by the dock. A team of three broke from the rank, and came up to align with its expected position. Thick ropes were flung from the deck, and used to heave the boat eventually close enough to glide easily off. Two large moldy anchors dropped into the water, the ship stopped. Finally, a wooden plank was ascent out to the dock by skinny platescales with no shirt. From there, the captain came to shore.

He stood upright, his wings folded, and his chest puffed some to express a sense of authority, or arrogance. His complexion ocean blue, with a green belly, and red spots along his plates. He wore expensive leather hide boots of iron and steel rings. His gloves were thick, and brown. He wore a torn up wartime navy captain's coat with rivets on the sleeves. Under it a vest, and a belt with a large buckle. On his side a simple short sword, and on his head a bicorne hat from the colonies. Behind him were curled horns, and two horns along his muzzle with breaks, and cracks down his lip scales. Most of his scales were broken in places. The base of his frills, and horns, showed a roughness which made Jennu look to be much older then he was told about in stories. However, not old enough to make him frail. He concealed any signs of age well as he walked to the gold man in front of the team.

"Captain Jennu, and the Loyal Treasure, arriving at port Freestride, dock-master Thelis."

"Yes. Noted," golden-scales Thelis marked something on a paper, "You are two days earlier then expected. Explain yourself?"

"We were refused port at two stops," the captain frowned some, "Local events, a fire, and a potential outlaw in town. We did not have to go through inland rivers to trade this time."

"So shall we be dealing with leftover cargo?"

"Yes. Our cargo is specific to its buyer."

The two continued discussion of manifests, and things of merchant news. All in imprecise words that Huron paid no ear to. He spent most of this time admiring the ship of Jennu's. He imagined his times at sea, and how peaceful, and boring they were. Staring upon endless water, and wishing for land. Sleeping his days away, or playing with other children in limited space.

A whistle from Thelis brought Huron to attention.

"We are to unload some cargo from the warehouse today. It is a small order of fifty crates. I want Fendle, and Huron carrying..."

A slap on the tail brought Huron to turn. He saw a green roughed man with large arms, and a seemingly excited smile down his maw. It is Fendle, Huron's associate, who was overly eager to prove his worth, and get paid.

"Let us get this done quick. I have a record to beat! Free fish dinner for the man who gets done before sunset!" He chattered excited.

Fendle lead Huron up to quartermaster of the ship. They

received a manifest with details of the crates they had to carry. He then read it, and showed it to Huron.

When asked about the content of them, the quartermaster said, "Fairly light. Three stones each at best. We will be on leave in town tonight, and provisions naught have to be loaded until tomorrow."

Dutifully, the two made their way to the hold. For what was maybe the rest of their shift, they carried all the crates from the hold to the top deck. A simple plan, with no expectation of trouble.

However, trouble made itself present. One of the crates, which was rotted along one side, gave its final break. Four others tumbled down, and broke along with it, the products rolled out onto the floor.

Fendle stared in horror at his failure. He looked as if he was about to weep for it. Huron remained calm, and ambivalent. It did not matter how bad the mess was, he knew that he could fix it. After all, Huron is a tool smith. He can use his tail to hammer a nail.

The items that were exposed were Jestarian, and abnormal. A bolt of silk of a Jester banner design was the first noticeable cargo. Another was a Jestarian dress, with obvious sides cut out for fins to hang through, and more leg space showing then there should be. Then there was the the Marsh Mellow, a purple flower found only in the Jestarian marshlands along the coast. There was plenty of it. It was clear that this was contraband, as a Skol embargo on Jestarian imports is in effect.

However, an object that Huron could not identify caught his eye. It was a tiny green sheet of glass, not transparent, but reflected like glass. Upon it were golden trim patterns. Setting within it were cut black stones, with thin metal strips melted to the sheet. The stones had patterns crossed under right into the way of the the trim. There was no order to it at all. Perhaps it was a child's toy from Jester? Or some decorative wall hanging? Finscales are queer enough to claim anything is art.

Huron stopped caring, and began to examine the crates to try to repair things. He tore off parts that were damaged, and broken. Fendle was scurrying around panicked, and anxious. His large form was unfitting for the quick, childlike motions.

"We are going to be skinned!" He squeaked, "They will starve us too. No fish dinners for us!"

Huron did not bother to answer. He managed to salvage enough wood to rebuild one of the boxes, but he needed to make some cheese glue to finish the job. He smiled just a little at the idea of going to the shipyard, and asking for cheese.

"What in the idle is this!" Jennu stormed oto the deck, and approached the pair.

Fendle ran up to Jennu, knelt down, and lowered his head, "I am sorry! They fell. We should have been more careful."

Jennu's proud, and noble act was now more savage as he growled loudly. He bypassed Fendle, and examined the mess. By now, Huron was stacking the Marsh Mellow on top of the lid of a crate he salvaged, so he could later move it quickly.

Jennu grabbed Huron, and glared into his big eyes. Huron was genuinely startled. He showed his fear with a concerned stare back, and ears drooping.

"What makes you so arrogant as to ignore your better!?" Jennu snarled.

Huron frowned, "I am sorry. I am trying to fix what I could."

"Fix it before I found out?" Jennu pushed Huron away from his work, and towards Fendle, "So you could tell the guards!"

Huron stumbled after the second push by Jennu. He fell onto his knees, and looked up at the captain. It was clear that he was in trouble. Jennu whistled, and motioned to one of his crew-mates. Who approached, and handed him a rolled up whip.

"You may not be my crew, but what you did must receive atonement." He said.

"Please no, sir! We will do better! Show mercy!" Fendle cried.

Huron accepted his fate, and looked down. If he was to be punished for fixing his own mess, then it would not be his position to refuse. He caused it, and so he must suffer for it.

"Jennu! Stop this!" yelled Zytle as he marched up to the deck board.

Jennu snarled, letting his whip unroll, and drop onto the deck. It was a heavy leather, likely horse hide. It was hard to tell, as it smells of saltwater.

"They know about things they do not belong knowing." Jennu did not face Zytle, "They should know only their place."

Zytle gripped Huron's arm, and urged him to stand, "This one is Kiri'grana. He deserves more respect."

"He did not acknowledge my presence! On my ship!" Jennu flexed his claws, and thrashed his tail.

"He is a Quirksettle. Like his father, he fixes things. A skilled smith looses himself in his work," Zytle replied, "He is a potential master of his craft."

"So what? Whipping insubordinate, and unobservant servants also can fix things, Zytle."

"He is not my servant. He is a peer," Huron noticed a trailing off slightly on Zytle's use of the word 'servant.' "I only whip my slaves."

Jennu gave the whip a piercing test crack. Fendle

whimpered, and held his hands on his muzzle. He laid on his belly on the floor, and stretched out his wings.

Jennu stared at Huron, and uttered with a sardonic tone, "Amazing..." was all Huron heard, because the demon returned to him.

One of his time with his father. Where when he saw a great Warlord, Vesuvious Vex holding his own whip. One made of Wyvern hide, with a set of nails along the tips. Huron once saw the warlord curse, and laugh as he lashed a insubordinate soldier upon the back scales.

He was stopped by a greater Warlord in stature, but a peer of rank. One who of blue, bearing the familiar patterns of his Selay. He held Vex's arm still just as Huron saw the exposed spine of the poor man. It was sad to say that Huron later learned this warrior died of his wounds. He never knew the reasons for such abuse by the Kiri'grana, but it was the moment that Huron's demon felt to use to stun him.

So no whip came, and Zytle had his hand on Jennu's shoulder. Jennu looked upon Huron, and pulled his head back. The captain knelt down to glare into Huron's eyes.

"You saw the war like I have. I can see the demon taking hold of you," Jennu seemed to lower his defenses, "Vex's first curse is within us both."

The broken-scaled captain sat down in front Huron for what seemed forever. Not a word spoken, as if they both knew what has come to consume them. The ghosts that keep them from enjoying peace bellowed within. They must suffer their sorrow. They are cowards, indulging in lies, and distorted memories.

Both lived the war. They are vessels for the innocent they slain. Who come from the Idle to pull them down. They Journey with us, by the declaration of repentance of Vex. Who uttered spells, and curses, when he slaughtered the family of cowards who signed the Uneasy Armistice: the treaty that stopped the world.

Huron's demon reminded him of the blood flowing from broken forms of his family. Rivers upon his feet. Jennu's demon was of farther fallen things, of innocent finscale eggs crushed by his own talons. Their unborn children floating in blood, and gasping.

Finally, Jennu broke the silence, "I should whip you until you scream. However, if you do me a favor, you can avoid punishment. This matter is urgent, and you must loose no time solving it. I may also trust you, brother. What say you?"

Kiven

CHAPTER TWENTY-THREE

We move alone, and this is not wise. We may be armed with the weapons, knowledge, and spirit. Though sadly in knowing, we see we are facing something far greater then one can manage. Let us call forth a formation.

Promise them a share of the treasure. They will not come for the bread, and comfort alone. They too demand entry into the eternal armies of the heavens.

The idea of appeasing others was lost to Selay, whose belly is filled with dissent. She has little gratitude openly, and refuses to submit to her betters. She takes joy in offense, and baths in the infamy.

She should bend knee to Brudge. His support for her trouble making should be reciprocated. He pampers her, as she awoke to a perfectly humid, and silent room. She was on her belly, in a bed of cotton, not straw. The sheets were satin, and the pillows exceptionally soft. This was a room for a queen, which Selay was going to squander. By intending to kick Brudge, and laugh as he rolled on the floor.

A candle flickered dimly by the nightstand, barely gleaming the room's stone walls. Selay swayed her tail fully while looking around. Her back stung from her wound. Her body is burning from her desperate attempt to save Brudge.

There was a wooden bowl, with a shard of glass resting inside it. A crimson cloth dangled from the side. She smelled her familiar stink on it, and wondered who treated her wound. Then scoffed at the idea of rewarding a finscale.

She is vulnerable, and thus sat up. Wisdom would be to stay laying, and rest, but she was left naked. She hissed at the pain as she moved. It was out of the question to be defenseless in Brudge's manor. Even though his stink was not lingering in the room, he could be nearby. If he pounced, she will kick him.

Once sitting on the edge of the bed, she felt a fierce jab on her rear. At first she expected a trap, but after examining it, she found her detached horn. Sighing in relief, she grasped it.

The mirror across the room let her see herself so as long as she squinted. There she learned she was still intoxicated, and puttered happily. This expression was enough motion to loosen a set of bandages wrapped around her body that she was unaware of previously. Wine does not make one prone to seeing everything, but it also makes you see twice as much. Selay removed, and tossed them to the floor. She saw they were only slightly stained with her blood.

Eventually she became bored of herself, got up with horn in hand, and moved towards the mirror. She glared, aligning the horn behind her head, and adjusted the ring, and bolts to reattach it. After a bit of fine adjustments she smiled at her symmetry, happy to look normal again.

Stumbling around the room, looking for something to wear, she chuckled. She fell onto a double-door dresser which contained a single dress. Throwing it to the side of the bed, she scoffed.

It was Jestarian, and quite exposing. The covering for the breasts was thick, but every other location, especially around the tail, was unappealing. The dress even lacked buttons to cover under the tail. The tailbelt was only silk. It was absolutely not designed for a platescale, or any person without fins.

Selay finally threw it aside in revolt. The front skirt was deliberately restrictive. She did not want to wear anything the would impeded her motion to kick Brudge, so if she willed it. It was better to be naked, then to dress like a Jestarian harlot. Selay could never let herself look like a member of a roost.

Again sitting alongside the bed, near the nightstand, she caught sight of plate of fruits. One was a clearly shaped pear, which caused her belly to roar at her. She lunged for it, and immediately bit into its soft skin.

So much travel, left Selay lacking on rations. Her fish jerky was consumed within less then a day, and she refused to stop to catch more. Now with saving Brudge behind, eating was something she could do. A pear, no matter how upsetting its flavor is, is welcomed.

Continuing to look around the room, there was nothing else to disdain. No pictures, and not a sign of her leather Armour. There was a door, and it was closed. On the nightstand, by the bowl of fruits, was a bloody sewing kit, showing they stitched her.

With the pear properly decimated, Selay moved onto her next victim. A round, stupid looking, green fruit with a hard shell. She never saw anything like it, and when she bit into it, failed to penetrate it. She hopelessly gnawed, failing to find a hole to puncture. Then examined it closer, and it reminded her of one of the eggs she whiteness consumed.

She threw the fruit away, and reeled back in horror. Her heart raced, and her blood boiled. She rose quickly, and slammed the door open as she left the room.

The dark, and stuffy hallway Selay entered was

immediately familiar. During her first stay, she would explore the entire complex, and found a basement where Brudge held private meetings. The conference room was adjoined by this hallway, which lead to store rooms, and now a bedroom.

Her feet thumped on the floor as she advanced, there was no need for stealth. The only threat in this hall could easily be kicked. When she was merely half through, a shorter Jestarian woman came out of another door, and stood in front of her.

"You cannot go upstairs until the Master says so," She immediately ordered.

She stunk of lilac, and was wearing a dress like the one Selay refused to wear. Her spots, and scales made her look like a dull minnow. Clearly this was one of Brudge's roost. Probably the better homemaker of them, as her fins were petite.

"Brudge is not my master. I demand to see him." Selay responded.

The woman looked over Selay, examining her entire body, "No! Go back to your room!"

"Out of my way!" Selay tried to push her, and found her easy. Diligently the finscale flanked, and reformed the blockade. She held her wings, and arms open to become a wall.

"I am commanded to hold you at bay! Brudge can not have you storming around here while the Heralds are patrolling!" she growled, "Especially without cloths!"

Selay tried once again to move past her. Then rumbled a bit at the challenge. When the second attempt failed, the platescale flung open her wings, stood to full height, puffed up her chest, then snarled.

"I will throw you to the ground if you not let me pass!"

The Jestarian squeaked, and looked up at Selay with wide eyes, and clear fear. It is easy to scare her, as Selay is taller, and bulkier. She is also preceded by her reputation of drunken destruction, and viscous combat.

"At least put something on," She stuttered.

"Where is my Armour?"

"Others took it to the river to be washed. It was covered in blood, and a smelly oil. We gave you a dress to wear," meekly spoke out the finscale.

Selay maintained her posture, "I will not be so low as to entertain him with my submission."

"The dress does not mea-"

"It means I will look like the rest of his roost. I prefer nothing at all."

The woman was offended, and used it to hide her fear. Selay tried to get in close, and the finscale looked to her side, thrashed her tail, bore some teeth, and held back a whimper, "Brudge loves us."

"I am not his whore! I will not look like one!" Selay scolded.

"Stop this!" The finscale rumbled as Selay got in close to her eyes, and bore her teeth, "Brudge takes care of us! You are one of us."

"Then as one of you I demand to see him," Selay loomed near her maw, where a deadly bite could be levied, "If he does not know what I know, then we all shall die."

"I have my task!" She held her ground.

Selay readied to slam the thick scales of her head upon the finscale's to scare her into a fight, or to flee. However, she unwittingly placed a hand on the woman's belly. With unclaimed egg's in her, she wined, and cried pitifully. A single push would have been enough kill her now. According to the size, she was a week until passing.

"He is sunbathing!" The Jestarian cried, "Do not do this!"

Selay pulled her claws back, and felt uncomfortable

with what she did. There are many places she never should rightfully go, and that was one. The platescale lowered her stance, and took a step back.

"Forgive me. I just wanted to move you. I was going to headbunt. I am sorry." She kept a snarl, but almost pleaded.

The minnow finscale bowed her head in submission, and sniffed. Selay frowned at herself. Then she walked by the woman calmly.

She knew she could overpower, and strike a deal with this woman. Perhaps enslave her? However the idea of keeping a Jestarian maidservant was lousy. They do not fair well in the wild lands, and if they do not swim regularly they will get sick all the time. She would be a burden, even though Selay could afford the costs with her new bounty.

With no more resistance, the platescale hussy stormed down the hallway in a staggering pattern. Into the conference room, she tripped. Then caught herself on the table.

The room is a dungeon for sinister affairs. Ready to use, after a quick cleaning. Everything was covered, and cobwebs were covering the covers. It has the Jestarian fish stink lingering within it too. It fit the requirements of good place to strangle someone.

Eventually she became familiar with her state of inebriation enough to walk steady. When she arrived by the hall before the wine cellar, with the broken doorway, and sunlight peering down, she took a breath. Then rightfully towards it, and left up the same stairs she climbed last night.

Two flights up, and several house staff were dotting about. They all gave the naked platescale threatening looks. However whenever she made eye contact, they looked away, and acted busy. Every face was familiar to Selay, all were the hapless mob who watched her kill to save their employer. They were all on guard.

The Sun Room was just across the hallway behind a set of double doors marked ironically with two suns. Selay swung them open. Inside is a room only a rich fool would want. A glass roof kept the place alight, there was a rock in the center.

The room was made into an artificial marsh plot. Where grass was grown on transplanted soil. Shrubs were carefully cut to not overgrow. Vines, and moss were allowed to climb columns, and rot the wood. Water bodies formed a basic irrigation system that kept the plants mostly green, and rich. Outside air was allowed in, making it comfortable, hot, and humid. There was a brick path that extended to just before the rock grove. Selay followed it.

Upon the rock was a most hideous sight. A naked Brudge. Which to say was not as fit as his clothing made him. Surrounding the rock was a collection of bottles, empty. Brudge himself was sprawled out upon the rock, limp, his head facing the door. His wings laid out erratically.

Selay steadied herself next to him. This mutually assured exposure she found disagreeable. Regrets of eating that pear were surfacing, but not fully enough to cause her to want to run. She only slightly felt the need to kick him.

Brudge made a foul lurching as he heard her footclaws tap on the stone path. He was unfortunately alive, and immediately lifted a bottle up for a drink. Once satisfied, he slowly opened his crossed eyes.

"Ua, why do you torment me by taking her form?" He mumbled a plea, "I serve you, and you refuse to give me your true splendor? I cared for your children. Please! I serve to see the truth!"

Brudge was clearly delusional, and Selay had no time for this. She crossed her arms defensively, and leaned some while shaking her head. She tapped a footclaw in preparation for a just kick to his nose.

Abruptly, Brudge rolled up. If by rolling up, it was meant to be falling to his feet from a laying position, then he most certainty was up. He was standing, that much could be established, when he was finished.

"Ua! I submit only to you! Embrace your son!" Brudge opened his wings, and arms. He stumbled towards Selay. Who put her hands out in ready to throw the man off her.

However his trajectory was all forsaken. With heavy stumbling, the naked, smelly finscale hugged the empty space well enough away to not even touch Selay. The hug was so intense that Brudge put his entire weight into it, and all that bulk went onto the floor at the same time. The wretched creature was so drunk, he saw two.

"I am not dead?" Brudge pouted on the floor.

"No. You do not get to sleep with your great adulteress," Selay gave a soft chuckle.

Brudge was rightly angered at this heretical insult of Ua, and tried to raise to his feet to confront Selay. As he rose he yelled, "Do not insult the Great Mother!"

It would have been somewhat threatening, but the entire assault was ended when Brudge fell back on his knees. He had no balance from his drinking, and neither any whit about him. It amused Selay to see him this way, daft, and easily mislead. Normally he would be sly, and confident, and reading his body posture was required. He seems pitiful, and broken now.

"Least Ain sings with you when he judges. Ua curls up with everyone," Selay began her heretical ministry with a divisive statement.

"Ua is not that way!" Brudge looked up towards Selay, and his eyes would not fixate on her face, "It is like a mother with her child."

"You clearly do not read the stories," Selay explained, "Ain's stories are all about teaching her not to curl with others."

"Not true! Those stories are clawed by pervert priests who do not know anything! Ua's tenderness is a mother's wing," Brudge stalled as he talked, his face gazing upward at Selay at he breathed in the embers of spring.

"Now that I have your attention." Selay swayed her hips, and turned around. She moved far out of Brudge's reach. When she turned to face she saw his eyes were staring right under her tail, "Whichever eye stares the lowest, I will eat."

Brudge laughed rolled onto his back on the ground. He kept staring, looking wherever he wanted, "You dare tell me not to look! You come here bare in springtime. That is a proposal for marriage at least."

"You did not give me a proper garment to wear. I am platescale. My scales catch, and tear thin silks. My body requires more space for bulkier plates. I do not have fins to hold up loose garments." Selay scolded.

"Then you should have waited for your cloths. Instead you offer me your glamour for the taking. If this is not your game, then what is it you play?" Brudge rubbed his forehead.

"I know who plots to kill us. I have their names. You must know too." Selay stated.

Brudge laughed, "You simpleton! It is easy too determine who. It is the Tributionalists in the chancellorship."

He continued, "Last meeting, I vetoed multiple requests to send payment to Skol. I called their names for this. They seek peace with Vex. They want to bribe him out of war. So they want me out of the way for obstructing them."

Selay rolled her eyes, Brudge did not notice. He had no idea. He immediately blames his rivals without proof.

Jestarian legislation is a terrible, and impossible, stone to move. Especially without a king. Every chancellor has veto rights, thus law requires unanimous support to pass. This means nothing ever is done, and the finscales waste time bickering. Brudge's Veto on a law is nothing new.

Back into a defensive pose, Selay saw how she could kick him. She targeted his ribs, but did not move to do so. After a period of silence, her thoughts dwell to the eggs consumed, and she growled.

"Brudge, that stupid Fordako Pact forbids violence in the chancellorship! You can not see that this is someone else? The enemy is far more worse then a bunch of eels who cannot vote to clean the mold off their asses."

Brudge laughed, "They do all have moldy asses for sure! My servants always complain of fester after one of them shows up. Still you make such a stupid claim. You are not my only spy in Jester. We all work through proximity. What do I not know?"

"Those who conspire against us are egg poachers," Selay's tail thrashed. She was having a hard time staying calm.

"Egg poachers? I do not deal in judgment for such a crime. I do not think the-"

"They eat them! I saw a whole clutch devoured!" Selay interrupted, "Journey's Rest theater is one of their fronts!"

Brudge sat up, glaring at Selay, "That is unheard of! I cannot accuse others of such a crime without proof. Especially the Quad family."

"It is true. They spoke of trying to murder you, and seize all your assets. When I heard, I ran. You took my Armour, I have proof on my pouches! I have the skull seal of the killers!" Selay yelled.

"That seal was on the one who tried to kill me. They are mercenaries. I do not trust your drunk memory, as I do not trust mine!" Brudge lifted himself up, and returned to his bathing rock to sit. He held his forehead, and swayed.

There was a strange pause, and Selay turned away. She displayed clear growls of frustration. The desire to go, and kill those she knew were behind this was unbearable. Brudge was helpless, this is not like him, she needed him to remain clever to help her.

He mumbled something, and it ended with him saying, "I should turn you in for a bounty."

Selay gave him the cold stare she would give only to something she intended to bite, "You dare?"

"They took everything. My businesses, my money. In less then a week my allies will abandon me. I am desperate, and I should send you back to Skol in chains for what you put me through."

"And that is?" Selay snarled.

"You stole the royal stave of Skolis, come to my home, refuse my courting, take from me, and murder someone in front of the entire staff. Then, you insult Ua, and stand before me like you are better," Brudge looked cold, and heartless, "You are better off turned in for your crimes, before the Heralds can can accuse me of all manner of things."

Selay clenched her fists, and was ready to charge at him. She felt betrayed, but not defeated. If he intends to betray her, she will have to kill him. He is beginning to sound complacent.

"Yes. I could give that little herald his story," Brudge thought out-loud, "A Skol spy trying to kill the one senator who refuses to bend to the Empire. I would gain the support of the people over night."

Such a knavery. Selay glared, and calculated her next move. She would kill him, escape, and hide. She bore her teeth, as he tried to stand. After she just acquired such wealth to buy her own home, she would be abandoned? Then it dawned on her, a means to prevent it.

"There is no bounty to collect. I claimed it myself."

Selay smiled.

"Such a shame," Brudge was up, and swaying about, "Then you will just have to surrender that money to me."

"Stop this tail pulling! You should have killed me in my sleep," Selay demanded, she lunged forward, and pushed Brudge, who fell right back on his tail with a startled roar.

He was quickly back to his feet, laughing, and opening his wings while puffing up his chest, "The bank seized my wealth. You may have saved me, but you owe me for the damage you wrought today! I am your debt master! Your earnings belong to me."

"I am not yours' to command! You cannot just take haphazardly!" Selay opened a claw, and prepared to slash at him, "You will have to fight me, if you want me to submit to you."

Brudge saw her ready. He crouched, and prepared to brawl. The Jestarian laughed pretentiously. He thrashed his finned tail threateningly behind him.

The two lingered in their pose. Neither wanting to take the first move. Eventually, Brudge cursed, and gave up, "I can not do this!"

Selay could, and she maintained her posture, "If you continue this betrayal talk, I will leave you dead in the same hole as Kiven will be."

"Kiven?" Brudge tilted his head, "My banker?"

Selay frowned, "Kiven is one of them. He is behind this. I shall kill him, his stomach will prove me right."

Brudge huffed, "I will not let you kill Kiven! I forbid it!"

"Then hope you can kill me here," Selay challenged, "I will not let this evil continue."

"Not Kiven!" Brudge scolded, "He has locked away my wealth! Not until I get it back!"

"And you do not call upon Aurix?" Selay snorted.

"It is a formal decree from the courts," Brudge sighed, "They claim things about not following regulations in my new homes."

"Why do you not have a chest of gold yourself?" Selay laughed.

"With you around? Stealing my wine! Never." Brudge pointed.

"Then seize the bank!" Selay yelled, "This is your domain. This is a fraud!"

"Not without a judge, and a reason."

"Threaten them!" snorted Selay.

"I am not a platescale!" Brudge shook his fist.

"Then I shall kill Kiven, and you can seize his bank in the liquidation."

"It will raise the alarm, and all my enemies will bring suit to me." Brudge explained, as he rubbed the side of his head. He looked as if he was about to feint.

"Then I do not need you to kill. I will do this myself." Selay turned, and walked away.

"No! Selay, you shall not kill. Or I will hunt you down." Brudge roared.

Selay ignored his command, and swayed her hips as she slowly walked towards the double doors. She took her time, so he could decide. Smiling spitefully.

"Selay! Stop!" He commanded.

She began to sing a rather out-of-tune song in mid-saunter, "They will die, Gew Vi' Jar, one bolt in his eye!"

She shook her rear to Brudge, and kept her tail low. Taunting, and teasing him. She sneered, as she lead him into actually doing more then just yelling. He must stop her.

She sung some more, "Vias Ea' Quad is fat, so three bolts will do! With blades for piercing his scales!"

She was halfway to the doors now, and gave her hind a smack. The taunt was enough to get Brudge to charge towards her.

"THAT IS ENOUGH!" Brudge roared as he flanked Selay, and stood in directly in front of her. "You are making me an accomplice to murder now!"

Selay smiled at him, "I think it is fair to know who your murderers will be."

She easily bypassed him, and made a faster move towards the door. Brudge did not let her get more then a few steps before he gripped, and pulled her tail. Selay tripped, and caught herself by her hands, only to be dragged back to where she started.

"I will need your money," he said. "Otherwise, we will never find Kiven."

Selay got back to her feet, and slapped the finscale's face for touching her, "You cannot demand what is not yours!"

"Then I will beat it out of you!" Brudge threatened.

"With what, a good time?" Selay chided. "My scales are from the Skolis Valley."

"Then I request you to credit it to me."

Selay became a bit more amiable on the spot, "I demand a fee of half the total value. If you want to use me like this, I must have something in return. I have to cover the soap costs of washing what you pay me."

Brudge nodded in agreement, he was lacking choice in the matter, "When I have the bank keys, I can afford that. Do not kill Kiven until then."

Selay smiled in agreement. She thought of the house she wanted to buy. One that she could hide in forever, and eventually bring Huron to.

"Now that we are not at each other's throats, Selay." Brudge opened his wings, and leaned his face towards her neck. "Let me thank you pro-OOOOPH"

He was met with a decisive kick to the belly. Once again crashing to the ground. Selay puffed up proudly at her victory.

"I never told you! My chosen is a farmhand named Huron in Tram. I will never betray him! You are not going to have me, for he is a very strong platescale. You do not wish to anger him, as he can rip your head off." Selay threatened.

Brudge was too winded to speak, and nodded in agreement. He looked disappointed as he curled up, gasping. His tail shook as it positioned to protect his soft belly. He would recover, Selay returned to a slow saunter out of the room.

She later forgave him, as she did provoke him with her teasing. She spent the evening preparing herself. A bath, a lot of food, and plenty of sleep. Her wounds cleaned with finscale wines, and plastered with honey. She later finally gave Brudge the credit he needed. When she did, he seemed joyous, and filled a chest with it. He gave a slip of credit, with the name: '"Rixor.'

He was his usual conniving finscale self again. Stern, hidden, and glaring.

Selay departed quickly. Brudge had the resources now, and so did she. She now moved in formation. Much stronger, and more apt to face what is coming.

Toumoistium

CHAPTER TWENTY-FOUR

There is a dire need to be true here. What is wrong must be challenged. Otherwise we would volley our attacks incorrectly.

All our vetting requires proof that should be observed, then collected. Things must be relative, and thus shine. The must alight the direction to face.

This is easier in war. Knowing what your army needs to march, in exact quantities, can be counted on ledgers. Our targets can be easily seen via banners. The truth is not so blatant in peace. It has become a silly game of manipulation, and a dance of deceit.

The drought of conflict has left us vulnerable to lies, and distortions. We succumb to the lull of security, and thus lower our guard. So much that even the senses of the rational are pushed aside.

Brudge's Jestarian mannerisms have lead him down a way he now deserves. Which is indebted to a contemptible platescale to keep his power. His nature turns to leveraging with morose allies in one last cry for conflict. War he will have, in the courthouse, and in the seas. He will rend a fire through the Marshlands of Jester.

The strings of this tapestry weave through all his staff. Servants spread talk to merchants, suggesting of a bounty of wealth for anything on his foes. Others began to swarm, and pull favor for special rights. His little enterprise stirs with new bickering. Although, not without a pay raise to stay quite about his pet platescale.

The roost in his manor bound together in an effort to appease. His time now consumed by a troop of them caring for his every scale. One always stationed nearby to guard him. Within this gaggle, there is snarling of arguments over everything. The only unifying force is protecting Brudge. Especially from Selay.

It was the day of the loan that Brudge had to deal with each quarter of his manor, but it was the night of the loan that the carrier pigeons flew. Along with a sprinting Selay. The morning after the incident, the Deep Lake Heralds began the assault.

The forces around Brudge began to counter the songs. Before noon a Seafarer Alchemist, one known for chewing lumps of coal, inked a response to the West Deep Lake Heralds. He hissed about the foul betrayals they made to the Derin family. He stood on his reputation in defense of the Chancellor, which was not worth a single hair off a northerner's backside.

The story made rounds in the gossip circles of the women in the city. After much empty talk about orgies, and roosting, Brudge's fate was sealed by supper. Since favor with the chancellor is a nepotism that could lead to wealth, gossip about Brudge was centered around how to impress him without angering their husbands. This unfathomable network erased any agitation from the morning's missive.

The Northern Heralds did not stand for such silence. They commissioned a small army of criers to go about the various districts of Northern Deep Lake. One stood, and rang bells in front of every tavern, and market. He roared a new set of stories about Brudge.

Most were aggressive insults scolding the Chancellor, and his allies. With a notice handed out titled: "Siege of Derin Estates." These were carefully sharpened claws grasping at the wind. Everyone gathered to listen, amused as legend of Brudge's sins were told. The situation became further frustrated by a buyout of lemons in the marketplace.

The cries of injustice went into the night. Leading to the Town Watch kicking the heralds off their stoops for keeping them from napping at their posts. Though no one could disperse the river poor who gathered to discuss. The conversations were heated, but nothing more then one baring of fangs was witnessed. The crowds dispersed in the early morn when everyone was too tired to care.

It was three days till the news reached Southern Deep Lake. All the heralds of the city are about it. It had to travel the roads along the coast, where it was posted in all places.

On their way to the courthouses, the Kiri'grana of the Tributionalists were pelted with, what is alleged to be, mud by angry river poor yelling, "Returning volley for Chancellor Derin!"

The Courthouse of Deep Lake opened to a ruckus of geese. Who then chased, and bit at everyone. These birds were found to be enlisted, and set loose, by two fowl distinct members of the Populists factions. These panksters were quickly whipped, stripped naked, placed in the pillory, and whipped again for good measure.

This event became the entertainment of the district. It was such a celebration that a local wine merchant gave a rather steep discount on his bulk supply in honor of the geese who 'were the delicious heroes of this whole affair.'

Such price fixation was a complete violation of

regulation. The sudden access of cheap drink for the poor in such ample supply upset the very fabric of Jestarian life. The Riverpoor mostly drink oat, or wheat beers, and had no tolerance for wine.

The morning heralds took upon their podiums to find the River Poor agitated, and demoniacal. The more scandalous stories created a reaction that will become a Deep Lake tradition for generations to come. In that custom, a smelly, unwashed crowd of festering finscales will uplift a town crier to dump him into a well. Then turn upon every warehouse, market wine stall, and tavern for looting. This event will be known to all as: The Deep Lake Well Riots.

However, the first time of this tradition caused an unnatural glut of drink. By supper, nobles of the Synyurl Loyalists Faction were eating fish dry. Which was enough to cause a significant response.

Within one fell swoop of a claw, they sent their Sergeant-at-Arms to North Deep Lake to put an end to the agitation. His name is Wer Di' Toumoistium. They handed him the seal of the Derin family, delivered by pigeon from Brudge.

He set to Northern Deep Lake via the ferry. Where he would spend the night in transport, and arrived the next day. He took a carriage out to the marketplace plaza, then walked the rest of the way.

He stopped to listen to the Herald speaking. Toumo stood out firmly in the crowd. He was pompous, constantly upright in his posture. His manor of dress was clearly of wealth, in so he wore a central black cape between his wings that covered enough to his tail to never show how it intended to sway. Which was never, due to careful training of oratory.

He wore a white overcoat, with fur cuffs, and a tunic. Like most Jestarian kind, frills showed where it need not be shown, including bare legs, arms, and sides. He carried a cane, which made him look full of self-importance.

Immaculately groomed, and polished. His red scales would shine in the sunlight. He was in his late middle age, with bags under his blue eyes from long nights studying Jestarian legal tradition.

He would be a gust of wind from a ghastly display, if not for the pouch along the side of his gold belly holding his cloths down. The bag was leather, plump with papers, and items that his profession required. He had no need to carry weapons. He had forms that would render anyone his vassal at any time if he so needed. Some gave him command of the guard.

His head was frilly, and finny like Jestarian faces are. Flowing waves of dark red strips on his forehead. He was wearing a monocle needed for reading, and bore no outward expression to the public. His maw was lengthy, and he forced his frown posture upward to show conscious displeasure towards everyone. It appears to work well in Jester, but in Skol, a platescale would think you were calling him a fish.

He observed the town crier ring his bell, singing.

"Hear ye! Fair Jestarian people! Descendants of great explorers, and lovers of Mother Ua! Chancellor Derin's manor has been under siege recently! Why does he insist on hiding the corpses?"

Murmurs in the crowd erupted. The little people were upset some. They were not drunk enough to be riotous, so Toumo did not feel threatened. What did threaten his entire position was a female who was clearly not smelling of lilac, and he had to withhold breathing nose to not look foolish in public.

"Chancellor Derin has been entirely foreclosed upon by all his investors! He has taken himself to retreat like a coward into his manor! By spring's end he shall be evicted, and his lands appropriated by the state he so serves! He will go to where he belongs for his frauds. To the river with the poor!"

Toumo could have ordered the crier arrested, but he knew better. He had to stop this at the guild headmaster. His Derin seal should be used sparingly. If he just ordered the arrest of town criers, a crisis would erupt, and there would be no end of it. This salacious nonsense is best contained with wisdom, and cunning.

Further, Brudge did not need money. He would have asked for it, it appears he is able to continue to pay his servants, and agents. Including Toumo's fees later, which would feed his family of six, soon to be ten.

"The reports of a platescale are not to be ignored. The body was carried off by servants to some unknown grave! We think the hand was finer, with more tender scales, and slender wrists! This may be a woman!"

Toumo wanted to laugh, but he resigned wisely. A platescale woman in Brudge's home was not a first. Brudge is strange indeed. During a gathering in his ballroom, Toumo remembered a blue platescale occupying a dedicated seat. She wore a dirty torn up rag for a dress, and glared at various attendees with hunter's eyes. Brudge called her the 'Ambassador of Skol,' but Toumo knew there was no women like this in the embassy, let alone dressed so terrible. She was obviously a mistress of Brudge, and he sure fawned over her as one.

"If this it true, Brudge may be nesting with a platescale! A foul thing indeed!" The herald opened his wings in fake outrage. He was bad at it, as he overly played the emotion, "No member of the council should let one so brutish near him serve our pact! Platescale women will cut off, and dine on your mast as they murder you!"

The lady with no lilac was now in plain view. Toumo felt his heart beat faster. He doused the fire with a memory of a time at Brudge's manor.

When too drunk, looking for a place to lay down, Toumo entered the room of a mistress of Brudge of different features. She was hairy, from a more northern region, but with Jestarian fins, and gills. He entered her chambers, as she was naked, and combing herself by a nightstand. She made a sweet smile as Toumo fell upon her bed to sleep. That lady later stalked him throughout the home that morning after. Brudge saw this, and discussed it. In exchange for loyalty, Toumo would be allowed to take her home to be an assistant. The next spring, they were married. Now Toumo can watch her comb, and groom every morning, at least, before the children woke.

He had no more ability to tolerate this, or hold his breath. So he continued his journey towards the Herald guild hall, which was just down the road. A brick building, fancy like all other guild halls, with a line of people waiting in front of it. They were all dressed as heralds, and wearing the guild seals.

Sharks circling after they smelled blood, which was being dumped into the waters aplenty. Toumo was not of the sharks, he was of the greater finscales who eat sharks. So he cut the line, only to be halted by two burly guards. He removed his Derin seal, and held it up.

"I am of the court! Stand aside!" He proclaimed loudly, getting everyone to watch.

One guard examined the seal, squinting at it, "Forgery! Derin is in a scandal! I expect confidence games here."

"I serve the Chancellors of Deep Lake! Do not make me override the town watch orders!"

Neither cared, nor expressed concern to care. One grabbed Toumo by the arm, and pushed him back, "Queue up like everyone else!"

There he fell on the ground, and dirtied his legs, and cape. Chuckles from the line were heard. Toumo got back up, and examined the guards: Mercenaries. They were out of his reach. If it was anyone from the watch, he could summon them to trial right away. Tua's little guild was clever.

Toumo surrendered, and stood in line. He spent all the time primping, and brushing the dirt off his cloths. The line moved slowly. Those who entered, came out with a bag full of documents, and one less bag of coins.

This is normal behavior for scribes. Though not of this volume. Springtime women's manuscripts were significant sellers. Combine that with a attempted murder of a Chancellor, and you have a fire sale.

When inside, Toumo could see the lobby was wretchedly small. It held five people who should never sway their tails, lest they desire to break someone's legs. There were three people, four if you considered the substantially fat finscale, with a grotesque chewing habit, that made Toumo feel uncomfortable.

A skinny young clerk was at the counter serving everyone diligently. He would give them a form to order from. Which was handed to a spry young assistant. Then he takes the money from the patron, who waits for the books to be gathered on the counter to be taken away.

Behind the clerk was the unending array of shelves, and artifacts. Farther behind them were silhouettes of people hunched over scribe desks writing. Each shadow's wings were tightened as they moved frantically, copying the demanded items.

Just before serving Toumo, the clerk left to investigate a book that was requested by this customer. Something titled, "Horse Tails to read While Gravid." to which the clerk shook his head, and said "We are out of that one." The customer sighed as he left, throwing his pack of documents over his shoulder.

The clerk made a happy smile at Toumo, seeing someone

dress as if he has a lot of money. He slide the listing of the news, and prices to his new customer. All of which were outrageous.

"To which you wish to purchase?" He said amiably.

Toumo read the form, adjusting his reading glasses to see. Curiosity got the better of him, as there were over twenty items of note. Half of them were related to Brudge, or one of his allies. Others were market sales, book reviews, and the usual government notices.

Toumo pushed the paper back, and gave his tail a solid knock on the floorboards, "I am a representative of the Derin Estates. I am tasked with putting a stop to these lies before it causes more disorder like it has done in the Southern districts."

The clerk held up the paper, displaying surprise. He tilted his head, as if he did not know what to think. Then he turned to the person behind Toumo, and shouted, "Next!"

Toumo was jaded at the disrespect, and slammed his cane up onto the counter top. The impact was heard across the hall, as one writing scribe cursed out. Books fell from somewhere unseen.

"I am Sir Toumoistium of the Court of Deep lake! I demand to speak to Scribe Tua!"

A spry blue man arrived to interrupt the event. His claws were black from ink. He appeared as if he has not slept much, "I am Tua, what is wrong?"

Toumo puffed his chest, "I am here to notify you of a cease, and deist from Chancellor Derin, and the Court."

Tua laughed, and waved a finger before holding out his hand, "Let me see the writ first."

The lawyer dug into his pouch, and removed a small scroll with a seal upon it. One of the Deep Lake courthouse in bold green tack. He handed it to Tua who unrolled it, and read.

A brief period of silence befallen Tua. He laughed, and threw the paper at Toumo. Who growled as it bounced off his chest.

"Charges of incitement, and defamation? By Ua and Ain, we only show what is true! I am not liable for the rowdy behavior of the others!"

"Truth? This is not truth!" Toumo made a wave of his hand, "Truth is in the sky being blue, and there are only two suns, and the moon is cracked. You soiled Chancellor Derin's name with the intent of enriching yourself. He wants justice!"

"Oh so he would! Which is why he bribed me!" Tua mocked Toumo by patting his snout, "You feckless flying snakes refuse to follow the law yourselves wrote by trying to buy me off."

Toumo held himself expressionless, he wanted to bite the little wretch.

Tua gave a smile, "Now begone. I have to write my next notice!" Before turning to walk back.

Toumo gave a quick head bob, then kicked the counter door. A crunch told him that is was once barred, and he destroyed it. Marching in, he grabbed Tua's wing, "Listen here..." he growled.

"You dare destroy guild property?" Tua bore fangs at the barrister.

The two locked gazes, and snarled at each other. They showed claws, ready to strike. No result came.

"Tua! Stop this before I throw you in the stocks myself!"

Both looked to see a rather massive man approaching. Where the spit chewing customer from earlier was large, this one looked like he ate him. He was barely wearing a tunic, with green trousers, and stunk of wine, and mackerel. With each step he heaved frightening breaths of desperation.

"Sorry, Master Accix, this man claims to be a state official." Tua bowed, and pointed to Toumo.

"He is!" the fat man arrived at last, "A dog of the Synyurl Loyalists, and should be tolerated, of not respected."

Toumo scowled, and returned to a upright frown, "You have a funny idea of respect, Guild Master?"

"Yes, of course I am the guild master around here," He seemed proud of that title, "You are deserving of the respect of a dog. You hold to the law of Jester without question. Which is the law of your masters."

Toumo corrected him, "I serve but Ua, and Ain's Justice."

"Yes, so we all do. Now, let us not talk about this where customers can hear." Accix motioned towards his office, "Scribe Tua has work to do. I will represent him in matters of diplomacy."

Both men made their way back to the office. The process was slow, and painful. Accix's massive figure barely fit through the double doors. He waddled into the office, and took a greedy drink from a pitcher of wine. Then sat down in his chair. It groaned, and cried from his weight as he settled in.

Toumo sat in front of the desk. He placed his cane directly in front of him, and held it with both hands. He remained expressionless.

"I am Kiwe Cir' Accix, and I know who you are Toumoistium," he huffed in desperation as he caught his breath, "I assume containment of Tua's work is your duty."

"If Tua refuses the cease, and desist order, I will take you all to court for this," Toumo explained.

"Nonsense. We are licensed, we have certain protections," the Guild Master leaned upon his desk, he chest spanned out like dough, "Tua went to Derin Manor himself, and wrote down what he saw."

Nonsense was the watch word, and Toumo knew that this defense was pathetically made. A licensed Herald's guild serves its lord. Since Brudge is the lord of this region, they cannot talk ill of him. The accusations levied by Tua were bordering traitorous.

"I am not denying the events at the manor," Toumo said, "The reports of false claims are more disheartening."

"Do we not have permission to speculate?" Kiwe chortled, "Things, such as a female platescale, premise deserve further investigation."

"You have license to do so, at Brudge's pleasure." Toumo reminded. "But you have not the permission to make the false assumptions you have."

"Well, we are not perfect. What assumptions have we made?" Kiwe confessed in this, then leaned back.

"Accusations that fall under the category of egregious." Toumo reached into his pouch, and held up a small number of papers, "Clearly done in a vindictive, and spiteful nature."

"What in the idle do you think you are doing? Brudge is clearly a traitor for vetoing treaty provisions. We are all ruffled by this," Kiwe gave a growl, which shook the fat along his neck, "We made no such insults elsewhere."

This was a deflection attempt now. He showed his bias. The treaty provisions are a Tribultionalist position, and an issue of the capital, not here. Toumo now just had to bring this to the court. His next move is to present an item of evidence before his action. He had it stowed within his bag, waiting for the opportune time to present it.

"These articles here, your guild states:

> 'Derin himself is a fool for such
> attention. His reckless self-importance
> makes him a figure among the river poor of

> *Jester. The flightless cheer his name as he*
> *provides   them   with   shelter   they   nay*
> *deserve...'"*

The guild master lifted his head higher, and frowned as Toumo began to list the insults levied.

> *"...There is much mention of Derin's*
> *disgraceful behavior in regards to mixing*
> *of clutches, and horseplay. His actions*
> *with women are vile, and he has frequently*
> *paid out to angry husbands for cases of*
> *adultery."*

"Adultery that is not true." Toumo added.

A growl emanated from the massive Jestarian. His chest could not puff, there was no room. Instead, he bore his forward teeth. "Now see he-"

He was cut off once again, "This is just the first two. Dare I read the worst?"

"We   have   been   granted   protection   from   the Tributionalists!" Kiwe roared.

Toumo stood up, leaning on his cane, and placed the notice on the table. He then removed, once more, an article from his satchel, and read.

> *"Derin   is   nothing   but   an   unabashed*
> *Platescale sympathizer. He is coordinating with*
> *Vesuvious Vex to slaughter all Jestarian in war.*
> *If only to escape with some hussy woman, who now*
> *has decided to back-stab him. Brudge should be*
> *charged for treason, and the flightless on the*
> *rivers should burn his estates."*

Toumo stopped reading there. He watched the rounded, and gluttonous man flex his digits, and huff. He could barely utter the saying, "We speak the truth."

Toumo threw this paper down next to the previous.

"Insults are not truth. Unless you can prove without a

question these are true. You have only said hearsay, and show malice. You incite violence in your intentionsm" Toumo then pulled out a second, fresh copy of the subpoena. Always careful to have a spare of the final order.

"I..." He began to state, "Sergeant-at-Arms Wer di' Toumoistium, servant of the Deep Lake Chancellorships, hereby summon Scribe Tua, and his master, Kiwe' Cir Avvix, to court. The charge is defamation, incitement, and slander of a state official. The date is ten days from this proclamation. Failure to do so, will result in punishment deemed worthy of contempt, at which the court will decide your fate to be that of excommunication."

Kiwe roared in rage, "You, and Derin are corruption incarnate!"

Toumo was already turning out to leave. He puffed his chest up as he steadily walked out the door. Everyone inside, clerk, and customer, watched as if he just killed Kiwe.

Finascales like Tua, are snakes like Brudge, and eels like Toumo, and his masters, all suffer the plight of the Jestarian. They go in lies, and deceit. One to profit from the misfortune of the other. The other, wrought with trouble because of his own deception. The last, a man doing so in lies told to him by the rest. All profiting in falsehood.

Cork

CHAPTER TWENTY-FIVE

The time we planned for is now. Ua and Ain give us one last chance at atonement. If we fail this, the world will burn. So this conflict is now loomed over by the Wyvern Order. We have the sole blessing of the power to tame the beasts of our nightmares. We shall catalog this song, to ensure we never forget why the world has stopped.

Let us observe this state once more. Vesuvious Vex, stole the throne of Skolis. The Order had no desire to keep Mek'velor, who was a coward, but has no inkling to allow Vex to slaughter again. We gave him only the mandate of domestic affairs, and forbade wars.

So the mandate regulates the sale of more Graceful objects. Some too dangerous to be in the hands of finscales, or flightless. They would grant power to destroy the Order, so they must be seized, and hoarded away.

This was ignored by Huron. He was willing to keep this unjust secret if it meant holding his station at the docks. He committed to the task of it by orders of the scoundrel Jennu.

Huron bore his usual rags, with a purse containing a few of his things carried over his shoulder. Light, and

steady his pace was when he set out the morning after to the
cliff-side. Quiet, and careful he was when he passed by the
workhouse he so diligently refused to sleep in. He took great
effort in avoiding the detection of a whiskered red woman.

At the walkway to Freestride's cliff wall, Huron
lingered to enjoy the warmth of the suns on his neck, and
face. Finding a rock to bath upon is something he had little
time to do since he left Tram. While dock work gave him
enough exposure to the suns to keep his muscles limber. He
still felt he needed it. As always said, 'just a morning upon
a rock is warmth for the week.'

Passing by him was a whole assortment of oblivious
Freestriders. They came from the workhouses, and various
holes. Many of the drunkards, and poor slept in hollowed out
caves in the canyon wall. Others from cliff side would glide
down.

They all came with a wide assortment of features from
many regions of the Empire. With faces that look vastly
distinct from each other. Even colonials were common, with
odd lack of ears, and fins. Tram is inland, and mostly rural,
which meant a range of common features. Here everyone smelled
in all sorts of offensive ways, showing that the city was the
hub between the the world, and the Empire.

It would have almost been a perfect morning. Sadly the
squawk of a familiar voice cut Huron's short-lived confidence
down. He winced as if he was in sheer pain, knowing he was a
failure at stealth.

"Huron! I am so glad to find you!" It was Tailya,
waddling up the street, springtime gravid, and wearing a
rather ragged dress stained with soup broth.

"Go away," Huron stated, trying to outpace her.

"I have to go to the top of the cliff! Better with
someone I know," Tailya said, with a cheery smile.

Huron gave a very low huff, it has all been ruined. He

then cut poorly into the crowd to make an escape. They formed a wall to protect their places from the forceful interloper. This allowed Tailya to close the distance into scent range.

Eventually the end of the lift line was properly visible. Gathered were an assortment of platescales. Huron, and Tailya stood in it.

There were two carts with wooden bodies. They were tied to chains, with gears that were pushed by water, and axles. They had only a four person capacity at most, but were usually loaded in groups of three. The long line hugged around the sides of the path. People entered either cart as it arrived, and the time to the cliff top was short.

No matter. Tailya tucked herself right between Huron's folded wings. She began to touch, and caress him. Some sort of cooing noise came out of her breaths. Huron tightened his neck muscles, and felt quite embarrassed.

"Why do you not sleep in the workhouse, Huron?" Tailya cooed.

"Because you do not belong asleep near me," Huron said back.

"Who will guard me though?" Tailya sighed.

She clutched onto Huron's wing like child holding its mother's tail. She took every step forward with him. Huron growled in offense to scare her off. She did not relent.

"The others in the workhouse are talking ill about us," Tailya began, "Some complaints about you not protecting your claim. They might report you to the watch for improper egg care."

"They are not my eggs. You eat big servings, and look fatter then you should for spring. Pass them already, and be done with me," Huron laid an attack on her, infuriated at her insistent attempts to make him break his promise to Selay.

"I am not fat!" Tailya dug a claw into Huron's wing, making him immediately regret his attack.

"I do not like this workhouse, Huron. It is musty, and unkempt. There is no floor. The roof leaks right onto the bed when it rains. No one cleans the buckets too. We should rent a house, maybe get a room at the inn. Anything is better then living with filthy flightless!"

Huron lowered his head, "These complaints, and attentions are not welcome, Tailya. Come summer. I will leave Freestride."

"But..." Tailya seemed to pet the wing she just dug into, and pulled it to cover herself in its webbing, "I have no one else to turn to..." she pleaded.

"The Church of Ua will always take strays, and is a short walk from here. Go there, and stop hiding behind my wings, that space belongs to someone else. They also need to heal." Huron finally was at the lift.

As it creaked open, two guards left with a young child. The child darted at full sprint by them. The guards kept a walking pace. One was green, short, and pudgy. The other red taller, and skinny. The green kept a poleaxe in his hand, and the red a sword on his belt. Both had eye coverings, but had no wings fit to fly with the Armour they wore. Which included dangling coifs that make no sense other then look like fools. That they were, for they spoke so loud that all could hear.

"Lying about that report was a good idea. Freestride customs work is easy, and boring." The green one churled.

"I am not happy for the pay cut. The soup is lousy," The red responded.

"But we sit on our tails all day. It is better then living under Vex's shadow in the capital." The green lifted a gloved claw to note.

"I suppose. If he knew that was a woman who beat us up, he would have thrown us in the Wyvern pens," The red said as they both were no longer close enough to hear.

Huron stepped onto the lift, and Tailya right next to

him. Finally she was out of his wings. Which Huron tightly folded to guard himself. In front of them, a typical laborer, with no special features outside of dirty, entrapped them in the lift together as it lurched upward.

Tailya turned to Huron, and squawked right into his earfin, "I do not like the church! It is stuffy. The Ua Priests like to do sermons naked while sunbathing. I saw the one here, and she is fat, and old. I saw cheese on her scales!"

The lift rose faster then it should, and creaked as it did. Halfway through Huron saw the other lift, with a rather fat, and rich looking blue merchant alone in it. His belly poked from the side. Huron was happy the extra weight would bless him less time then needed to the clifftop. There he would attempt a full outpacing of Tailya, and escape.

"Huron! Do you hear me!?" Tailya screeched into his ear as loud as possible.

"Keep yelling so I will no longer!" Huron replied.

"I said the Ua priestess has cheese on her scales!" Tailya jeremiad.

"Then she should bath more. Or you should collect it for sale to the marketplace to pay for your lodging! I will not tend you a home, for you are not my chosen," Huron reaffirmed.

"Where is your chosen? She abandoned you!" Tailya scolded, "You should take another."

"That is not how it works. I must find out what happened to her," Huron said, "It is not good to simply abandon family."

The lift topped off finally. It opened to a small stone junction that went to the main market road. About five blocks away was a rather impressive market plaza. There, crowds gathered towards it to shop for everything. Just off to the side was the Herald's office. Also a tavern with some of the worst food Huron ever tasted outside of Selay's fish jerky.

Huron was quite familiar with most of the street from a long time ago. He once lived in Freestride. It was just after his family returned from war, for roughly a month. He only recounted what he saw from his window, and from trips to the market with his father. His demons then were much worse, and made him too scared of the world around him.

Huron's course was towards the market, but not entirely there. The plume of smoke that came out from a gap between the homes was where he had to go. His old home, the smithy.

His best walking pace was not fast enough. Tailya, despite her extra weight, was more then able to keep up. She seemed to bounce.

"Huron, let us go towards a cobbler to get something for our feet! I think all this walking must make us both hurt!" She levied another complaint.

He ignored Tailya by faking as if he was checking the door numbers of the homes, and felt a strange urge to just run. However, running would make attention, and the guards might think him a thief. So he paced, and looked dumbfounded. Which he was good at. He hoped the whole town could see the stalking, obsessive, impostor noble-woman was as silly as she carried herself.

Tailya did not yield her protests, somehow she went from shoes to curtains. This then went down buying a pot, then a strip of leather. Then some strange thing involving a spoon, a sac, and a cotter pin. She was unrelenting, agitated at being clearly ignored.

To cancel out his own annoyance, Huron tapped a claw on every wooden beam, or fence post he found. Eventually he came to the smith's fence, and then the gate through. He felt happy to be halfway done with her.

The smithy was occupied by a green man with off proportions. His head was smaller then his body, his biceps were large, and his belly had a large spread. His girth made him look as if he leaned back constantly. The perspective made no sense, but he managed to handle his tasks perfectly.

In one massive hand he held a small iron pliers, pinching onto a silver-steel plated boot of immaculate design. In the other, he had a really small hammer that he would tap onto the plates to bend in masterful impacts. He shifted his massive body back, and forth. Then finely adjusted his results with few more bends, and taps. A master smith, also is a jeweler at the same time.

Huron readied his inventory, and after rummaging in his sac he he produced a writ with the seal of the Amour's guild. The smith noticed him during that, and smiled at the seal. He then stood up, put his tools down, took off his gloves, and set them next to his work.

"Zytle sent the payment last night," he said, "So you must be for it then?"

His voice was rough, and charred. Like any smith in a forge that always burns. Few had good work though, necessary work. The entire city stood upon its smiths.

"I am here for a chest," said Huron, placing the writ back into his pouch.

Tailya somehow arrived behind Huron's wings again. She brushed against him, and was poking her head up from behind him, and watching the smith. When Huron noticed he turned to glare coldly at her.

Her eyes widened, and she just blurted out, "You look like Talsworth!"

The smith glared back at the annoying woman, and smiled, "I am his brother, two clutches removed. Who might you be?"

Tailya expressed excitement at meeting someone new. She waddled out from behind Huron, and made a curtsy, "I am Tailya Mek'velor, princess of Skolis."

The man rumbled a belly laugh. He did not believe her, "Hah, and I am Ain's Master Smith for his forge!" He turned to Huron, "Where did you find her?"

Clearly Tailya felt offended at the broadside mockery, and turned away. She thrashed her tail, folded her arms, and held her nose pretentiously up in the air. A whimper once was heard, but nothing else. Her tail kicked Huron's legs, and he kicked her tail out of the way.

"I found her in a rotting hole in Tram. I agreed to leave her in a hole in this city with those that think themselves possessed," Huron ironically replied.

"Smart man," the smith said, "It is much better to build a nest with one who thinks herself a popper, then a lord without wealth. What is your name, young man?"

"Huron Quirksettle. My family sold this establishment to you after the war."

The smith became joyous over the name, and held out his arms in a merchant welcome, "Huron! I thought that ball snout, and ears were familiar! You are so big! His son you are! How is your old man?"

"Calm, and reserved. He profits from debt servants on the farm," Huron began to feel a bit homesick.

"The state must pay good for servant farm hands. Anyway, I am Cork Talsworth. You might not remember me. You were so young, and absent when I saw you."

Cork was right. Huron had no memory of the man, just of the sale of the forge. His feelings of that time were of just wanting to be held by his mother again. He yearned for her wing, and could hear her purring as if it was a song.

He had to stop this, "I must hurry. Jennu is expecting me to deliver this thing."

Cork nodded, "Wait here. I will fetch it."

He stood up, quite slowly. Then strode off into the house, and vanished a bit. The door frame was wider then

Huron remembered, he must have changed it.

Tailya was still nose up, and posing offended. Huron turned to examine the forge. Everything was in better shape then he last saw. Elaborate, and sophisticated mechanisms were available on every step. Regulations for bellow timing, a small grid of plates that could guide molten metal into multiple casts, and every piece of bulk part set in the expected order to assemble by. Cork must be able to produce three times as much as during the wars with this design. Perhaps even set everything in standard lengths.

Cork eventually returned, hold in his hands a small oak chest. With etching, and gold trim on it, this clearly was a a valued treasure. He was gleeful as he approached Huron.

"This little thing will clear the loan with the guild. I can then start a family next spring!" The smile on his chubby small cheeks was gentle, and true. Though there was no presence of any woman who would be his.

"A chest for a merchant? I do not think they are that valuable?" Huron took it up, and examined it.

"Inside there is some metal that makes it so much more valuable then it looks," Cork nearly opened it to show but instead gave it to Huron.

"This must be the purest gold on Allya then," Huron looked upon all sides of the chest in examination.

"Yes! The very purest of them all!" Cork then returned to his boot, and sat down to continue hammering at its imperfection, "Why does the only son of Quirksettle venture this far from home? You should be caring for children?" He inured.

"My wife, and children are kidnapped. I am trying to find them." Huron answered.

Selay's voice came into Huron's mind. Clearly, and distinctly her whispering, "find me" as she darted into the woods, and played hiding, and hunting with Huron. When Huron found her, they would curl up in the grass, and nuzzle. Only to play again with Huron hiding, and Selay hunting.

"Oh, so sad..." it was hard to tell if Cork was genuine, "What does she look like?"

"Blue as slate, with a milk white belly. A set of plates on her cheeks, and no ears like a colonial. Her horns are jagged, but only once at the tip," Huron rattle off, happy to never forget these details.

Cork looked a bit surprised, "That sounds an awful lot like that hussy at the Keg. My brother complains about her. He keeps saying she needs to get pegged, but everyone who gets close gets assaulted."

"Really!? That could be her!" Huron nearly fell over, so he put the box down, and leaned forward on the table, "You must know when she will be back?"

"I do not know. She showed up early spring time, and it has been over a month since my brother has complained about her. She started a legendary fight," Cork explained, "She vanished since then."

"You must know more!" Huron demanded.

"Well... the tab really is what my brother complains about the most. He never saw one so high."

Huron kept asking for more details. Yes, this was the profile of Selay he was following. Someone with her exact features, but a traveled drunk who is foul, and perverse. Selay's lack of any decency was a trait of all of Huron's memories with her. She yelled, and cussed the room over. Her behavior was something he never was told to expect in any woman.

Tailya eventually became bored of acting offended, and began to play with the box. Huron noticed her movements out of the corner of his eye. He did not say it, but if she broke it he would have to sell her to Jennu, and pray to the gods that was enough to not become a debt slave to the guild.

Eventually Tailya gasped loud. Huron then turned to threaten her, but stopped shortly when he saw the box was merely opened. There stood a wide-eyed Tailya jaw open.

Huron matched her look entirely. For the impossible became reality in his eyes, and the stories, and legends of explorers, and lullabies stared back at him. The contents of the box would not be easy to see, except it made itself known.

A perfectly molded, and empty coin, twice the size of a regular gold coin was in view. It would have been placed upon a silk padding of red, but it was not. Instead, its gold reflection mirrored Huron, and Tailya's expression back towards them as it wobbled in the air, and rose slowly higher. It was a miracle.

Both knelt to examine closer. It stopped ascending. It leveled to Huron's eyes, and stayed above the chest. It stopped its wobble, and stayed level to the horizon, and spun just ever slowly.

Cork blurted out, "You better put that back in the box before someone sees it!"

"How is this real?" Huron asked.

"Yes, it is. Graceful Gold. A metal from the forge of Ain."

Huron pinched it between his two claws, and tugged it from the air. He immediately felt as if he should lift his entire arm up, but he effortlessly overpowered it.

Tailya was staring at it in pure awe, "This is contraband! If the Order, or Emperor know of this!"

Cork never broke a stride tapping on the metal boots, "The guild is the Empire out here. Zytle will see it arrives in Skolis. Jennu is loyal, he is taking it there. All this must be secret, for Finscales are collecting it too."

Huron examined both sides of the coin, and imagined how Ain could make such a thing. He thought that maybe Ain would beat his wings to power the forge, and cast the metal into an ingot, and press it down with immense fury. Eventually when the metal fights back, the ingot would take for itself some of Ain's flight, and such able to rise on its own. Of course, Huron could not grasp any way to reproduce it himself. Even as a smith's son, there is just no way he could compete with this work.

"Smith Cork!" boomed a rather fine, and noble voice from behind the fence, "Your brother basted all his food with beer, and now I might be drunk!"

"Sir Gintrix, that is a good thing!" Cork looked up at the new arrival.

A tall, and gray man, clad in gold Armour, clearly older, entered the smithy with authority. Causing Huron to place the coin into its chest, and close it securely. He looked up at the man, and saw the horns of Srica Gintrix, highest elected knight of the Order.

Huron was awestruck, and felt frightened at the sight of someone so powerful. He said nothing, and held his arm on the chest. Nobel Gintrix, equal only to Kings, who tolerates no disputes with followers of the Twin Gods. Slayer of Finscale heathens. Kiri'grana that flies higher then all the rest.

Two town guards escorted him at all times. Which is wise. He was swaying drunk, and he may need a post to lean on. They stood opposed at the entrance in wait.

"How are my boots, good smith?" Gintrix queried politely, shaking himself back to a bit of balance.

"I have been tapping on them all night," Cork lauded, "I think the dents are all correctly in order. They are replaced with various assortments of other dents that look like lovely patterns."

Gintrix took the boot off its stand, "Ah splendid, a dent that looks intentional means no one shall notice a thing!" He smiled at the craftsmanship, "Now to test the fitting."

Huron, and Tailya watched from the corner as Gintrix lifted his leg, and hopped around as he pushed his foot into the boot. He looked like a complete fool, and his typical regal, and nobility were briefly gone as he danced around. When eventually he hopped to facing them, he saw Tailya, and squinted.

Tailya began to panic as Gintrix said slowly, "I know those whiskers..."

With no time, Tailya began to flee. Or perhaps waddle at amazing speed. She let out a protesting whine as she clearly was moving at a pace that risked her health. She left towards the alleys in the direction of the cliff wall.

"Hold up! Stop her!" Gintrix yelled to the guards, who ran after her. He then faced Huron, and pointed, "You stay here! You are under detention!"

Huron had no thought other then run. He kept the chest tight to him, as he darted fast on his powerful legs in the same direction as Tailya. No demons came, but his heart raced. Gintrix cursed out at him as he knew that he must put on his other boot before he could give chase. Which meant more dancing.

"Stop that man with the horned tail, and the small chest! Stop that red woman with the whiskers! Ring the bells!" Gintrix shouted, pulling his boot as he stumbled out of the smith into a barrel.

The alleyway was the only option, so Tailya fled through it. Huron followed. Tailya trotting ahead of him, hopping up, and flapping her wings to move faster. She let out panicked breaths that echoed from afar.

Each side street was blockaded by the town watch, who shouted orders at each other. The town bells rang in alarm, and the people looked from windows. There was only one way, there was only the cliff, and the light of the gods before them rising on the western horizon.

Huron caught up to Tailya, and saw pure fear. This same fear he saw when she was helpless, and that thief girl threaten to press on her belly. There was no way to stop her anxiety, as Huron had no way to stop his own.

When they broke to the street before the cliff facing, Huron turned back to see the silhouette of Gintrix limping as he adjusted his boots. He was moving fast, and alone. He would be here shortly.

Tailya stopped running when she stared down the cliff facing. The lift was blocked by two guards, the green, and red from before. Both yelled "Halt!" and began to carefully approach them. About six watchmen were gaining from other roads.

Tailya opened her wings, then stood out. She hesitated as the wind gusted. She then quickly grabbed Huron, and ripped the chest from his arms. She opened it, removed the coin, dropping the chest, and tucked it right down her dress so that it pinched on her fat belly. Turning back to Huron, moving as if she was not gravid, the red woman grabbed him, and threw him off the cliff. She dove afterwards just as Gintrix cast judgment.

"Tailya Mek'velor! You are the property of Emperor Vesuvious Vex! Surrender! You, young man, will be beheaded on site for this!"

The wind beat against Huron's body. He could see the world upside down, and a desire to turn, and spread his wings wide overtook him. When upright, he saw Tailya's wings stretched wide, and with sun rays spreading across her body. Her tail swayed, and steered her perfectly. For a moment, Huron wanted to catch her.

However, he had to gain his control back, so he flapped his large wings, and winced when he felt his wound remind him of its presence. Yet he stayed lifted, but with no good balance. A lifetime of gliding games allowed him to follow Tailya without recourse. They banked towards the docks.

Huron looked behind, and saw the guards on the cliff, with Gintrix clearly standing out in his Armour. The man could not fly, not because he could not, but because silver-steel is too heavy. So he stayed there, watching, and made a rather piercing whistle.

The Wyvern screamed. Huron, and Tailya, fled to Jennu's ship. Enemies are here, and now comes the moment of judgment.

Rixor

CHAPTER TWENTY-SIX

Eyes open, and see what is coming. If we do not look, we go in the wrong direction. We do not wish to appear like cowards, when we are just silly fools.

Beware of the tall grasses, for enemies will lie in ambush. Such things are not beyond any weak foe. Burn all fields, things, and woodland suspect of their presence. Then expose them out to face us fair.

Of course this is metaphoric in peace. Now is politics. We engage in secrecy ourselves to prevent worse things. Our words are our arrow volleys, aflame to lead our foe into the open. We must be the warlords of clever. A bribe here, and threat there. Saver swords for back alleys, for we wage the suffering of peace.

Jestarian folk are habitual to these practices, and are thus twisted. In some ways, finscales were apt to take vantage of the culture of platscales. Mainly that of the alluring power of beer.

Once, a Jestarian brigade won a siege by establishing a camp upstream of their fortresses. Boarding all the water sources to deny clean drink. Where there was wells, they dumped all their excess wine. Finally abandoning the defense.

This migration allowed the Skol Armies to take the hold without a fight, and before winter.

The nature of platescales is territorial, and strong. Sadly, the nature becomes exasperated when enough alcohol is introduced into the system. For in this fortress, a celebration ensues like no other, upon discovering the well was flavored. When winter came, and dehydration set in, fighting among the rank became unmanageable. Injury ensued, and without water, the army had to abandon their catch.

The retreating scouts witnessed the Jestarian forces return the without conflict. Snowfall came, thus ending all chance of a siege until summer. The finscale snakes spent winter in peace, and comfort, for exploitation of ourselves in ways we failed to foresee.

The enemy unseen was ourselves then. If we would have struck a water source elsewhere, the fortress would never have been lost. We could have enjoyed a winter drunk, warm, and with boiling pots of stew to keep us happy. A penchant for excess folly is common among all Allyians.

Today Chancellor Brudge is his own folly. He is bumbling ineptly within a plot set about because he was too busy to swear fealty to any factions. He is now making mistakes. Mistakes that should cost him his life. Such as his choice of highwaymen.

He poisoned his own well in the act of hiring a forester to siege a castle. For that, you find an engineer. Employment of Rixor's band of robbers for this task was a clear mistake. One that was painfully obvious to the drunken daughter of an engineer, Selay.

She would have done a better job. Her path of destruction already proved her merit. Her siege of Anya, and repeated sieges of Brudge's wine cellar, turned with great profit. However, Brudge was deliberate in ordering her out of his affairs after delivering the letter to Rixor.

She gave the letter in proper order. After reading it, of course. Rixor's band lived in a dug out hovel. One scout kept watch there always. She easily found it, since it was the best place for a kidnapping in Deep Lake. Selay wore her travel robe, and kept a dagger in her hand.

The letter she read was quite typical of Brudge. It was not formally sealed. It was written in his fake, pompous, and self-important nobleman tone. It complained about the day's events. He levied the hardest complaints on the Banker Kiven. He claimed that the man did not see reason, and explained that he needed a small item withdrawn from Kiven's bank before he left tonight for Port Selis.

Rixor, a tall, skinny fellow, always wore a coat that made him look like a tree. Green, dirty, and his frills were like branches. He was polite to Selay, and refrained from any commentary. She met him before, this constant professionalism made her always want to bite him. However, she knew not to risk biting a swamp finscale. She would not want the plague.

She left when she realized he was examining her. His sinus was flaring, and his highly trained sense of smell was making him unable to look away. It was impossible for even the best urine to hide Selay's fire from Rixor's honed sense. Quickly she left, as she had drinking to do.

The band trekked into town from the Northeasterly route. They left their hovel unattended, and lonely. They cleared out their old home, intending to not return for some time.

The target was the obvious bank of Deep Lake, run by Kiven. They took a cart, a thick pry bar, two barrels of sulfur, and all the bags they could. Finally, they buried everything else in the woods. A siege was prepared, they dawned batter leather, and torn chain-mail Armour.

Upon their first moment in town, the guards began to stalk them. The band had to hide in a alleyway to advance.

Selay encountered them there, while drinking mighty on someone's balcony. She took to perching on rooftops. The afternoon suns were showing supper was just over. For all, it was too late to turn back.

The platescale followed them to the bank, and took a position on a row home roof down the road. She regulated her intake. Drunk only enough keep a mostly accurate headcount, and not fall off the roof.

The bank was a neat little structure, perhaps the size of a tavern. It was of strong stone, with sturdy columns, and spaced upon its own city block. The front entrance was a lobby, with large decorative windows, and doors with plated trim. One could open their wings, and loose themselves in the space where everyone waited to be served. Tables of fine craftsmanship were set for the tellers to service patrons.

The brigade entered the front door. The cart was parked on the side alley. They immediately began firing crossbows into the guards, who fled. Then all the bank customers, and tellers were chased out. A rouge quickly began to examine the gate entry to the vault room, and jerked the lever to open the door.

By this time the robbers were already failing. A noisy bird began to panic. A security system, made from a simple bag of gas just aside the gate, was set off by the latch. A needle pushed in the wrong direction, broke the bag, and scared the bird. This alerted the guard in the back alley, who rang the town alarm. Deep Lake's Bailiff, and his militia, descended upon the bank from their patrols. The streets were quickly cleared.

Selay watched the town guards sort out their entry plan. Snaps of crossbows could be herd. Out of the front came volley of bolts, and arrows. The guards scattered. A standoff ensued, and roars, and curses flung between all. Selay took a swig from her bottle, and was amused.

Rixor, and another took one of the barrels of sulfur into the bank through the side door. At that moment, Selay was now sure of the vault's location. The side was for deliveries so that less time was needed transport, and catalog, that meant the vault was there too.

An explosion was set off from inside, and scared every bird into flight. At least one woman, gravid, came out of a hiding spot. She chittered nervously, and hopped as she fled down an empty road.

By this time, the guards overcame their innate cowardice, and laziness. They ripped a merchant cart apart. About five held the side of the cart as a rather cumbersome shield towards the entrance. The whole watch moved closer to the building from behind it. Two men broke for the alley, only to be shot down on site. The rest stormed the bank, with three bolts per man flying past them. One guard stood up to look at the entry, but was shot in the throat.

The second explosion was the barrel in the lobby, the flicker of a flaming arrow could be seen as the cause. The chaos was enough to knock the guards aside, and deafen everyone. Rixor's team was now fleeing out of the side exit. In tow, every bag they could fill.

As if one last display of heroism, the rouges all banded to push the cart down the ally. One of the members of the team lingered, and a short sword entered his forehead. Rixor continued to light fires using sulfur bags on arrow tips to create a cloud of smoke to loose the guards.

It worked. The guards regrouped, and were joined by others, then broke to search the town. Selay sighed, and pouted over how quickly it ended. The entry to the bank was decimated, and barred up. The bird alarm was carried out, dead, a guard later cooked it, and ate it. The side door was covered in crates. The watch stacked the bodies, and took inventory. The bailiff was distraught, and when he thought he was alone, would cover his face with his hands, and growl at himself. This was a catastrophe for Deep Lake.

Selay took a short nap while upon the roof, and woke later that night. There was no good way to sleep here. If she wanted to rest, she must sit up, and grasp the roof with her foot claws properly. She could not, so she went from dosing to drinking, to waiting.

By mid night, the watch was reduced to three lonely men. One patrolling outside, and two camping in front of the vault inside. It was a literal camp, with a fire, and pot. When she was sure it was only three, Selay plotted her course.

The failure of Rixor's plan was stupendous. He did not foresee adversity, and just ran into the bank. The guard out back should have been dealt with. However, there are more enemies.

First of them is the twin suns. The guards could easily see, and stalked them in the afternoon light. Crimes of this level are never done in the day.

Next, was the clerks, and guards in the bank. The method of entry did not secure any leverage to keep the town watch at bay. If they took prisoners, time could be bargained for a thorough search of the vault, and an inspection of the security system.

Third, was that bird. It just could have been killed while it was calm. Which a single bolt would suffice. Combined with correctly resolving the other two complaints, there would be really no trouble.

Then the sulfur, a big misstep that everyone can hear. If the other avenues were traveled correctly, sulfur would be unnecessary. All the night could be taken to open the vault.

Finally, even with all the time ever to break in. The sight of a cart full of gold, and valuables would cause an alarm. So stealing everything is pointless, only a small hoard should do. Every bit of effort should have been on the target relic. No handcarts, one bag, and no noise. Perhaps not even more then two cohorts.

In all this, stealthiness is the rightful way. Nothing but the most quiet approach would do. The best point of entry for it was not where one would expect, but the second floor window. Which is where Selay threw a large rock.

The glass shatter awoke animals dormant at night. Resettled birds flew off, and strays yelped. A rather fat looking, possibly tasty, rat screeched as it ran from Selay's approach. No alarm bells sounded, a guard ordered another to look around. Selay scaled the wall, then tumbled into the window.

It was a dark administrator's office. Only the light from the night sky came into the room. It shone upon a desk with an engraved finscale woman with her wings open. Upon the desk was a nice stack of books on trade, and a single piece of paper. It was a notice. Selay took it, and held it to the window to read:

> *To assignments,*
> *I have urgent business in Port Selis, and*
> *shall not be in town for about a month. Deffer*
> *all appointments to the next in line.*
> *Kiven Di' Noach*

It was now clear that Kiven was not finished with Brudge's destruction. He was fleeing town to avoid the chancellor's response. Given the lateness of spring, he must also be heading to this "Great Feast" event Quad mentioned. Which is clearly now in Port Selis, the Capital of Jester.

She stuffed the note down her leather cuirass. A regular hiding place for papers on route. She turned to the rest of the room, and began to rifle through for anything with unmitigated destruction. She decimated, and threw all she touched onto the floor. Her drunken rampage, upon a finscale's records of deceit, gave her great amusement.

Eventually, she came onto a round iron ball. It was in a bowl, settled near a strange hole that went into a pipe. Perhaps a vent? The area the pipe entered was the network of vent pipes reserved for the foul odors of waiting customers. So perhaps Kiven kept his own vent for private affairs?

Selay did not bother to look for sure, because a guard was already charging into the room after her.

"Robber! Stop!" he was green, and carrying a short sword, no helmet, for his fins were too big.

Selay immediately used both hands to throw the ball at him. It substantially missed, and the guard was unimpressed. She then threw an account book, and that was more impactfull. He had to move his sword arm to evade. This prevented any swing, and gave Selay the chance to duck, and spin. She used her heavy tail to uproot the guard. As he tried to get back up, she grabbed him by the chain mail shirt, and firmly slammed her plated forehead into his. He was stunned, and disarmed. After a delay, he fainted.

There is now little time until the rest of the guards find her. So she began to rummage for anything. She found a box of full leather bags full of something. Clearly replacement gas for security inside the vault. She took two in her hands, and left towards the office door.

Kiven's office opened immediately to a balcony that looked upon the lobby. This gave Selay a near perfect view of the ruined entryway. Also the camping guard inside was standing at attention, and looking into various shadows for anything. His fellow came behind him, and they began discussing their plans. Both looked scared, and rightly so, for a platescale is near.

Selay lobbed a bag into the lobby fire. Its shadow alerted the guards, but its impact with the fire made a bang, and a spark of flames erupted briefly. This caused them to leap for cover. One guard had his whiskers set a lite, and he had to put out a fire on them, smacking his face.

Selay swooped down onto the least suspecting whiskered guard. She slammed his head into the stone floor, and defeated him right away. She ran right back up to the second floor balcony as other guard followed.

Catching a glance at the vault. Selay saw two doors. A rail door, removed, and set aside. Then the inner vault door, which was off its hinges, and angled. This would mean no trouble for entry.

The guard chased her up the steps in haste, and easily saw her. To which the blue platescale ducked into the darkened office. He made no hesitation to enter, and immediately ran to his fainted friend on the floor. Selay made a growl, then relocated into another shadow. She pulled back her arm to her side, and threw the second gas bag at the back of his head.

He had these dainty horns. They were enough to break the gas bag, which he immediately inhaled. The reeking smell made him gag, and cough. He was stunned long enough for Selay to gain speed for her charge, but he stumbled to face her, and ruined her flank. She used her hand in this rush to push on his face, and tripped him off his feet.

He was not finished, but Selay had him under control. Using a book, she hit him upside the head, but it was not enough. Some guards did not use their heads much, so they took more blows before they feinted.

It did enrage him. He bore his fangs, and his tail thrashed. Unable to win this way, Selay ran towards the broken office window to stand in what little light there was.

The guard was on his feet quickly, and glared at her. Selay threw off her travel robe, and let it fall to the floor. She let him see her wings wide open, and gave him a flirting smile.

"You will not seduce me, platescale." He said, stepping towards her.

Selay was not intending that. She was blocking his access to light. When he moved to catch her, he grabbed her wrists, and held on strongly. While intimidating her in a growl, Selay beat her wings.

A full set of flightfull wings, and the palms of their hands, slammed into both sides of the finscale's softer head as quickly as they began. He fell feint at last.

Selay winced from the pain it caused, and she inspected her wings for damage. They were fine, but hollow bones should not be weapons against even Jestarian hide.

With her foes dispatched, Selay finally could get into the vault. After pushing open the door, it was immediately too dark. She used flame from the camp to light a wall candle, then whatever she found in the vault chamber.

The whole place was ravaged clean. Rixor's siege was damaging to the lock-boxes. The pry-bar was still laying on the floor. This meant that it may not be possible to acquire what Brudge demanded anymore. However, Selay thought that if she could find at least one thing to fence, it would not be such a waist.

She had all the time of the night to stand, and ponder where to go next. Obviously Kiven had to die, but the thing Brudge demanded of Rixor was also of paramount. Without it, Brudge may die soon, and with his demise, Selay's expectations of funds to kill all those egg eaters.

If Kiven has it on him, that could mean he is one step ahead of her. Which is strange, as Kiven should not expect her to be alive. He should also expect Brudge to be unable to raise his claw in vengeance by now as he ensured the Chancellor's bankruptcy, and murder. There is no way to expect Selay's issuing of credit, nor her success in saving his life. However, finscales can be clever, and perhaps Port

Selis is a trap, and Kiven took this thing with him?

It was completely speculative. Selay would have kept pondering if not for a rather disturbing, and painful snag tugging at her footclaw. She noticed she was pacing some, and became stuck on a loose floor tile. A loose tile in one of the most secure room in Deep Lake?

Selay freed her claw, then examined it, no damage other then a lingering, and fading, discomfort. She turned to the tile, and its unusual position. It was deliberately made loose. She took the pry-bar left behind, and used it to uproot it, and bring forth an opening. A secret chamber.

Taking the wall candle, Selay went down. There was a ladder, but she just hopped, as it was not too far down. She shone the candlelight around this room.

It was fairly dusty, and a few spiders glared from their webs before running. One spider looked like it would make a rather great snack. Though Selay was not hungry. She was more interested in a track that was near a pipe.

The track went from the back of the room into a groove that was carefully sized. Selay could look into it, and see the other end was a lever. Also a set of gears, with some weights, and a latch.

Then there was the door, and there was no way to open it. It was iron, but with no lock, and no handle. When pushed, the door did not move, and a small tapping sound indicated it was barred.

A secret vault, in a vault, with a special puzzle. A strange thing, new in her eyes, and smelling of engineering from some crazy Jestarian coal-eater that thought too much of clever machines. Selay once delivered a letter to him for Brudge. In his workshop she heard him rambling to himself about tiny creatures beyond where the eye can see everywhere, fighting each other like armies at war.

Then that pipe, it was the same size of the pipe in

Kiven's office. If Kiven had a private latrine, he should have it with a smell cover. The ball was of the same size too, and if dropped might end here. It was reasonable to think, that the ball would be able to follow the groove, and touch the latch on the far end. If so, the latch just needed to be pushed, and the door could open.

Selay left the staff back in the forest area she secluded her father's book in as well. She thought it would not have been useful on this journey. However, she had a pry-bar, a long knife, and wraps on the upper half of her feet.

Using this, she constructed a sort of pry-bar knife. Or more so, she tied a knife to the pry-bar. She shoved this revolutionary tool into the grove, and nudged at the lever. When she could just tap upon it, she jabbed forward while keeping the knife blade pressed into it. It easily shifted, unlatching the mechanism.

A sliding metal gear creaked, and a something thumped. The iron door, once immobile, breathed opened just a bit. Selay pushed it, and it gave no resistance. The secret vault, in a vault, with a puzzle was was now open, and Selay disassembled her new lock-picking pry-bar knife, and wrapped her foot back up.

The room was not spectacular, and was more of a closet. It was cluttered with chests of exquisite design, and items of unknown meaning. Objects so fantastic, that they clearly were the playthings of the kings around Allya. She wondered which one she could ransom off for a murder.

She determined that it was a small green plate, which was cold. Upon it was a series of gold trim in straight patterns. The trim ended at black squares. They had no meaning. After determining it has no use, Selay threw it to the side.

Next she glared at a statue. A bare naked image of Ua, holding a scroll with her tail around a clutch of eggs. The statue's scales were all made of gemstones. Some of the ones in her extended wings were missing. This clearly was the source of some of the bounty Kiven paid, and Selay collected, then loaned to Brudge for a fee.

At last it was there. Just as Brudge described. Inside a worthless copper pot sat a long scroll. It was wrapped in a leather cover, and with two ribbons of royal Jestarian blue silk. A center ribbon dangled a golden seal. The seal of the Synyurl dynasty.

Selay did not open it. Normally she would be privy to joyously reading other's private affairs. This time she was fairly understanding of Finscale bureaucracy. That seal must be kept until it was ready to be used. I would not benefit her to read it before Brudge, lest she loose her investment. She had an idea of what it was: a King's Writ.

Selay took it, and left out of the office window. That morning, she left the northeasterly gate out towards Port Selis. Alone, with her purse containing her father's book, the staff, this writ, fish jerky made in Brudge's kitchen, and three bottles of wine from Brudge's cellar to drink along the way.

Her trip will be uneventful, and serve as good rest. Those who would be a threat to her, were diverted mysteriously by misfortune, as a band of polite highwaymen were about. Who were better at guarding this hussy then robbing banks.

Chancellor Dos

CHAPTER TWENTY-SEVEN

The fields are now ash. Next is to contend with the great foes in this Journey. Let us gaze inward. For our blood lust has lead us to thus. It nips upon our tails, and we fear what it will make us become. We want to fly away. Not the strongest suit of armor can can provide defense here. So we must defeat it with a shield of will.

Jestarian nature is of rusted Armour. They soak in their rivers as always. Their own treachery creates many heads snapping. They snarl not at where they should, but at each other. A monster cannot move without agreement, and Jester views only motility upon itself.

Such is not the way of the platescale, who serves Ain, and Ua in Task. We will endure to control ourselves. This shall make us worthy of an empire that spans the whole of the world, and slays the Fordako hydra.

In Finscales, a rousing is occurring. One reluctant to find a unified cause. Thus leading to a meeting in the great halls of Port Selis. Once a place where explorers were commissioned to map the world. Now it sits as the hall of the worst government to burden it. A state that should have ceased when it lost its king, but still carries on as a headless corpse.

They shall hang themselves on a treaty, one signed in blood of Fordako. His linage ruled until Synurl's death. Now, the Jestarian debate their unity seasonally. Some hold the rope, and others put their heads inside to dare them to pull.

One of the many heads is Chancellor Grov Dos. His name is old Jestarian for Wood Wall. It was odd in its lack of reference to anything seafaring. Its meaning still stuck with him, for he was about as brittle as one.

He stays firm to his finscale culture. With a thick Jestarian accent that refused to bend to any platescale syllables. This made him sound like he was gurgling water, and constantly overused jaw clamps.

Prideful of his heritage. He helped save his kind from death a mere two generations ago. He idolizes great explorers, even Titani Featherscale, who was no Jestarian. He adores the valorous nature of Fordako. Although, it was not hard, as so few finscales were valorous.

Dos tried not to puff his chest up in pride when Herald Haiyear Choonadi mentioned Fordako. If he did, he would face tipping his chair back, and falling over. He did not want to spoil the interview.

"Yes. Chancellors like myself do all we can to maintain the Fordako pact. We try to live in the image of the first Chancellorship. We all are required to swear upon the original treaty."

"Where is the treaty now?"

Choonadi is a large red man, not of fat, but of muscle. His cloths are baggy. He is flightless, and clearly colonial by his ears. With frills, and fins along his limbs, tail, wings, and head. With plates, and patches of fish scales, he is an abomination. One of the Restavias brood.

Chancellor Dos bares impressive fins, including large ears. With green, blue, shining fish scales. A set of whiskers on his nose were so fine they waved around his box maw at the slightest upset. His horns spiraled, and curved. Like all of his kind, he hid his expressions skillfully.

"The pact is in the care of the Jestarian Twin Suns Church, the first Order, in this city." he replied, "No single Jestarian is without their copies for reference."

"What is the role of a Chancellor?" Haiyer read from a paper full of claw holes.

"We are the liaisons to the regional guilds, and Kiri'grana of Jester for the most part. Some of us, like myself, are leaders of internal factions," Dos explained, "We set tax rates, manage licensees, and propose new laws. However, our most important role is to set up regional armies in the service of The Pact in the time of war."

"What about you?" the red herald thrashed his tail, and tapped his footclaw.

"I am the leader of the river poor families in the Port Selis River districts. I spend a lot of my extra time with them. I coordinate with other chancellors in the city to help find labor."

"How are Chancellor's determined?"

"By tradition of the district, or choice the king. I used to be a steward on the islands. After Synurl's post-war reforms, I was reassigned to be closer to him. I provided finscale refugees with safe passage to the Marsh."

"I remember many folk escaping. Though I was a hatchling more concerned with standing, and eating bugs. Until they came for my family." Choonadi lulled.

Dos chuckled, "You should try the fireflies around here. They are quite delicious."

Choonadi smiled, "I prefer brown moths. What of the business of the Chancellor's lately?"

"The usual."

"I have to write something more then that, sir."

"Another attempt by every faction to loot the treasury. Thraalin wants more money for his pet projects, and Menurut wants more for troop deployment along the Great Crack."

The herald perked up, "Is Jester planning a war with the Skol Empire?"

Dos shook his head, "More like Vex is testing us. Our ships are not the problem, we can ram Skol galleys, and board quickly. The canyon is too vast for any army to safely cross, so we are defended. Our problem is those damned Wyverns. They are not restricted by land."

Choonadi wrote down details, "I suppose a serrated blade, or arrow, can handle a platescale. Wyverns are a far more durable enemy, ballistic fire is not able to slow one down."

Choonadi appeared rather excited at the talk of warfare, "Is it not heresy to kill a holy Knight?"

Dos leaned forward as if he was telling a secret, "Yes. But we do not care. The Order should be wise, and stay away from the Skol Empire. It chose a side, and thus must be dealt with when the time comes. Politically, we have made great pains to separate our church from the main branch in Skolis."

The herald injected, "The Order could raise a flanking army of finscales, or bring the North with easy bearing upon Jester."

"It naught matter. The riders will have to die if they war with Jester. It would be petty. They elected to serve Vex in his quest to slaughter any gilled person. It is either them, or us, if they continue Vex's plans."

Choonadi put his big hand on his gill, and solemnly rubbed them. His breaths became more agitated, and puffy. Dos remembered how he first met the man.

His parents were beheaded in a mass slaughter by Skol. He was a vengeful child, and wanted to fight in the army. He would try to sign up multiple times, only to be carried out by his head fins. Until he stewed away on a marine ship, that was boarded, where he fought, and killed a platescale.

He was sent to the islands, where Dos was a steward. There he became an informant within the refugees from the colonies. Dos was then given his promotion, and like all Chancellors, requires spies. In this case, Dos sent him to New Freestride to work as a Herald to spy on Skol. Today, upon the insistence of the Herald, he sits in front of his sponsor Chancellor.

The thought was stricken from Dos when a familiar musky scent came. Both Choonadi, and Dos turned to see Dos's chosen. Her burning fire was bright. She wore a long gown over her green body, with the typical spots, and frills poking out.

She delivered a rather small roll of paper with a tie to Dos, "This is from the pigeon of Derin's. I hope it is news of him married," she fluttered, before growling, and climbing closer to bite on Dos's headfin.

"Choonadi, I think you must leave now," The chancellor said, examining his chosen, who began to wiggle, and open her wings in front of him.

The red herald nodded, then got up to leave, but stopped just shy, "Sir, my sponsorship?"

"The tavern we mentioned knows the word. You can stay as long as you must. However, if you must show identity, you will find a fabricated writ in your tavern room."

Choonadi left. Immediately Dos opened the message. The seal of Chancellor Derin was drawn upon it in claw, rather then feather. A number was the location in Port Selis to travel to, with the expected date of one day from now. The pigeons give no time to prepare.

That day was spent by Dos entertaining his chosen. For him, it would have been better if it never ended. He ached, and yearned for more with her. However, there is work to be done.

The destination was Brudge's manor in the southern bay area. It was evening, around supper. A great bustling was present. Staff gathered on the lower floor with rooms alight, and food prepared. They were all servants Dos saw before.

Overall, there was very little difference between this manor, and Deep Lake. Brudge did not like to vary his style, as he enjoyed brooding in familiar settings. This place is just as much of an eyesore as the other, as the colors did not match any homes in the neighborhood.

At the entry, a manservant greeted Dos, and escorted him in. No casual conversations, or pleasantries were exchanged. Just quick rerouting through the ballroom.

It was crowded with every lady in Brudge's harem. The flock barely wore cloths, and were playing as if they were nobility. Dos felt quite secure from view as he passed through the room, some unfolded wings in front of windows to block any onlookers. The rest chattered, and churl as they evaluated the latest gossip. This was a spy network clearly operating.

The lower kitchen was with one cook taking stock. It smelled of bread. The cook did not appear rushed, and seemed to be playing with rather odd spices, and mixtures of brown mushrooms with pointy tips in a pot.

Through the empty hall, into the stairs, and down in the basement. There was no candle unlit, and the stone halls were perfectly silent. Dos noticed an oddity in the form of a chair barring the doorway to the wine cellar. This was despite it having multiple bolt locks, and its own metal bar.

They continued down the hallway. They went left, then to a pair of old double doors. They were opened, and through a moldy stone archway there was a large meeting room.

This was the place, and the first person noticeable upon entry was Chancellor Derin himself gazing back from across a short table. He sat on a stack of pillows. His arrogance was made lude by the rather affectionate woman aside of him, that he wrapped his wing around.

Dos nodded a friendly greeting, "Hello my fellows. Am I late?"

Brudge opened his hand, and motioned to the right of him, "Not at all. This seat is yours."

Dos made his way to his perch. An overly frilly blue man happily barked from opposite of his wine glass, "Chancellor Dos can never be late! We are late for him! Chancellor Ki' Wyrenair on the other hand, has a lot to answer for."

Dos sat down right next to the lady comforting Brudge. She wore nothing along her backside, but was covered in enough lilac to not irritate. She used her claws to rummage out dirt under Brudge's scales, and sniffed at him. Her reward was Brudge's well-practiced strokes all along her fins, and back.

"Have you defied Ua? Did Brudge chose someone at long last?" Dos teased.

Brudge gave a devious smile, "I only choose what would rile up the Tributionalists. My ladies are happy to care for my appearance."

"How comforting. Though come summer, you will be lacking the chastity you have now," Dos replied, "Half of finscales will be checking their wash basins for you. The other half will be inviting you to their wash basins."

Brudge chuckled, "All should worry! I am fickle about my clean scales," he took a sip from his wine, and then traded a nose bump with the lady.

Dos took stock of the membership of this meeting. The faction leaders are present. He noted them all.

Chancellor Thaw, of the Synyurl Loyalists. Those who seek to restore a Synyurl to the throne sat at the left of

Brudge. He was sort of sleeping, or not, Dos could not tell. He was smiling, and rumbling softly.

Chancellor Menurut sat to the Right of Dos. Representing the Jestarian armies. He was at this moment digging a claw into a piece of bread, and looking at it with like he wanted to kill it.

Chancellor Allyater sat at the left of Thaw. He is the leader of the Fordako Pact faction. A roost of stuffy know-it-alls who lectured all about the application of the Fordako treaty. He was rather observant, gazing back. He seemed amiable, his overly-frilly greeting earlier had no malice in it.

Then there was DasturRios' Esh' Thraalin. A big chested man in a navy admiral uniform. Head tart of the Seafarers. A collection of merchants, and navy officers, who made up the Navy. Thraalin was rather enjoying his wine more then he should, and had to hold his glass with two hands to keep it upright.

Everyone was here, except one faction leader. The Tributionalist leader, Wyrenair. Which is not a surprise, since the Tributionalists are boiling mad over the recent obstruction of their protection scheme with Skol.

Dos did not notice the doors were closed shut until a solid wrapping echoed from them. Everyone looked at the door. Brudge sighed, then leaned to his lady, and gave a fin on her tail a good tug, and her rear a pat. She stood up, and adjusted herself. Then sauntered to the entrance, and opened the doors.

In came a man so arrogant his chin always was hoisted up. He wore blindingly golden robes that matched his scales, and seemed as if he could not frown any more so. Brudge's lady intercepted him, and examined his posture, which he gave her a threatening glance. She snorted at him, and left, with the servants closing the doors behind her.

"My fellows, musty, and mold is not the place for such Kiri'grana as us to meet." The arrogant man proclaimed, "The indoor lake is swampy, and is best suited for Jestarian elite."

"Then Wyrenair, you can spend this entire meeting soaking up in the lake. We shall stay close to the wine room, and be drunk, and festive down here!" Thraalin cheered as he pulled a piece of bread from his loaf, and lobbed it at Menurut. The marine was startled from his strategic analysis of his own loaf, and gave his fellow a glare.

The regal Wyrenair huffed as he examined the two, "More like with children. For if this was not a proper seal, I would not have bothered. What are we summoned for Chancellor Derin?"

Brudge slowly stood up. He set his hand on his sword handle. Then growled, and opened his wings to gain attention.

"The Fordako Pact is broken. There is a plot on my life."

Everyone, including Dos, was not paying their utmost attention to Brudge's presentation. So he took stock, and drew his blade. He growled with every word.

"This is an organized plot! I have good reason to accuse someone in the council of this. People with Banker Kiven, who betrayed me by sending an assassin."

Wyrenair laughed, "This is a issue for courts, not Chancellors. Derin, stop trying to play as if you are pure. You are probably mixing some poor lady's clutch, and are the target of her husband's vengeance."

Brudge pointed his sword at Wyrenair, "Your faction, Chancellor Wyrenair, has been increasing the pace of their slander against me. I should bring an investigation upon you by formal decree."

"Nonsense!" Wyrenair laughed, he sat down, "Slander is great fun, and riches. Entertain me! For I may not be loved, but my Gills are dry, and need wetting."

"Kiven, and others, have seized my assets in Journey's Rest without a permit," Brudge sat down glaring into Wyrenair's eyes. "My North Freestride wineries have had supplies cut off. My North Isle estates, despite being carefully designed, are now condemned by all local governments. Kiven has refused access to my accounts, and vaults, and thus betrayed me. This pattern requires protection, and thus a conspiracy on me at the senate level."

Wyrenair poured a glass of wine. Of course he was careful, and he took the bottle from one that he saw Thaw drink out of. Though, with how Thaw swims in the swamp lakes, it might make no difference then a poison.

"Again, the courts, and spies can resolve this better then us Chancellors."

Allyater frills lifted, and fell as he spoke, "Yet if the pact is broken, and this is a fellow Chancellor. This can become a crisis with a suspect. You better have evidence, Derin."

Brudge sighed, "Every holding, and asset seizure was in regions operated by regents who expressed a desire to appease the Skol Empire. This happens directly after our winter deliberation. I have lead the Jestarian nation back to sovereignty, and refused to pay off Vex. The coin should house the river poor. The Trubutionalists have no desire to graft off their own kind it seams."

Wyrenair growled, "And you are going to kill us all! Platescales thirst for war against us! My agents in North Freestride hear nothing but word that Skol is debasing it currency in preparation for something."

"You are swimming backwards, Wyrenair!" Brudge scolded, "My spies across the Empire show that Vex is minting gold to keep the empire together after the tax revolt in the colonies! He has all his armies overseas!"

"Your spies are lousy, Brudge Char' Derin. To whence your entire efforts to defame me are as well."

Brudge sat up, and crossed his arms. He gave a jaw snap, and Chancellor Thaw reached under the table to remove stacks of hemp paper. He threw them on the center of the table.

"Here is a record of all the defamation that you have paid the heralds to write, Wyrenair. False claims, and praises for the Tributionalists."

"Paying someone in the Heralds to write about Derin's misadventures with our wives is not illegal!" Wyrenair defended.

"Neither is owning a guild in another Chancellor's district," Dos injected, only to get a strange look from Brudge, and Thaw.

Thraalin chimed in, "It also is not traditionally polite for Chancellors to attack their opponents outside of issues. We attack each other, but usually before the winter, or summer meetings."

Wyrenair returned to holding his head up arrogantly, "It is late spring, and you must have been twirling too much during your morning swims, and thus dizzy. Getting ahead of your opponent is good strategy."

Thrallin harrumphed, and snorted. He shook his head, and his bulb bounced between his eyes. It was oiled, and glowing, and it caused the shadows to dance in the room.

Menurut snorted back at Thrallin, and took his vengeance for the bread assault earlier, "Does not your wife clean you, Thrallin? That bulb is swollen I think!"

Thrallin defensively lead his head back, and stiffened, "How dare you! Leave my bulb, and wife, out of this!"

The battle began in earnest. Dos watched Brudge continue to glare into the eyes of Wyrenair. He received a gaze back, as the others began to banter, and bicker as they always do.

"Your wife does not stand a chance! What is that name she gave you? Dastypuff?" Menurut teased.

Thraalin became a bit nervous, he blinked, and looked scared, his cheeks turned red, "No! Too far!"

Menurut reached over Dos, and grabbed a pillow next to Brudge. One where the woman was sat on earlier. He lobbed the pillow at Thraalin, who puffed up his chest, and fell backwards trying to avoid it.

"Just the mere threat of fire from any woman, and he becomes a loaf of bread rising!" Menurut laughed, "He spends so much time at sea, and now his chosen cannot touch him without seeing him capsize!"

Thraalin laid upon the ground, slain by this pillow. Dos saw him faking as if he fainted to hide from the embarrassment. Which everyone laughed at, and thought was more adorable then a problem for the man.

Everyone felt at some point like Thraalin, a unending desire to display, and impress upon others your size. It feels good to show her you can guard her. All unnecessary if she is already shadowing you. Thraalin never got over the initial habit of doing so.

The banter continued, everyone but Dos, and Brudge participated. Brudge lost control of the meeting rather quickly, and he momentarily held his head down in shame. Although there was a slight curl in his lips of amusement.

Eventually, Brudge got up, and walked across the room. It was long after Wyrenair was absorbed in the drunken revelry. So he did not see his rival move about.

Dos watched Wyrenair freeze in place when Brudge placed his hands on his shoulders. Then, quickly, Brudge roared as he threw his fellow Chancellor onto the table. Everything was upset, including the banter.

"I KNOW IT WAS YOU! YOU ORDERED KIVEN TO PUT A PRICE ON

ME! IT IS YOUR FACTION!" Brudge roared.

Wyrenair turned to look up. He immediately surrendered by opening his wings. His tail shook in fear.

"You are mad, Derin! I may slander! I may want to pay off Skol! But only until we can fight back! I honor our Pact!" He pleaded.

Allyater immediately pulled his sword, and took a mediator position, "What is wrong with you, Chancellor Derin? Honor the will of Fordako! Non aggression among allies."

Brudge drew his sword again, "There can be no pact if there is vile members like Wyrenair plotting to slay us."

At this point, all had to stand to attention. Members were forced to pick sides. Dos stood too, rather confused.

No fangs were born, no growls sounded. Anger was well kept, and everyone remained calm. Tails were still, and everyone just examined each other.

Thaw gave away the fact they planned to intimidate Wyrenair. He did so by not having his hand on his sword. Same of the military chancellors, who are first to arms in real conflict. Dos immediately decided to play along, and put his claw on his sword. This lead all others to do the same in silent acknowledgment of the conspiracy.

For you see, The Fordako Pact faction is the initiator of mediation. In trying to stop Brudge from harming Wyrenair, they actually cause the Chancellorship to intervene. His faction is the legal backbone of the nation, and bound to tradition. The push closer to violence is now a crisis. Even if it was fake. They shall vote for mediation, and cause an emergency meeting.

Brudge circled his sword, and remained stern, and angry. He moved it quickly past Allyater's block. It was easy. The block was a gesture, not an actual attempt to stop Brudge. Brudge jabbed the blade at the face of Wyrenair.

All that arrogance was gone from the man, along with

the shine in his wine-stained cloths, "PLEASE! I did nothing! I just bought the heralds, and used them to get an early advantage come next meeting!" Tears came down his face.

"You are a filthy liar!" Brudge growled, "Now I cut off your tail one segment at a time until you confess!"

"No! Please!" Wyrenair begged, his entire body quaking, "They..."

Brudge gazed at his other chancellors. He asserted himself with a snarl. He grabbed Wyrenair's arm, and threw him on his belly. The man gave no resistance as Brudge held his tail, and readied his blade.

"Fordako murdered traitors! He did not give them this much mercy!" Brudge explained, "Tails grow back, but heads do not."

Allyater was about to interfere. He was stopped by the sounds of yelling, and cursing from behind the doors. Whatever ruse they were all playing, no longer was present.

Those doors were violently kicked open, dislodged from their hinges. In the archway, stood a hunched over, and unkempt creature. In the wake of its entry a stench of a thousand burning fish engulfed the room. Thraalin fell over from his reaction, and everyone turned to gaze into this nightmare.

It was clearly a woman, platescale, and blue. Growling, and somehow able to stare into everyone at the same time. On her body was the least womanly outfit Dos ever saw. It was an old Skol Warlord suit, mixed with a leather cuirass, and patchworks of improvements, and repairs. A red skirt covered her waste, with green, and gold in the traditional pre-armistice loincloth. The rusty plates were only on one side, and two daggers, with some pouches were on the other.

It was a nightmare to examine her face. A Jestarian is taught to recognize the scales, and faces of great warlords, and this one was of similar. One who commanded fear. Lambana

Kitsuna, in the form of a woman, the man who killed thousands of finscale eggs, stood here.

In her left hand was a sealed scroll covered in leather. In her right, the Staff of the Skol Empire. There was no way out of this room but through her, and she looked rabid. She was a monster, one from a known line of them.

Chancellor Derin returned a glare at this woman. She paid him no return. She instead shuffled up past him, and to the table. She deposited the scroll onto the back of Chancellor Wyrenair.

"The Jestarian people are infested with the rash of a faction who feast upon your young!" She growled, "I will hunt them. I need to know the location of something called 'The Great Feast.' They shall be there, and I will kill them all."

Everyone panicked, Menurut pulled his sword, and snarled at this platescale. She did not care about him. Allyater, Thaw, and Wyrenair ran to the far side of the room, and huddled together. Thraalin readied his blade, and stood in defense of the others. Chancellor Dos joined behind Thrallin, fearing he too should not face down a platescale.

"Remove this beast!" Thaw yelled.

Menurut tried to approach her, and she snarled at him, "Listen! I have seen people at the Theater in Journey's Rest eat their own children. Kiven Di' Noach supplied them with the eggs to eat! They talked of murdering Chancellors!"

Wyrenair pointed, and bore his fangs, "THIS PLATESCALE IS WITH DERIN! HE IS A TRAITOR! REMOVE HER! SLIT HER THROAT! I CALL FOR DERIN'S HEAD FOR THIS!"

Menurut kept this woman distracted as Brudge grabbed her, and used his body to contain her staff arm. The marine chancellor grabbed her other arm. He slipped as he pulled on her, and yelled, "What is this oily substance!" Then he pulled her by her wing arm instead.

"ONE OF YOU MUST BE AN EGG-EATER! I WILL FIND OUT, AND

KILL YOU! YOU ARE NOT SAFE ANYWHERE!" She roared as she was pulled out of the room, Menurut closed the door, and Brudge remained outside.

The Great Feast. Chancellor Dos remembered something of that. Choonadi was talking about going to some kind of feast soon, but talked of no details.

"What in Ain's Forge was that about?" Allyater asked, as the room returned to order.

No one answered. All eyes fixated upon the sealed scroll. It managed to roll to show great seal of Synurl.

"Is that a Writ?" Thrallin said, finally able to breath again, "A platescale brings us a writ?"

"A forgery! All King's Writs by Synurl were read." Wyrenair crawled to his feet, and tried to clean off his cloths. The writ fell from his back onto the table.

"Apparently not," Dos answered.

"By Ain's Valor, and Ua's Grace, is this why they want Chancellor Derin dead?" Chancellor Thaw theorized.

"Article 6, all Laws with the Royal Seal can only be read, and open in the chamber." Allyater detailed, "Regardless of forgery, or if a platescale touched it, we have laws."

Brudge reentered the room looking rather upset. Something of joy, and disgust appeared when he saw the writ. Everyone was circling around it like birds, or plague-infected fish.

He spoke rather calmly, and in awe, "I request an emergency session of the Jestarian Chancellorship. Under article 6 of the Fordako Pact, to read, and deliberate upon this writ. Written by King Synurl himself, and given to me before his death. Recovered by my spies."

"Your platescale spies?" Allyater pointed.

"You all have platescales working for you since at least the New Freestride blockades. So yes, my platescale spy." Brudge sneered.

All Chancellors in the room refused to argue, and agreed. Even Wyrenair, who was to second the request. Simply because he had to know is was fake. This removed the last doubt from Brudge that the man was plotting to kill him.

Dos lingered as everyone left. Brudge was solemn, and brooding from that point forward. He eventually left to his study. He brought the writ, and stowed it on a bookshelf.

Dos entered the study with a glass in claw. Brudge had grape juice, not wine. He was sober this whole time, and it was uncomfortable to see, it meant he was being a true Finscale. He was ahead of the whole affair somehow.

Dos joined his friend at the window to brood, and stared at the night sky. Then admired the moonlit gardens.

"What happened there, friend?" Dos asked.

"You were too late to plot on how to handle this." Brudge said quite content.

"Shame, you all looked obvious." Dos churled.

"No! That was my desperate plan. I was not expecting my true plan to come through," Brudge sipped his grape juice, "This frightens me more. I can see what is coming, and it is a school of sharks that smell blood. My desperate plan was safer."

"Is it because of that platescale?"

"No. She is my spy, and she is right. I just can not side with her yet."

"Then what?"

A thud outside in the garden caught Dos's attention. Out of seemingly nowhere, that platescale woman was stumbling into view. She was drinking wildly, and spreading her wings open while on some prowl.

"Brudge, why do you entertain this creature in your home? Spies are supposed to be secret, like how Thraalin uses pirates?" Dos asked, as the platescale woman fell into a bush.

Brudge was not watching her, he was watching the clouds, but he heard Dos. He shook his glass. He smiled some, then returned to a solemn look.

He said softly, "Sometimes, monsters are necessary to deal with other kinds of monsters, while you figure out what must be done."

Visek Jennu

CHAPTER TWENTY-EIGHT

Our mind is clear, and we now charge. Let our foes tremble in the rumble of our feet. We thunder upon the field towards them.

Huron, and Tailya fled. The warm wing of fear has them in its hold. They left Freestride at sight of Gintrix. Escaping into the Ocean of The White, thinking its calm will bring safety.

There shall be none to be have, for the Skol Navy peruses these cowards. Its rage makes its range endless, and enduring. Rage for death of the great Zyrko, rage for the treachery of the Fardako pact.

The upper hold of the schooner 'Loyal Treasure' creaked, and groaned as both Huron, and Tailya rotted away in it. Their heads low, and their scales dirty. Sitting apart, opposed, and across a cabin walkway, they shivered from the damp cool air around them. Lack of time to set up beds made rest impossible, as splinters dug under their scales.

Two days ago this began, with both begging to be taken on board. Captain Jennu obliged, giving Tailya the job of guarding that thing they acquired. Jennu did not know what trouble he was in, for Gintrix rallied a terrible fleet of warships from the navy docks to hunt them down.

Tailya spent the bulk of her time across from Huron in the same position he first met her in. With wings extended, and a glare. Huron avoided her eyes at all times, and tried to look out of a nearby window. Her wings must be stiff by now, as no one could keep them unfolded for such a long time. She is trying to desperately get Huron to agree to closer contact, which he foolishly refused.

In regard to this nightmare, Tailya was the only cause of it. If he did not get stuck in the dungeon in Tram, he would not be here. He should have left Freestride immediately when she entered town. Then he would have no reason to fear Gintrix. In her company, he has become a traitor to the Empire, terrified that he will now die for it soon.

Jennu's promise of escape was about the only comfort Huron had in this time. The captain's ship was tiny, and fast, compared to the large triple-decked Skol caravels. One Skol ship bore the weight of one-hundred, and fifty crew, and Jennu has merely thirty. With effort, and a good wind, Jennu will outrun them all.

However, the wind was not welcoming, and unstable these days due to spring rains on the coasts. While it kept the Skol vessels out of battle range, the Loyal Treasure could not gain to fullest speed. So began the endless pursuit outward into the darkest oceans. Hopes of finding large islands to hide on were expected. In the distance, the five ships towered like haunting specters, never growing closer, never growing farther. If only they were ghosts.

Every so often, Jennu could be heard above ordering sails to full, or lower. He held the helm himself sometimes, other times he managed the crew shifts. He plotted courses to islands, which never appeared, and eventually became lost. Only knowing his direction is away from the Empire, a course he was well founded at.

By the second day, the crew was rotated in shifts of three. Tired men of each shift would come in looking exhausted, and disappear into the dark corners. Others would appear from nowhere, and go up top to begin work. Every member was ragged, with broken scales, cracked fins, chipped horns, and dirt covering.

At the afternoon of the second day Jennu ordered the ship turn at a small five degree angle. Leading from a westward heading to north. There was argument among him, and his crew. He ordered it again, with more force, and they complied.

Soon a lazy fog covered the ocean. Underneath a vast colorful patch of coral appeared. Huron thought a moment this was a coastline. It was not. It was the great Coral Shield Wall of Jester's ocean territory. The historical feature of pride for finscales, and thus most populated by Jestarian ships.

The helmsman above shouted, "Coral! We are entering Finscale waters!"

Jennu laughed, "Those platescale ships will not chase us through here! Keep sails full, angle north towards the rise of the moon!"

The ship adjusted, staying along the reef, but moving deeper within. Huron could not tell where the Empire's ships were anymore, and it made him relax. He tried to get some sleep.

Tailya was holding a rather strange expression. A wicked grin, with fangs exposed, as if she was possessed. Huron never liked that kind of smile. It was common among warriors while they slaughtered their opponents.

This state continued until an early shift was rotated. Jennu himself came down with his crew, barely able to stand upright. His tail thumped, and drug along the wood. As he approached he growled softly, stiff from a three day shift.

The captain came to rest on a crate aside of Huron. He had no quarters this trip as well? He grunted, and sighed in relief as his weight shifted off his backside, and along the hull of his ship.

"The Skol Navy is not stupid. I do not expect them to peruse us any more," He said, "So we can finally get to the business of setting up quarters, and warehousing. To which I hope you help with, Huron."

Huron sighed in relief, "What about food? I cannot work when starving."

"There is food, but buried in the lower hold. However..." he perked up, turned behind himself, digging in a bag on his belt.

Huron glanced over to the side, he could not smell a thing. Jennu procured a cloth rag, and uncovered a small supply of fish jerky. He offered some.

"Always better to be practical, and hide some extras where no one looks!" the captain smiled.

Tailya plucked a piece from the stack, and began to gnaw at it. Huron joined, and Jennu took his own piece. All were voraciously hungry.

As Huron bit into the overly salty meat, he noticed it was amazingly better then Selay's fish jerky. It did not taste like charcoal. It also tore easily.

Jennu said, "You really need to do something about your woman here."

"She is not mine. I do not control her!" Huron scolded.

"She clearly thinks different. If you do not show you are stronger then her, she shall control you," Jennu leaned back into the ship hull, "I know what those whiskers mean. Royal family, titles, and treasures to come with!"

"I do not care about whiskers, and titles. I can make my own fortune with my crafts," Huron scoffed, "I am married, and refuse her. Besides, she is clearly a fraud."

"Yet the Order peruses us with desperation. Someone must want her." Jennu wiggled a piece of fish in his hand at he spoke, "Those eggs must have two weeks left. Soon she will give up, and have the first fiend who offers. Which will be someone from my crew."

"Good! Get rid of her for me!" Huron smiled, and enjoyed the idea of this finally coming to a close.

Tailya gave a snarl, listening intently, "Stop talking as if I do not hear you! Huron, you almost had me in that dungeon!"

"What dungeon?" Jennu said while chewing.

Huron growled, and thought about that moment. He did not want her, his demons did, he retreated in full as soon as he had a glimmer of control. What he did was inappropriate, and its consequences are not to be lightly agitated. Two clutches of children, one elsewhere, another nearby, and in transit would be unmanageable. Selay must be found, and the brood brought home.

"I want you to leave me alone, Tailya!" Huron finally snarled, "You were only promised my help until Freestride. You now sit here, and want the rest of my life?"

Tailya's eyes widened, and she puffed up, "I am entitled to my choice of suitor!"

"No you are not! Stop deluding yourself into thinking you are some princess!"

They continue to fight, and Jennu continued to eat his fish. He watched amused, and even purred like a buffoon at the first meal in two days. He was also enjoying the site of an attractive woman before him. However, this came to an end when Huron stood up, and left for the top deck. He left Tailya whimpering.

"Ho! Does this mean I can have her now?" Jennu got up, and yelled.

There was no reaction from Huron. At the top deck he

looked upon a busy ship. The crew was gliding from the dual sails, walking calmly to check ropes, and climbing masts. A whistle sounded as Jennu came to the deck.

The fog was impenetrable. The sky was as devoid of features as the idle. No one could see them, and they saw no one.

Yet it quickly darkened into a mysterious shape. Which then formed out of the mist into a massive nimble ship. It made no time towards.

"Jestarian ramming vessel! Brace!" roared someone as a sudden bang erupted.

Jennu began to roar as he dashed into action, "Weights, and anchors, to port-side! Stabilize before we capsize! Survey team to lower hold!"

The smaller schooner, about one deck smaller, began to tip, and roll. Huron lost his footing, and fell onto the railing on the starboard side. The crew were more sure, and they all moved crates, sandbags, and themselves to cause the ship to balance back some. This worked, poorly, but they were able to stay upright.

The nearby Jestarian ship was indeed a ramming vessel. It was designed with two systems for splintering hulls broadside. The first was simple thick bronze hooks that would swipe like claws upon the lower hull of the ship. Second, spring-loaded harpoons that would tear through that same hull, eviscerating cargo, and crew. Any vessel that survived, would find itself out of supplies, and nearly immobile due to this. With three sails, a lever, and gear rowing system, this ship was far faster then anything put to sea.

The Jestarian ship took immediate control of all direction of the Loyal Treasure. This in spite of the desperate orders of Jennu to break free. With that, they were now captured, and helpless.

The survey crew returned to the top, "Captain, water in

the lower deck. Hold is sealed off!"

Jennu roared, "Damnit all, we lost our rations. Set sails to half, lets face down these water lilies! We dine on finscale for this!"

Huron took up position along the stairs, and a short finscale, with one strange spike up the center of his head, perched up on the rail of the other ship. Behind him was a contingent of rather wet, and cleaned-uniformed sailors with equally angry expressions.

"Skol Scooner! You dare enter our reef! This act of aggression shall not be tolerated!"

Jennu struggled to take him seriously. Huron saw the captain's maw curl from laughter at this tough little fish-head. His tail thrashed.

"How dare you! I am Visek Jennu! Privateer, and merchant! You are clearly new to captaining!"

The Jestarian captain bore some teeth in disgust, "Pirates then! Mold to be licked off the bottom of the ocean! Dirt worms in my sea, eating the roots of my coral!"

"What nonsense are you spewing!?" Jennu teased, "You must have been out at sea too long, and have cabin fever! We are not pirates! We travel with tobacco north!"

"No you do not, Jennu. I was told to drown platescales like you on site!" The little man roared, "Prepare to be boarded!"

Jennu did not have to order his men to respond, for immediately everyone took to weapons. Like a disorganize choir they also shouted obscenities, and various creative insults at the Jestarians. The finscales delayed.

The crew began to swarm near to Jennu in a circle. One of them pointed to Huron, and yelled, "You! Civilian! Either fight, or get below deck!"

Huron nodded, and decided to go below. Fleeing is in his nature. He made his way back down the stairs. However, before he could open the door, he felt the entire ship lurch again to the side, and braced.

He saw the glow of fire erupt, and a defining sound of the whipping cloth sails. He stared in awe as the Jestarian vessel's center mast snapped, and crashing into the fore sail.

The Jestarian crew retreated from boarding before they started, as the captain shouted to fall back. The harpoons were cut, and the hookclaws were severed. Like a scared isolated fish, the finscale vessel turned away.

"Skol Navy! Five capital class ships! Three Sails! Looks like Iron plated hull!" Some Jestarian could be heard shouting.

The captain roared, "Ready! Turn to starboard at sixty degrees, prepare rowing gears!"

Long wooden rows extended on cue from the sides of the ship. They began to row desperately. The ship began to pick up speed.

"Like I said, Water lilies!" Jennu shouted, "Pull weights! Full sail, lets get away from that fleet!"

The crew glided as they untied the sails to full. The chain to the anchor was severed as it could not be raised, leaving it into the sea. The ship slowly floated forward, but it was not nearly enough to escape. The water in the hold was too heavy.

Huron remained on the top deck, interested in the sites. It was far better to watch this then to deal with a smelly woman below. He stood next to Jennu, and squinted into the fog behind them.

The hull of the Treasure snapped, and groaned, and Jennu cursed himself, "Dammit. We are loosing wood, we may not make it. Ain, save us."

In the shadows, five lights, perfectly apart could be seen moving. They all arched high into the air towards the broadside of the Jestarian ship. They were ballistas that struck along the rower hull. Splinters of wood flew high into the air, and a puff of smoke erupted. Huron could see a few bodies falling down the sides. Some were dead, some finscales screamed.

Jennu was also looking, he hung his head lower, "It appears we now hold the weight of nations on our wings," he grieved, knowing he just started a war.

In a show of retaliation, the Jestarian vessel's top deck erupted into a nearly endless volley of fire laden arrows. The Skol vessels all retracted sails to avoid damage. They still maintained course, swaying along the flow of the sea.

However, a final volley of ballista bolts, each the size of a tree trunk, broke through the Jestarian ship's structure. With that, the ship split apart, and the arrows stopped. The crew dove into the surrounding water to swim away. They would likely survive, but what was left of the ship capsized over with a sad groan.

Jennu, and Huron stared into the abyss, and the fog cleared enough to see the five Skol ships. Just as before, slowly swaying, and coming closer. They were wrong about Gintrix avoiding finscale waters.

Even in the darkness, the faint shadow of a large Wyvern was seen. It stood ready on the deck in the center ship. It extended its wings, and let out a scream that echoed into the sky.

"Huron, below deck!" Jennu said.

Huron ran below, and down the stairs. He heard the roar of Jennu's crew as their captain rallied them with a call. The Wyvern screamed more piercing.

"It is clear the Empire is willing to persecute a war with Jester! If Vex wants blood, let him drown in it! We are scuttled, but we can take their ships, and have ourselves a whole fleet if we fight!"

Huron ducked down into the hold. The floor was flooded somewhat, and the water was icy cold. Cargo was thrown all around but a few crates. On them Tailya curled up to escape the encroaching wetness.

Above, the sounds of snapping wood, and hammers, erupted as the crew tore apart the ship. All settled into it being lost. They fashioned spikes, and fortified the top deck in ready for an assault. Others came down below, and retrieved oils, spears, archery kits, and anything that could be used as a weapon.

"Ready the first volley, ignite arrows!" Jennu ordered, "Fire!" and the twangs of many bows could be heard.

Huron felt a small assurance in the organization of Jennu's crew. They stood tall, and firm-scaled, in spite of facing the Empire. They were calmer then even the finscales in the face of death.

Tailya showed none of that here. She was huddled up, and shivering, her cloths soaked. Huron snorted, and cared little about her. She has killed him. All he could do is find some crates across the hold to sit upon to keep dry, while waiting for this nightmare to end.

Then the comfort all left Huron, and was replaced by sheer terror. The shouts of the crew, and the impact of their bodies in the counter-attack was obvious. Following, a deafening smash as the ballistas tore apart the masts of the ship. Huron huddled himself up into a small ball, knowing there is no where to run to now. All he could do is let his demons take over.

His mind drifted to sadness, and peace. He imagined the comfort of his mother's heavy tail curled around him as when he was little. Huron's ocean trips would be filled with nights of such warmth, as the sea is cold, and cold is not welcome to a hatchling.

This momentary lapse into memory was never fully realized, for even Huron's demons fled in terror. The crew above him screamed, and Huron's heart raced. The chaos above was interrupted by the screams of a thousand dying in terror. The Wyvern has arrived.

"Shoot it! Throw spears! By Ain's forge! Its eyes are soft like ours!" Jennu scolded.

It was no good, the creature crashed firmly into the center of the ship. Its foot, the size of one man per talon, splintered the floorboards of the deck, and crushed into the hold. Tailya screamed in pure terror as the creature tore the roof out near her. What little light there is shown through as the force of its landing also ripped through into the flooded lower cargo hold. Then it flew off. Water spewed into the rest of the ship quicker now.

Tailya looked for Huron, and saw him terrified. The hole created was between both. Crates fell from their place. With one last snap of the hull, the ship began to float apart. Tailya appeared desperate. She whimpered, as she did before she became Huron's burden.

Gliding in from the deck above, clad in a heavy silver steel, and holding no weapon, came Gintrix. He landed stable, and assessed the situation, first looking at Tailya, then Huron.

"Justice be served. Traitors all shall die here," He judged, then pointed at Tailya, "I am here to bring to to the Emperor, Tailya Mek'Valor."

Gintrix stood across the hole from Tailya. He began to value his leaping distance for flight across, and open his wings. Huron began to breath heavy, and all the sounds around him seemed to leave. He saw before him not Gintrix, but the sight of a soldier. This shadow leaving the tent his family slept in. Between him, and this specter, the blank face of mother Dask, the severed head of babies Fikki, and Ifpesp, and the cut belly of beloved brother Oflin all laid. Their blood flowed towards Huron Quirksettle's feet while he held a freshly sharpened dagger. Yes, Huron could do nothing but rip apart that soldier. With his demon's call for vengeance singing, he charged in full.

The man turned at the sound of Huron's rage, and was greeted with the full body of a fit platescale. He flung into the dark abyss of water. His arms, and wings flailed as Huron clutched upon his neck. There was no color in this shadow, just something that must be destroyed. Venenge must be sated here.

The idle of the ocean surrounded Huron. He did not shiver, or feel cold anymore. He did not breath, nor think about it, he just dug his claws into this shadow. It struggled to fight him off by hitting his strong arms. It was no good, Huron is much stronger.

Eventually the wreck above shifted, and light shone upon them. Briefly Huron awakened from his possession. It was too late, for his claw already pierced, and blood clouded the water back into darkness. Gintrix stared at Huron with shock as he ceased his struggle. The spark of life left the great rider, and Huron let go. They drifted apart, as Gintrix's heavy armor sunk him into the coral below. It reflected what little light there was to see, and the coral seemed to open to embrace Gintix like mother's wings.

Huron knew exactly what he did. He, and his demons, took upon themselves the right to be the authority above all in who faces Ain's judgment. He made himself judge upon all of the world in taking the life of the leader of the Holy Order of Wyverns. Gintrixm, the supreme divine watchman of the Grateful Task, is now dead. In taking the divine right from Gintrix, Huron now shall be outside of the law. In this revolt from the Grateful Tasking, he is now branded a heretic, and only death can redeem him.

So Huron decided on redemption. He hung there, accepting his fate, and waited. Huron stayed in the idle quiet of the sea, as the world above him burned, and warred from what he did. He hung before, but with no rope this time, in the icy embrace of the nothing. He gazed down into the abyss, and wanted to whimper but could not.

He felt the cold again, then quickly he felt a rushing wind. The light around him grew, and his ears woodshed softly, and finally erupted into a flurry of sounds. A chorus of blades clashing, and a horrible singing came from every direction:

> *To the east with two spires,*
> *Our fair king ruled,*
> *To the west water flows,*
> *Our ships shall explore and go,*
> *Ua protect us, Ain we fight for you,*
> *We are the men of Skol,*
> *Our valor and justice be known,*
> *Vex is not fit to rule,*
> *All those who serve him are fools,*

Huron could not move, he would not, and it did not matter. The warm embrace of a wing, like mother's, came upon him. Huron could see the embers of the war above. The weight of nations, and lives of all brought to bear because of his cowardice. The only thought left, is the selfish thought of his Selay, just before it all went dark.

Gawudon

CHAPTER TWENTY-NINE

The beings of our darkest impulses ordained this conflict. Our shadows made us fall from our place. Now as they prey upon us in our momentary weakness, they seek to establish their own authority. Chaos endures, as dark wings spread to form the lonesome abyss

Smile, for we revel in chaos. Gather your will, and strength, we have a foe to fight. It stands before us as our enemy. It is time for the butcher to slaughter again.

The dim light of candles in Brudge's Selis Manor did nothing to chase away the abyss of night. It was peaceful. Until Selay determined that the shrubbery wall of the inner garden was worthy of wrath.

She knew that this battle was decisive. For the pricks, and pokes of various branches soothed some of the her lingering pains, calming her. She was immediately thrown off the bush by her own attempts to position herself to the best comforting distribution. Landing square in the darkness of the inner garden, Selay was defeated. Defeated by a hedge.

The realization that Brudge now has a ruined flowerbed struck her great satisfaction. So she sprawled out her wings, and thrashed her tail. This would add more cost to her rampage by digging up bulbs, and upsetting dirt. She laughed at the feeling of the stalks of innocent roses breaking, their thorns unable to threaten her plated body.

Selay huffed in relief. The rather inebriated woman thought just how much more she could lay siege to Brudge's expensive yard. Perhaps by assaulting the shrubbery again? She might be able to launch herself in the right way to decimate that innate fountain, with the transplanted lily pads, and the statue of a naked ugly finscale woman spouting water from the wings.

Yes, this would do. Selay was sure that a broken statue, and a ruined garden would be the perfect Casus Belli for Brudge. Let the war between the Platesacale, and Finscale empires begin anew here! Although, it would be easier if she did not leave the Royal Staff of Skolis elsewhere. For she could ruin that too, and enrage all of history.

Many amusing thoughts dulled Selay's momentum. She ceased her assault on Brudge's flowers to rest her head on her arm. She took a hefty drink from her bottle of salty bitter cooking wine she stole from the kitchen.

The foul wine settled violently. She rather enjoyed its destructive results. It is drink, and it kept the thoughts of finding, and abducting Huron, and what she would do to him, away. It warmed her, fogged her vision, and made her thirsty for a fight.

She plotted on how to stop Kiven. He is here in Port Selis, and must suffer. No court would be impartial enough to render Kiven to a proper sentence of death. Further, none in Jester would listen to the testimony of a platescale interloper. This justice must be forced by some other means, and Selay would not be happy if it was not done, so she must enforce it herself.

This Great Feast: where, and what is it? Is it some ritual? Is it just a meeting? Wherever it is, springtime is not a place for a feast, as harvest is the time to enjoy the fresh food. This must be some strange opposite to the main practice of the Order. To find its location is going to be easy. Look for a lot of ugly finscales. Though the guilty do not travel in the open often, do they?

Port Selis is one of the largest cities in the world. Untouched by any war, and defended. The city is layers of old structures. One generation always trying to rise over the previous. This maze of buildings allowed for anything to happen in isolation. Top it off with the stench of fish in every direction, and the finscales are impossible to tell apart.

One cannot just go to Port Selis, and expect to find anyone easily. No things stood out, except government buildings. So a different means to find this event should be done.

Perhaps if Selay acquired the schedule of all the known officials in the city? This would take a long time, but it would produce gaps of times where a lot of Kiri'grana would be absent or vague. There would be definite reference to The Feast there.

Although using the maidens in Brudge's keep would be quicker. They are his potential suitors, who should be infighting. They might be hostile to a platescale who Brudge clearly shows interest in. Yet these chain-mail links spread far into other homes which would definitely hold feast goers.

Before thinking on which one to try first, she took another drink. Then suddenly had to fight off a need to gag. The pull was so strong Selay immediately sat up, and puffed her chest up to tighten all of her resolve. It worked, and she softly rumbled when she released her breath.

She is in a small square artificial grove, with hedges, and flowerbeds outlining all sides. At the center, a column with a ship facing towards the exit of stone. This is a place for sinister plotting, and the tree's on each corner provide enough cover to allow any sort of privacy. The perfect hole to strangle someone, a mainstay ascetic of Brude's manor.

It obviously is Jestarian. The western side was the only escape, and there was that boat statue, so it must mark the exploration westward by the finscales. The walkways in the center are shaped to further guide anyone in that direction. They were to remind one of the great explorers from Jester's past days of colonization. Brudge was quite careful to design allusions to finscale history in his properties.

The north is exposed to the wide bay side of Port Selis. Although the manor was farther out into the rural district of the city, the spires, and lights of activity are in clear view. Along with a whole armada of Jestarian vessels coming through to port. The ships are covered in meandering wisps of lights as the crew moved about with lamps. Some lights dove around masts, between ships, and even climbed the sides of the hulls. Port Selis bay was in itself a marvel, and a blight on the landscape, a living contradiction.

Selay took another firm drink, and glared outward. She made a sigh, and from that a scent of old fish, and frog urine made itself known. Someone else is wearing scent covering.

The platescale rose up to her feet, and staggered masterfully. Peering around a full perspective, she could see nothing among the shadows that could be surely identified. However, she did smell at least four distinct variants of stink from all directions.

If anyone were to enter this manor secretly, it would be from the north, along the wall, and into the trees. That would require a swim, which explains why they would need a scent mask. The trees provided perfect cover in the darkness. They would likely be finscale, so they already stank to begin with, making detection, once aware, easy.

Selay held her head up, and swayed as she called out her find, "You all smell like full waste buckets! Come down here, or I shall go up there, and and throw you all down!"

She staggered towards the center. She leaned on the boat column, tipping it. Then retreating from using it.

She is an open target, and did not care. If they intended attack, they should do so before she smelled them. They had plenty of time, so they wanted something else.

She looked into all four scent directions, nearly tripping over her tail as she staggered. Taking another comforting drink, she grunted. Cooking wine does its best to keep your balance off, and she is deserving of all suffering for drinking it.

The trees rustled, but it was a gust of wind. With it, the stench only was more apparent. Someone is hiding in there, and it is not anyone in Brudge's manor, who all had to wash today for the meeting.

"The smell of frog piss, and compost is undeniable! You do not even know how to hide properly! Show yourselves! I like insulting finscales to their faces!" Selay opened her arms wide, and puffed her chest in a show of defiance.

Another rustle, and the slap of weight onto the ground was heard in the southern side of the grove. Selay could only see the movement of a branch from the tree, but a set of tall burdensome frills rose above the hedges. Someone was there, and now moving towards the entry.

When the light exposed this someone, Selay squinted her eyes to glare. This is clearly a Jestarian woman, lanky, with rear protruding backwards. She covered herself in a expensive silk robe. Tied with a belt that was violet silk wrapped loosely around leather. The sides, and shoulders were cut to shape along her frills. All features were light blue, just as her belly was exposed a little, which was a lighter blue similar to Selay's white belly scales. A soaked wet scarf coiled around her neck, and covered her short blunt feminine muzzle. Her eyes, red, and her face just as blue. Her hands were contained in large sleeves that folded in front of her. Then finally, down between her petite breasts, a necklace of a Ua's Shadow rested.

She opened her wings as a show of peace, "Pardon me, is Chancellor Derin here?"

Selay's nostrils flared up as she tried to find this woman's seasonal fire. It was not present, but she was covered in scent masking ointments. It agitated the platescale, for she thought that was a recipe unique to her father. So she tipped her bottle, aggressively. She then examined her drink, and frowned, as it was halfway empty. This is most distressing.

She shook the bottle, and answered, "On this night? Who would entertain a horned fish like him?"

The lady bowed politely, "I am Priestess Gawundon Esh' Pabeh of the Chapel of Ua's List. Chancellor Derin, and I have a private arrangement tonight."

Selay had to turn, and pace to stay upright, as her state was becoming more unsettled. When the woman said she has a private thing with Brudge, first thoughts would mean something. However, her name, something Selay knew, meant something else.

Selay pointed, and mocked, "Jestarian with similar conjunctions in their name are better to avoid fornication. Their children might swim angled, or be born hermaphrodites!"

"You are rude. That is not how you talk to a priestess of Ua. Especially as platescale in our capital," Gawundon responded calmly.

"Priestess my left horn!" Selay swiped a claw as nothing, "There are three other stenches of fish-heads circling around nearby. Call them here! Ua and Ain would be so mad to find their priestess allowing her followers to get their tails sliced off for flanking a platescale."

"There are no others. Your tone is annoying. What do you think you are talking about?" Gawundon asked, "I am bearing the necklace of the church, anointed by Kityun. That gives me authority. Learn your place. Where is the Chancellor?"

"You are certainly the authority onto but foulest types of perfume!" Selay swayed, and reached into her pouch. She procured two of the symbols born by the assassins she fought, and threw them at the feet of the priestess, "Typical lying finscale you are!"

The priestess spent an awkward amount of time glaring upon the logos presented. She became upset. Perhaps a motherly protection was shared for those thugs? She revealed her hands, and flexed her claws, covered in black leather gloves.

Gawundon bent over, and picked up the seals, "These mean nothing more then Ua's shadow. They are worn by any who follow the mother," She replied, but Selay saw her shaking, even with her blurred vision.

"Ua's Shadow, Ain's Forged Blade," Selay repeated what Fuil said, "I only need to know what you call yourselves other then the whores of Kiven."

"What?" Gawundon looked up sharply, "I know of none of these things!"

Selay knew better. Brudge only entertained her appearance in the base of night. This is an attack. It was clear that they were going to use a larger force this second time, in the advent of failure to collect Brudge's scales. Their hesitation also meant they knew who Selay is, and they came for her too.

She must expose Gawundon, and get under her tail as a severe pain. This would provoke a proper response, and then give Selay what she craved tonight most: a fight. This required slowly chipping away at the priestess's composure.

"I wonder," Selay put her talon on her chin, "If Kiven's original payment were to be taken by the target, and hidden away... what ends would you whores go to get it? I bet you would jump into a Wyvern nest if need be."

"What? Do not call us this, my dear," Gawundon said, and gave her troupe away with it.

"Us?" Selay smiled, fanned opened her wings, and arms, "This is going to be too easy!"

Turning her back, and laughing, she then took a solid drink of cooking wine. She let her wings drop, and stretched, and cracked her back, and spine. *Soon*, she thought, so she should prepare to be agile.

"I, uh... apologize. I am not of these things you say!" Gawundon made a poor effort at lying.

"Tell me! Can I get you to strip naked for a fancy gemstone?" Selay looked back over her wing at Gawundon.

"No. I am not a crass harlot like you!" Gawundon yelled.

Another drink, and it was much more enjoyable. The company of a victim for harassment made just about anything more pleasurable. After shoring up her inebriated state, Selay wiped her arm on her maw, and grinned.

"I have a gemstone. I stole it from a den under the theater in Journey's Rest." Selay rummaged into her pouches, "The fool I stole it from calls himself Fuil Esh' Garam. He had one eye. Till I punched the good one. Now he has a half an eye. I also taught him how to drown a fish. For this, he told me all I wanted to know about where bounties are, and what bankers paid him. He also said your name."

Gawundon made an audible growl from behind Selay. One of someone warding off a trespasser. It was clear that Fuil was more then some guild mate.

Selay turned around, holding up a white sparkling gemstone. It twinkled in the little light of the bay.

"See here! Now take off that flea-ridden blanket you call a priest robe!"

Gawundon was glaring, and clamping her jaw, clearly angry, she put a hand on her belly, and growled, "Fuil? That was you?" No more was she acting. "Whore of Brudge! I am his immediate master!"

Selay nodded in approval at the true tyrant within Gawundon, "Much more appropriate. Yes."

Gawondun shook her talon at Selay, "Justice is needed! He is mine! He told me the town watch did that. We hung two of their most valorous guards in vengeance from the wall!"

Selay stroked her chin, and tilted her hip, "I did not want him to lie to you. I just tied him to a table, and took his pants. That vengeance was all your stupidity. Besides, you can not possibly find the bounty without dealing with me."

"Dealing!? You dishonored us with your insults, and now demand parlay?" Gawundon growled, "You are nothing but the bitch that Derin keeps in his back yard! We prefer someone nicer."

Selay laughed, and held up again the lone gemstone to her eye. Both knew that it was genuine, and that it must have been from the bank. Its worth to Selay was to pay off a bar tab somewhere. To Gawundon, it was worth some blood.

"I am the bitch who defaulted your contracts. I have the entire balance. Kiven's bank is tinder, and I am hunting for him here."

Gawundon held her head back in Jestarian arrogance, "You are too foul, and simple to ruin a bank. Lying your way out of Ua's Justice shall not spare you."

Selay gripped the stone in her palm, and tucked it back into her side pouch. She looked into the trees, and scoffed at the shadows now moving. Locations of all were more obvious, as they were the best places to leap down, and stab the platescale.

"Justice be done in the light. Call them down, and we shall talk reciprocity. I would let you have Brudge if you convinced me," She offered.

The finscale snorted, she took a breath, then pointed her maw into the air to make a few click sounds. Such vocals that were of no use to language. She finalized this with a clamp of her jaw.

Three hopped out of the trees, and formed a surrounding wall to entrap Selay. The platescale resumed her drinking, and examined them all. Each one a finscale, and each one completely masked like the Forged Blade hunters she killed before. Cowards hiding in darkness, and not giving their enemies the right of knowing who slain them. They all stood defensively, holding various knives, poised to lunge at any command. They are loyal dogs.

Gawundon stepped towards her troops, and made sure Selay was encircled, "A lone sapphire is still not proof you still have the entire payment. Nor that Kiven's vault is destroyed. So I shall leave, and let you be the supper of my blades. I can track the Chancellor myself."

Gawundon turned to the exit, and Selay yelled, "What a stupid coward! I knew I should of let Fuil run, rather then tell you he is not man enough anymore!"

Gawundon stopped as a snarf called her attention. She turned to one of her minions. The agent whispered into her ear. The priestess sighed, and growled in frustration. Selay heard them mumbling between themselves in a most disagreeable way. The platescale rouge then took a joyful tilt of her bottle once again.

The wine was stronger, and nearing its end. Selay may have to resort to total violence to get through to the cellar for a refill. There must be drink, or no one shall live.

Gawundon sauntered back towards Selay, "You were not lying about the vault's ruin. I was hasty to leave. Kiven's Bank in Deep Lake was robbed entirely some days ago. My client is now in default."

Selay was measuring her remaining drink by shaking the bottle, and staring at it, she frowned, "I tell many truths," Selay began, "Ua is a mere whore, and Ain does more intimacy with the tails of men then I care to speak of. You will kill only if you get paid."

Selay poked her talon in the bottle, and wiggled it, then removed, and licked it, "I also know you hide behind Ua's stench more then her shadow."

Someone growled in offense outside of Selay's view. It did not matter, for everyone should be properly offended. It is the best way to fight.

"You dare to insult the mother goddess?" Gawundon growled, "I am her blade! Her priestess! I serve under her warm wings!"

"More like you lay on a rock naked, and tell everyone stories!" Selay came back, "Then lead a pack of children, who do not know the evil they do, to their death. You should know a platescale is twice as tough as a finscale."

Gawundon snarled, "Lies, and insinuation! I have the authority of the Order. Its seal is upon my back! The Wyvern approved me with its own claws! They are the agents of our gods! How dare you insult the ch-"

Selay popped her finger in the bottle, "Question a church? I killed Zyrko. He bleeds, and his bones break just like the rest of us. No god's saved him. Delos is probably still holding a steak upon his fat eye."

The finscale was now on irrational terms, insults are one thing, but hearsay is a violation of the divine. She was also sensitive to what happened to Fuil, as he is clearly a lover of sorts. Now Selay needed one more blow, and this would get her what she wants.

Gawundon pointed and bore her teeth, "I declare you blasphemer! You bow to the gods! Bow to this priestess, or loose your head!"

Selay chucked, a dual then. Just perfect. For she was liquored, and ready to render asunder the world around her. She gave one last hard drink to complete this moment, and finish her cooking wine.

"I do not bow. You must dual, and force me to bow!" Selay challenged.

The Ua priestess was inflamed, and threw off her robe. Fortunately, and not to Selay's complete surprise, she was wearing something under it. There was a girdle, and an upper cuirass, with a skirt that would protect her legs. All brown, or black. Straps, and belts formed hangers for daggers, and pouches, all in quick reach for dispatch. Not so different then Selay's patchwork armour.

The scarf also was discarded, and a rather elaborate set of flowing frills, and long earfins were displayed. Her fangs protruded cutely, other teeth were shown in her anger.

"A dual? No! Submit to Ua's love, and be spared!" She offered.

"A dual! Yes!" Selay countered, "The only truth is violence! Ua must show she is stronger then I, and thus more true! Fight me!"

Gawundon glanced to her flock, she seemed to hesitate. Finscales are fearful of platescales, so this was expected. Selay had to push her just a bit more.

Selay licked her lips, "A priestess of the order should be willing to put her life on the line for Ua. Are you?"

"Ua is my life! I will die for her love!" Gawundon yelled in zeal.

"Then prove it!" Selay snarled.

"Only if your defeat means your submission to me for this trouble! I want you to pay in misery for what you did to my kin!" Gawundon threatened.

"If I win. You call off your agreements with Kiven, and tell me where I can find him!" Selay countered.

"No! Kiven is protected!" Gawundon tried to leverage.

"Kiven kidnaps eggs! I must kill him. Ua demands the same of you, and you are an accomplice for daring to protect such a creature!" Selay bargained.

Gawundon leaned back in surprise, "Kiven what?" she frowned, "Egg poachers? Not Kiven? Such nonsense! Stop toying."

"Finscales are easy to toy with, but this matter is not a toy. All of Allya stopped warring to protect our nests! I may even pay you for the trouble." Selay reinforced.

"I do agree with your moral cause, but I do not believe you," Gawundon said, "If you win, I may help you find these nest poachers, even without payment! Though I demand proof for their behaviors before I shed any blood."

Once again, Gawundon held her hand to her belly. She was wincing in the thought of it. She retracted, and stated, "A dual then."

"Finally!" Selay twirled her empty bottle by the neck, to hold like a sword, and crouched into a combat position, "Until one of us cannot stand anymore!"

Gawundon joined in agreement by taking her her own fighting pose. The discussion is over. Neither hesitated to charge towards each other in earnest.

First, Gawundon ducked, and Selay swung her bottle horizontally. Selay missed, while Gawudon skirted aside, and struck her hand into Selay's lower right body.

Selay only grunted softly as her hard scales absorb the impact. She aimed a downward bottle swing into Gawundon's head, but quickly had to retract to block a kick from

Gawundon as she spun back up. Selay's arm absorbed most of the force. This could have ended there if Selay did not rouse a defense.

She was facing Gawundon's large, and heavy tail, it was impossible to stop, and stung like a whip along her side. It was also controlling Selay's weight, and Selay could not escape it without stepping backwards. Gawundon followed with two solid punches into Selay's collarbones with intention to break. It only hurt.

Selay escaped this by swinging the bottle blindly. Gawundon had to change to defensive evades. Several swings, and misses later, Selay's left bottle hand was angled very high. A downward, and blind swing from the left impacted Gawundon's thick neck, and gills. Where it shattered, and caused her to yelp, the supple gills were vulnerable, and when squeezed, were very distressing to a finscale.

No shards were inside Gawundon's gills, and this allowed her to quickly shake it off. No blood, no abrasions, it was a quite professional bar brawler swing.

The lack of blood scent displeased Selay. It would be preferable to the others. She sought to remedy this by raking her right claw into Gawundon's shoulder, which resolved nothing as it made no impact. However, Selay followed with a stab into the finscales belly with her broken bottle.

Again nothing came, and in this Gawundon latched upon Selay's bottle arm wrist in desperation, and twisted it firmly, making the platescale hiss loudly. Selay dropped her bottle, and pulled her full weight into Gawundon's body, which took all control, and pressure from the finscale's grip.

Her larger body shook the finscale, and ensnared both together. This immobilized both of Selay's arms, and Gawundon's right arm. With her left claws, Gawundon slashed Selay's face, landing a solid scratch upon Selay's big muzzle.

Both pushed free, and snarled at each other. They stood opposed, and the others just supervised, following some quiet code of non-interference expected in an honor dual. It must be done correctly, or none of them would be able to extract their sadistic vengeance upon the platescale. A platescale who dares to disobey the divine contract of Ua.

"Brutish drunk, you bleed first! Give up! I shall let you take blade contracts if you surrender now!" Gawundon offered.

Selay wiped her maw, and looked upon her blood. She designed that the smell of blood was good now, and she is right. Her blood reeked of alcohol, and the pain cleared her head.

The platescale abruptly charged towards Gawundon. Deciding to match the wider angle, and speed of her opponent's trickery. Selay dove, and rolled her shoulders into Gawundon's feet. The finscale had to jump, and Selay jumped as well by catching her footing, and lifted Gawundon higher then the finscale planned. Selay turned to her side, and gripped Gawundon's ankle, and pulled, forcing her opponent into the center column, and shattering the stone boat.

There some scales broke. Though it was not upon anything other then her right side where she hit the statue. The priestess snarled, and managed to vault upwards, where she ran into the darkness to recompose.

Selay paused, as Gawundon dove over the hedge Selay previously lost a fight to. Selay remained stationary. Best not to involve her previous challenger, and that she was well intoxicated, and should not jump without a good launching point.

Gawundon climbed one of the tree trunks, then vaulted off towards Selay. They collided. The platescale was unable to maintain balance from the weight of the finscale, she simply decided to absorb the whole attack. Landing Selay a painful collision with the stone walkways onto her back.

Gawundon stood up, and stomped on Selay's chest. She put her footclaw upon the sore collarbone she previously attacked, and displayed herself in victory.

"Yield, platscale! Be mine!" Gawundon demanded.

Selay tried to deal with the pain, but every time she relocated, and appeared to care, Gawundon twisted her claw. This punctured her harder chest scale, and if not careful, her throat. Selay laughed when she realized that boat was now pebbles.

"Yield!" Gawundon's teeth bore as she grew intolerant.

"Not sober yet!" Selay laughed, and with both her arms she hugged Gawundon's foot, and twisted to roll.

This dug the finscale's claws solidly in Selay's chest, and it hurt enough to make her sound out. However, this took control of Gawundon's leg. Forcing her to pull back to free herself, and avoid having it break.

However, Gawundon was to receive a firm footclaw into the buttox just as she hopped free. Selay kicked her feet up, and the finscale tripped, and fell forward.

Then the platescale pushed her claws into her opponent's abdominal scales just so lightly. Recounting the times Gawundon gripped there, and assumed there was more to that. Selay was right, and the finscale trembled, and gasped, then desperately ran to a safe location. Her claws digging up Brudge's ground as she nearly panicked.

Rising to her feet, Selay looked sideways from Gawundon. Both examined briefly, looking for weakness, and momentarily factored a plan. Again they charged, and resumed their battle.

Selay gave a blind, but full, upward cut to disorient the finscale. However, Gawundon recovered too fast, and introduced a spin, and a full knee to Selay's side. The introduction was met with a turn that impacted to Selay's back scales, which were solid, and firm, so she barely felt it. Selay gave a left arm swing straight into Gawundon's maw. Gawundon recoiled but quickly recovered. She then used both her claws to quickly, and recklessly swipe Selay's now exposed belly scales.

Selay roared loudly as her white plates easily tore. This pain made her fall back, and nearly falter. However, impulse overtook her, and she charged back without a second thought.

She saw that Gawundon's right side was bruised when she broke that stupid ship. So Gawundon's right side must be the focus, and Selay applied a forceful right kick to push Gawundon away, and charged again.

Gawundon caught Selay's left leg, and she kicked the left foot of the finscale with her other leg to make her let go. A strike on Selay's face landed hard. The platescale let the impact take its toll on her maw, as now was not the time to be defensive.

Leaning to the right, and sidestepping, Selay let two jabs on her opponent's right side. Gawundon yelped at the second one.

The finscale spun tried a very forceful left arm swing, and a grapple to catch Selay's neck. This landed on an arm instead, and Selay was already behind Gawundon. Selay once again kicked Gawundon in the tail, who had to stumble forward.

The finscale tripped, and turned right back with a kick herself. Selay grappled her leg, throwing Gawundon to her side, and exposing her right again. There Selay placed two light fast jabs into her right breast.

Gawundon cried in pain, and held her balance, then met Selay with a solid, and fierce upward hit to her ribs. The force was heavy, and painful, and Selay felt herself loosing wind. She had to bite her tongue, and finally slapped the finscale over her head.

Gawundon began swiping again with her claw. Now it was too late, as the previous swing into Selay's hurt belly took all of the finscale's strength. So Selay managed to land five very light pummels into the her right side. Gawundon was becoming swollen at this point, balancing out Selay's bleeding wounds now.

The priestess escaped this descent by faking out Selay in another charge. She ran right. Her right flank protected her as she gave a grapple on Selay's neck with her arm, and a single solid impact on Selay's plated head made her fall to the ground.

Gripping her side, and breathing heavy, the finscale stumbled to a short distance. Her tongue hung out, and waved as the other blades were watching in either amusement, or surprise.

Selay, who took on long deep breath, and then stood up, was using her drunken state to ignore the pain. Back on her feet, she glared at the finscale, and stood like a stone statue with bleeding wounds. Gawundon became panicked, and was tired, and then turned to run to acquire a better vantage.

Selay gave chase to catch the assassin. Through the western path, and to the main servant's hall they ran. Gawundon immediately lept onto a large wooden beam, and used her claws to climb to the rooftops.

Selay stopped, and watched, then ran the southerly direction. She scaled up another beam. She was faster, as breaking into Brudge's home was nothing new, and she knew all the right spots. She used her speed to gain a momentum, and take flight off of the wall.

Gawundon made a panicked screech. The sight of a

flightfull Selay was unexpected. She did not know that Selay could fly. The finscale scrambled onto the roof, and ran southerly along it towards the great hall.

Selay gained distance, and was about to grab Gawundon with a dive when the assassin ducked left, and westward towards the living manor. Gawundon struck a glide, and crashed into the roof, kicking up stone shingles, and scrambling to the peak.

Selay flapped, and gained some air, but could not hold her flight for much longer. The platescale banked, and landed on the southern side of the living area, then turned, and sprinted to Gawundon.

The fleeing finscale pulled a spin, and threw two of her four daggers at once towards Selay. The platescale hussy was already diving, and crawling on all fours, as her inebriation failed at producing a good, and balanced landing. The daggers careened between Selay's extended wings, as she just charged bestiality for a pounce.

Gawundon slide down the roof, and took a charge along the side. She kicked up pieces of shingles, and caught behind Selay when she returned. She kicked Selay's tail, chuckling, but it was short lived.

Selay immediately spun, and kicked at Gawundon. She removed her daggers, and stabbed fore. Then swung with her right arm, and Gawundon stepped back. Then with her left, Selay followed up in a slash, blood trickled from a cut along the collarbone, and leather straps of the priestess. Who looked wide eyed at the rules changing so quickly.

Selay followed with her right arm that missed into Gawundon's side, but the finscale used all her strength to deflect, and twist Selay's next swing. Gawundon was shaking in her efforts, this was fear, and weakness showing.

Selay dropped her first knife, and Gawundon slammed her forehead into Selay's left forearm, which was guarding her face from this headbutt trickery. Selay bore her teeth, and dropped her second knife, and pulled her arm away.

The finscale twisted Selay's right arm, and was slow in mustering force. Last time she used her body, but this time, Selay took her solid head, and slammed square into Gawundon's eye. The finscale yelled, and stumbled back. Never headbutt a platescale.

Selay's lungs began to burn, and her head felt lighter. Disorientation, fatigue, and overheating were settling in. She refused all that with her will, and tightened her jaw to divert from holding her tongue out. She must not look weak.

Selay first hopped back, and roared as she charged. Her full weight, and speed now in effort as she made for one more assault. Gawundon was dizzy, and holding her eye. She panted, just as overheated as Selay is.

Selay did not land her attack, nor kick, or duck, but bypassed, and spun Gawundon. She grappled her arm, and slid a hand on Gawundon's side, and dove feet first. The dive landed Selay a distance enough away for another charge.

Gawundon took all her effort to stay upright on the angled rooftop, and was unprepared to react. Selay, who spends quiet a lot of time climbing buildings, was skilled in perching, even when very drunk. This let her charge again, and Selay spun the finscale, and was right behind her once more.

One final move, and this time a bounding kick to send Gawundon tumbling off the roof. This was not so, and Gawundon recouped her balance. Quickly the finscale grappled onto Selay's leg, then threw the platescale hard off the northern edge of the building.

Selay's heavier, and thicker body decimated all in the way. She fell like a sack of rocks through a few tree branches. The final stretch was the naked statue of the finscale woman, to which Selay shattered through unabated.

Dust, and chipped stone spread across the garden, and Selay splashed face down into the pond, tearing the lily pads apart.

When the dust settled, Gawundon came down. Landing from a glide, she limped over, with low posture. Her breathing ragged.

Selay's blood colored the water, but the incomprehensible hussy was, unfortunately, still alive. She rose her head, breathing heavy, her tongue out, and down full. The platescale quaked, and shuttered from the pain of the impact, with perhaps bones broken, she still laughed joyfully.

Gawundon stepped into the fountain to exert authority. She placed her footclaw onto Selay's back, and yelled, "You dare laugh! You are beaten, and I shall now cut your wing membranes so you never fly away from me!"

Selay looked from the side of towards her opponent, "Finscale blood smells so much more potent then platescale tonight. Do not you agree?"

Gawundon was to have none of this, and attempted to push Selay into the water to drown her. However, her foot, and leg shook violently. She was unable to summon any strength, and she fell.

"No!" she hissed in absolute pain as she crashed into the water.

With immediacy, the blades came out of the darkness, and surrounded the dueling women. Selay rolled to her side, and sat up. She took inventory, and smiled.

In huffs she concluded, "You cannot stand anymore. I win! Contract is called off!"

Gawundon was able to handle any water, she is a finscale. Though she was shivering, and faced Selay.

"You win. I yield." She shuttered, "Contract resented. We will not take business from Kiven."

Selay turned the finscale to her side, and ripped out a knife from her back. It was one of the two remaining knives Gawudon had left on her side. Selay took in in the first charge on the roof. Then in the second, stabbed her just right of her spine in the weakened scales.

"You are absolutely *stupid* for using knives," Selay said, as she twirled the bloody dagger, "Kiven's whereabouts?"

"He is in hiding, but we were to deliver reports of success soon at the old Synurl Family Fortress in central Selis. Many clients we serve also will be there with additional work," Gawundon tried to prop herself up, but failed.

Selay examined the wound, and saw it was as intended. She did not try to strike anywhere but the kidney. Since there are two of those, it would be less fatal. It would end the dual. The wound bled profusely, and the blood diluted the water far more then it was before. Gawundon could be recovered, stitched, and spend the rest of the summer in a bed.

"Whore of Brudge, I demand to know your name. I should know it for when I tell stories to my flock," Gawundon winced.

"Selay Quirksettle, of Tram, Daughter of Lambana Kitsuna, chosen of Huron Quirksettle." She stated.

"Lambana? I was not beaten by some drunk at the local tavern? Now I understan,." Gawundon laughed, and hissed at the same time.

"People call me a traveled drunk. I have tabs in all the major cities to pay. Sometimes, it can be both." Selay smiled.

"Kiven really is egg-poaching?" Gawundon asked.

"Yes. He also eats them, with others. I will kill them all," Selay replied softly.

"Why must you?"

"Because I must."

Gawundon smiled, "You do Ua's work then. Help me back up, and I shall join you in bringing Ua's justice to your enemies."

Selay twirled the blade in her hand again, and examined the blood upon it. She then placed it at the side of the fountain. She looked back at Gawundon, who was helpless now. Then at the others, who serve Gawundun, who looked confused. She helped the rouge sit up, who put her hand near he abdomen.

"Does Fuil know you are with his eggs?" Selay asked.

"Such personal things to ask about? Spring never came for us," Gawundon growled.

In determined that to do the things we so ordained, and do not have to explain again in this passing, we do. Now, we are in our first resolution in this conflict. We are presented with our first enemy. Our Shadows.

Selay quickly retook the dagger, and impaled straight through Gawundon's eye. The knife easily shattered bone. All life severed instantly from the finscale.

Selay was distant, and absent of any expression of life herself in the ascension of her absolute authority. No songs or rituals to perform as the Ua priestess gave no more sounds of pain. She fell into the water, then floated upward to its surface, her maw hanging open, and the knife lodged in her skull.

Selay stood, stained in blood, with her own wounds bleeding some still. The assassins around her all watching. She left the plaza slowly, as if she was a wraith, and into the shadows without any opposition. The contract was called off after all.

The blades all surrounded Gawundon's corpse. They knelt, and removed the lifeless finscale, rolled her in her robe, and carried her into the shadows where they all came from. They also collected the seals of their two fallen. They silently left.

The office window dimmed above. Brudge saw the whole affair. Watching the monsters do what they do so well.

Haiyear Choonadi

CHAPTER THIRTY

Let the first enemy fall to our sword. Continue immediately to preserve the advantage of shock, and force. Each step we take spreads the fire so wrought in this conflict. We butcher, and become like ash wraiths upon the field. Become the darkness that is terror to those who do not follow the Grateful Task.

In how they are, they must be afraid. This *Order of the Egg* knows it should be destroyed. They stir upon things that we had to stop history to resolve. Using finscale, and platescale arms, let us hold the world still until they are purged from it.

Port Selis may be Jester's capital, but Synurl Manor is not Jestarian anymore. A segregated fortress surrounded by a forest, walled off within the city. This was the place that the finscale kingdom was created. There Fordako lived, so did the Synyurl dynasty, and others. Prior to Synurl's death, it hosted the largest roost. Now it is home to rats, and moths.

The church of Jester was given hold of the estate. This prevented abuse by the squabbling Chancellors. It was not spared from contemptible priests, and neglectful ministers who would forget about it. The sovereignty of Jester, a joke of a thing, was not well-respected by its own mediators.

Tonight the embers of intrigue flickered. A curfew was called, and it allowed the guards to arrest plenty of the destitute, so none had a chance to see. Except one who had license to know by only his own authority.

Sounding cracked branches, and crushed leaves as he moved, Haiyear Choonadi was like a lumbering Wyvern through the estate's forests. For him, this was a masterful feat, for he is a large, and fit finscale, and platescale mutt. It was impressive in the mere idea that no guard heard him.

His trespass has the purpose of locating the Order Priest Raviwr Ricin. From Tram, now much farther north. His cart, and him were seen outside of the embassy. This is an indication of something of import happening, as an Order Priest should have no business in Jester in this current climatic weather. Old platescales can suffer swamp sickness, and feuding finscales have ideas, and knives. In fact, only a Wyvern Rider should be able to roam any bit free. Ones as Yelvian, or Oth, who are better suited for diplomacy with conniving finscales.

Ricin made no secret of his presence. A clearly marked cart with the seals of Tram, Skol, and the Order was first found stuck in a crowd by Choonadi as he moved about the market today. Its driver was swearing, and threatening the finscales around him, who in turn displayed mockery, and laughter. They considered his threats lacking water, and his words dry.

When the irritated platescale driver bore teeth, and claw, a small group of finscales showed full bottom at him. This made him try to run them over, and rush to the embassy. The scene was so obvious that Choonadi could only follow suit.

Soon the Tram Metropolitan departed once again, in the dark of the night after curfew. Naturally the herald's stalking resumed, and ended here. To the Synyurl Estates. The gate let the platescale priest in without a fuss. Choonadi let himself in with a glide over the wall, and made his way through the dark woodland.

This epicenter of finscale history was so awkwardly active. In his month in Port Selis, not once did the estate have bright lights such as this. This was also quite secluded. It could only mean something secret is happening. Where there is secrets, there are stories to sell.

Now the final bush gave way to a open cobblestone walkway that was covered in moss. Just by it was the complex. Choonadi stood in awe at the towering structure. An old Jestarian coastal fortress, impervious to the strongest of sieges, and armies.

Every window was alight, and people were inside. Like ghosts, maroon robed figures were about in pairs. Their wings shown strong with flight. Maws could be seen moving behind white cloth masks in conversations. When walking, they sometimes appeared to be floating room to room, and drank from glass cups.

Over at the entrance, Choonadi saw Ricin leaving his coach. He dawned the same mask, and a robe of a brighter red with gold trim. It was too dark to see much else, but the priest walked with his cane into the building. Following were two guards in robes. His carriage immediately left.

It was clear that Choonadi was woefully unready to enter the front door. There was someone guarding it who had a bulb on his tail with spikes. So he searched the premise for a better way in.

As expected in this late warm spring, someone opened a window on the second floor. A quick climb, a glide, and Choonadi grasped onto the frame, and pulled himself into the room.

The reason why this window must be opened is now known.

This was a washroom, and it was recently used. It was damp, and there was a coal burner under the brick tub that was still hot. Perfume, and soap are nearby. However, its previous user has recently moved on.

Choonadi moved on as well, seeing no robes, or masks, he had to explore elsewhere. The big man somehow silently crept down the hallway into a roosting hall unseen. Once this hall was clearly a nursery for the many children of Jester's royal family, and their mothers. Tonight this place is for private meetings between strange wraiths.

A man left a room down the hall, and Choonadi hid in another room, and peered out. The person was in costume, and hung another mask on the door handle. A signaling that someone else was there? *A murder?* The robed figure left with no sense of urgency.

Choonadi came to the door, and took the mask. He tucked it under his arm as he slowly crept inside. He reeled in disgust at what he saw.

A rather fat green man laid face down, naked upon the bed. He growled a choking snore of such immense volume that it could be confused for dying. He was not dying, he was a drunken mess. His robe flung over the foot of the bed.

Choonadi guessed that the hooked pattern, balled tail, and dual spikes made him someone from the Barum nations. He could not verify it, if he did, that would mean smelling him. His origin would be confirmed if he smelled of potato, and Choonadi was not ready to risk his stomach. So he just took the robe, and left as quietly as he came.

A sense of futility was sudden at the feeling of some sort of crust cracking in the folds of the fine silk. It would do, because he doubted he could get such a broad size anywhere else. After adjusting his wings, the New Freestride Herald took a walking posture that hid his details perfectly, and made his way towards the more populated halls.

It was perplexing now, that someone from Barum was here. Just as perplexing as a platescale regional priest. If Jestarian folk were to find out their royal estate were like this, they would all consider this a just cause for war with Skol. Then again, any *thing* is a just cause for war on Allya, for it turns the world. So the flavor of the gathering is not important, but the consequences shall always be.

He felt observed as he maneuvered through the halls of the main manor. Small talk, gossip, but nothing stood out as worthy of note so far. There was a soft sense an anticipation of something big to come, as several would seem to be nervous in their body motions.

Eventually Choonadi came onto the second floor of a vast gallery. Adorned upon the walls were paintings, all covered in cloth to protect from dust. The floor below was where the largest gathering appeared, and a flight of stairs were on the far side from where Choonadi entered.

Centerfold, to the back of the room, were two immense wooden statues of Ua, and Ain. They were rather shoddy, and of planks. Between them, and on the lower floor, an alter that they faced away from. Clearly assembled in large pieces, and painted gray to look as if they were stone. Both gods were naked, Ua held a scroll rolled shut with a seal bearing the words of Mother, Statecraft, Law. Ain held a sword, and shield with no immediately visible etchings. Both of them poised in defense, with their wings held high, as if they were holding up the ceiling.

Choonadi smiled in awe at the handicraft that must have gone into their design. As rickety as they were, they could be respected for their sheer scale. Ua's head, and eyes seemed to look back at him. He could only raze his head so she could see her child, and imagined her giving him a view of her glamour.

"Gewj, my boy! This person you shall meet will fund our

new project!" a rather annoying voice squawked, interrupting Choonadi's moment.

"I hope so, Vias," said a younger man, a bit nervous, "A story about a flying vigilante dispensing justice in Freestride is not going to be good without supporting cast, and the best props."

Choonadi scouted for the source of the voices. He found a plump man, reeking of lilac, pass by him. In his shadow a skinny figure, almost female, followed. They walked like a dog, and its master, one submissive, the other sure. The fat man gave a waddle as if he was gravid, which must have hurt his pelvis as he stepped.

"Of course, if he asks for special attentions you must be kind enough to give him some," Said the fat one.

"What kind?" Gewj sounded off defensive, "I cannot do anything that will displease my chosen!"

"Just offer him a show, a performance." Vias said as Choonadi began to follow, "He shall not want more then a preening."

"No! She will be mad at me!"

The two entered a doorway into another hall, which seemed endless. The door closed, then locked, and Choonadi was blocked from access. All he heard was a scolding Vias, "You will simply just not tell her."

Snorting, the herald had to move onward. Adultery, and nepotism is meaningless, and commonplace. He must have better. So he turned right, onto the balcony behind the statues. It was hauntingly dark, and private. There were already two men talking. Two broad men, right behind the Ain statue. The shadow of the shield only barely hiding them.

"This is bothersome. Lutivia proclaiming friendship with Barum Decor is going to upset the Talon Order, and thus the whole power balance of the coalition!" One said in a scratchy voice.

"Do not fret of it. bandits have already seized the bribe money. Barum looks foolish now that they promised a gift, and failed to protect its transport," the other said confidently, "Just advise the king to send a gift, and there shall be no change."

Sighing, the scratchy voice said, "I hope so, for the sake of the whole order. The coalition wills it otherwise, and neither of us can face Vex alone if this goes afoul."

"Aye, but it shall not," the other nearly sung, "Vex wants finscale blood more then ours. We must only seem stronger then Jester. Which is why we are here, to discuses how to weaken the Chancellorship."

The other snorted, "We would be talking more officially if we did not have to initiate someone this year."

The other seemed mildly bothered by something, he leaned down to watch the crowd, "That new member would be Kiven Di' Noach, some of the money of Jester we can siphon into our own ends."

The other just gave a growling laugh, "What a catch! I suspected that is the man who shoved that peg into Derin's filthy, and pretentious ass?"

"That is him."

"The news of the riots is amusing. A herald down a well. What a show!" The scruffy man coughed a few as his excitement was too much. He was clearly ill.

The other man stayed calm, "Kiven is a brother of chaos in our little order."

The other took a sip of wine, and growled. He continued a bit of a coughing fit, and signaled agreement, "Foul Jestarian air!" he gagged.

His companion roared down, "Will someone close the window, this draft is drying!"

"Now we just need to deal with Thraalin, and his new boats," the coughing man said, drumming up phlegm, and spitting upon one of the covered paintings. Choonadi did his utmost to stay back.

"One of his privateers was caught in a skirmish with a navy ramming ship not too long ago. He will have to answer for it in the session coming," The other smiled, "Our finscale brothers shall deal with him there."

"Good. That oaf needs to be tied up, and fired from a ballista. My spies caught him playing with toy boats in the wash basin like a hatchling would."

"He is a bit mad," the other said.

Choonadi had to rest himself on a wooden beam. Those two were talking so eagerly of the fate of nations as if they controlled it themselves. This was no simple gathering, this was a secret fellowship of some sorts. The dealings, the clear innuendos, and the lack of women, who would gossip about it, made it abundantly clear. He must find a way to tell everyone, Chancellor Dos must be told.

If the colonies knew, the Restavias council could muster a defense in ready. He could advise in warning about plotters with purpose though Freestride. Though he must get this purpose first.

He began to pass by those men, who glared at him. They knew he was listening, and still talked. He walked down the stairs, and into the crowd. He felt scared for his life at this point, as if not only the gods, but some shadow from the idle was now intently seeing him. He continued on anyway to see two men were discussing over empty wine. A very short one, and a tall broad man.

"This is not prudent, or pragmatic, it is reckless," the smaller one said irate, "If he dies right in the public, it will end the life of his killer."

"So be it. Chaos is what matters most. Just the thing we need to stop the emergency session," said the taller, "Jestarian legislators will not be meeting for another three months if we can stop this. They are fickle enough to cancel the meeting over a corpse like his."

"I hate it! This will draw too much attention to one of our members," the little man growled.

"Not with the outrage the herald's are creating. Everyone shall call for Derin's head no matter the writ's contents. Derin will take up sympathy with the killer for eliminating his rival, and we shall have a spy right in our enemy's employ," the taller explained, "Understand, friend?"

"I still hate it. This is going to escalate, and maybe backfire."

"It is what Ricin says is the Grateful Tasking. We must do this. We must control both sides of what is to come, and rend the wounds we make so wide that the finscale hydra dies."

This was more for what Choonadi needed. A grand conspiracy to control the flow of history in some direction. Though for what end? They are not profiting with coin, they are in fact going to loose vast estates, and fortunes if Jester falls. Something bigger is afoot, and Choonadi must strive to find it. He must do this, for his fellow finscales.

A bell sounded, clear, and omnipresent. Choonadi could not find any direction it was from, but it was there. A soft horn followed up, in a low pitch of sorrow. Everyone ceased their prattling, and faced towards the alter. They shifted into a formation of rows, seemingly preassigned.

One man off in the corner gagged, and growled after touching the wall. He could not say anything, but someone apparently spilled an oily substance upon it, and he touched the results. He was staring at his hand, and using his robe to clean it. He then joined into the crowd, vanishing.

The bell sounded again, and everyone was stopped. Everyone but one, as he was sleeping, and locked in his room. Replaced by a Herald who was going to tell the world of this thing. The smell of smoke from somewhere was detectable.

"In the end, nothing matters! All born shall die! What we create shall be destroyed!" boomed a voice from everywhere in the hall, with a clear platescale gruff.

Choonadi gazed upward to see the eyes of the great idles light. Someone has candles in the heads of the statues, or more aptly torches, as there was clear smoke.

"The only thing that is eternal, that has no end, is the Gods of the Twin Suns! Who radiate forever!"

The mouth of Ua opened, and let out a cloud of smoke. Choonadi saw the ropes on the jaw, and also the glitter dust that was of chalk that toned the smoke orange of fire. Obviously, it would be stupid to use real flame in this tight room.

"Ua our beautiful mother! Her eternal warm wing!"

Immediately Ain's maw opened the same, breathing the same colors of smoke. The room became hazy some.

"Ain our father, we seek to be strong like him!"

The maws closed, and there was just a brief silence.

"However, they are in eternal war, and chaos. To defend the nest, and prepare for the great war to come. Only in spring do they call for peace, to see to their children. Who are us."

"However, in the betrayal of Numril, they demand eternal punishment! We are the All Ua Ain's, the children of Ua, and Ain's nest! Ain has cut the wings of the All Ua Numril, the children of Numril. Thus we, and them, now must face trial before we can join them!"

"There are those who fly, we are they! We are the given the Grateful Tasking. The duty to command, and rule the children of Numril until they pass the trial, and regain their flightfull wings!"

"So we guide them!"

Choonadi saw two people from behind the statues. They

held torches of fire that broke through the darkness behind the alter. One was a finscale woman, the other a platescale man. They were naked, healthy, and strong. They were slaves, as when they opened their wings there was no webbing to be had. They exposed their naked bodies to the crowd from by the alter, and stared emotionless, like statues.

"These are the flightless, our flock. Those who come from Numril. We must take good care of them, and guide them. They are required to *obey* the Grateful Task, and *kneel* before us in it!"

Both knelt down, and then lowered their head in submission. Their tails curled around their ankles, and they remained still. In exposing their necks, there was no protection from death, showing pure surrender.

"Finscale, and Platescale are alike in they follow the creed of Ua, and Ain, along with us all. They may be rivals, but they are not dissimilar in their way of the Grateful Tasking." The voice continued.

"What be the Grateful Task? Ua, and Ain demand them to contest, but they signed an Armistice. They have betrayed the Task. There is no reward for peaceful armies in the Trial."

A bitter smell eased into the room, and Choonadi felt his heart race. He was excited, and this was shared in the crowd by tail motions. The thing of this smell clearly had aphrodisiac properties.

"In the end we have prepared the world for what is to come! Because what we create *must be destroyed*! We created Skol, and we created Jester, in their totality, and now we shall see their finality! The Grateful Task demands the union of these peoples as one! Land, and sea *must combine*! As so many have unified into our creations before!"

The two slaves stood up, and faced each other. They opened their wings, and struck rather alluring poses. Gills glistened on the woman finscale, and the man bore his chest scales to signify his solid defense.

"In this union, there shall be a more pure people birthed!"

The coupled approached each other, and embraced. They spend moments staring into each other's eyes like long lost lovers. Choonadi felt this was a genuine expression between these two, and the act was both staged, and real. Or they were well-trained.

They guided each other back behind the alter, and into the darkness. Or more perhaps as dark curtain hung below the balcony that Choonadi once stood on. He only noticed it now in its first upset.

"Spring is over, and the warmth of the gods is greater now in the summer! So to warm our hearts to this coming union, and the rebirth of the Trial. Let us Feast!"

The couple came out, and they held together a large prop of an egg. No, it was not a prop, it is *real*!

"Behold! This egg is the product of the union of a platescale, and a finscale! Proof they are both of Ua, and Ain's love!" proclaimed the voice.

The couple placed the egg upon the alter, and light coal under it into a burst of brilliant fire. The egg itself illuminated, and showed the world its contents. The darkened form of a living child, curled, and pathetic. Its tiny wings, arms, and tail would twitch a little as it was sensitive to the new heat.

Choonadi was concerned, for this was not proper egg care. It should be with its mother, and should be nestled in a nest of softness. The shell is brittle, the child's scales are unformed. It must stay where it was laid until hatching. What are these people doing? This was wrong of them.

The voice resumed, growing softer, and tender, "This child, subtle, and innocent of all this, is *cursed*!"

Choonadi now was most attentive. A curse? This child

was a mixture like him. No one thought this mix in such way. It would be stupid for the Kiri'grana to think this too.

"Like all born today who are not cleansed. They are subject to Vex's curse he laid forth when he took power. Unworthy of his task, he bathed in the blood of innocents. In ritual sacrifice of his own peers, he demanded the gods to bring back the souls he wronged to posses his servants in all the nest. This possession consumes us all, the rot, the plague, the greed, and entitlement of Jestarian, and Skolis alike is evidence of our its hold. We have strayed from the Task."

Once again both slaves knelt down, they held their wings open, "However, we are free of the demons of Vex."

The slaves lowered their wings, and struck submissive poses again. Behind them, center of the alter, a tall robed man slowly came forward. He then stood on some crate that made him tower over the egg, and fanned his wings out. It was Ricin, he was the voice, this is his performance.

"Those free of Vex's curse can once again take upon the Grateful Tasking! We have overcame his sins to return to our rightful place in the heavenly order! This egg represents the vessel to purify!"

Then Ricin lifted upwards a long metal object. It was like a elongated needle for sewing. Glistening of silversteel, and so long it made Choonadi gulp nervously.

Ricin held it over the egg in presentation, "The soul of the child in this egg, like all children who die of simple rot, return to Ua, and Ain to be born again."

He angled the needle to the side of the egg, and simply pushed it inside the shell. Impaling through the clear albumen, which spilled out in small droplets down its side, he came to the neck of the child.

The horror Choonadi felt made it challenging to contain his disguise. His eyes were widened, and he had to flex his claws to not go into a rage. It took everything to keep his tail from thrashing. This is what he was looking for. This is the hidden truth that would be impossible to explain. Who could believe him? Did not the world stop over this? Did all not make peace to prevent this?

The needle touched upon the poor baby, and it began to squirm at the intrusion into its sac. Then with sure force, Ricin plunged the tip into the neck. The child's mouth opened in a muted shout of agony, and its limbs violently thrashed, and flailed. It took no effort to dislodge the vertebra of the neck, and tear apart the thin hide of the child. Ricin blew into the end of the needle, it was hollow, which completed the process, and split the child's head from its body. It became stiff, just as the blood blotted out the figure, and a ring formed around the outer shell of the egg.

"We free this child of the trial, so we may free ourselves to pass your judgment, Twin Gods!" Ricin said, then began singing a song in a dialect that Choonadi could not identify as Jestarian, or Skol. A wholly different, but familiar, language.

The room joined in unison, they all feigned sorrow for the now murdered hatchling. If Choonadi just had a sword, he would cut all their heads off, and send them to Ain's trial to face the child they just destroyed. They would have to tell a naive soul that lie. It is a lie, this is not what Ua, and Ain demand of us.

When the hymn ended, Ricin removed the needle from the egg. That was when the blood poured out, and then clotted. Ricin dipped his talon in a bowl of water, recently placed by a slave. Choonadi could see both slaves tried desperately to hide their eyes. Their maws were glistening with tears, as this was their child.

"This vessel is ready for the Great Feast! Our newest brother is to come forth to capture his demon in it, and be purified!"

From the crowd, a man of medium size came to the center of the room. He then opened his wings, and slid off his robe. His mask also fell to the floor, and he was exposed naked to the alter.

He was finscale, white with yellow tones dotted around him. His maw of medium length, and his eyes were green. The fins on his head, tail, and legs dangled as he waited.

Ricin held a claw out to beckon him, "Kiven Di' Noach."

"Kiven Di' Noach..." the crowd longingly said, and those near touched the naked man as he began to slowly saunter to the alter.

Kiven the banker, a dead child, a preacher, and plotting people from all over. This society must not be allowed to be secret anymore. There is too much power here, too much rotting. Choonadi began to feel sick now, and stepped back some to prepare to leave.

As Kiven took his position at the alter, a feeling of terror began to overtake Choonadi. The herald felt his scales stiffen. A frightful monster was felt glaring over this whole affair. Ua, and Ain must be coming, he felt, they must stop this.

Ricin took his position behind the egg, and opened his wings in a towering display again, "Ua, and Ain, your warrior seeks to be free of Vex's control! He shall slay your enemies, and serve only you! Let the new trial commence!"

The slave couple stood up, and obediently guided Kiven to his correct position by the alter. They turned him to the crowd, and began to clean his body. They used their maws to pick dirt from his scales, and then wet towels to care for his gills.

When Kiven glistened, and shone, the slaves left, and he then knelt down, and Ricin spoke, "Now brother, sing your song!"

Kiven bowed his head, and glared down his maw, "I am Kiven Di' Noach, a flightfull finscale follower of Ua. I have provisioned armies in the war for Jester, made full the bellies of the unready. Gave homes to innocents. I have amassed a king's fortune for the Trial to come."

The crowd repeated what Kiven said. They chanted it together in various tones, and styles. Some proud, others not.

"I have seen a rat scurry through Jester, pretending to be more then he is. I once regarded this rat as my sworn ally. However, he is arrogant, and defies the Grateful Task of unification. He worked to build his own armies, and so I struck him with fire. The Derin Estates shall collapse forever within the week. This is my offering of Chaos."

The crowd sung with spirit when they spoke the last line about Chancellor Derin. Choonadi saw smiles, and heard churls from members. How did Derin make these enemies? The man was very much loved among the kingdom.

Ricin said firmly, "Now Kiven, you are loyal to the gods. You have overcame your demonic curse, and idleness. Now take the final step towards salvation. Take the egg, begin the Great Feast."

Kiven rose up, and turned away from the crowd. He stood tall, and waited for Ricin to get into position. He was just near the egg.

"KIVEN DI' NOACH!" roared a haunting feminine voice from the darkness above.

Kiven ceased his advance to stare up. A glass jar of oil slammed into the floor behind him, and oozed out slowly in all directions. Between Kiven, and the egg landed a large creature. It flung its wings open, and a dust spread away from it. It was a woman, a platescale woman, clad in leather armor, blue with white belly scales, pronounced cheek plates, and a blood red war skirt. She stood so fearsome, that all others shrunk.

The crowd was looking at each other, unsure if this was the show, or not. However it was meant to be, Ricin fled quickly, and could be seen running from the side of the Ain statue, and into the shadows. He was scared of this woman, so this must not be his doing.

There was on her back, this staff. It was not just a lonesome stick, but it was one of the seal of Ua, and Ain. It was *the* staff, the same one that Vex should be guarding. By now the news of its theft is established, so is the death of Zyrko, and the wanton chaos around it.

Kiven seemed to know for sure who this was. He could only fall to his knees, and squeal out a pitiful cry. His true finscale nature is now shown to the room.

His pleas were not of mercy, but of a desperate acceptance of the inevitable, as a glistening long stiletto blade rose up above his head. Then suddenly, it was driven through his skull, and lodged surely there. Ending his lamentable noises. No effort was made to collect the knife, and the woman pushed Kiven's head to face the crowd. His face stared with wide eyes, and open maw while blood spilled upon her feet. Then pandemonium broke loose.

Some began to charge her, but a single flick, by her tail, of burning a coal from the alter fire struck upon the oil. The smoke erupted, and even the air caught fire. Everyone fell back, and coughed, including Choonadi who could only stare at this woman.

She stood as a statue. Her burning green eyes examining, and clearly memorizing everyone in the room she could. When she looked upon Choondi, all he felt was a need to fly away.

The flames consumed, and torn through the wooden statues now. The fear of this platescale became fear of burning to death. Others in the room were running out in every direction. However, every door was burning, and every wall was made of some stone. There was no viable exit other then a window. Which the first through it was on fire, and died instantly from the attempt. Everyone else desperately climbed out of the window in terror.

"There is no where you can hide! I shall find, and kill you all!" swore this woman.

Before any thought could be made, the head of Ua cracked, and crashed between the woman, and Choonadi. Causing the herald to run, and dive through the window, consumed by panic.

As he landed, he veered off into the darkness, and did not stop running until he was enough away to loose his robe. He raked his claws in rage over it, and tore it apart. Then removed the mask, and shredded it with no mercy.

What he just saw was nothing as he expected. He thought some secret order, advisers hiding out for a day making favor, would be a fun way to sell intrigue. However, the child, the egg, that platescale woman, all said something worse.

Those that rule us, the Kiri'grana, killed that child. This was not their duty. They did so calling for the death of all in their own wars. Wars we all want to see, but not without rules.

Did Choonadi even want war? He did not right now. He just wanted to go back, and save that egg to make sure it hatched. He saw the child's dumb little face staring at him from just out of the egg smiling. Then back to the ritual. The veneration of the act, and the blood on the shell. A life denied its trial.

Choonadi bore his fangs at nothing, he snarled, and spittle fell from his maw. His breathing ragged. He wanted to go back to break every neck in that Great Feast he could.

He thought again of the egg, and fell down. He threw up

right there, and tried to crawl back up. He was not strong enough.

Then he tore at the ground with his claws, and snarled. He thought he could write a story about it in the heralds, and have the criers talk about it. Then he realized that no one would believe him, they will call him mad.

He rolled over, and curled his large body into the same position the child in the egg was. He shuttered, and imagined himself curled around it, guarding it from the world. He felt his soul cry in pain, and bellowed in agony. He felt as if he died tonight, his ties to those who rule over him began to sever. All he could moan was:

"I have seen evil."

Tailya

CHAPTER THIRTY-ONE

So falls our foes upon the field. This conflict is resolved in the proper way. Give only the smallest sorrow for the evil that had to be done, and celebrate our triumph.

Bury our foes, then sing their songs to announce their merit. We must ensure they get proper station. Tend to the spoils. Bloody swords to clean, chipped axes to sharpen, and dented shields to reshape smooth. All things, once theirs, now is ours. Weapons reforged, cities to rule, flightless subdued, and fields to sew.

Our Kiri'grana divide best all this treasure. The Flightless do not have the capacity to be above worldly burdens. Save for the ones skilled enough to count without use of claws should make good indexers, they can help carry the parchments.

They receive this privilege from being of the linage of the Ki'Grana dynasty. From the great maternal care they gave, and order they established. They sit upon the top as sovereign to all. Dictators of the Task, from in Skolis, the world capital, and all her clients.

Tailya laid on her back, gazing at the towering plumes

of smoke that rose high above the various ships she recently escaped from. The conflict, now so distant, was silent. She could tell the ships were sailing apart from each other, the cloud from the flaming hulls becoming wider at its base. The Skol Empire vessels were the only ones remaining, now haunting towers anchored in formation away.

She also knew that no one would come to collect her. The battles of men, more interested in their own tails then that of their betters, was not to be interrupted on the mere plight of a some platescale woman stuck on an island. Even if she was a flightfull. There is death to be dealt, Ain thirsts for blood, and this battle is the igniting spark of war that shall turn this world anew.

All Tailya could do was shiver in her soaked heavy dress, sit up, and hug her knees. There she was, on a lonely island in a small chain of them. With no insects, some fish carcasses, and a rib of some raft rotting.

This misfortune was one deserved for rescuing Huron from drowning. He did, after all, refuse her. Though she feared that without him, she could never cope with what she is to face. Late spring, and the pain of being alone, were unbearable thoughts.

The swim to this beach was rough, and the jostling on Tailya's body has her now concerned about broken shells. If the damage is done, it would only be a matter of time before she would feel searing pain, and bloat from bleeding. Then feint from it, only to die mere moments later, and face Ua in disgrace. Broken shells lead to laceration, and hemorrhages.

With this fear now in her mind, she rest her chin on her knees, then wept. She gazed out to the sea. Her face pleading to the gods for death come faster.

Some discomfort came on her belly, and Tailya leaned back to rub, and give inspection. Under her skirt, pressed hard on her scales was a tarnished metal coin. Tailya tossed it away, as what good was such things where she is?

This unfinished coin lifted into the air. It pushed sand out of its way easily. This made Tailya distressed, and she made a desperate whining. This stupid thing defied even her rejection of it, as its lack of immediate value turned into a mockery of Tailya's fate. In its pretentious floating, it became of such import that it could buy her safety, food, and a doctor, if only she were on the mainland. The Graceful coin, that Jennu wanted to guard, has its irony now painful to gaze upon. Jennu, for all he is worth, drowned in that sea in front of her.

Suppose that this was a fitting conclusion for one so pure of stock as Tailya Mek'velor. A life of isolation, confusion, and enslavement. Never was she free to so as much as dress herself. Recently, with this journey with Huron, she tasted some semblance of autonomy. She hated it. However, around Huron, she felt more secure, in a way not unlike when she was with her mother a lifetime ago.

A lifetime ago, it seemed, that Tailya was able to climb every tall cabinet, and shelf. One where hanging from wooden beams by her tail, and squeaking, was her great accomplishment of the day. Or feasting on fat cockroaches, and flies. Or dodging a leaky roof, and cowering in her mother's arms when the wind would cause the house to creek suddenly.

This was life in the eastern peninsula on Ilimnus, where the Empire was least interested in government. There, Tailya was left to live in poverty in a fishing village with her mother, who was the gemstone in the eyes of many of the men there. They called her queen, and gave her trinkets, and food in tribute.

A night that began curled up on her mother's chest, became a morning awakened in a horse-drawn carriage. With that, the soft purrs of safety, and love became the cold glares of power hungry nobles. All who made her a pawn in a great game she had no idea about. When the priests of the Order loomed, and sentenced her to isolation, she cried for mother, only to become eventually caged by them. Now, in her first year of adulthood, she cries out to return to the old pens, and her mother's wings, where it is warm, and safe.

No harm was ever brought upon her directly, as the church cared for their leverage well. Tailya was fed, clothed, and groomed to perfection. Locked away, in moldy keeps, and given entire floors of castles to roam alone, or with a regular troop of caretakers to watch over her.

Not once would she be allowed to leave. Never were the boys allowed near her, and most certainty she was denied any books that were worth reading. In fact, she was always read to, and kept ignorant on to the goings on in the world.

When she was upright, around seven, a Ua priestess tutored her. She was told how to stand, be proper, treat frills, and given simple flying lessons. Most importantly, she was given a pillow filled with beans, shaped like an egg, and told to curl around it as if it was her own. She was told, in no doubt, that she is to be a mother. Her life was the nest, and to her future husband.

She was told that her children would be the generation of kings to rule the entire world. The mandate of Ua and Ain, and their Grateful Task, she was responsible for. In all this, Tailya was made most special then others, and thus not allowed to befriend them, lest they betray the gods like Numril did. Or so they preached.

For Tailya, was the last title holder of the liquidated Mek'velor Kingdom of Skolis. When the shameful Warlord Vesuvious Vex slaughtered his way to power, he incorporated an Empire, not a Kingdom. This meant he created a title in place of another, he usurped.

The Wyvern Order recognized this technicality, and

refused Vex's calls for centralization of power. Skolis was a master of clients conquered, and Skol seeks to be absolute. In this, there was no ability to call an organized state of total war, and Vex could not make one until all disputes are resolved. Tailya was taught, in no uncertain terms, she is that dispute's resolution.

Tailya's marriage would give Vex's son the full claim on all the Skolis vassals, and thus they could resume their claims on Jester. Also, their further claims on the entire egg of Allya. This was Ordained when the Order's Wyvern migrated to Skolis. All she had to do was to bear children with the son of her father's murderer.

Alas, in statecraft, all things must be difficult. Tailya was kidnapped two years ago, by dukes, and petty lords of the western regions. Each one trying to use her to impress the Emperor Vex, and each one resorting to trickery to prevent such things.

The final hands were of rebels, who opted to liberate her, and restore her as a Queen of Peace. With its leader offering his hand in marriage. Tailya was not impressed. Of course, these rebels were slaughtered, and the dukes reclaimed her.

The many holds, and basements, she was forced to hide in, were places of people who died shortly later. All becoming increasingly more lonely, impoverished. Her term in them shorter as chaos circled daily in the upper halls. She was unable to understand much of it.

The dukes that held her were arrested en mass by an illegal encroachment of the Tram church in the region. These white gowned thugs spirited her away to meet with someone named Ehtah, who then took Tailya to Tram. During which, her first fire erupted, and made all around become zealous, and desire her. Like all women in first seasons, she was confused, and terrified.

She was thrown for too long in a dungeon in Tram, there she met Huron. Who was a statue. Who came from the darkness. He was consumed in her fire, until he became scared, and made her continue to suffer.

Today, that fire raged unyielding in her. Tailya wanted it to end, and it would end in pain at this pace. A pain that was clearly slow to arrive. With only just the discomfort of eggs pressing inside her, she continued to wait, drawing memories to divert herself from lessor thoughts.

Over to her side was the large, and still, form of Huron. He washed up about two wings away from her, on his side. Tailya saw no life in him, and yearned for him to be around now. She wanted to hear his timid deep voice, even if he insulted her. She felt Huron to be now lost forever, and she cried out to the sky in sorrow.

Then, she growled. If she was to die here, Tailya decided it would be against someone she chose. This made her more confident, and bold. So the woman drug her gravid body towards Huron. She wanted to feel him once again near her, like when she was behind his wings in Freestride.

She touched Huron's wing-hand gently first, and jumped a little as it twitched. It loosened itself at contact. She let back as it tried to tighten again. Huron has not gone yet! He is still here! Tailya continued to rub her hand on his his wing arm, and climbed along his body.

His scales were icy cold, his cloths heavy, and wet like hers. When Tailya leaned her body to his, Huron began to shiver. His breaths staggered.

The weight of her belly was becoming too much. It was clear the swim strained her body. In response, Tailya crawled back to the coin, and plucked it from its defiant hover. She shoved it between her breasts, and crawled on all fours back to Huron, instantly lightened by the coin's flight. She covered Huron's entire torso with hers, and caressed him.

The shivering grew worse, and the cold was made more uncomfortable by the warm spring wind along Tailya's now opened wings. Huron began to make a soft, and desperate gulping sound, as if he was drinking.

She was terrified that Huron was going to die soon. She pawed her hands on Huron's chest. Making wines, and pleaded at him as she did when he fell at that flaming manor.

A full cry was not enough to make Huron rise to face her this time. So she simply laid her head on his chest, and listened to his heart. It was beating desperately, unsteady, and chaotic.

Tailya was blaming herself now. this whole thing began when she ran from Gintrix. If she let him capture her, Huron would go free, and she would be eating cake in some office somewhere. A comfortable life as a breeder to child of someone who murdered her family would be better then this. It was not like Vex's son was as bad as his father? Of course, this life would be empty, with no purpose other then to populate the government with new rulers. Huron would be alive though, and Tailya could maybe have visited him, and rewarded him for his protection of her.

Now the quaking was terrible. Huron, and Tailya's cloths combined to make the cold worse. She stripped herself, and now naked, pulled Huron's cloths, but only could lift his shirt, and remove his trousers.

Immediately she felt the roughness of his scales, and her shivering abated when what little warmth they had met. She leveled herself with him, and pressed her hands on Huron's chest to hold herself. He should die warm, and in comfort.

She took pity on him at this point, and curled tighter. Her tail wrapped around his. She choose then that if its time to die, she shall choose Huron officially.

She really chosen him when they first met. She did not

understand how she could not do so. He was all she could hope in her perfect husband. He is dumb, strong, and cute. From first touch she wanted to be his. Tailya lifted herself back up, and tried to nose bump Huron, knowing this is her last moments with him.

Such a virtuous man he was. Huron's quest was to leave home to find his lost love. Most would never risk such things, but this 'Selay' he called for in his moments of pain was his lost gemstone. His family he swore to never abandon. In his expression of loyalty for her in his every moment, Huron earned himself worthy of it in return. These virtues Tailya wished for in her Kingdom, the Kingdom Vex had taken from her. The Kingdom lost when the world stopped.

Tonight though, on this Island, Tailya was her own queen. While in Skolis Tailya should sit, her authority here on this atoll is recognized now by her own self-appointment. She decided that she was to make Huron her King on this island tonight, and no one could tell her otherwise.

It was her divine right to her subjects to direct their policy. Huron is her subject, and she proclaims him her's in all ways possible. No longer can he be 'Selay's,' simply because Selay abandoned him. Tailya would never do such a thing. His refusal of her prior, is now vetoed. So she held herself against him, and did not let go now, gripping tightly.

Besides, Huron is owed a reward. He suffered through all this for no good reason other then Tailya's lack of wisdom. When she had no place to sleep, or to turn to in Freestride, Huron handed her his things. He slept outside, and Tailya was warm inside. A person of Huron's manors should never be denied happiness as long as Huron has been.

For three years without contact is agony for anyone. If this 'Selay' was alive, because clearly she is dead now, she would have been apt to return to her husband, and comfort him. She did not, and so her whereabouts matter none. Tailya is here, and in Huron's last moments, he should be loved, and in with someone who owes him herself.

She owed Huron at least this. If she was in her proper throne, she could have paid him in riches for protecting her in her most vulnerable times from the minions of the illegitimate Emperor. Who sees her as a thing to use for his own gains.

Tailya sat up, and growled into the sky. She pressed her hands on Huron's chest, and let the gods hear her position on this. She is nothing but a tool in a bigger game. A breeder to lay eggs, and distribute land. In this, she had no control over her fate, her trial in Ua's eyes was a poor joke. This cannot be allowed any more. Damn Ua's Tasking. Vex does not deserve his little plans. Rebel, did Tailya, in this final moment.

So, in this, Tailya queries Ua. The great story of Numril, and the betrayal come to mind. So be it, Tailya chooses, she chooses to follow Ua in her betrayal of Ain.

Except, Numeral encouraged the betray, and Ua fell for it. Tailya will be Numril this time, and Huron shall be Ua. It is time to divide the world again, she felt.

Tailya threw her head up, and roared to the gods in in full. Then, she held still, and waited. Below her, Huron coughed, and gagged as water came from his maw. Then, when he fell still, Tailya laid across his chest, listening to the beating heart of her mighty Chosen all night. She was not to abandon her family now, as they naught her. Her head was finally clear, and the fire doused. She waited for the pain of the egg shells to appear, and Huron's heart to finally be still. None of these things would come, and they both slept soundly.

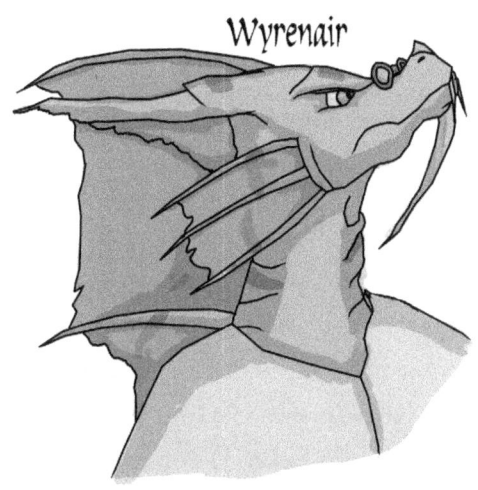

Wyrenair

CHAPTER THIRTY-TWO

The suns set upon crimson-irrigated fields. With evil deeds completed, we retire to our camps. When we rest, we dream to fly our banners over the Great Hall of Selis. The burdensome quarrels of the queer members of the Fordako Pact we shall suffer no more. For platescales prepare to bring proper order. Jester's end will ripple across the world, and force all to rise to face us. In this, we shall return to the grace of the Twin Gods, and light the Trial anew.

This tormented Brudge as he climbed the endless stairs in front of the hall. He did not risk flying up, as his thoughts left him pensive. The sight of flying into the wall would be an additional scandal to deal with, and he must maintain discretion.

He brought with him a pair of mercenaries hired for mere trinkets. He gave them armor, taught them hand singles, and various barks, and made sure they seemed somewhat fit. He needed dogs to bring upon leashes to show he was still strong.

The guards at the top of the stairs let open the door, and Brudge passed through into the darkened lobby. To a floor glistening ocean blue marble, and walls, and ceiling bearing

paintings of historical events. From the signing of the
Fordako pact, to many navy adventures, to the wars that
defeated the platescales. The final piece showing the funeral
of Fordako, which took place in this room. The story of
Jester continued into the branching offices, and main forum.

The blue tone made Brudge think of his little
platescale. She returned rather quietly to his estate last
night. For once, she was not keen to insult him, and hid
away. This was very strange of her, and made Brudge upset. He
yearned for her attacks like a glutton, and was mired in the
show she gave him in Deep Lake. He had to stop to control his
awkward feelings. He needed to be reigned in.

When this is over, Brudge will order Selay to be his.
By force. His platescale was so savage, and unkempt, but he
found her quarreling nature rather desirable. She is loud,
and smelly. She defiled things civil, and he saw her
admirable. When her desires were set on something she was
unstoppable, destructive, and violent. Where others in his
flock hide under his wings, Selay would trash the room on her
way out, lash Brudge, and everyone else with insults, and
ugly truth. There were no kind words from Selay, but Brudge
found her manipulations attractive, and profitable,
nonetheless.

He then noted about Selay some thing. It destroyed his
hope of ever having a productive marriage. She showed no
concern over being gravid this spring. With no effort to
protect her belly, and even entertaining viscous combat. This
meant infertility, and this disrupted Brudge's thoughts of
her enough to calm him. She would be a useful wife, but not
in the most vital ways he required.

Brudge had to curse himself for thinking what he did.
This was a circular fixation on one foul woman, who would see
him crushed under his own bookshelf, rather then protecting
her. She lied about her marriage with some pathetic scoundrel

in Skol to ward him off. She deflects, assaults him, and scams him into her crimes. She eats off his plate, pays him naught, but he still returns to help her. She then showed herself to all the leaders of the Chancellorship. This game is becoming too dangerous, she may need to be contained.

He indexed other women in his hold to settle for. All suited him equally, as they preen just as well. However, none would be able to handle power, and such were unsuitable. Someone must be chosen for him soon, as his enemies plot, and they may win. Kiven, the Tributionalists, the Heralds, and how many more chancellors are waiting to kill him in his sleep? This is a new era of Finscale politics, where knives replace bribes.

After today, Brudge will be challenging for the entire coral reef. His hard-built business is on sticks, and muddy ground. If he stays still, he dies. He must only advance now, with cunning. A cunning he was not too sure he was ready for.

For unsatisfied sharks will antagonize fish in the sea. They will separate the school, and consume the one who will swim away. This is Brudge's school, and he swam in front, so his leadership directs the whole.

One man's loss shall be another one's gain. For a Riverpoor family fed in a random act of kindness shall make a complex series of eventualities come forth. This happy family shall anger a merchant, who did not get his sale. This merchant will be short in taxes, which will anger the tax collectors. They will further anger the regional lords. All in this shall need appeasement. Even if Brudge merely buys a loaf of bread from the market himself to throw into the sea, all must be appeased to have unity.

However, Brudge delighted in one idea. He thought that creating diversions for the whole would be good leverage. One idea, a large trade adventure, could be profitable, and popular. He could sponsor it, bring Thraalin in to plan it, and watch the whole kingdom follow. Thraalin is very loud, and oddly entranced by anything that looks like a boat. He would bring so much attention to it that no one would see Brudge deal with rivals.

Thoughts of how to deal with Wyrenair, and his faction, were entertaining. Brudge figured about how to arrest them, or better, call upon an audit to burden them with distractions, as he shut down their businesses, and tore apart their platescale relationships. He grinned, and felt sure, and vindictive as proper. He was ready to do his duty as Chancellor now.

With his face of stone, he pushed open the door very quietly, and squeezed in. He chattered to his bodyguards to be discrete, and they were. Modesty for now, to be quiet, and raise his earfin to hear all.

The chamber was circular, but not fully utilized. Half the room was set up with tiered rising rows of tables, and chairs. In each one was an assigned chancellor of the kingdom. The wooden seats were comfortable enough, set with ample room for tails to sway briskly.

The other opposing side was a large, and regal chair setting in front of banners. The chair was the Throne of Jester. There was plenty of empty space. Historically, other chairs for the Royal family could be set to allow attendance. Since there is no king, the chair was lonely, and empty. Aside it leaned the staff of Jester, a mockery of the Skol Royal Staff.

Between them was a large circular floor mosaic tile. In a pattern like the lobby. This was the presenting area, where ceiling windows would cast shimmering rays onto the speaker. There the great case would be made wings wide.

Thaw was supposed to be overseeing this whole room today. He was the Synyurl Leader, and thus the King's party. He was not doing anything but foraging at his desk, sorting through a large stack of papers.

Where there is a lack of order, there is always someone attempting to sew chaos. This time it was Wyrenair. Who stood in the light, and held open his wings, as he hissed his complaints.

"This whole meeting is an embarrassment to the Chancellorship!" he lobbied. "I move immediately to censure Chancellor Derin here so we can all go back to our tasks. Chancellor Thaw, call to order on it!"

Brudge remained in the shadows, his black cape kept him hidden. He snarfed quietly to his guards to hold the entrance. Wyrenair was irritating him, and he resisted the desire to order them to stab the creature.

"Derin's estates are foreclosed upon!" Wyrenair held himself with perfection, "He is a suspect in the murder of a child, a town watchman, and Kiven Di' Noach. I also have good witnesses who can claim he may not only harbor platescale spies, but he might have relations with one too!"

Chortling came from within the rows, as others felt amused at the idea.

Then came the roar of Menurut, "Wyrenair lies once again! Give this up! You agreed to have this meeting too."

Wyrenair laughed, "Derin's platescale, you laid hands on her to protect us all that night! She is blue, and was clearly made aware of our meeting by our host. We may argue to bribe the platescales away, but Brudge curls with her while he argues to sacrifice ourselves in conflict to Vex! A finscale cannot swim two ways at the same time! He wants us dead!"

"Tribute is pointless!" Thraalin huffed, "The Empire has recently incurred into our coral reef with a fleet of warships! They sunk one of our patrols, and levy we killed Srica Gintrix! We stand near war! Our trinkets, and Brudge, contributed nothing to this!"

An unseen chancellor shouted down, "No more humiliation for us finscales! Vex has taken the reef! We must give him nothing more until he retreats!"

Next to Thraw, a fellow Loyalist bellowed, "Now would be a great opportunity to remind other nations we have sovereignty in foreign things!"

Wyrenair seemed surprised, "You all are mad! Even in its pathetic state, Skolis shall overcome us in a month from total war!"

Menurut growled, "Tread lightly. This room talks the business of army. Maws stay shut on our provisions, and positions. Spies watch, and wait."

Wyrenair pleaded, "Chancellor Menurut, all spies know that you have not the force strength to defend the south eastern routes through the mountains. This is the season Vex could simply go through there."

"Do not tell me how to fend those roads!" Menurut crossed his arms, "Nonsense upon your claims too. Platescales hate the cold too much to risk there!"

"I am a peer of the Alliance, and such can advise freely here! Yes, I will tell you!" Wyrenair grunted, "You leave that route exposed. We would be better to pay our due, and then propose an additional offer to buy back the reef. I think we should allow the empire to locate Gintrix's corpse, then pay them to leave. Offer to help, so this resolves quickly. The cooperation could make things easier. I further want the seized Derin estates to be sold, then their proceedings given to Vex. It should be enough to please him, as it is valued as much as his colonial taxes."

"And what? Fund the invasion forces?" Thraw barked.

"I will not tolerate our waters to be ransomed!" Menurut scowled.

Brudge flexed his claws at the sound of such a cowardly proposal. Wyrenair is a scoundrel under all that noble garb, and how he so willingly sells his fellows to his own fear is terrifying alone. His need to expose Selay is low, as he runs spies in the Armour's Guild of Freestride just the same.

Thaw finished collating his papers, he locked his desk, and took the sheets to his chest, and stood up.

"Wyrenair, I despise your constant problem-making with Chancellor Derin. I have warned you once before about how close we all think you tread with sedition against the Fordako Pact."

Thaw began his way down into the center. He gave Wyrenair a glare. The Trubutionalist leader stepped aside, and left the center towards his chair obediently.

Thaw stood large, and slammed his tail on the floor. Out of the darkness, behind the throne, came two ladies. One brought a table, and another brought a folded white gown with a necklace. They set the table in front of the Chancellor.

Thaw placed his papers on the table, then took off the more cumbersome articles of cloths he had, such as his pouches, and gloves. He nodded to the ladies, and they then draped this dress over him. Then tied the necklace of Ua, and Ain.

This would be a bit queer, if it was not Jestarians being quiet queer to begin with. Thaw was wearing the dress of a Ua priestess, effectively fit for a woman. It was slack in the chest, and on the tail, and was not good for his figure.

However, he assumes the role of Ua, the mediator, during the times of her teaching her children of how to do statecraft. It was required to be worn by the king, or his chosen, during sessions, making him stand out, and glimmer in the light so that no one would miss his commandments.

Thaw took up his papers, and the stewards collected his things, the table, and left into the darkness. Brudge wondered who they both were, but had no chance to look at anything reveling.

All the usual hissing, and growling between peers was silenced. With Thaw's ritual, came the simple call to decorum. Formality, and rules of the Chancellorship, were taking hold.

The chairman dragged his tail as he walked up to the throne. He sat in it, and glared into the eyes of all. His papers set in his lap. He saw forward, his wings dropping open. The man maintained a posture of holding a great burden, knowing that he carries history on him now.

"We must remind ourselves that we value our lives, and that of our families!" Wyrenair stood, and shouted, "No fish ever survived long after treading into the darkened waters. I motion the Chancellorship to recognize that Chancellor Derin's call to default is to be seen as an act of war to our enemies! Which is doom upon us, as we are not strong! He must be disciplined for this!"

Thaw roared, "I call this chamber to order! A King's Writ is present in the room! Its presence supersedes all our petty issues of the day! It is why we are here, so it must be read!"

Wyrenair pointed at Thaw, and scolded, "I deny not the Pact's authority, or my vassalage! However, Jester has been king-less for so long that it is impossible that a new Writ exists! I call its authenticity into question! Especially considering it comes out of Chancellor Derin's claws following such a dire situation for him!"

Chancellor Dos stood up, and pointed to Wyrenair, "You are a guppy! You delay the proceedings out of spite! We all know its seal is authentic, obstructionist!"

Brudge decided to finally enter this discourse. He chuckled, and smiled while he stepped through the light towards his seat.

"Derin! I see you laughing!" Wyrenair shouted, "You

find it amusing that you play with the lives of finscales as you do?"

Brudge was hoping Wyrenair gave him reason to respond, and he stepped into the light, and opened his wings, "My peers, what good is the life of a finscale if we are denied our right to swim freely in the sea! Our reef is taken from us, and we fight like gulls over a fish carcass! The writ is here, and if we do not read it, then I say damn this Fordako pact, and I will go home to muster my own marines, and take back the reef myself! If we will not enforce its whole purpose, to fend off platescale invasions, then I do not want it!"

"Brudge is absolutely mad!" Wyrenair mocked, "Authenticate the writ before it is read! It is a forgery!"

Brudge glared up at Wyrenair, and decided it was a good idea to borrow a page of Selay's book, "You will get your authentication. If you succeed in blocking this writ with your lies Wyrenair. I shall kill you here, and now! I tire of this rivalry!"

"ORDER!" Thaw slammed his tail hard upon the floor, "Gods be forgiving to us. Chancellor Derin, this is uncalled for! The Fordako Pact states no alliance member shall harm another! Present the Writ now, let us authenticate it, or I shall have you, and Wyrenair disbarred."

Brudge turned to Thaw, and when sure Wyrenair did not see, he smirked. He plucked the writ from under a belt, wrapped in a red ribbon, and leather, stamped sealed with thick wax. He then threw back his cape, and held the paper into the air.

"King Synurl, beloved, brings us direction from Ua's gardens! This King's Writ is the target of Kiven's seizures. We acquired it years ago together, and know nothing of its contents! The traitor wanted to take it from me. With it now under siege, I call for its immediate authentication, reading into record, and to law! I present this to the Chancellorship now!"

Thaw set his stack of papers on the floor, and rose from the throne, "Faction leaders, arise! Approach for the authentication of the seal using etching."

Thaw entered the center of the room, and into the light. Behind Brudge all faction leaders entered as well. Chancellor Dos of the Populists, Chancellor Wyrenair of the Tributionalists, Chancellor Allyater of the Fodako Pact, Chancellor Thraalin of the Seafarers, Chancellor Menurut of the Alliance Ventrines, and Chancellor Thaw of the Synurl Loyalists, and finally Chancellor Derin, who stands alone.

They formed a circle around Brudge. From behind Thaw came the same two ladies from before. One held a locked box, and the other held the same table. They set up in front of him, and between Brudge. Then they set the box on the table.

Thaw returned to the throne to pick up the the staff of Jester. On its neck was a key, and he removed it, and came back to the box. Which he used to open it.

He removed a parchment, then a wooden king's seal. This was the same seal that was used to create the writ. Thaw then removed a granite stone, and scraped it across the covered seal, where it imprinted upon the parchment. He did this once for every paper, and handed it to each chancellor.

Brudge took a stand near Chancellor Dos, and Chancellor Thaw. He handed Dos the writ. Dos examined his sheet, and the writ, and then passed the writ to Wyrenair, who passed it on after extra scrutiny, and a snort. Finally, the writ arrived back to Thaw.

When satisfied, Thaw collected the papers, and returned the seal, granite, and sheets to the box. He locked it. He then returned to the staff, and retied the key. Then came back to take the writ.

The room remained quiet until he finally slammed his

tail on the floor. The stewardesses removed the table, and the box. They once again vanished.

Thaw returned to stand in the center of the circle now, and held the writ up into the air for all to see again.

"By the Grace of Ua, and Justice of Ain. We record, and witness, that this day of spring in the Era of the Skol Empire, over thirty years from the signing of the Uneasy Armistice, that the Jestarian Chancellorship unanimously authenticates this King's Writ. The seal is from our beloved King Synurl."

All leaders stepped behind Thaw in a military formation. Brudge stood just off behind Thaw's left wing. The chamber sounded in unison with a tail slam, "All hail King Synurl the Peacemaker!"

"Upon the breaking of this seal, this new law shall be read, and its proceedings be honored!" Thaw explained, and held up a claw to the wax seal, he slipped it under the fold.

There was sudden bated silence. Older members came to closer seats to watch, many shifted to get a better view. Thaw had to wait for everyone to settle, because all chancellors must see the seal breaking clearly.

Silently, with no noise, Thaw simply swiped his talon through the wax.

"The seal breaks! Long may our Alliance live! Long live Jester!"

"Long live Jester!" Everyone chanted, expressing some sense of joy, and relief.

This was the most dull of processes. Such a long series of confirmations, authentication, announcements, logging. This made sure spies saw. Later, the older chancellors would pen in their memoirs the story of this writ, which is some of the most dry reading ever. This all upheld the centuries of traditions laid forth by Hitiwa Fordako in the beginnings of this strange nation.

Thaw clutched the writ, and lowered into a huddle to read it. As he read, then reread, he looked at Brudge from his side in disbelief. Then he tightened his frills to hide some anger.

Brudge smiled, and nodded. He took stock of his fellows standing beside him. Thraalin smiled, but was absent-minded. Brudge swore he saw the flames of a burning ship in his eyes, lost in some battle at sea.

Dos was watching everyone in the crowd. Menurut was still, and unreadable. Wyrenair was either scared, or angry. Allyater however, was clearly drunk, and almost tipping over.

Thaw held the writ high, "By the grace of Ua, and the Righteousness of Ain. This Proclamation is authorized under the Grateful Tasks of they to the Kiri'grana lords. Who Ordained King Hitiwa Fordako with the authority of administration over all of the Jestarian Peoples. Defined by the Fordako Pact, and our oath of vassalage. King Synyurl is Authorized to proclaim this King's Writ to the members of the Chancellorship of Jester."

Brudge sighed, drawing up rather old memories of the regal style of his late liege. A style that was exemplified most in Synyurl's final crisis before his death: the refugees from the colonies. Brudge maintained every detail, and frowned knowing that today the poor sleep on mud from neglect by their lords. It was good to Synyurl it one last time.

"Section one: Conditions. In the state of affairs today, King Synurl's wounds have resulted in no heir to his estates. In that, inheritance must be decided upon, for when the time of Judgment before Ua, and Ain comes for him. Therefore, the purpose of this King's Writ is to finally settle this judgment."

The crowd murmured, and someone stood up to relocate. A few Chancellors whispered scolding words, but eventually settled down in the Trubutionalists section of seats. The factions were collecting themselves.

"Section Two, Provisions. Provision A. This King's Writ is solely owned by Chancellor Brudge Char' Derin. Who is tasked with its safe keeping, and administration until when, and after, it is spoken in the Great Hall."

"Provision B. Chancellor Derin speaks to the finscale people, their suffering, and need for vengeance through his zeal for the Pact. Authority is placed in him for his continued loyalty to it."

There was protesting conversations in the crowd. Whispers sounded as chancellors leaned to each other to talk. Many were becoming agitated from their own personal envy.

"Order now!" Allyator calmly slurred, "Chancellors, remember your place is below King Synurl!"

Thaw made a stinging glare at the upset chancellors, who all returned to silence, "Provision C. Chancellor Derin has received this writ, sealed, with instructions that it remain under his care until after Synyurl passes, and is ordered to destroy it if Synyurl produces an Heir. It is only to be open when the Chancellorship is under great danger."

Thaw turned to Brudge, "Chancellor, Did you agree to these conditions?"

Brudge nodded, "I have. Synyurl placed this seal in my presence, with those instructions mere days before his death."

Thaw tilted his head, "How did you loose this writ?"

"It was stolen. I spent much time recovering it. It is the true reason for my neutrality." Brudge affirmed.

Thaw glared, "Then why did Kiven take it?"

"I gave it to Kiven's vault to store after he helped me rescue it. He illegally seized it when he betrayed me. He is a traitor, and puts us all in danger," Brudge explained.

"Yes. The Pact is in great danger. Skol invades us," Thaw smiled at Brudge, and turned back to the chamber.

"Section 3: Upon Reading, the Fordako Pact is provisionally suspended until a new Martial Leader is properly anointed. Chancellor Derin is to immediately be selected to be voted for said position, and the title of King of Jester."

The room became riotous. Many stood, and threw over their tables. The chancellors all were beginning to yell down at the same time. The many heads of the hydra snarled so envious, that none could be heard.

"Silence! The reading is not finished! Silence or the guards will arrest you all!" Thaw barked.

The protests were softened, and the reading continued, "The Chancellors must agree, and cast on blood stone vote to grant him the Grateful Tasking. Upon Majority, Chancellor Derin shall surrender his prior holdings to an heir, and receive the holdings of the Synyurl family estates."

Thaw snarled at the chamber, which had a few members stirring again, "Summery: The Chancellorship shall vote for Derin to be King, upon majority he shall be made. Upon failure, the Fordako Pact is disbanded, and the Kingdom of Jester is no more. The pact requires a leader, or it will not face the coming wrath of Vesuvious Vex."

With that, a great torrent was unleashed. The tables were destroyed, and papers scoured over the floors. Objects were thrown into the center, fortunately no one was hit.

It Is clear the whole chancellorship is so troubled that it shall no longer survive without a King. Brudge hung his head still, knowing he just put his nation up for ransom. His lungs took much more effort to breath, as if he felt older now. He regretted reveling in this earlier.

Oddly, despite all this chaos, Brudge was able to hear the yelling, and hissing from outside in the lobby. Someone was laying siege on the Hall, and Brudge signaled his guards, and pointed to the lobby. They left quickly, drawing their maces.

Thaw roared, "Faction leaders! Reign in your members for voting! Prepare the blood stones, and raise them to the gods!"

Brudge was the first to remove his, always gently sitting in a pouch just under his sword. He made sure his other arm was under his cape. Thaw glared at Brudge before slamming his tail hard on the floor again.

Brudge made sure he was in the light, and all could see, "I present here the Derin Bloodstone. For the first vote, I state my reasoning. I vote against myself! I do not wish to be king for my own private desire, but based on the need of us all to have a navigator in this dangerous sea of history we face today! All the world has lost its virtue after the last war, and we stand on the precipice of our annihilation."

The crowd was oddly calmed by this, murmurs, and upset faces were visible. Brudge's show of modesty quelled fears of most of the junior membership. He took a gamble by making the appeal to humility.

The stewards came with bronze bowls, a table, and set up in the center with Thaw. The bowls were painted with various images of Ua, and Ain in the roles the seasons of the year, along with their handles, and rims decorated with gemstones.

Brudge then faced away from his peers. He dropped his bloodstone into the left bowl with Thaw watching. He then turned to go back to his seat.

"Chancellor Brudge," Thaw spoke, "Stand, and present yourself, the subject of the vote, near me. We all must see into your eyes before we decide to submit to you."

Brudge had to squeeze his eyes briefly to hide his worry. He was planning to cower in his seat until the vote was over. He just destroyed his nation, and sacrificed all his security, and had to deal with his growing fear. He did obey Thaw, and stood behind the voting table, let all see him for the coward he is.

"Now let us cast our vote! Right is for, and left is against!" Thaw commanded.

One by one the chancellors came from their perch to cast their votes. Each vote clanged as a bell when the blood stone fell into place. Each returned to their place.

The siege in the lobby was not over, and its sound overtook the calm of the chamber. Thuds, and clangs broke out, and the doors shook from the impact of a heavy object.

A clear female voice squawked, "You shall all let me through! Or so be, I will tie your tails around your necks, and shove those maces up your holes!"

Thaw turned, and groaned, "What in the idle is..."

Then those great doors parted in force, one of Brudge's guards tripped through them striding backwards. His helmet was gone, and his tail was somehow around his arm, and neck. He fell over, not from lack of balance without his tail, but the lack of mobility from having his trousers pulled to his ankles.

The wide open doors to the hall were exposing the darkness of the lobby. Between them, holding a staff of Ua, and Ain, was a savage sight. Selay dared to storm the finscale capital. Her wings were apart, and open, and her posture low as she stomped into the chamber. She had a satchel over her back. Everyone panicked, and took to the opposing side, except for Brudge, and the guards.

"Platescales attack! Skolis is here! To arms!" Roared Chancellor Menurut.

The sliding of swords resounded from around the chamber. Brudge readied his as well. The platescale glared with the look of amusement at everyone's stance.

He glared into her eyes. There she was, her arrogance,

her defiance. She is mad to come here. If she does not have good reason, Brudge will have to kill her here so no one realizes that she works for him. She is going to ruin this whole meeting.

Selay let out a roar in a hysterical rage. The guards began to encircle her, and she fanned out her wings, and entered the light. Forcing herself into the chamber.

"There are finscales in this place who put eggs at risk! Present yourselves for execution! Face me!" She demanded.

Brudge saw she was maddened, and screaming again her nonsense without evidence. There cannot be anyone in this room that does as she claims. It it unfathomable to consume the unhatched.

Almost as if she read his expression, Selay snarled, and approached him, "I have the proof right here, Brudge!" She held up the sack.

Wyrenair yelled across the room, always the opportunist, "There is Derin's platescale! She invites herself to the whole chamber to show just where his loyalty lies!"

Brudge examined the bag, but did not touch it. From how it sagged from its straps, it clearly was heavy. At the corner, the contents barely showed. When Brudge saw what it was, he stepped back. He lost all form, and his eyes widened in horror. His sword clanged on the floor, and he opened his maw.

"Remove her! Kill her outside!" Ordered Thaw, as he motioned his hands at the guards.

A large group of guards formed a wall between Selay, and Brudge. They pushed her back, and boxed her in. The blue platescale began to do what she was best at, curse, spit, and brawl.

"You all say you love your kind! You all only swim

together in hopes no one eats you first!" She taunted.

One guard immediately grabbed Selay's arm, and his hand slipped off her as he looked in pure confusion, and yelled, "What is this oily substance!?" He sniffed it, and gagged, then backed off.

The guards eventually pushed Selay back, and out of the room. Or, as Brudge saw, Selay left on her own accord. She lobbied the entire chamber with fouled curses, but backed off without so much as harming another guard. She clearly enjoyed this.

There was a brief outbreak of fighting in the lobby that quickly died off. Brudge felt unsure, for if Selay was dead, then he shall have issues for quiet some time over her. If she survived, he is going to have a lot to answer for.

The cold stare of his peers brought him back to sense. He then went to collect his fallen sword, and returned to the voting table. Hiding his unease poorly.

Thaw looked upon Brudge with concern, "Are you fine? You seemed bothered by her?"

Brudge was bothered. He saw nothing but what was in the pack, and he wanted to throw up, and fly away. He held himself tightly, but felt weaker from it.

It became much worse when he realized that he was faint now. If this vote was lost, he was going to die today. So Brudge began to have a absent look upon him.

"I am fine now," he lied, "Let us finish this."

Slow, and systematic this was. The single clang of a rock every few moments was all that broke this silence. Eventually the dullness broke again.

Wyrenair roared at his time to vote as he lost all ability to self-govern, "Derin is a traitor! For the sake of the Jestarian way I must stop you!"

Wyrenair drew his sword, and launched in full flight into the air. He dove at Brudge quickly, preventing the large man from responding. It did not matter. Brudge was distracted by what Selay did up until the floor impacted his backside.

Wyrenair was pulled off Brudge, and disarmed by other Chancellors. However, somehow, he broke free, and pinned Brudge down to scrape at his face. The wounds bled, and were going to scar, but before anything worse could happen, Wyrenair was held back by Brudge's allies once again.

The chamber broke into chaos. The Pact Faction members joined with the Tributionalists in a full brawl. It resembled a typical bar fight in Freestride. This is the moment everyone realized that there was no more Fordako Pact, they were all sovereign. This is the end of Jester.

Thaw was isolated in the middle of the room, and he roared to no avail, "Everyone, stop this chaos! Lest Vex naught have to kill us, we can do that ourselves!"

The fighting spread towards the center, and the voting table made a deafening crash as it fell. Thaw tried to catch the table, however he tripped, and fell to his knees, and bellowed, "Oh bother. I cannot hold them anymore."

The blood stones scattered across the room, and slid ageist Brudge. He saw Thaw surrendering to his weakness at last here. He had no choice now but to stand, and take his Sword.

The tall, cunning finscale laughed at the searing pain of his newly fashioned claw marks. A desire for vengeance came, and gone, when he concluded that these were his doom scars. All his paintings shall be redone with them post haste.

Wyrenair was still held in place by his peers, and just scowled at Brudge. Around them was chaos, and the fall of everything. Brudge glared into his rival's eyes, and saw something he did not expect. Wyrenair looked saddened. He shared his sympathy with Thaw. Did he truly care?

Wyrenair prepared to say something, but he began to

choke. Blood came out of his maw, and he became blatantly frightened. His eyes widened, then lost all life, and he fell limp. The others let him go, and they all panicked at the site of the Chancellor. Wyrenair was lifeless on the floor.

The killer was still standing there, and he dropped his bloody knife. Not a single person knew who he was.

Menurut roared, "Guards! Chain him down, and cut his wings!"

"All Hail King Derin! Long May he Live!" the man shouted as the guards swarmed, and slammed him to the ground.

He was chained around his neck, and a knife was taken to his wing webbing. It was a bloody dissection, and he wailed from it. Then he was drug out of the room crying in pain. He continued to shout in support of Brudge until he was too far to hear.

Brudge's greatest political enemy was dead. There was genuine despair. For what Brudge did, Wyrenair's assault was justified. Jester was Wyrenair's security, and Brudge destroyed it.

Everyone was disturbed by the immediacy of the death of Wyrenair. The most annoying person in the room is quiet forever. Fellow faction members, and his allies moved closer, but nothing could be done other then to wait for the guards to carry his body out.

The room returned to calm eventually, though much more ugly then prior. Swollen lips, pulled, and torn frills, claw marks, one bit nose, and a lot of black eyes were about. Everyone settled down, and appeared insecure, but relieved.

Thaw collected, and cleaned the bloodstones. He then placed them together in one of the bowls. When done, he slammed his tail, and said with less confidence then before, "Everyone, with order, come, and collect your stone, and return to your seats. We shall have to vote once again. Since this is Jester's future, and I have the martial authority, I will kill anyone who does not vote tonight. You are all now my hostages."

Several guards closed, and barred tight the doors to trap them all in. With calm, and silence they retrieved their stones, one at a time. With calm, and mourning silence they sat down. They tried to reassemble the room some, but to no avail.

Brudge retrieved his stone, and once again stood to vote. Thaw said, "Again" as Brudge dropped the stone again, and declared he will vote against himself for the same reasons.

As before, but much slower, and more painful, every Chancellor voted. One stone rang at a time for each one. Some made changes, others hesitated, and mulled over their choice longer then before.

Eventually Chancellor Thraalin approached, and held his hand to the left bowl. He gazed into Brudge's eyes, and hesitated. Brudge looked back at his friend, and the large finscale looked down.

"We have lost ourselves today? Have we, Brudge?" he said sorrowful while gazing back.

Brudge wanted to say something affirming, but what today has given him was a world with no Finscale homeland. Further, a world where finscale eggs are soon to be destroyed in the coming march of Vex. A world where no gill-bearing Allyian is going to live.

There was no chance to answer, for the windows that light the center were shattered from above. Looking up, sparkling shards of glass, and someone was falling down the whole three floors of the chamber. It landed with open wings across the floor, and a thrashing tail.

Selay returned. Brudge knew every vein, and blemish on her wings. This time, he did not opt to kill her.

Thraalin had that intent, and he drew his sword, and

prepared to swing it. However, Selay simply rose up, and tapped her talon on Thraalin's nose. The large man became excited. He puffed up, and lost all breathing before he fell over in defeat. Selay knew exactly where to strike the Great Dastypuff.

The platescale chuckled at her newly slain adversary. Then, she glared at Brudge, then Thaw, and held up her pack. She opened her wings, and faced a crowd of finscales that was only so irate. They were tired from the fight, and only glared as she removed its contents, and tossed the sack away.

There was no doubt anymore when Selay lifted an egg up into the sunlight. It was a finscale egg, and it was dead. The blood ring was there, and the blood inside the egg blotted out where the child would be. However, the chamber gazed upon a trail of blood that dried external of the shell, and the shadow of a severed head, its mouth open as it showed it died in horrible pain. The struggle for life was so intense, it broke out before it was ready to.

There was nothing but silence, and attention towards Selay. For the first time in history a placescale held the floor of the Jestarian Chamber.

"This egg was killed by Raviwr Ricin in a ritual," Selay began, "It was meant to be consumed by Kiven Di' Noach. It was murdered in Synurl Manor, and was a mixture of a finscale, and platescale. Those who enabled this are here among you as a secret faction. As well as within Skol, and other nations."

"You are lying, platescale." Someone shouted down, "You killed that yourself."

Selay removed a long silver stiletto from her side belts. She lowered the egg, and held the knife up.

"Inspect this knife, it is the sister weapon of the one found in the skull of Kiven. I killed him by impaling his skull. It was forged by a finscale in this city."

"Kiven is dead? This cannot be true, is it?" Thaw asked.

He immediately received an answer, as a guard came, and whispered to his earfin. The surprised caused his fins to perk up. They lowered when he realized what this meant.

Thaw murmured, "This is really awful."

Selay examined the crowd, and she seemed to fixate on someone in the chamber. Without any hesitation she threw the knife into the group. It missed its target, who began to run.

Selay began to track him with her gaze, but he vanished. She then held the egg back up for the room to see.

"There goes Chancellor Quad of Journey's Rest. Cut open his stomach before I find him, and see who is right," She ordained.

"You shall do no such thing!" Thaw growled, "You are declaring war on finscales with these words."

Thraalin stood up, and immediately was cut back down by Selay pressing his nose. She then glared at Thaw from her side, and scoffed.

"I give no damns about what you worthless lot think. I am here to warn you." She growled, "This dead child is one of five eggs killed I know of. I will find every member of this faction, and I will kill each, and every one of them, and their supporters. My justification is in what is right, not what some corrupt chamber votes upon."

Thaw snarled at Selay, "We are the arbiters of the Grateful Task! You dare go outside our commands?"

"I do not care about the Grateful Task. This is a threat I deliver to you all," Selay brought the egg to her, and stroked it as if it was still alive, "If you help me, this would be good of you all. If you oppose me, I will hold you all accountable, and thus kill you. If you get out of my way, you at least live with the shame of knowing you work alongside those who continue the work of Vex."

This was the time for Brudge to intervene. He now is sure Selay is right, she has risked herself today to show this, and she is going to not stop until she fulfills her promises. He could help, and perhaps give Jester some sense of virtue.

Brudge walked up to Selay, and held out his hands, "Let me look at it."

Selay handed him the egg. She gave him a sure look of "I told you" that did not help her case. Brudge examined it.

The dried blood on the shell began from a small puncture. It was done using trained hands, trained in surgery. Someone familiar with eggs, and anatomy. A priest of the church is usually educated enough to know how to learn this. Selay could learn this too, but Brudge knew she would rather be drinking in his cellar. He had to both investigate, and help her at this point, for it could unify Jester whole again, and give the finscales life anew. Thraalin is right.

So Brudge held the egg up, and shouted, "We have lost who were are, and this is our proof!" Brudge then brought the egg close to him. "Before the war ended, we all became evil, and smashed platescale eggs, and burned nests. So did the platescales in kind to us. We made peace to stop our evil. Now one of the enemy grants us a path to redemption. Are you all blind enough to refuse it?"

Brudge carried himself to the voting table. He sat the egg down between the bowls. He smiled at his peers, and enemies.

"I am Brudge Char' Derin. I am done with this game of power. I just want to avenge this child's death. I want to find who did this, and show the world what happens to egg killers."

"Ua and Ain give us this trial so we can prove ourselves in it. Their reason for the test is to prove if we will defend the nest along with them when the time comes."

Chancellor Thaw pulled out his bloodstone, and dropped it into the right bowl. He looked stern, and sure. The sound seemed to ring more pure then the other times. He then took a position behind Brudge, like a guard.

"If you vote me king, or end the Pact today, I no longer care," Brudge closed, "I am dedicating myself to avenging this egg. With, or without you all."

Thraalin pulled himself up. He tried to crawl away from Selay, lest he face another harrowing assault, but he came to.

"Let us find ourselves again, Brudge." he said, regaining his composure, and dropping his stone in the right jar, "My captains, and their ships will gladly join this cause." Thraalin stood behind Brudge.

Chancellor Dos eventually cast his stone. He cast for Brudge, but only after glaring at Selay. She smiled rather frightening at him. He too stood behind Brudge.

Then Chancellor Menurut came down, and set his stone right too. He nodded, and stood behind his choice without any incident.

Allyater came down, and he frowned. He swayed a bit drunk, and then cast his stone right. He looked upon Brudge, and then stumbled as he returned to his seat.

What remained voted. Those who voted for Brudge stayed behind him, and those who did not sat back down. Left, and right, orderly, and calm. From out of the splinters of the chamber, came a new order.

Thaw began to inventory the stones. Counting each one slowly. During this, Selay simply left without warning. Brudge stared at her sauntering, and swaying tail. Someone should arrest her, for the world would be better then. However, no one dared to arrest someone who was right.

The tally ended, and Chancellor Thaw called out for order. The final vote was forty to twenty. Brudge received the majority.

"All hail King Brudge Char' Derin!" Thaw roared happily, "The Fordako Pact is restored! Let the world know that Jester has chosen its new king! Finscales have their protector, and champion!"

Other chancellors who voted against Brudge stood up to leave that moment. The time to protest was over. You were of the new Pact, or not.

Brudge turned to his new throne, it seemed much larger then he remembered today. It also lost all its beauty now that it belongs to him. He quietly loomed over it as the stewardesses dressed him in the royal Armour, that Armour did not fit him, so it hung loose. They then handed Brudge the staff of Jester.

He was supposed to sit with the staff, and Armour, as his subjects bowed to him. However, he could not do it. Something stopped him.

Brudge thought of nothing other then that egg, and how foul he was for using it to propel himself to the throne. He did not even think twice about it when he did. Normally such a thing requires him to think beforehand to avoid stuttering. This did not.

An emptiness filled his heart, and Brudge saw a vision of what was the burning hull of a Jestarian ship. In the distance, Skol ships anchored in the Jestarian coral reef.

Brudge turned to face the room, and he saw all his supporters bowing to him with their arms over their chest, wings open, and heads down. They were ready to be beheaded if Brudge was displeased.

Then he transfixed upon the egg in the center of the room. He was compelled to walk to it. He felt a burning need to protect it, to make sure it hatched. To reach into the idle, and pull the child in so it may live the Trial.

Brudge dropped the staff, and pulled his armor off. He

then took the egg into his arms, and held it to his body. He walked back toward the throne.

As he saw, he saw visions. Things of war. A dark burning sky, a forest burned to become a battlefield. He saw the great crack in the world. Upon it there were two large flames.

Brudge curled his tail around the egg and set it in his lap. He glanced at his new subjects, all still bowing. Then lowered his nose to bump upon the shell. Immediately Brudge saw fire, and blood, fearsome Wyverns of the Order, the death of all around him. He saw the cities of Selis, and Skolis burning bright into the darkest nights. He saw an army crossing by flight over the great crack, where uncountable numbers spilled. All cut down by arrows as they fly to their death. He saw flames from clouds, things he did not understand yet. What he saw caused him to weep, for he knew it was bound to happen, and he was ready to cause it. Over this pathetic egg.

The Uneasy Armistice is broken.

End of Volume One